WHERE SHALL I FLEE?

WHERE SHALL I FLEE?

Anne Clare

PUBLISHED BY ANNE CLARE

Where Shall I Flee?

COVER DESIGN AND INTERIOR FORMATTING: Amanda Ruehle

Apennine Mountains
Adriatic
Sea
Rome
Cassino
Anzio
Naples
Mediterranean
Sea
Messina
Sicily
ITALY

DEDICATION

To those who served and sacrificed under the thin shield of a red cross, trying to preserve life in the midst of death.

Where can I go from Your Spirit?
Or where can I flee from Your presence?
If I ascend into heaven, You are there;
If I make my bed in hell, behold, You are there.
If I take the wings of the morning,
And dwell in the uttermost parts of the sea,
Even there Your hand shall lead me,
And Your right hand shall hold me.

Psalm 139: 7–10

Prologue

February 24, 1944

Blood flowed warm over Jean's hand as her eyes slid closed. Leroy's voice called as if through deep water. She couldn't answer, couldn't force her mouth open. A shiver wracked her heavy limbs. *This must be what going into shock feels like.*

An arm slipped under her shoulders. Leroy's voice cut through, pulling her back. "Jean? Jeannie, you gotta wake up. Jeannie—"

She tried again to respond. "Leroy?" *After everything, it can't end like this*—but the world around her dissolved into hazy gray. Straining to find thought, she offered one last prayer. *God, please, if this is the end, forgive me. I'm so sorry. I was so angry…and proud, and I'm so sorry—*

Darkness swallowed her.

Part One

ONE

February 9, 1944

JEAN HOFF FIXED HER EYES on the dark horizon, the LST's narrow railing digging into her palms. Gulping breaths of sharp, salty air, she tried to ignore the way the deck rolled under her feet.

I should've known better than to eat so much before we embarked. If they hadn't kept talking about how it was the last decent meal we're going to get for a while... She tightened her lips.

Closing her eyes, she tried to imagine that she was out fishing walleye with Grandad in his little motorboat. The wind was a chilly precursor to a summer thunderstorm. The tossing waves were ripples on Elbow Lake.

Imagination failed. Grandad's boat would never survive waves of this size. The cold wind rushing past her pushed back the stink of the ship—mingled scents of gasoline and closely crowded humans—but it wasn't anything like the cool breezes through the pines. The ship lurched over another swell then dropped, leaving her stomach behind. Swallowing hard, she gripped the rail until her hands ached. *Can't ever imagine away the facts, can you Jean?*

"You ok, doll?"

Jean opened her eyes to slits. One of the men had materialized out of the night, sympathetic grin stretched under a helmet that looked too big for his long, freckled face.

She said nothing, just stared down at him—sometimes it paid to be too tall—letting her eyebrows slowly rise.

His grin wilted. Adjusting his helmet, he shuffled past with a muttered, "Never mind…Lieutenant…" and disappeared into the dark.

Turning her gaze back to the horizon, Jean pursed her lips. *Am I going to have to stare down every guy in the Army? You'd think eventually they'd get the hint.* It almost made her consider returning to her bunk below—almost, if it weren't for the stench of the other nurses' vomit that had driven her topside.

The deck dropped, and the bile rose in her throat. Squeezing her eyes shut, she swallowed it down, along with the irritation. What was the point of getting upset? He'd gone, and she was blessedly alone—as alone as she could be on this tub—

A warm arm bumped her elbow. Her eyes snapping open, she turned, ready to tell whomever it was to back off, but it was just Stan. With a sigh, she relaxed, until he spoke.

"You sure like scaring them off, dontcha Jeannie?"

Her stomach soured further. *Oh swell. He saw.* She shrugged, and the boat heaved again, giving her an excuse to keep her eyes fixed on the horizon.

Undeterred, Stan leaned against the rail next to her, wind whipping his salt and pepper hair back from his lean, lined face. "Y'know, it might be better to go to the other side of the boat. Wind to your back. Unless you want a face full when it comes up."

She risked opening her mouth to answer. "I'm trying *not* to throw up, Stan."

"Hmmm. Good luck."

Pulling a deep breath in through her nose, she imagined the salt air cleansing her lungs. She spared him a glance. "Don't the waves bother you?"

Stan shrugged. "Twenty years of surgery leaves you with a strong stomach." He pulled out his pipe and tapped it on the rail, looking up and considering the strength of the wind. "So. What'd that boy do to earn your ire?"

Trying to sound calm, professional, she answered. "He called me doll."

"Whew." Stan grinned. "From the look on your face, I figured he'd tried to pull something worse."

"Come on. Think that'd fly with any of the male officers?"

He snorted. "Well, no, I don't suppose so, but then I don't think 'doll' is really an apt description for me. Handsome, maybe, but—"

Not feeling like giving him a courtesy laugh, she refocused on the rolling, gray sea.

"He's brand new. A little tetchy, aren't you?"

Her shoulders stiffened, a wave of heat replacing the sick feeling in her belly. "He's enlisted." She bit out the words. "I'm an officer. He might as well learn to keep that straight from the get-go. Besides, I'm not in the mood to have some guy I've never met—"

"I suppose," he spoke over her, "it isn't your never mind that that boy could be all shot up in a few hours. A little kindness—"

She ignored him. " come on to me. I'm here to be a nurse, not a flirt, and I'm a darn good one—you know I am."

"Sure. No complaints on your work. Socially, though…" he twirled his pipe through his long fingers. "Your Major said there'd been some friction."

"What—have you been checking up on me? You've got no business—"

"If I don't, who does? My point is, if you can be civil in the OR—"

"That's work. But it's been four months since I shipped over, and I'm tired of the skirt chasing, wolf-whistling…I thought the ring might've at least been a deterrent." She gripped the rail a little tighter.

That shut his mouth. With a look down at her hand—at the little diamond winking even in the dim light—Stan heaved a sigh and turned to stare out at the horizon. Remembering Joe, just like she was.

The silence didn't last long—it never did with Stan. He shook his head, then reached over to give her shoulder a squeeze. "I know, I know. But it wouldn't hurt if you didn't stare daggers at every little comment—especially when the boy was probably just trying to be nice. If any of them really *do* get fresh, well, they'll learn that this old dog still has some teeth. But, until that time... Teams work better when they work together, Jeannie."

"Jean."

He tucked the pipe into his pocket. "If we're going to be that way, maybe I should just call you lieutenant? You were always Jeannie to me, kid."

"I'm not hanging around the surgery in pigtails anymore."

"Maybe not, but when you signed up, I promised your old man..." he trailed off, the weight of the history between them too heavy for words. Stan had been almost part of the family, coming home with Dad most nights after the clinic was closed, eager for one of Mom's huge suppers at the worn and dented oak table. Always present—until he wasn't. Until he left. And then Joe left.

She shook herself and looked over at him. Elbows braced on the railing, shoulders slumped, and head bowed, he looked his age. *It's not his fault—none of this is.*

Softening, she risked releasing the rail and put her hand over his. "Stan, I'm fine. I'm going to be fine."

"Yeah?" He squeezed her fingers. "How long you gonna wear that ring?"

Pulling back, she dropped her hand. "I have a chain for it for when we're working. I just like to have it close." She turned back to the horizon, wishing the wind wouldn't make her eyes water. Silently they stood, side by side, thoughts lost in the past.

Finally, Stan straightened. "Ok, Jeanni...*Jean.* I'll keep my nose out of your business, but just...try to play nice, won't you?"

The deck dropped, and her irritation rose. "I intend to be perfectly professional, *sir.*"

"Sure thing, *lieutenant.*" He shoved his hands in his pockets and pushed away from the side. After two steps, he turned back. "Better make sure your gear's in order and try to get some sleep. Word is, once we land, we're gonna be busy."

Her mouth went dry. Licking her lips, she nodded. His footsteps were swallowed by the sounds of the sea, but Jean did not move. She didn't feel like sleeping, and she'd checked everything already. Twice. She was prepared.

Of course, from what I've heard about Anzio, there might not be any 'prepared.'

The rumors had reached her outfit while still down in Riardo. First, rumors that the landings behind German lines on the Anzio beachhead would be the key, unlocking the road to Rome. Then, rumors that the beachhead had become a trap. The soldiers and support staff were just waiting to be pushed back into the sea. Rumors, too, about just how badly the 95th Evacuation Hospital—the group they were coming to replace—had been hit. A shiver that had nothing to do with the cold traveled up her spine as she tried not to picture the devastation a load of anti-personnel bombs could do in a hospital tent.

Shaking herself, she straightened her shoulders. *I don't want rumors. The fact of the matter is, this is where we're needed. And after all, I wanted to get into the thick of it.*

She raised her eyes from the horizon line and squinted toward the land beyond. Could she see it, or was her imagination filling in the blank space? Did a dark silhouette stand against the eastern sky, far away but growing ever closer? Could those little irregularities be the Alban Hills she'd heard so much about? She couldn't tell. One of her old Sunday school verses floated through her mind. *I will lift up my eyes to the hills— From whence comes my help?*

Well, not from those *hills.* She squinted harder, as if by the effort she could see the tanks and artillery rumor said waited—German forces perched above the narrow Allied beachhead like vultures picking at their bones. *No. More like a red-tailed hawk eyeing its prey. And here I am, just another mouse scurrying into the hunting grounds.*

Another shiver shook her. When she had signed up, she'd thought she was ready. Ready for a combat zone. Ready to prove that she could be brave. She'd done alright so far, joining the hospital group on Sicily and moving up with it through southern Italy. But here…here, the sick feeling in the pit of her stomach, stronger and longer lasting than any bout of seasickness, foreboded that maybe she had been wrong.

God, what was I thinking? What were YOU *thinking?* The ship dropped, but the urge to be sick had passed, at least for the moment. *Enough. Stan was right. Better head back to my berth. Check my musette bag one more time. Try to sleep.*

Making her way across the deck, she wove around groups of soldiers—replacements—sprawled about. Some paced. Others slept. One sat cross legged, leaning against the side of a jeep lashed to the deck, scooping cold beans out of a can.

I suppose heading to the beachhead with a whole crew full of soldiers ought to make me feel a little less exposed—

It didn't. She knew just how ineffective their protection could be.

"Hey, George, catch!"

Squinting through thin, pre-dawn light, George Novak stretched his scarred, sun-browned hands up just in time to snag the piece of packing crate Leroy had tossed. "Perfect."

"Will that finish it off?"

George knelt and carefully fit the board into the last empty slot of mud. He sat back on his haunches and surveyed the makeshift wooden sidewalk running in front of the embankment where he and

Leroy had dug in. "Looks like it. Whaddya think?"

"Hmm, let's see." Making a big show of inspecting each board, Leroy Anderson walked the length of their creation—all ten yards of it. His slow grin spread from one prominent ear to the other. "Swell!" He hopped up and down a couple of times, packing the boards into the earth, then stuck his hands in his pockets and strolled over to George. "Feels like I'm walking down Main Street back home in Tower."

"Ha! Main Street Anzio." George stood and stretched his shoulders. He was shorter than Leroy, but broader, a few more years of hard work under his belt. He reached under his helmet and scratched his dark, curly head, then nodded toward the echoes of sporadic fire from farther up. "I dunno, kid. What about the sound effects?"

Leroy hesitated. "Well...walking in a thunderstorm, maybe?"

Laughing, George shook his head. "What a storm! You'd be better off indoors."

"I'll bring an umbrella. Maybe find a nice girl to share it."

"Aw, Leroy. You romantic." George took a swig out of his canteen, then grimaced at the oily aftertaste. *But that's what you get when they bring the water up in empty gas cans.* "Sadly, there's a shortage of girls just now—nice or otherwise. But maybe that's for the best—gives me a chance to coach you, so next time you see one you can actually talk to her." Besides being the youngest member of George's squad, Leroy had gotten some ribbing in Naples for losing the power of speech whenever they found themselves in female company.

Another squad member, Pete, stuck his brown head out of a dugout farther down, like a gopher out of its hole. "Hey, we talking girls? Take a look at this." Reverently, he unfolded a Betty Grable pin-up. "My kid brother sent her over—snuck her into Mom's package of cookies."

The dawn light was growing brighter—bright enough to see color, George noted, as the picture made the tips of Leroy's ears flush pink under his blond hair. *We're gonna need to keep our heads down pretty quick.* The first air raid of the morning had flown over not long ago.

More would be coming. Still, they had a few minutes before the Teds could get a good look at them. "Your brother's a good kid, Petey. Can we put in requests?"

From the direction of the latrines, Shorty came sauntering up and made a swipe for the picture. Pete tried to dodge, but Shorty grabbed it, holding it as high as his limited stature permitted. "Lemme see."

Snatching at it, Pete said, "Hey, knock it off—you're gonna rip her!"

Ignoring Pete's protests, Shorty took his time to peruse the picture. "Shucks, Petey, if she's gonna be on your wall, I might have to visit more. Hey, George, she almost looks like that spicy little number you were going around Naples with—don't she, Leroy?"

The kid shrugged.

"What was her name, Georgie—another Maria or Teresa or sumpthin?"

George fished in his pocket for a cigarette. He could picture the girl Shorty meant—pretty enough that the comparison worked. Good dancer. But her name? *Luciana? No, never could get a date with her. Gia. It was Gia. Not that it matters. Ain't like I'm going back to find her waiting for me.* He took his time lighting up. "Why, you thinking of calling her up for a date, Shorty? Naples is a long way from here."

Shorty sneered. "Maybe next time we get leave. After all, it's not fair that you always snag the best lookers. Every town we end up in—how do you find 'em?"

Holding his smoke in the corner of his mouth, George plucked the pin-up from Shorty's fingers and handed it back to Pete. "We've all got our gifts, Shorty. Maybe someday you'll find a lady who'll appreciate your personal brand of charm."

Shorty bristled. "My old lady likes me just fine, thanks—"

"When she's not sending you Dear John letters and threatening to run off," muttered Pete, but only George heard him. Shorty was still talking. *Never knows when to shut up.*

"—and maybe someday you'll find one you can't get away from

when you're bored, or they'll get wise to what a heel you are—"

Leroy stepped up behind George. "Hey, Shorty, how about you shut up, huh? Just cuz you know you shouldn't be dating anyway—"

George's grin couldn't quite hide his gritted teeth as he interrupted. "Settle down, fellas." Looking up, he was grateful to find a ready distraction. "Hey, Wally, I mean *sir*! What's the time?"

Skinny Wally, gangly legs carrying him along the edge of their new boardwalk, barely paused. Swallowing down his prominent Adam's apple, his gaze stayed fixed on the letter he was frowning over. "Dunno—not your clock."

George stepped smoothly in front of him, blocking his path. Playing along, Leroy joined him. Wally stopped, looked at them, then kept reading.

Folding his arms, George looked over at Leroy. "Whew! Power's gone to his head!"

Leroy nodded, solemn.

George stepped forward and draped an arm over Wally's shoulder. "What, *Sarge*, you can't talk with the rest of us lowly dogfaces no more?" Even while joking, he couldn't help eyeing the new stripe on Wally's sleeve. *Figured I'd get mine first for sure. Ah well...everyone's gotta start somewhere. And corporal's not so bad.* "After all, you're using the sidewalk me and Leroy built."

Wally looked down at the boards and snorted. "Stupid waste of time. How often you think you're gonna get to walk around on it? Just cuz they aren't bombing right this second—"

Patting Wally's shoulder, George cut in. "Ok, ok. Settle down, Wall. It's been a few hours, and I'm just wanting to know what time it is when Annie sounds off again."

"Didn't you hear? They blew her up last night."

"We've heard that before." The Army Air Force had been busily hunting for Anzio Annie since the enormous gun had begun flinging shells into the beachhead just under a week ago. Each shell roared like a freight train passing overhead, and the places they hit looked as bad as if a train really had crashed into them. Every time hopeful gossip said that the bombs had finally silenced good old Annie, another blast debunked it.

"Naw, they're sure this time." Wally shrugged George's hand off.

"How much?"

Wally hesitated, and George stepped back and put his hands in his pockets, nonchalant. Leroy grinned. Glancing back at his papers, Wally shifted his feet. "I…don't bet."

George laughed. "Who's betting? I just got a mess of smokes today and wondered if you'd like a few *if* good ol' Anzio Annie were to miss firing off this morning. Celebratory. And I wondered if you have anything good you'd like to share if you were to come by after she fires. We're just being friendly, see?"

Wally paused a moment more. "What kind of smokes?"

"Lucky Strikes."

Licking his lips, Wally folded his letter and stuck it in his hip pocket. "Well…I got two chocolate bars. Good stuff, not D rations."

George stuck out his hand. "Done. And what time…?"

Wally pulled back the cover of his watch. "About a minute after seven. Why do you care so much about Annie? You that lonesome for a girl?" A pallid beam of sunlight stretching across the embankment caught his eye. "Better get our heads down." The whistle of a shell to the north punctuated his statement.

"Sure. Wanna stick around for a while? See what happens? I got a new deck of cards too."

"What—it your birthday or something? At least these won't be marked." Wally kept grumbling, but he followed, ducking after George into the dugout he and Leroy shared. Leroy straggled in, and Shorty elbowed past, uninvited.

"Pull up a chair," George said, waving to the packing boxes he and Leroy had scrounged.

Wally grunted. "Not bad for a hole in the ground."

"Well, a fella does what he can. Better than sitting in the dirt for weeks." Silly as he knew it was, George felt a little swell of pride at the compliment. Besides the boxes, he and Leroy had lined the walls with cardboard and some pictures Leroy's sisters had sent from magazines and newspapers. A stove, rigged up from an empty oil drum with some cardboard shell casings serving as part of the pipe, kept the room warm and helped it feel more like a home than a damp hole in the earth. The high water table meant they all had to stoop under the low ceiling, but once they were seated it was hardly noticeable. Leroy lit the lamp he'd rigged up from odds and ends as George dealt.

"So." George set the deck on the table for Wally to cut. "Any word on the Limeys?" He'd met a few of the British soldiers during the early days, back on Sicily and on leave in Naples. Seemed like nice enough guys. They'd had a friendly argument over the merits of tea versus coffee. "Haven't seen any of 'em since landing."

Wally grunted. "Sounds like they're still having a rough time over there by the Factory."

George dealt. "At least they're holding on. After what happened to the Rangers trying to take Cisterna—" He fell silent. What was there to say about Darby's Rangers—crawling through the mud, quiet and careful, into an ambush. Of over seven hundred men, six had made it back to the beachhead. George cleared his throat and set down his cards to pat his pockets for a fresh smoke.

Shorty cursed his cards without any real emotion. "This place is hell. What're we even doing here? Did the brass even have a plan?"

"Course they did, Shorty." George laughed. "Plans always look great on paper. Us coming in from the sea, taking on the Teds from behind—the boys from Cassino taking 'em on from the front...I'll bet it sounded foolproof in the White House."

"Yeah, well, then I guess General Lucas was a bigger fool than they'd reckoned on—" Shorty began, but Leroy interrupted.

"Why don't you stop shooting your mouth off like you know strategy?"

A grin pulled at the corner of George's mouth. *Wow, he sure reminds me of Norrie. Always ready to jump in to defend anyone.* The smile faded.

Shorty spluttered. "What? You think you know better than me? You're just some hayseed from the North Woods, kid. And you're stuck here, stuck under those hills, just like the rest of us."

George held up his hands in a pacifying gesture. "Fellas, fellas… First of all," he turned to Leroy, "do they even grow hay way up there, Leroy?"

The kid just shrugged, glowering at Shorty.

Lighting his cigarette, George continued. "Whether the general knew what he was doing or not don't really matter just now, does it? The real question is, who's bidding?" Looking at his own cards, he added, "For my part, I'm not sure we'd be much better off if we'd pushed forward before we got the beachhead all secure. We might've gotten cut off from our supplies, and then where'd we be?"

Holding his hand out for another card, Wally said, "The Jerries are tough—I'll give 'em that."

George took a long drag of smoke. "I wouldn't give 'em anything. Old Neville Chamberlin tried that, and they just kept taking."

Leroy laughed—he was a reader too. Shorty, who'd probably never even heard of Britain's former Prime Minister or his attempts to pacify Hitler before the war got going, pretended to get the joke and laughed too hard. Wally just grunted again.

Hungry for information, George tried to keep Wally talking. "So, rumor has it we might be sent over to help at the hospital with hauling."

"Hauling what?" Leroy looked up, bright-eyed and curious.

"Stiffs." Shorty grunted, then grinned at Leroy's horrified expression.

The kid looked at George, then at Wally, obviously hoping one of them would contradict the statement.

"No, not bodies," Wally answered the unspoken question. "Wounded." He shrugged. "Well, mostly anyway. Gotta get 'em on the hospital boats, but the Jerries just won't let up. The beds in the wards are filled and then some. It's bad."

"Don't they have enough fellas working down there already?"

"Probably, but you know Greer. He likes his ideas."

A chorus of snorts and oaths rounded the table. Spit and polish Lieutenant Greer had taken over their platoon just before the landings, fresh from stateside, boasting about all his ideas for changes.

"Anyways," Wally continued, "he says since we're sitting in reserve just now, we might as well head over and see if we can't help out. Suppose it kind of makes sense—maybe they're shorthanded after what happened to the 95th Evac."

Silence fell again. It was one kind of terrible when the fighting men got bombed. It was another kind when the Germans hit the wounded in the hospital tents. And the doctors. And the nurses.

They exchanged cards in silence, until George drew. "So." He laid down a straight to groans from all. "Anyway, it's a change of scenery, and at least it's farther from the guns. Hopefully. Sounds like you never do know in Hell's Half Acre."

"Aaaaand," Shorty took the deck to deal the next hand, "word is some more nurses will be coming in." He waggled his eyebrows with a lecherous grin.

"Yeah?" asked Leroy, interested again.

"What, kid, you figgering on being a ladies' man like your buddy—" Shorty began.

"Don't matter," said Wally, shaking his head at his cards and tossing them back on the table. "They're all second lieutenants or higher. Can't fraternize with us anyhow."

"Well..." Shorty kicked George around the table. "They aren't *supposed* to."

George ignored him.

"Oh. Right." Leroy shrugged. "Still, it'd be nice to see a girl again."

George laughed. "Not worth it, kid—whoop! There she is! The

only lady I was worrying about this morning!"

Even dug in, the roar of Anzio Annie shook their bones.

Wally cursed without any real anger. "You always win, dontcha George?"

George gave him his biggest grin and lied. "Sure do, Wally."

Two

Jean bared her teeth in what she hoped was a passable smile. *I just have to hang on until we start our regular shifts. Even Stan would have to admit I'm trying.*

After all, she hadn't told off any more of the hopeful enlisted men who tried to strike up conversations with her or tried to press her with cigarettes or chewing gum.

She'd listened silently to the captain who'd told her a sob story about the Dear John letter he'd just gotten in a clumsy attempt to get her to promise to go dancing with him next leave.

She'd even gone out of her way to be helpful. When they'd been waiting and waiting to get permission to pull into Anzio harbor and most of the other nurses had been sick into their communal bucket, she'd shared her canteen so the woman next to her could rinse out her mouth. Sure, she'd found an excuse to walk away when the woman had tried to chat afterwards, but she hadn't felt much like opening her mouth and risking her own humiliation.

When they had finally—*finally*—gotten permission to pull up to the shore, she hadn't even smacked the seaman who'd grabbed her waist to steady her when they were disembarking. She hadn't asked for the help but had accepted it without complaint. She felt proud of her forbearance.

But this was too much. She counted to three before she spoke. "No," she said, holding her smile in place, "I'd really prefer you call me Jean."

Betty Sanderson, a petite brunette with wide blue eyes, sprawling on the cot across from her pouted. "But Jeannie's so cute!"

"It really is," the blonde, Gladys, threw over her shoulder. She'd insisted on taking the cot in the back—crammed in with even less space around it than the other two. This tent had been built for two; hopefully, the mix-up would be sorted out quickly and they could get more space. Gladys's backside barely fit into the narrow aisle between Jean and Betty's beds as she bent over her musette bag. "Just like that song, you know, that they were playing on the radio all the time—"

Betty clapped her hands—actually clapped her hands—and giggled. "Oh yes! *I dreaaaam of Jeannie with the light brown hair…*"

"NO." The growling protest ripped out of Jean's throat.

Betty stared, mouth hanging open, her eyes even wider.

She looks like a fish on a line. Ugh. No, c'mon, gotta play nice. Jean took a deep breath. *Now they'll just ask more questions.* She swallowed and leveled her voice. "No, thank you. I…some people used to sing that song to me. It gets old fast."

"Oh, you poor dear." Gladys finished puttering, straightened, and shook her finger at Betty. "You shouldn't tease her, Betty. If she likes Jean, she likes Jean." Her bed groaned as she plopped down on its sagging middle.

I don't need a mom over here thank you very much! Still, what would Stan say? Taking a deep breath, she smiled—sort of—again. "Thanks."

"Of course. You know, we never really got to know you at Riardo. I'm so glad we have a chance now…" Gladys glanced over at Betty, then said firmly, "Jean."

Betty could roll those huge blue eyes more dramatically than anyone Jean had ever seen. "All right. Not Jeannie." She leaned forward, looking at the ring Jean still wore.

Oh no. "Well, I'm due to assist in the operating room in an hour, so—"

"Hello? Anyone home?" A big, raw-boned girl with auburn hair stuck her head in through the tent flaps. A diminutive blonde peeked around her shoulder.

Mama Gladys jumped in at once. "Yes! Hello! We're just getting settled in. I'm Gladys Grady!"

Both newcomers offered smiles, but they were a little too tight, too strained, and their eyes looked as if they hadn't had much sleep. *No wonder, with all the artillery we've been hearing.*

As if on cue, a shell shrieked overhead, landing with a crashing boom somewhere farther back, toward the harbor. Jean jumped, Gladys flinched, and Betty curled up a little tighter on her cot. The visitors didn't react, except for tightening their jaws and fists. "Do you mind if we come in?" the blonde girl asked.

Betty reluctantly sat up halfway to make room, and the bigger girl sat next to her. The blonde looked for room next to Jean. Jean scooted over until she was balanced in the minimum necessary space, trying to smile again as her skin cringed from the unwanted contact.

The first visitor grinned. "Thanks, neighbors! Whew, it's comfy as sardines in a can!" She had a sharp laugh, more like the neigh of a horse than anything. It irritated the headache that had started behind Jean's eyes. "I'm Madge Hill. This is Lynn Holtz. Just finished our shift and stopped by to welcome you all to Hell's Half Acre."

In a moment of silence, the newcomers all stared at her. Slowly, Betty sat up straighter. "Hell's...?"

Madge laughed again, but Lynn answered in a soft voice. "Don't mind Madge." Looking down at her hands, she stretched her fingers over her knees. "It just means...I think it was someone's idea of a joke. *This* is Hell's Half Acre—the whole medical area." Another crash sounded from outside, punctuating the statement with force.

"Why?" Betty asked.

Madge laughed—*does she do anything else?* —but Lynn shrugged. "Well, you know. Usually the medical compound's in the rear, but there isn't really a rear here. Just the Mediterranean. And, well, I don't know if the Germans have bad aim or bad intentions, but we just seem to attract bombs." She let her hands fall, empty, into her lap.

They all stared at her, uncertain what to say next. Lynn blinked, then pulled another tired smile over her face. "You got in last night, didn't you?" She stretched, an involuntary movement for stiff shoulders. "At least it was quiet when you landed."

"On the beach, anyway," Madge said. "Don't suppose you heard about the hit on the nurses' tents yesterday? You might want to find a way to dig in." Lynn bowed her head and crossed herself.

Hit on the nurses' tents. The words froze Jean where she sat. *Yesterday. If we'd been here a day earlier, or if we hadn't wasted all that time waiting to land, it might be over already.* She refocused on the conversation as she heard Mama Gladys say, "How was it when you came in?"

Madge didn't manage a full neigh, but she still chuckled. "We had such a hard landing, I thought I was done before I'd even treated a soldier. Then we got ashore, and the boys all told us we'd be better off getting back on the boats and out of here. Not the most encouraging welcome."

"But…" They all turned their eyes on her, and Jean regretted opening her mouth. Still, they couldn't be saying what it sounded like they were saying. "But I still don't understand what happened with the nurses yesterday, and the 95th. It must have been some kind of mistake. They can't bomb the hospital. I saw the wards when we came up—the tents are all bunched together so they can't miss them…They're all marked with red crosses, aren't they? The Geneva Convention—"

Madge shook her head and pulled a box of cigarettes out of her pocket. "Means diddly squat right here and now, honey. I had friends on that hospital ship, the *St. David*, when she went down. They made it off. Some of the crew weren't so lucky." She proffered the smokes to the other girls. Betty and Lynn both took one. Madge lit up, closed her eyes, and inhaled deeply. "The Jerries bomb us all the time. Oh, they'll say it was an accident, that we're just too close to the legitimate targets, which we are, but still. With the hits we've taken—" Her eyes opened again, reflecting weary pain. "Guess things weren't so bad down south, huh?"

Betty's languid face was grim, her lips a thin line. Even Gladys looked a little pale. Lynn pursed her lips. "Oh Madge, you've scared them."

Madge shrugged and took a long drag of her cigarette. "Might as well tell them the truth, Lynnie. Besides, whatever we've got coming at us, the boys have it worse. That's why we're here, right?"

Nodding, Gladys said, "Of course."

Betty spoke up in what was meant to be a nonchalant voice, betrayed only by a slight quaver. "I think you're all missing the more important questions." She pulled her bag over onto her lap and fished around. With a little grin of triumph, she pulled out a compact. As they waited for her important revelation, she examined her face in the mirror, pursing her lips and patting her dark hair.

"Yes, Betty?" Mama Gladys prompted.

Betty shook her head. "What I wouldn't give for a visit to the hairdresser..." She snapped the compact shut, crossed her arms on her knees, and leaned forward. "What are the chances of getting a decent date around here?"

The tension broke, and the other girls laughed.

"Oh honey," hooted Marge, "where're you gonna go? It's not like there's an officer's club, and even the baseball diamond's got foxholes!"

Jean rolled her eyes.

Betty caught her. "Well, maybe you don't need to worry about it Jeanni...Jean." She jabbed the compact towards Jean's hand. "Just who gave you that sweet little diamond?"

The question slapped Jean, and she stiffened as all eyes turned towards her. Gulping a breath, she tried to steady herself. *This shouldn't bother me so much anymore.*

Mama Gladys caught her look. "Betty, you shouldn't be so nosy."

"Oh, you know you wondered too." Betty picked up the cigarette she had set aside and accepted Madge's proffered match with a nod. "And you know you'd just die if Major Fillbert offered you one of those. Maybe she could give you some advice." She gave a wicked smile as she took a drag, looking away from Gladys's blushing cheeks to focus on Jean. "So?"

The interruption gave Jean a moment to get her bearings. She pulled in another deep breath. "His name was Josiah Johnson. He's dead."

"Oh Jean…" Mama Gladys squeezed in beside her, hand on her arm. Jean closed her eyes, willing herself still, willing herself not to pull away. Lynn and Madge, to their credit, just nodded and kept quiet. Betty nodded too. She looked as if she might ask another question, but Jean decided to forestall her.

"I'd rather not talk about it anymore." She pulled her arm away from Gladys and stood, her hair brushing the roof of the tent. "We have plenty of work to do here without living in the past." She leaned forward to catch Lynn's eye. *She, at least, seems sensible.*

"I wonder, is there anything, anything in particular we ought to know before we start? Anything that will help us care for the men better and keep us from…" Her voice caught and died, and she hated herself for it.

Madge swooped in and saved her with another neighing laugh. "Keep you from playing those heavenly harps sooner rather than later?"

Jean nodded.

"Well, you'll want to know where the nurses' bomb shelter is. Wouldn't be a bad idea to see if you can dig in here, too, if the water table will let you."

Lynn shook her head. "I think it's too high."

Madge said, "Ok, the shelter it is, then. Otherwise, how are you at duck-walking?"

"Duck... *what?*"

FOURTEEN HOURS LATER, at the end of her twelve-hour shift as Stan's surgical nurse, Jean wished she'd never heard of duck walking—or the Anzio Amble as some of the fellas called it. She returned to her tent, walking in a low sort of squat with her head thrust forward for balance, her thighs burning. Reaching her tent, she collapsed on her bunk. With a groan, she stretched to her full length, joints popping.

Still, it's just about the only way to travel. The other nurses hadn't exaggerated about the dangers of the hospital area. She'd seen Stan striding out to the latrines, standing straight as if he dared any enemy to shoot him, but any temptation she'd felt to throw caution to the winds fizzled as she treated the wounds of men who'd met those hazards firsthand. With the risk of shrapnel and stray bullets, it was either folding her height into a duck walk or crawling. Pride wouldn't let her crawl.

She shifted on the unyielding cot. *I knew it wouldn't be glamorous, but I didn't expect a chafing girdle. Maybe I should just give it up—I pretty much look like the fellas anyway. It still feels a little funny wearing pants. Like I stole some of Joe's clothes. Not that I've even got that much of him.* She touched the ring, now dangling from a chain around her neck. The one thing she did have, evidence that he had been real, that he'd loved her. With a sigh, she raised her gaze to the canvas roof—an olive drab haven from the smells and sights of human misery.

Well, maybe not the smells. She wrinkled her nose. *I'm pretty ripe.* It wasn't bad enough to entice her to heave herself out of bed, though. Sleep tugged at her eyelids and weighed her limbs down. Pulling the scratchy wool blanket over her shoulders, she slept.

Even in sleep, rest was elusive. It seemed that she still stood in the rows of hospital beds.

She stands in the full ward. The stink permeates everything—the stink of blood and medicine and plaster and of the men—boys—who need a good wash and meal. But first they need to be stitched up, the missing bits repaired or replaced. Everywhere she looks are the tubes and the pipes and the haunted eyes.

A blond boy grabs her sleeve as she passes. "Don't send me down Purple Heart Highway! I don't wanna go to Naples—what if they hit the road again, nurse? Don't send me there—just send me back to my foxhole. I promise, I'm ok..." And she wonders if he remembers he's missing his left foot. Maybe the morphine has clouded his mind enough that he doesn't, and anyway, she can't help because her hands are full of instruments that need to be sterilized and Stan needs her in at the operating table—

But then his face is Joe's, his eyes accusing. "Why won't you help, Jeannie? Still too scared?"

She tries to open her mouth to respond, but her lips are stitched together. The scream tears at her throat—

BOOM

Jean's gritty eyes snapped open.

WsssshhhhhhBOOM

They're bombing us! Frozen, staring at the canvas roof, she bit her lips until salty blood spread across her tongue.

The red alert sounded—*A little late, isn't it?*—and another explosion's aftershock shivered through the air and vibrated in her bones, making the walls tremble. BOOM. A banshee's monstrous shriek passed overhead.

Slow reflexes kicked in, and she rolled off her cot. Crawling under and grabbing her helmet from her bedside, she pulled it down tight around her ears and wrapped her arms around her face. The earth trembled beneath her, or maybe she was the one trembling.

*Breathe, I've got to breathe. I've done what I can do. I've taken shelter—as if hiding under my bed will make any difference. Maybe I should run to the nurse bomb shelter—*But that would mean going outside.

Into the dark that wasn't dark because of the glowing flares and the flashes of light and explosions.

Jean squinched her eyes shut. Tried not to picture the broken men in the hospital. Tried not to picture those nurses who were hit in their own tents. *Nothing left. They said there was almost nothing left... God, please... if it's me, don't let me feel it... I couldn't stand to be crippled or... please. Just let me die... then at least I'll see Joe again.* She hated herself for the neediness of the thought but didn't take the prayer back.

The shell impacts sounded closer, louder. Jean flinched with each crash and wished that someone—even mothering Gladys or vapid Betty—were with her. *And I was so happy we were working opposite shifts. God, I don't want to die alone.*

A small eternity passed until the terror tightening her belly and drying her mouth was numbed by exhaustion. Her heavy eyes started to droop—until something odd, unfamiliar, opened them again. Silence echoed strangely in her ears.

It's stopped. It's over, and I'm still... I'm still here. The shivers took her; the damp chill had seeped through her wool coveralls and into her bones.

Got to move.

Another shiver wracked her. *I don't want to get up. I don't want to. I don't want to go out there...*

Hurrying feet and voices passed her canvas walls.

Jean closed her eyes, tight.

Coward. Joe was right.

Her eyes snapped open. She rolled out from under the cot, brushed herself off, and straightened her helmet.

GEORGE YAWNED and rubbed the sleep out of his eyes. Sure enough, as soon as darkness fell and the first enemy fire of the evening had settled down, Wally had come around saying Greer wanted them all loaded up to go to the hospital area double-quick. Two squads had piled into the deuce and a half truck to sit in the weary dark, straining their ears over engine noise for sounds of the enemy.

Wedged in between Pete and Leroy, George tried to doze. Pete kept fidgeting, craning his neck to look behind them, back towards the hills. With a sigh, George turned to him. "What's eating you?"

"Think they can see us?" Pete fingered the St. Michael medallion around his neck.

George was about to answer, but Lieutenant Greer's snort interrupted him. "That's why we don't use headlights, son, remember?"

Never mind that you're just about as green as Petey, here. Greener—at least he came in before we got to Naples.

Pete wasn't buying it either. "Sure. Sure, but they know where the roads are and—"

"Getting twitchy for your foxhole, Petey?" asked George, smiling so the other man could hear it in his voice. "Don't worry—this is just a little vacation. You and Betty'll be back together soon."

Maybe steadied by the remembrance of his waiting pin-up girl, Pete quieted down.

Despite George's talk, any chance of sleep had fled. *After all, Petey's not wrong.* Most likely, the Germans had this route all ranged for artillery—it seemed like they had all the roads and crossroads figured out. The beachhead being so small, this truck would almost certainly pass ammo and fuel dumps—places that would fry 'em up good if they happened to pass during an air raid. And their destination, the hospital compound, hadn't been dubbed Hell's Half Acre for nothing. He grimaced and fumbled for the cigarette behind his ear, even though he knew he shouldn't light it. *Never liked doctors, even when appointments came without the risk of being blown to bits.*

Leroy cleared his throat. "So, how long's it gonna take us to get there?"

The kid's nerves helped George shake off his own. He forced a grin. "Not long—after all, we've only got, what, five miles to cover?

Not near as far as we had to march on Sicily—and that was the time my bootlaces got stole. Did I ever tell you about that?" He launched into the ridiculous story, glad for the distraction as the dark miles wound away. By the time they'd reached the hospital compound and been set to work evacuating casualties, he'd found his confidence again—good thing, because Leroy needed someone to steady him.

"Pssst. George, did you see that one?" Leroy whispered in a library-quiet voice.

Subtle, kid. George strained to keep a straight face. He positioned his side of the stretcher next to the bed of the patient they were to move before asking, "Which what?"

Leroy leaned in and lowered his voice another notch. "The nurse. The tall one over there—with the kinda light brown or dark blonde hair."

"Nope." George grunted as he lifted the groaning patient onto the stretcher. "Gimme a hand?"

"Sorry." Leroy hustled to his end, helping position the patient's feet, still sneaking glances over his shoulder at the nurse. "She has about the prettiest green eyes—"

"Yup." George couldn't see her face—she was leaning over another patient—but it was easier to agree. He gave her a quick look as he straightened. *Too tall. Kinda skinny, but to each his own. How could the kid even make out eye color in this light?* She turned her head and snapped at another nurse, who hurried over with some bandages. *Not too friendly, either.* Something around her neck sparkled on a short, silver chain. "And a ring. Didn't you notice?"

Leroy focused hard on the stretcher handles.

"She outranks you anyway, kid. Remember? They aren't supposed to fraternize with dogfaces. Unless they can't help it, like for you, you lucky guy." George grinned at the boy on the stretcher. The soldier's pale face, twisted in pain, eased for a moment into half a smile. Then he coughed and groaned.

George frowned. "Hang in there—" he glanced at the dog tags, "Martin. We'll get you to the boats; then off you go!"

Martin shook his head weakly. "Naw, I don't wanna go to Naples… Purple Heart Highway…"

Mustering another grin, George shook his head, "Don't worry about that part, buddy. You just hang on for that little bit, and then you'll be home free! Just wait and see."

"Home." Martin echoed the word, a tired gasp. He coughed again, then closed his eyes.

Leroy caught George's eye. "Purple Heart Highway?" he mouthed.

Shaking his head, George nodded down to Martin's still face. He'd explain the nickname to the kid later—the road they'd travelled during the dark wasn't the only one the Germans had ranged, and some guys said it was more dangerous to be evacuated than to just stay put.

Pete came up beside George, helping Shorty haul another stretcher and trying to adjust to their vast difference in height. "Why'd they have to make all the nurses lieutenants anyways? It's not like the officers don't get enough attention. Will ya look at that?" He nodded over to Lieutenant Greer, who was chatting up a pretty brunette as she straightened the lines going into a patient.

"Why do you think he suddenly got all philanthropic and volunteered us to lend a hand?" George caught the nurse's eye and gave her a grin and a wink. She flushed and gave him a saucy half-smile in return. Greer shot a glare over his shoulder, and Leroy sniggered.

"How does an ugly cuss like you always do it?" Shorty grunted.

George ignored him, focused on keeping Martin's stretcher level. Glancing down at the wounded kid's face, he frowned. *He doesn't look good—too pale.* Martin groaned again, and his body twisted.

Mustering a hearty grin, George said, "Hey, buddy…what are ya gonna do first when you get home? Find a date, go to the movies, or get a good meal?"

Martin moaned. George straightened, lips tight. *He's not gonna make it.*

Leroy knew something was up too. He caught George's eye. "What should we..."

The nurse Leroy had been watching was nearest. "Nurse!" George called. She looked up, took in Martin's face, and hurried over. Leroy flushed and averted his eyes.

It didn't look like she noticed. She ignored both of them as she pursed her lips and checked Martin over, long fingers pressing his abdomen. He barely responded.

She looked up. *The kid was right about the eyes anyway. Pretty, sure, but brrr, cold!* Her voice wasn't any warmer, but she sounded like she knew what she was doing. "Bring him back. Now."

That got a response. "No... I'm going home," Martin groaned, but she didn't listen. She spun on her heel and hurried back through the ward, toward the OR receiving area. George and Leroy followed as they could, weaving around personnel, trying to keep the stretcher steady.

The nurse didn't even look back as she hailed one of the Majors. "Stan, I'm pretty sure he's bleeding again." The surgeon immediately began barking orders, and a couple of enlisted hospital workers came to take Martin back.

George stood, watching. *Poor guy.*

One of the medical fellas barked at him "C'mon there—get back to the others. We need to get that truck out." George shook himself, gave the guy a half salute and a grin, and looked over at Leroy.

The kid was gawking at the exit his green-eyed girl had taken. George tugged on his arm "C'mon. Let's get outta the way."

Their next evacuee was a burly fellow, almost too big for his stretcher. When they bent to lift him, Leroy grunted in surprise. George gave the man's uninjured arm a playful half punch. "Hey, fella, you been sneaking some real food from somewhere?"

The big guy laughed, then coughed. Flecks of pink spittle dotted his chest. "Sure, sure. Hey, thanks, fellas. Keep up the good work—haul the rest of us outta here. That way there'll be space when it's your turn."

George hefted him up. "Nah, I don't think I'll be visiting Hell's Half Acre anytime soon. Yikes! Seriously, how'd ya keep this much skin on your bones on rations?"

The big guy ignored the last comment. "We all said we wouldn't come here. Wait till they send you up to the front. You'll figure you're lucky to get back." He coughed again.

Leroy chimed in. "I figure we're gonna break through any day now."

That set the big guy laughing again, then coughing. The nurse Greer had been bothering rushed over, shushing him. He brushed her away and spat over the side of his stretcher. Wiping his mouth with the back of his hand, he said, "Kid, the only place you're going is on an evac boat or into a pine box. If'n they've even got boxes and they're not just feeding fellas to the fish." He grinned, his yellowed teeth big as tombstones.

Leroy swallowed and shook his head. "No, we're…"

George gritted his teeth and interrupted. "Buddy, since we're the ones getting you on your evac boat, maybe you'd better can it and let us work."

"Hey, I'm just…"

George jostled the stretcher a little extra as he hefted it higher. The big lout gripped the sides, cursed, and shut up.

They dropped him off at the truck—his stretcher was the last. The engine rumbled to life, and George dredged up a little of his old Sunday School experience to mutter a quick prayer for their safe arrival—even if that meant the big idiot would make it out too. With a sigh, he turned back toward the tent wards where more rows of wounded waited. "C'mon kid. Let's see what else needs doing."

"Ok." After a few steps, Leroy said, "So. She seemed like she knows her stuff."

"Who?"

"You know. That nurse. The one with—"

"Riiight. The blonde or brown hair. If you're gonna go all swoony over her, you'd better decide which. Personally, I'd call it brown. It'll be easier to rhyme when you start writing poetry."

Leroy smacked him. Then, his face grew sober. "Think the guy—Martin—will be ok?"

George shrugged and opened his mouth to respond. He froze. Leroy took a couple of steps more, then looked back. "Hey, Georgie?"

George didn't hear him, focused on the form approaching through the dark to their right.

Him. Even in the blackout conditions with nothing but a hint of starlight, George knew him. Knew his walk, his stooped shoulders, his heavy jaw so incongruous on his thin, still face.

The oncoming man stopped a few paces away. After a moment of silence, he said, "Hullo, George."

George's head jerked down, then back up, a nod as stiff and contrived as a marionette's. "Hey, Frank." He plastered on his easy grin and folded his arms. "What're you doing here? Feelin' poorly?" *As if I'd be so lucky.*

"No. The old man sent me over—I'm looking for Greer. He's your lieutenant, isn't he?"

"Sure is. What you want old Greer of the Rear for?"

Frank looked past him. "Orders. It's urgent. Could you show me where he is?"

Pointing toward the tent they were returning to, George said, "Follow the sound of nurses' voices. You'll find him."

"Thanks." He started to turn. George meant to let him go, but he couldn't stop himself.

"Hey, Frank, how's Lil?"

The other man turned back slowly. "Lilly's just fine. I got a letter this morning—she said everyone back home is doing just fine. Thanks." The next words came out as if they were forced. "Should I say anything from you, to her, when I write back?"

George laughed. "Naw, I don't think so. You can always give her a hello and send my regards, but I suppose she knows she's got those. I'm glad you've heard from her, though. Glad she's doing well. Good she's keeping busy writing too. She does best when her time is fully occupied, doesn't she?"

The dark line of Frank's shoulders straightened. "I know she'll be relieved that you haven't had to move up yet. Keeping safe in reserve, way back from the line. I'm sure you're enjoying that."

With a low sound in his throat, Leroy stepped forward. George sidestepped in front of him and shook his head. *Settle down, kid. This worm's not worth it.* "Well, we can't all be buddies with the Major and keep busy running messages, can we? But here I am, digressing, and you with a message to deliver. I guess we'll have to catch up later."

Frank smiled, a cold, thin smile. "I suppose so, George. I hope we get the chance. All the best."

George watched him go, then with a sigh followed. Leroy hustled up beside him and leaned over. "Who's he, George?"

"No one to worry about."

"Yeah, but what a fat-head. It, uh, it seemed like there was…well, maybe some bad blood there."

"I suppose you could say that." George pulled out his cigarette and almost lit up before remembering blackout regulations. With a low curse, he stuck it in his mouth, unlit. Stupid how Frank could still set his nerves on edge. "He's the only fella I ever considered killing who wasn't on the other side of a battlefield." That stopped Leroy in his tracks. He whistled, but George just shook his head and walked on. *I said too much.* That's *a road I don't want to go down again.* "Now what's got me wondering is why we see a fella like him, here, with a message from the old man to our Greer." He shook his head. "Kid, I've got a feeling we're not going to like that message."

To the north, the rumbling, shrieking, booming shells echoed through the beachhead.

THE NEXT EVENING, George ducked into the dugout, kicking the walls. One of the pieces of cardboard lining fell to the ground.

Leroy looked up from the letter he was writing. "Hey, careful! I just fixed that."

"Sorry, kid." George leaned over to right it. "Better get the place in order—we'll have to leave it behind for a while."

"What? Are we moving up?"

"That's the word. Did some asking around. Sounds like the fellas in the 45th are heading up and over to buck up the Limey lines by Via Anziate. It's been hot over there—bad luck for them. We're going pretty much straight north, towards..." He pulled out the rough map he'd sketched. He jabbed it with his finger. "Padiglione. Well, over to the east of it, I guess, so we aren't stepping on any Thunderbird toes."

George pulled the cigarette out from behind his ear and his matchbook from his breast pocket. Pausing, he looked over at his friend. Leroy stared into space, pale. George tucked his matchbook away. "Hey, got a light?"

Blinking, Leroy shook himself. "Sure." He dug out his pristine matchbook. The kid hadn't taken to smoking, but he liked to carry one around, just in case. He threw it to George, who snagged it.

"Thanks." He lit up and took a long drag. "Wally says it shouldn't be long up front. Good news—I'd hate to have someone take over this little place while we're out. Mom always said renters never take care of a place like owners, ya know?"

Leroy forced a chuckle. "Yep, I suppose." He bent his head back to his letter, though his pen hung poised over the paper. "Not long? Was Wally pretty sure?"

"Weeeell, you know Wally. Always a sour puss, but even he didn't think we'd be up more than a few days. Give the guys up front a break."

"Sure—and you figure we'll be breaking through soon, right?"

George opened his mouth, then closed it. Shorty's curses echoed through the door, and he burst in waving a letter.

"Look at this. Just look at this! Another one!"

Sticking the cigarette in the corner of his mouth, George reached for the letter. He perused it and whistled. "Your old lady again?"

"Yeah. Today of all days..." Shorty's string of invectives was extensive, if not very creative. He accepted a match from Leroy and lit up.

Leroy said, "Who's she leaving you for this time?"

"Yeah, Shorty," George said, "doesn't this make three Dear John letters you've got from her? 'Course, look at the bright side—she always comes back."

"Smart guy aren't ya? This time it's the baker. Can you believe—"

George nodded and made sympathetic noises from time to time, glad, for once, of the interruption. With any luck, by the time Shorty was out of steam, Leroy would have forgotten his last question. Unfortunately, George couldn't.

Long after turning in, he lay awake. *If we'd only made it farther that first day on the beach. Or the second. I can't blame Lucas for hesitating, for keeping us back until the beachhead was built up, but he must've known that if we got trapped here we wouldn't have anywhere else to go. If only we could've reached those cursed hills before the Teds took 'em. Or if our landing had done enough so the boys down at Cassino could've broken through...*

For the hundredth time, he thought through the maps he'd studied in days past, trying to see how things could've gone differently. He closed his eyes and pictured Italy, that sexy high heeled boot stretched across the Mediterranean. He imagined a red line across the calf—the Gustav Line where the bulk of the Army was trapped. It had seemed to make sense, sending him and the rest of his force north by sea, to come in from behind the lines, to attack while the main army attacked from the south.

Maybe it could've worked if they'd been able to send a bigger group up here, or if the other guys had broken through. Or if we'd just been able to advance, even a little. If we could've just got some breathing room, some space for a rear echelon...Heck, while I'm wishing, I might as well wish we'd been able to march right up to Rome!

Rome, like he'd read about in all the books. The eternal city, the ruins, the history. He'd always wanted to see Rome. He and Lil had talked about going there when things settled down. Frank's chilly face floated across his mind, and he rolled over. That didn't bear thinking about. Rome was only important as the first Axis capitol, almost within their grasp.

Almost, though it sure doesn't seem to be getting any closer, no matter what the brass says. Shows what they know. And those are the guys who hold my life—all our lives, all the fellas...and the kid. Poor kid's scared stiff. He shouldn't be here—he's too good for this, too much like Norrie—

He rolled onto his side.

Gotta stop chewing on that. They've gotta have a plan, down there by Cassino, they've gotta. And when they break through, so will we. We'll whip the Teds yet.

Flopping over to his back again, he sighed.

Just get through this time up front. Just get through it, and get back again. No problem. Get the fellas through it. Maybe get a few more stripes to wear home. That'll show 'em. He clutched the edge of his blanket and clung to the bright image of his triumphant return to keep back the surrounding dark.

Three

Leroy dreamed of home. Of the mine.

The door shuts with a final, clanging thud, a metallic coffin. As the motors on the mine hoist start up, Leroy stares straight ahead. He doesn't care to look up, to where the sun is receding. The mine feels like a great mouth swallowing him up, and he doesn't much like to watch the 'gulp.'

Nothing's gonna go wrong. Never has, has it? He clenches his sweaty palms.

A sharp, shimmying motion shakes the car. Dad mutters under his breath. Another jolt. A wailing shriek echoes up the shaft as metal pulls away from metal. He knows they're going to fall. Down into the black grave, already dug for them—

Leroy's eyes snapped open. The smell of earth, of damp darkness still surrounded him, with the stench of his own dried sweat and unwashed clothes, and that shriek—the angry shriek still pierced his ears. His clawed fingers covered his head, trying to shut it out—

I'm buried alive! I'm…

The shriek passed, as did the sensation of falling. As he blinked the sleep from his eyes, everything came back. He was on Anzio. Not buried—unless he considered their little dugout a tomb. The shriek—*It was just that darned big gun. Of course, just another shell.* Here came the next one, loud as the first.

He wiped his hands across his brow, scrubbed them over the stubble on his face. *It's good I'm hearing them. After all, don't they say that you don't hear the one that gets you?*

If that were true, he was safe from an awful lot of shells. One shriek ended; another began, then another. The roof of the dugout trembled, shaking loose dirt and sand over him. Eyes streaming, he told himself to curl up, to protect his head, but he couldn't tear his gaze away from the earthen roof that might come crashing down.

Gradually, the din decreased.

Gosh I'm a chicken. Gulping a deep breath, he forced himself to sit up. He folded his hands. "The LORD is my shepherd; I shall not want…. Yea, though I walk through the valley of the shadow of death, I will fear no evil; For You are with me…"

A sharp image flashed through his mind: Mom's big hands, dried out from scrubbing floors and washing clothes for six children, wrapped around his. On the nights when Dad worked late at the mine, when Leroy couldn't sleep for fear of a cave-in, she'd come in and whisper prayers in his ear until he could sleep. Her words lit up the dark.

His heart slowed, but his eyes couldn't close—wouldn't close—what if they didn't open again? *Thank God we aren't out patrolling in this, or on the front*—but they would be soon enough. Then what?

With a last echoing rumble, the shelling stopped. Leroy closed his eyes, forced himself to breathe, to lie back down.

It was no good. *Tomorrow. No, it's a new day. Tonight. Tonight, we move up.*

The sensations from the first patrol after they landed flooded him—the tension clutching his belly as he followed George, creeping through the silent buildings of Anzio, nerves on edge. The flood of relief when they reported that they hadn't encountered any of the enemy. Safe.

But now, the hills were full. Full of the enemy, looking down, firing down. Nowhere was safe anymore. The Germans, or the *Tedeschi,* as the Italians called them, waited, massing up to destroy the little beachhead.

And tonight, we're going out to meet them. His sweat went cold. He shivered.

Lord, it's not like I expected to sit in reserve the whole war. It's just that I didn't expect to be here. *Sitting here, waiting for some Ted's lucky shell. I thought when I left home, decided not to work in the mines, I'd be leaving holes in the ground. Starting fresh. Moving forward.*

Maybe Dad was right.

When Leroy had first proposed the idea of the military in '39, just a sophomore in high school starting to look ahead, his dad tried to talk him out of it. "C'mon, Lee, what's the Army got? With all this mess in Europe...well. Even if we get involved, they'll need healthy young fellas here just as much as over there to go get all shot up." He'd shaken his head and gone back to his newspaper. "It's stupid, that's what it is. Another war in Europe. Maybe Lindberg and the rest of them are right—we should just take care of our own." Leroy had let it drop.

Of course, that was before Pearl Harbor. Once the word of the Japanese attack came over the radio, it didn't matter that most of the folks up in Tower, Minnesota didn't know where Pearl Harbor was, they'd all been steamed. America attacked on her own soil!

Even Dad had to bend a little. "But not till you're done with school, son. It's only, what, five months till graduation? Go then if you're bound to."

And though it chafed, Leroy had waited, even when his older sister, Marty, went off to Washington state to work in the Navy Yard. No one gave her any grief. Even the younger girls found things to do, helping with scrap drives and knitting for the "Bundles for Britain" drive at church with Mom.

The months wore on, and every chance he got, Dad took Leroy along to the mine. He introduced him to the foreman, to the men who ran the machinery, hoping something would strike his fancy. "They'll need iron, son, you just wait. The way our mine's producing, there'll be a little Minnesota iron in every plane the Allies send up soon!"

The look on Dad's face when Leroy came home the evening of his graduation and announced that he was taking a bus down to Fort Snelling in the morning sent guilt twisting through his middle. *I guess he really thought he could convince me to stay, work at the mine.*

Rolling over, he sighed. He was only four when word of the accident at the Barnes-Hecker Mine in Michigan had reached his family. Still, his memory was seared with the image of Mom crying on Dad's shoulder because her brother had been working over there and she didn't know if he'd survived. Not many had—the shaft had flooded too quickly, trapping more than fifty men underground. One man managed to climb out faster than the rushing water; the others were drowned or buried alive. Dad spent years trying to convince Leroy that the Soudan Mine was different—strong, reinforced by the iron they dug out, but Leroy hated the feeling of claustrophobia that seized him in the dark, half mile ride down into the earth. He hated the heavy walls lit only by flickering, artificial lights.

Life underground wasn't for him. So he'd left, enlisted, shipped abroad, and now, here he was, stuck underground after all. With a sigh, he gave up on getting comfortable.

Trying not to disturb George, he eased himself up and slipped the little paperback of *The Great Gatsby* off their "bookshelf" crate. *Whoever thought up shrinking novels into these little "Armed Services Edition" books ought to get a medal.* He didn't like this one quite as much as *Davy Crockett*, but it sure beat reading the labels on ration boxes or serial stories in the papers where the next installment might not come for a month, or at all.

Outside, the dawn was just starting to paint the horizon gray. Even in the dim light he kept a low profile, sitting cross-legged on their makeshift sidewalk. Looking down at it, he grinned. Wally was right. What was the point of a sidewalk in all this mess? But it had given them something to do and cheered Georgie up a little. All the waiting nearly drove him nuts.

Leroy trailed his finger along the lines of words until he found his spot. Right. Gatsby and that other fella—the one who was married to Gatsby's old girl—were about to have it out. His finger froze, poised over the first word of the chapter. *George and that guy at the hospital had history, that's for sure. The way they looked at each other…I wouldn't like to see what'd happen if they ran into each other where no one was watching.*

Leroy had been friends with George since he'd joined this outfit as a replacement after the Salerno invasion. In those months he'd never seen George rattled—not during that fistfight in Naples, not during the training or the sailing over here in that hellish storm, with boats breaking apart and getting stuck in the waves. *Kept his head enough to save my life, anyway. But whoever that guy—Frank—is, he's sure gotten under George's skin.*

Wonder what he did to him. Not that it's any of my business. He pulled out a piece of gum. *Sounded like it had to do with a girl. Well, that's no big surprise.*

Closing his eyes, he savored the tang of spearmint that flooded his tongue. He'd given up on trying to figure out the way George was with girls. *He's not the wolf Shorty makes him out to be—don't know why he puts up with that. But…* But it was true that his friend was hardly ever without a date. He'd wine them and dine them and dance and smooch, then say goodnight at the end of the evening, and that would be that. At breakfast he'd laugh about how they'd tried to squeeze him for money or a free trip to America—the more mercenary a girl was, the better. The only time things were different was with that one girl in Naples—the one Shorty had teased about. Gia Something or Other. *Three dates. He took her out three times. Then, after I said that he must really like this one, George never took her out again.*

Leroy grimaced. The taste of the gum faded too fast, leaving behind the taste of stale rations and dirt. A rumble rolled through the earth at his back—someone on the road. He pushed himself up and eased his nose over the embankment. The trucks pulling past bore big red crosses on a white background.

Wounded. Wonder if they're from up where we're going?

Three ambulances trundled past, followed by an open jeep. Leroy felt pretty sure he knew at least one guy sitting in the back. Whitey Stevens from down Lake Itasca way—they'd come over together. He was easy to spot because on the ride over he'd gotten ahold of a British helmet—looked like so far no one'd called him on being out of uniform, though that'd probably change now he wasn't being shot at. Whitey's bandage-wrapped leg rested on the edge of the jeep door.

The light slowly grew as the ambulances passed, and Leroy's ears caught the buzz of the first planes of the morning. He looked to the skies. *Huh. Air raid running late today. Dear God, look out for those vehicles, please?* A memory of green eyes prompted him to add, *And the people over at the hospital, too.*

The sound of muttered cursing got his attention, and he turned, looking down his sidewalk. Along it hustled Wally, packet of papers in hand. Mid-invective, he raised his head, his eyes meeting Leroy's. He grunted, then nodded.

"Hey! You see some ambulances go past?"

Leroy nodded. "Sure."

"Well, look. Greer wants this info from the forward OP to get to Cap'n Paulson, quick. Not sure what he'll do with it in the hospital area but," Wally shrugged away his superiors' fickleness with a sour grimace. "You just hustle over there and get it delivered, will ya?"

Leroy hesitated. He'd be heading in the same direction those planes had been. As he opened his mouth to answer, thunder sounded in his ears—the oncoming roar of a freight train. *Anzio Annie.*

He hollered but couldn't hear himself. Barely felt the thud as he rolled off the embankment. In the dirt beside him, Wally's open mouth flapped like Harold Lloyd's on the silver screen, but instead of an organ accompanying this silent film, Annie's roar filled every sense. Squinching his eyes shut, Leroy prayed but could only manage, "Please....please..."

The thundering shriek passed overhead, then careened deeper into the beachhead.

Leroy listened to his heart pound. Slowly, his clenched hands loosened. Taking a deep breath, he rolled over. His gaze landed on his book, crumpled in the dirt. "Oh, shoot!" He brushed off *The Great Gatsby* with the edge of his filthy shirt.

Wally rolled over, too, and spat. "Never mind that. Here." He held out the sheaf of papers.

He wanted to protest, tell Wally that the roads weren't safe, but the words stuck in his throat. *I'm not much safer here, anyway, not if Annie looks this direction.* A little spark of hope lit in him. *And if I end up in the hospital area, I might see her...* He found his feet. "Yessir, Wally. Sure thing."

He turned on his heel, debating whether to wake George, but George already stood beside him, grinning. "Whew. Annie makes a good alarm clock, don't she? Off to the nurses we go again, huh?"

Hoofing it up to the road, they met another jeep headed toward the rear. Highway 7 was a dangerous place with the sun rising, but Leroy and George looked at each other and shrugged. Flagging the driver down, they bummed a quick ride. The pale illumination in the east—behind the German emplacements—grew, lighting up the road and the land around it. The strange, wet landscape was sliced up by ditches and canals. Supposedly, it had been drained to make way for farmland, but the Germans had re-flooded it to prepare for their arrival. Half-drowned farmhouses and stands of trees stuck out of cold, stagnant water. Leroy shivered, and pulled his collar tighter around his neck.

All things considered, it wasn't a bad trip—they only had to stop and hit the dirt three times. Twice, Annie's roar sent them into the muddy ditch, then the planes Leroy had watched that morning strafed them as they returned east. When some shells started whining overhead, the driver just cursed and hit the gas while they held on.

The hospital area was buzzing with activity. *Of course, I don't suppose it's ever quiet.* Ambulances parked by the receiving tent. Enlisted men with stretchers unloaded the wounded. Shells whistled and whined over to the north, but most of the hospital workers paid no attention, and the sirens stayed silent.

George took the lead, asking around for Paulson. Leroy followed, peering around, trying to appear casual. He started as a nurse rushed out to check a man's vitals, then relaxed. *Not her.* George caught his eye and winked, and heat flushed the back of Leroy's neck.

The first familiar person they found was Whitey, sitting outside the receiving tent with his bloody, bandaged leg stretched out before him. A tired grin pulled at his face as he waved Leroy over. "Hey, Minnesota! Don't suppose you've got any smokes?"

Leroy grinned back as George fished out a cigarette. Whitey took it with a nod, lit up, leaned back, and sighed. "Thanks. Boy, that's the ticket. How you doing, Georgie-boy?"

"Not too bad, 'cept I hear you guys left a mess up front, and now we gotta go clean it up. Thought by now, crack troops like you, you'd have the Teds running." George grinned to take any sting out of the jibe.

Whitey cursed at him good naturedly. *Good thing they know each other*, Leroy thought. *If someone'd said that to me after coming off the front, I might've slugged him.*

"Naw," Whitey said, "we figured if we did, you'd be sore about not getting in on the fun. We figured we'd come back, take a rest, play a little ball. Now we've got 'em softened up, you can head in and finish the job for us." He leaned his head back. "Let me know what the view's like from the top of them hills, will ya?"

George shook his head. "Tell ya what, buddy—next time, don't trouble yourself about doing me any favors, ok?" He pulled out a smoke for himself. "How's everyone else doing—is Rialto here, too, or is he still…" his speech slowed as Whitey shook his head and took another long drag.

"Naw, he's not here. Who knows where he is? Rialto's squad went out on patrol a couple nights ago. None of 'em came back. We went out in the same direction last night—that's where I got the souvenir." He gestured to his leg with his cigarette. "Found one body—Wayne Wilson, you know him? Didn't find nothing else but lots of spent shells. Little blood maybe, but who can tell in all the muck? I figure they're on their way to a POW palace."

Leroy's stomach clenched. He'd heard stories about the German camps. If you were an officer prisoner of war, they were supposed to treat you ok, if they were abiding by the Geneva Convention anyway. He wasn't as sure about how they'd treat a no-rank dogface.

George shook his head. "Well. That's a shame. Hope they come out of it ok."

Whitey blew out a puff of smoke. "Maybe you'll be saying howdy to them yourself, soon. The front's no joke. You might get lucky, get taken prisoner..."

"You call that lucky?"

"Better than dead, ain't it?"

George shrugged. "Maybe, maybe not. After all, we've all gotta cash it in sometime. If it's between that and trusting Jerry-style kindness…"

"Easy to talk big about going down guns ablazin' when you're sitting pretty in the rear." Whitey took another drag. "You think Anzio's bad here? Just wait until you get up front. Up there, it's not just the shells, not just the planes, it's *them*, liable to climb right into your foxhole and slit your throat." He shrugged. "I figure any fella who gets out of there alive is lucky—by any means possible."

George raised his eyebrows. "So, how'd your leg get shot? Was it really the Teds, or...?"

Leroy twitched at the question. George had guts to say it aloud. Guts, or maybe not too many brains.

Whitey flicked the cigarette butt at George. "S mine. Just lucky it didn't take nothing else with it. And nope, I stepped on it honestly, Georgie Porgie. So, why dontcha shut up and do what you came here to do, huh?" He leaned back his head and closed his eyes.

George opened his mouth, but Leroy interrupted him. "Sure, Whitey. Get well soon." George echoed him.

Moving away, Leroy scanned the camp again, looking for someone who could tell him where to find Paulson. A nurse came over to check on Whitey—she had darker brown hair than the girl he was looking for—and he intercepted her. "Excuse me..." He snapped a quick salute, then froze, trying to remember if he was supposed to salute the nurses or not. Dropping his hand awkwardly to his side, he fumbled for his voice. "Um...lieutenant, Nurse, um, do you know where Captain Paulson is?" She smiled and directed him to the next receiving tent. On reaching it, he realized that George hadn't followed him. *Where's he gotten to? Oh well—first things first.*

After a few more queries, he found the captain and delivered his missives. *Ok. Now I just gotta find George, and maybe we can get another ride back.* George, however, was nowhere in sight. He'd probably found someone else who'd come back from the front—he was always digging for more information.

As Leroy hesitated between the receiving tent and the one across the way—looked like pre-operative patients in there—the red alert sounded.

Oh shoot.

Looking from side to side, he tried to get his bearings. Medical staff—enlisted men, nurses, doctors—were still hurrying around, keeping on with their jobs while shooting occasional glances at the sky. And then, there she was. The green-eyed girl, hustling into the tent to his right, probably just coming on for her shift.

Without thinking, he followed her as under the warning siren, the drone of planes grew. *Sounds like a bunch of them coming. Sheoot.* Ducking to peer into the tent, he saw her, another nurse, and a couple of enlisted hospital workers. Some patients had rolled onto the floor, covering their heads. Others who could not move lay helpless on their cots. At the bed nearest him, she leaned over a man, shielding his head with her own while fiddling with the tubes going into his arm. An impact—too near—made the glass bottles rattle and the bag of plasma beside the boy shake as he groaned, "Not again, please, God, not again. Get me outta here—"

Her voice carried over his, calm and cool. "Settle down, soldier. It'll be done soon."

Another crash—much closer—and Leroy flung himself into the tent. "Ma'am, get down. I'll watch him—you get yourself down, ok?"

The nurse looked at him, her eyes wide with surprise. Then they narrowed. "What are you doing in here? You need to—" The drone of planes was so near that it seemed as if they must crash into the tent. Her eyes flicked upward, her lips tightened, and she bent back over her patient.

Fine. Ignore me—but I'm not going anywhere till this is over. "What can I do?"

She scowled, then bit her lip. Her eyes flicked to the side where another man lay, all hooked up to tubes, out cold, by the looks of it. "Can you cover him?"

To the shakes and rattles of another blast, he pulled the man's blanket higher, and tried to shield him. Twice more, engines swooped overhead, then faded away. The alert sirens quieted. Leroy turned back to the nurse.

Still bent over her patient, she was checking the man's lines. There was no sign of what she'd just been through other than a little tremor in her hands.

Several more enlisted men and another nurse rushed in, and Leroy shuffled his feet, aware that he was out of place. He cleared his throat, wanting to say something to her while he had the chance. She straightened. Awkward silence reigned for a moment, then to his surprise she breathed, "Thanks."

"Oh." Leroy shrugged, uncomfortable. "Sure. I—"

An older man—*officer, a surgeon, maybe*—hustled over, unlit pipe clenched between his teeth. He gave Leroy an appraising look from under heavy black and white brows and growled at the nurse, "Dangit, Jeannie, when're you going to stop yammering and start getting me some more plasma? We need to get operating."

She gave him a cool look and spun on her heel with a "Yessir," which somehow sounded less respectful than if she'd called him a name.

Leroy grinned, but the older fella caught him and glared. Leroy snapped to a straighter stance. "Sorry, sir," he said, not sure what he was apologizing for. "I'll—"

The surgeon just waved him away. "I don't care what you do—just go and do it wherever you're supposed to. Morphine?!" The last was shouted over the doc's shoulder. One of the enlisted medical staff hurried over, and Leroy ducked out.

Jeannie. He grinned to himself. *Pretty name. And maybe not as cold as she looks. Don't suppose that matters, though. I wonder who gave her that ring—*

Lost in thought, he jumped when George appeared and draped an arm over his shoulder. He was cracking wise about something or other, and Leroy sighed. George was a good buddy, but not the easiest guy to think around—he was all talk and action.

Brushing aside thoughts of the girl and worries over whether they'd reach their hole before the next raid and what tomorrow would bring, Leroy zeroed in on what George was saying just in time to hear, "I don't care what Whitey says, kid. A POW camp is not the end of this war for me. Nossir."

Another lovely night. Jean huddled in a corner of the nurses' air raid shelter, her shaking arms a weak shield to protect her weary body. Another blast shook the dark hole. Bits of earth drifted down onto the crush of elbows and mingled smells of body odor and stale perfume. Closing her eyes, she wished to be anywhere but here. *If only I'd been able to dig down by my tent.*

She'd tried during her off hours despite Gladys reminding her what the other nurses had said about the high water table. She'd smiled and thanked her and kept going once she was gone, muttering to herself that life would be easier here if people could mind their own business. She had managed a decent-sized hole that extended under her cot—something she could just roll into—and gone to the worship service at which she sang "Jesus, Savior Pilot Me," and wondered if she really wanted that if He chose to send her to places like this. Still, she had her hole dug. She began her next 12-hour shift satisfied.

When she'd returned to find her hole half full of water and one of her socks floating in the sludge, she blinked back tears. Mama Gladys tried to laugh it off. "Well, maybe we could use it to soak our laundry?" Jean bit her lip and managed not to answer with any of the scathing comments that raced through her mind.

Shifting on the hard bench, she tried to press herself into the wall. One of the other off-duty nurses started to sing— "Blues in the Night." Jean wrinkled her nose; she didn't have the voice for it, but a couple of the other girls, Madge included, joined in, laughing. At least the girls on her bench were quiet, heads bent together, talking between blasts. The redhead on the bench across the way looked like she was asleep.

Leaning her head back, Jean tried to follow her example as the earth shook around her again. A yawn nearly split her face in two, and she hugged herself tighter. *If I could just get warm enough, I probably* could *sleep, even here.* Another blast whistled over. *And if they'd just quit it…*

They didn't—it felt like a longer raid than usual. In spite of the cacophony from outside and the singers who had moved on to "There'll Be Bluebirds Over the White Cliffs of Dover," Jean must have dozed, because she found herself back home.

Jeannie stands in the office Dad and Uncle Stan built onto the side of the house. Everything says HOME: the pale-blue walls, the lithograph of Jesus the Good Shepherd behind the admission desk, the worn green couch, the potted philodendron in the corner. Her nose wrinkles at the mingled scents of iodine and rubbing alcohol and Stan's tobacco, contrasting with the rich smell of pound cake drifting from Mom's kitchen.

Walking through the door to the exam room, she clambers up on a stool next to the table. Uncle Stan's warm hand on her shoulder steadies her. He helps her with the ear tips of the stethoscope and shows her how to position it on Mrs. Larson's swollen belly. Mrs. Larson laughs at Jeannie's face as she hears the baby's heartbeat, a soft, miraculous flutter.

She beams up at Uncle Stan, "I heard it!" And then she looks past him, out the window, where Fred is walking up the sidewalk with a boy she doesn't know, tall and golden-haired, and her own heart gives a little flutter as she bends back to get a better look…

"Hey, Jean? Want some?"

The dream faded and cruel reality crashed in with a shell's whistle. She focused her bleary eyes on Madge.

"Wha…?" She blinked again, and resentment replaced her confusion. *Can't she even let me dream in peace?* During training, the other nurses at Camp McCoy had learned to give her space. She'd managed to stave off unwanted friendships at Riardo. But here, here there was nowhere to go. Nowhere to get away. No space. *Is it so bad that I just want to do my job and not have to play like I want to be friends?*

"Jean?" Madge still stood over her, holding a cup of…something. The smell coming off it made Jean wrinkle her nose in disgust. "Sorry, honey, did I wake you? Just thought you might like a drink." She laughed. "It's one way to warm up!"

"What…what *is* that?" Jean cringed at the smell. *Grapefruit? Ugh, rancid grapefruit?*

Madge laughed again—that braying neigh that set her teeth on edge. "A little cocktail one of the enlisted fellas dropped off for us for our next little 'air raid party.'"

"Cocktails? Where in the world..."

"Well, it's not much." She took a sip and wrinkled her nose. "Medical alcohol and grapefruit juice. He insists it'll grow hair on our chest. I had to remind him that that's not what most of us are going for." She laughed again and held it out.

"No. Thank you."

Madge shrugged. "Suit yourself." She lowered her voice and lowered her bulk to the bench. "Look, are you doing alright?"

"I'm fine."

Studying her face, Madge shrugged again and took a swig. "Okey-dokey. No offense, you just have seemed a little—" She shrugged for a third time.

Does she do anything besides wiggle her shoulders? "Like I said, I'm fine."

Nodding, Madge took another drink. "Sure." She hesitated, then shrugged again. "Just so you know, though, you're getting yourself a bit of a reputation."

Jean bristled. "What do you mean?"

"Well…you hardly ever talk to anyone. Not even at mess. Not even when you're off."

"What, is this a social club now? I thought we were here to work…"

"Sure, sure." Madge raised her hand. "I know that—none of us came here expecting to sit around curling each other's hair. It's just..." She took another sip of her concoction. "It's just that, this place. This is a terrible place, Jean." The shriek of a shell interrupted her.

When it faded, Jean answered, "I hadn't noticed."

Madge didn't laugh for that one. "We've gotta be able to work together, to stick together. Support each other." Another sip. "Isolating yourself isn't gonna help anything. Neither is snubbing people who try to be nice to you. Or staring down your nose at your fellow nurses—even if they can't sing the best."

Jean looked away, warmth flooding her cheeks.

Madge continued. "We're all professionals, and we'll all do what we've got to do, but, well, let's face it. You're not the only...let's say 'strong personality' out here. But that job we came to do? I figure it's hard enough without distractions to make it harder." Another shriek echoed outside. "Well, except the distractions we can't do anything about."

Did Stan put her up to this? Jean reflected on the past few days—and squirmed a little. *No. This shouldn't matter. I'm a good nurse.* Jean sat up and met Madge's eyes. In a perverse way, she was grateful for diversion from the air raid. "What, and boozing up on a sad excuse of a cocktail will show everyone that I'm ready to be best friends forever, and *poof*, that'll save more lives?"

Madge shrugged yet again. "Maybe not. But walking around like you've been sucking on lemons doesn't do much for morale—for the boys or your fellow nurses." She laughed. "Not saying I care, or you've wounded my morale by not having a drink. But..." she paused as a particularly loud blast went off. "If things go bad and you want anyone to have anything nice to say for your funeral, you really should try loosening up a little." She tossed back a swig of the "cocktail" and sidled through the other nurses to a more friendly spot.

Refusing to watch her go, Jean leaned back. *So what? I don't care. I'm not here for a popularity contest. I'm here to do a job. It's not fair...* She could almost hear Stan's answer. *Sure, it's not fair. Life's not fair,*

Jeannie. What good do you think pouting about it will do?

I just need to sleep.

She tried—tried to relax and shake her unease. Eventually, she dozed again, just enough sleep to leave her painfully weary as she trudged to the mess hall for coffee and some thin oatmeal, then back to the hospital for another nightmare of a shift. One patient, sterilize, scrub, then another—the operating room blurred before her eyes.

She made a run to the latrine as the sun was westering, nearly nodding off on the wooden seat. Returning, she saw the ambulances unloading another round of casualties and gritted her teeth.

If the weariness ever touched Stan, it only made his fingers more nimble. As soon as she returned, he was on her, barking, "Faster, Nurse, Faster!" A boy lay on the table—red-haired and freckled—limp as a rag doll. Jean positioned his limbs, and Stan made the incision.

One of the enlisted men hurried over. "We've got more coming in. Colonel Blake says we need to work faster.

Stan muttered as he pulled a stitch taut, "Well the Colonel can just get his butt in here and—" The boy began to twitch and shake, and it was over.

Stan bowed his head and exhaled. "Ok. Next."

Jean nodded, but she couldn't look away from the freckles on the soldier's pale face. Was it her imagination, or was his face familiar? *Is he the one who checked up on me on the boat over? The one who called me doll? The one Stan said I should be nicer to?* She swallowed, hard.

A couple of men came with a stretcher to take him away and bring in the next one. Bullets, maybe shrapnel. Pierced liver.

Her hands shook; her body ached for sleep. It didn't help that she'd started out tired. She blinked her bleary eyes as the scalpel wavered in front of them. Stan's shouting snapped her out of it. One of the other surgeons had come in.

"…whaddya mean we shouldn't operate? He's…"

"…we need to prioritize better. We've got a line-up, more coming in…"

"…and with all the time you're wasting we could've taken care of how many more…"

Jean just kept prepping. Stan would win—he always did.

Then the lights flickered. The first shell fell, near enough that she felt the impact in her bones. The equipment rattled, and the lights blinked out again. Cursing, Stan said, "Grab a flashlight in case they go out."

Obeying, she flicked it on and tried to keep it steady, but the beam quivered. She closed her eyes and gripped harder. *Yea, though I walk through the valley of the shadow of death…or stand stock still while bombs are exploding around me. Lord, I must be out of my mind.*

"Nurse? Hold it steady or take cover." Stan spared her a glance, sharp, worried.

"Need me to take it?" asked one of the enlisted men.

She pressed her lips into a grim line. Another crash shook the air, and her mind screamed to hide, but her voice said, "No."

"You sure? You look a little—"

"I said *no.*"

Stan leaned back over the boy on the table. "Got one." A bullet fell into the waiting tray with a *ping.*

By the time the shelling had stopped, he'd closed, and they were on to a new patient—sucking chest wound. The surgeon Stan had been yelling at muttered something about "stubborn cuss," but he said it with a grin. Then, he took one look at Jean and sent her to bed.

Jean didn't remember much of the walk to her tent. She passed Betty and Lynn on the way, and they asked if she was going to the mess hall. Could it be time to eat? She pictured that lifeless, freckled face on the operating table. Shaking her head, she brushed past them. Stumbling into her tent, she collapsed onto her cot and tumbled into dreams of Joe.

Of North Africa, of a sandy beach.

Of a stubborn, golden-haired medic who ran forward.

He ran forward into danger and away from her forever.

She spent her dreams chasing his retreating back and calling after him, but he never turned around.

Four

George grunted as he stumbled over Pete's bent back. "Whoa, Petey! Whatcha doing there?"

"Sorry, my boot lace is all…shoot. Figures it'd break tonight. Everything else is going wrong. Just when I got the dugout finished…" Petey stood and continued forward, still muttering under his breath.

Shorty bumped George's elbow as he pushed forward. "Petey, you still going on about your hole in the ground? I think we've got worse problems." The sneer in Shorty's voice was clear even in the dark.

Petey spun around. "Shut up, Shorty, I worked hard on that…"

"Sure ya did, Pete." George elbowed Shorty out of the way. "Hey, we shouldn't be up front that long—you'll probably be back to it soon. Your dugout with Betty smiling from the wall, mess in walking distance—all the comforts of home."

Leroy added from behind them, "Unless we break through. I'm hoping we'll see Rome in a week or two!"

George focused his eyes straight ahead and kept walking. Pete did the same. Shorty, however, turned around and laughed in the kid's face.

"Anderson, we're gonna be here forever. Or at least until the Teds stomp us—"

Leroy wasn't just an optimist—he was stubborn. "No way. Even if it's not us doing it, we'll get through. Either the boys at Cassino will break 'em or we'll mass up enough here on the beach—the brass have it planned, don't they George?"

"Sure, Leroy. They got a plan. We'll get off this beachhead, eventually." George tried to sound convincing, but he knew he'd been a little too quick.

"Yeah, but will we still be breathing when we do?" Shorty yelped as George passed him and trod heavily on his foot.

Leroy just wouldn't shut up. "Naw, Shorty, George here thinks…"

In a falsetto, Shorty mimicked him. "George thinks. George thinks. Georgie oughta be a general for all the stock you put in his brains. Maybe I should call him that—General George. How's that?"

George laughed it off. "Do I get a salute with the nickname?"

"Kiss my…"

George spun and stood toe to toe with him, straightening to his full height. It wasn't much more than Shorty's, but his glare added inches. "Whoa, now. Do you *really* wanna finish that thought, buddy?" Shorty dropped his eyes.

George turned away and hiked his pack higher on his shoulders. He looked up as tracers streaked across the indigo sky and rubbed his chin. He noticed Leroy watching him though, so he smiled and clapped him on the shoulder. "C'mon, fellas. We better spread out and quiet down."

In the dark hours before dawn, they reached their new positions, right up in front with only the tomb quiet of no-man's-land beyond. George tried a grin on the fella whose foxhole he took over. The other guy didn't even meet his eyes, just hauled himself out and shuffled towards the back.

The hours of frigid darkness dragged. Odd noises drifted across the blank, furrowed marshland ahead. A few sporadic artillery shells burst, though nothing came too close. Tedium and tension vied with each other.

After a while, George's strained senses scented tobacco drifting from the next foxhole over. The fellas here had been doing some tunneling too. The foxholes were connected with a series of trenches, stirring up images of the last war. Squinting through the narrow alley between his and Leroy's hole and the one Shorty and Pete had taken over, he could just make out the burning orange ember on the end of Shorty's cigarette. It lit up his and Petey's silhouettes. He opened his mouth to say something, but Wally beat him to it.

"Put that out!" Wally barked through the dark, then lowered his voice to a hiss. "If you wanna be Bosch target practice, do it on your own time, Shorty."

Shorty grumbled an apology, but Wally must've turned away because George could see the embers brighten as he pulled in one last drag.

Petey cussed him out and slapped the cigarette into the mud. "You wanna get us shot?"

"Like they can't see us anyway."

Petey spluttered, "Not in the *dark*, idiot. Not unless we give em a light to aim by..."

"What, you think they can see this little—"

"Maybe they can!"

George spoke low and smiled into the dark. "Getting too loud might not be the best idea either, Pete." They quieted, and he closed his eyes with a sigh. He couldn't entirely blame Shorty. He fingered the Lucky Strike he'd stuck behind his ear, then put it in his mouth without lighting it.

Beside him, Leroy stirred, then rose to a crouch and peered out of their hole. "I can't see anything out there."

George grunted. "Nothing to see, yet. I'll keep watch. Why don't you try to get some sleep?"

"I'm never gonna sleep tonight. You go ahead."

Opening his mouth to argue, George yawned instead. "Maybe I could. Sure. Thanks."

He rolled himself into his blanket and overcoat, surrounding himself with familiar scents of damp earth and wet wool. Curling up against one of the almost vertical walls, he wasn't warm, but almost, nearly, on the edge of warm. Weariness allowed him to relax, to start to drift away.

The sound of water sloshing into a helmet liner and the incongruous smell of soap pulled him back. "W…what're you doing? Leroy, are you shaving? Here?"

"Well…yeah." George could picture Leroy's sheepish expression. "It itches."

"Oh for…" George laughed. "Kid…do what you gotta do, but can you do it quietly?"

"Sure. Sorry."

George had almost drifted off again to the rhythmic scrape of the razor against the kid's stubble when Leroy cleared his throat. "Hey, George? You still awake?"

He sighed. "Yeah."

"Think we'll make it back?"

"Sure kid."

"Really? Cuz Shorty said…"

George tried to get comfortable again. "Shorty likes to talk. Wake me up when it's my turn to watch, ok?"

"Ok. But…you do think we'll make it back?"

Petey hissed from the dark to their left, "You might not if you don't shut up."

"Sorry."

George rubbed his drooping eyes. "Look, I aim to do my level best to get you back, safe, home and on that Main Street with your girl on your arm. If you want more than that, better talk to the Big Guy. Ok?"

"Ok."

George closed his eyes again, but sleep was a long time coming.

DAWN WAS PAINTING the sky in broad strokes of orange by the time Jean's shift ended. As she staggered to her tent, all she could think of was sleep. Ducking inside, she saw Betty's empty bunk and sighed with relief. *Finally, some time alone—*

"Oh, hi, Jean!" Gladys chirped, sitting up from her bunk in the back.

Jumping, Jean gasped, then replied wearily, "Oh, hi, Gladys." *Be polite.* "How are you?"

"Pretty good. I got some sleep." A yawn interrupted her. "Hmm, I think I'm still ready for some coffee. You?"

"I just finished my shift. Hoping for some sleep, too." She sat on her bunk and pulled her boots off, wrinkling her nose. *Ugh. I need clean socks. And a bubble bath, please.*

"Oh, I'm glad you get a break."

Jean gritted her teeth. The words were kind, but did Gladys always have to take on that mothering tone?

She continued, while rummaging through her musette bag. "Did you go to the air raid shelter last evening? I was hoping, when the sirens went off, that you'd had sense enough to take cover. After that hole you dug flooded—" She pulled out a comb with a little "Ah-ha!" of triumph.

Sense enough to take cover? "I can take care of myself." Jean bit the words off, one by one.

Comb halfway through a lock of hair, Gladys stopped and stared at her. "Of course you can. I didn't mean…" She resumed combing. "Look, I'll get out of here so that you can get some rest."

"Thank you." Jean lay down, unable to suppress a groan as her weary muscles stretched to their full length for the first time in hours. She felt a twinge of guilt. The mention of the shelter reminder her of Madge's words. *I ought to apologize for being short with her—* but Gladys was speaking again.

"I didn't mean that you don't have sense. It's just, Jean..." She hesitated. "I just hope you're going to do whatever it takes to stay safe. I worry about you."

"Safe?" Weariness mingled with frustration, and Jean gave a half-hysterical laugh. "Safe? Gladys, there is no safe. I could get killed in the wards, in bed here, or sitting on the latrine!"

"Oh honey," Sporting that mothering tone again, Gladys sat on the edge of Jean's bed and patted her leg. "You're not going to die..."

Jean swung her legs out of the bed, knocking Gladys' hand off and stood. "How do you know? Nobody knows." The tears stinging her eyes surprised her, made her angrier. For a moment, she saw the Western Union telegram again, those hateful, sterile typed words "The secretary of war desires me to express his deep regret..." She shook the vision away and wiped her eyes. "Gladys, will you please back off and stop being such a mother hen?"

Gladys blinked and stood, stepping back. "I'm not trying to...Jean, I'm your friend..."

"I never asked you to be."

Gladys's face crumpled, then smoothed out. "All right." She turned and left without another word.

Watching her go, Jean pulled in a deep breath, then another. *Alone at last.* The old pleasure in the thought was absent. She lay back down, pulling her blanket over her shoulders.

Though she slept for several hours, Jean still felt sluggish when she woke. After washing up, she made her way to the nurses' mess, hoping some coffee would clear her fuzzy mind. She sat near the end of a table and said grace. Glancing to her left, her eyes caught Gladys's—in her hurry, she hadn't noticed the other nurse sitting at the same table. Gladys's gaze slid away from hers without any reaction except for a brief, polite smile. Jean felt a little flush creep up her neck. *Good.*

She'll finally give me some privacy. The words sounded right, but her food stuck in her throat. She downed the coffee and headed to work.

Being back in the surgery steadied her, helped her ignore the nagging feeling in her belly that she'd done wrong. All went well until they were just about to operate on the last patient of the day—some nasty shrapnel wounds to the face and shoulder. Stan was just beginning his first incision when the enlisted man assisting at her table bumped her arm.

Normally, she'd have steadied herself, avoided the tray of instruments, but not today. Not when she was fuzzy-headed and slow-fingered from lack of sleep and unrest of mind. They crashed to the floor as she stared, helpless. She spun on the man in a fury. "Just look what you made me do! Now we'll have to sterilize all of this again—we don't have time for this kind of incompetent—"

"Nurse Hoff." Stan's voice was soft but sharp, cutting through her tirade as if he'd sliced it with the glittering scalpel in his hand. "This boy—the one here, on the table? He doesn't need this. We need to take care of this mess, now, so that we can take care of him. Is that understood?"

"Yes. Sir."

Together, they did it. The surgery went well, and, mercifully, the shift was over.

Jean hesitated outside of the OR, peering into the thick blanket of dark. *I wonder if Gladys's shift has started yet or if she's in the tent. Maybe if I stall a little...*

"Hey, Jeannie?"

Jean signed and squared her shoulders. *He's never going to get it right.* Somehow, tonight, it didn't matter so much. "Yes, Stan."

"Give me a hand, will you?" He nodded to a box, twin to the one he was carrying. Obediently, she hefted it up and trailed behind him through the hospital area to a waiting jeep. Loading the boxes into the back, Stan climbed in beside them.

Curiosity finally penetrated her tired mind. "What's all this? Where are you going?"

"3rd Division Clearing Station got moved up a ways—to Acciarella—yesterday."

The name meant nothing to Jean, but she nodded. "Ok. And?"

"I got a couple buddies in that outfit. I want to go take a look at where they're at. See what shape the fellas are in when they're admitted. Too many cases of trench foot coming back to us, so I scrounged some extra socks and things to drop off."

While vehicles could move more freely in the dark, he couldn't mean… "Isn't that dangerous? Going farther up?"

Stan snorted. "I'm not jumping on the front lines or anything. Don't figure they're more of a target than here."

"Ooook…." Her brain was running slow from weariness, and her eyes felt red and raw. "I guess if you've gotta…."

"So glad you approve."

"I'll come too." The words left her lips before she realized they were coming.

That stopped him. "What?"

"If it's safe enough for you, it's safe enough for me."

He stood for a moment, rooted to the spot, then nodded. "Ok. I'd like a word, anyway."

"Sir?" the driver looked anxious as Stan handed Jean up. "We're going pretty far forward. Shouldn't the nurse—I mean the lieutenant—I mean, is this a good…?"

Stan said, as he climbed in, "What's your name, son? Your first name, I mean."

"Uh…Jim. Sir."

"We'll be fine, Jim. In and out. Right?"

"Right, but, I mean, the nurses are rear echelon."

"Are we going to the front?"

"Well…no, but I've never driven up to Acciarella, and…"

"But you'll find it, won't you?"

Jean closed her eyes. Just another argument for the old man to win. Maybe she could sneak a nap.

Stan continued, "And unless the Krauts plan a major offensive for tonight, are we in any more danger than being in the hospital area?"

"Well…I don't suppose so."

"Then let's get moving."

As they jolted into gear and pulled out into the dark, Stan pulled out his pipe and beat it against his hand, clearly wishing he were able to light it. "So. What's going on?"

She tried to deflect him. "Oh, nothing new. I'm settling in. Oh, just yesterday, at mess, Major Thompson complimented me—us, really—on what a good surgical team we are. And I've been working on my bedside manner, really…"

He just looked at her, wind whipping his hair back from his forehead, and she sighed, the protests dying on her lips. Wishing the conversation could be had more quietly, she admitted, "Ok, Stan. I know. I'm trying; I really am. It's just, being packed in with the other nurses is…if I could just get a little privacy…"

"Privacy? Where do you think you are?"

"I…" Any time she tried to defend herself to Stan she felt like she was just a child again, caught sneaking one of the lollipops they saved for kids after their checkups.

Stan heaved a sigh loud enough to be heard over the engine and the crunch of the tires. "Doesn't matter. Jeannie, if you don't cut this selfish garbage, get yourself under control, you're gonna get booted back home or someone killed."

"How…"

"Think distracted nurses work well?" His voice was a harsh growl.

Jean raised her chin. "I just…" her chin quivered. "Stan, I…" She closed her eyes, nothing left to say, tired of trying to explain herself. Silence surrounded them, apart from the jeep's noises and the occasional sound of artillery fire to the north and ahead of them. The steady sounds lulled her into a doze until Stan's voice snapped her out of it.

"What's the trouble?" She opened her eyes, prepared for another onslaught of Stan's advice, but he wasn't talking to her. He'd leaned forward, towards the driver whose helmeted head was swiveling right and left as he scanned the road. The dark wrapped around them, turning all the world into vague, dark smudges of gray and deeper shadow. The blacked-out headlights gave no light.

Jim turned, his face a paler shadow. "I'm not....Sir, I'm not sure we're in the right spot—the map doesn't match up. If we can get to a crossroads and I can find an MP or..."

A flare burst overhead, bathing the world in eerie, unnatural light. A farmhouse jumped out of the dark to their left, jeeps parked behind it. Ahead, a scrubby stand of trees stood, skeletal branches stretching to the sky. The ground was pockmarked with holes—foxholes? A cold hand of fear gripped Jean's belly. *How far up are we?*

There was a foxhole just below the road at her left. A soldier lifted his head, his face half in light and half in dark. His wide eyes, white in his filthy face, met hers. His mouth opened. He was calling something, but his voice was drowned in a whistling scream.

The road just ahead of them blew apart. Jean's head jerked back. A cloud of dust and dirt blew over the top of the jeep. Rocks pinged against the windshield. Her body slid into Stan's as Jim cursed and swerved, pulling the jeep around in a U-turn. He hit the gas. Dust stung her streaming eyes.

Another shell hit the road behind them—pushed Jean's head forward. Jim was shouting in the front seat "...us ranged! We gotta..." Another landed off to the right. Yanking the steering wheel, Jim swung the jeep across the road. The tires hit the mud at the verge, wobbled, spun, caught again.

The flare faded. Jean strained her dazzled eyes. She could see nothing, but her ears still rang with a shrill keening. Touching them, she wondered if her eardrums were damaged.

The shriek paused, then began again. It was a voice—a voice from the right where the foxholes were, where the third shell had landed. *Oh no.*

Stan was shouting at Jim. "Stop, Stop, by all that's holy, STOP," and he vaulted out of the jeep.

"Nosir—you can't, the medics will…"

Without turning, Stan hollered, "Jeannie, stay put!" He strode off—not running, still the cool, confident 'old man.' He strode across the field just like he'd stride across the hospital floor, and Jean didn't need to see it to know his expression—the firm chin, the unyielding line of his mouth. Jim's continued shouts would do no good.

Bile rose in Jean's throat. "Stan…?" she croaked. *He's leaving. He's leaving me.* Her hands shook, but her legs took control. She shrugged off Jim's restraining arm and jumped down to the muddy road. Running, she bent her head low as if her steel helmet would do any good against a shell. *Oh God, what am I doing?*

A cloud of pale dust hung in the air ahead—it was from there the cries came. She could make out a word in the keening now, "Doc! Doc!" Following the sound, she ran forward, not watching her feet.

The ground opened beneath her. Dirt and rocks scraped her calves and back. She landed with a gasp and a thump.

Trying to get her bearings, she half stood, then fell back with a cry as her ankle twinged. The hole was only a few feet deep, but longer than wide. Ahead, a soldier crouched in the dark. He stared at her, wide eyes in a pale face. Stan knelt beside him, working on something on the ground. Glancing up and meeting her eyes, he betrayed no surprise. "Quick, Jeannie."

She crept over to him, favoring the ankle. A man lay on the ground, the dark, spreading stain on his torso black in the night. Stan grabbed her hands and put them on the man's chest. "Press down!" He fumbled through a first-aid kit, and she wondered where he'd found that and where the medic was until her eyes took in the red cross on the helmet beside the fallen man. *Oh, no.* She pushed harder as the warm blood rose over her hands, over her wrists—

Pulling out the sulfa powder, Stan barked, "Harder, Jeannie!"

Leaning in, she pushed harder, but she knew—and Stan must've known—it was no use.

WhhhhshhhhhhHHHH. The shell's whistle grew louder, followed closely by another – falling, crashing, shaking the earth and filling the air with debris and more cries. Cries rose from the trenches all around— "Medic! Medic!" they called, not knowing their medic lay bleeding out under Jean's hands.

With a heave, Stan stood. He vaulted over the top, drawn to the cries. He turned back once to call, "Jeannie, stay with him! Stretcher bearers will be here soon."

"Stan!" She screamed his name again and again, but he'd vanished.

The medic coughed violently. Blood spattered her uniform, and she pressed harder. His eyes went blank. His body went slack. It didn't matter—if she just pressed harder, maybe it would be ok—

Closing her eyes, she took in a deep breath. The medic was dead. She couldn't do more. But what should she do? She pulled her hands out of his blood and stood.

Where's Stan? I don't know what to do. God, I don't know what to do here—*I'm supposed to be at the hospital—*

A noise like a freight train roared through the sky.

The other soldier, the living one—she saw him clearly now, bloodshot eyes, bristles on his unshaven face—lunged for her and grabbed her wrist and screamed something at her as he pushed her down, but she couldn't hear him, couldn't hear anything.

Then the crash came, so big, so loud, it couldn't be real. As if from a great distance, she felt her body leave the ground, then strike the back of the trench. Earth fell about her like rain. The air left her lungs in a painful whoosh, and she couldn't bring it back in. She couldn't breathe. Couldn't see. Couldn't hear. A fish out of water, gasping, twitching on the lakeshore. Grandad said it would be over soon, but she hated to see it suffer as it flopped—

Breathe. Air rushed into her hungry lungs.

She coughed, hacking and choking, and breathed again. And again.

It was a marvel, drawing air in and out of her lungs—she alternated coughing and pulling it in with big, grateful gulps.

Slowly, her other senses returned. Then a thought: *I'm alive.*

Almost afraid to try, she moved, wiggling fingers, toes, her head and neck, and finally sitting up, patting down her body once, then checking again. Somehow, she was still all there. All limbs intact.

There was another man here... What could have happened to him? She tried to make sense of it. She'd been hit, or no, maybe she hadn't...

The shell. It didn't hit here; it was just close enough and big enough that I felt the impact. I'm lucky the concussion didn't kill me. But where did it...

A certainty she couldn't explain, clutched her belly.

Stan.

She still didn't see the other soldier, but there was no time to look for him. Up—she had to get up. She scrambled to the edge of the trench, scrabbled at the dirt with her hands and feet to get up the edge, then scuttled like a lizard across the blasted ground, calling, angry that Stan wouldn't answer.

She tumbled into the trench he had run to—but it wasn't a trench, it was a huge furrow, littered with pieces of metal and—

He was there, and he was gone, and the little that was left...

Was this how Joe looked?

She retched onto the ground. Her shaking knees unable to bear her farther, she fell to the earth.

The world stopped. Nothing was real anymore—

Nothing was real.

Until the shot, right above her.

With an effort of will, Jean raised her head. Someone stood at the edge of the furrow, looking down at her. The boots—she saw the boots first. They didn't look right. Her eyes widened. She raised her eyes farther. Pants—field gray instead of olive drab. She began to tremble. The curve of the helmet, almost right, but not—

Slowly, Jean rose to face the German soldier and raised her blood-streaked hands.

FIVE

THE EARTH BUCKED and kicked under George. Forgetting for a moment where he was, he scrambled to his feet. A screaming artillery wail ending in thunder over to the left brought his memory back. As the roars and shrieks of falling metal blended into one tremendous din, he threw himself back onto the ground. Bits of dirt and rock pelted him. Teeth and bones rattling with each crash, he lay, face pressed into the damp soil. A sharp pebble dug into his cheek. Wheezing through dust-clogged nostrils, he willed his heart to slow before it burst. The heavy pressure of overwhelming sound pinned him helpless to the earth.

It might have been a few minutes, or it might have been an hour before the world quieted. Still he lay, cold, stiff limbs rigid as a corpse.

Slowly, he came back to himself. Pulling in a deep breath, he coughed. *See? You're not dead yet. C'mon now Georgie, got a job to do. Wake up—what's first?*

Weapon, of course. Most likely the Teds would be following a barrage like that with some infantry. He groped at the earth until he found his Garand. It only took two tries for his shaky hands to get his bayonet fixed.

He rolled onto his back and forced his eyes open. Swinging himself to lean against the earth wall, he turned his face towards no-man's land. Smoke and dust and haze draped indistinct forms.

Clearing his throat and spitting, he managed to croak, "Hey, Leroy? You ok?"

A dark form bumped his shoulder, and he jumped. "Yeah, I'm fine. Whew. That was something."

A glowing stream of tracers streaked over from behind. Pulling on his old grin, just in case the kid looked over, George rose to a crouch, trying to get a look at something, anything, that would clarify their situation. Over to the left, where Petey and Shorty were presumably still alive, he saw nothing but a splotch of darker black in the shadows. The others in the platoon were spread out across this line, but no cries or small arms shots reached his straining ears.

Good enough. He leaned back, the chill of damp earth seeping through his uniform.

Water sloshed against metal—Leroy taking a sip from his canteen. "So. What do we do now?"

"Do?" *There's nothing to do, kid, but wait for orders. Or for a German to come sliding down into our hole and blow us to kingdom come.* A shiver of cold fear sliced through his belly, and he shook it off. "Well, I guess I'll watch now if you wanna sleep."

Leroy managed a weak laugh but said nothing. They sat together in the dark.

A small eternity passed. George held his rifle, chill fingers cramping around the unforgiving metal and wood, eyes straining into the dark. His feet and legs slowly went numb.

He must have dozed. His eyes opened after what had seemed like a long blink and saw light above the rim of his hole—pale, pre-dawn light. Relief washed over him. *Finally.* He pulled the waiting smoke from behind his ear and licked his parched lips. Lighting up and taking that first long drag, he half stood, then fell back against the dirt wall, pins and needles shooting down his legs. Staying in a half crouch, he tried to stomp circulation back into his feet. Beside him, Leroy did the same.

The wind brushed against his left cheek, blowing down from the hills to the north east, from the direction of the Germans and of the British salient. It carried sounds, so faint that he might be imagining them. Singing. Shouting. Small arms fire. And louder, the big guns, firing from the direction of the sea, answered by others from the hills.

Leroy's head swung toward the sounds, like a hound catching a scent. "Whaddya figure?"

"Sounds like the Limeys are getting hammered."

"Didn't some fellas from the 45th head up there, too?"

"Yeah. Couple regiments, I think."

"God help 'em. Do you think…" Leroy trailed off.

Do I think they'll hit our line here, too? Good question, kid.

The growing light brought their surroundings into focus. George caught sight of Shorty looking back at him, dark eyes wild. His mouth was working—probably grumbling—and he had his rifle in one hand and something white in the other. Most likely that rabbit's foot from his missus. Petey leaned against the wall next to him, playing with his rosary.

George's fingers twitched toward the breast-pocket Bible he'd been issued—mom had asked in her last letter if he was carrying it. Instead, he reached for his pack and pulled out a can. "Whaddya think, franks and beans for breakfast today?"

Leroy opened his mouth to answer, then froze, staring up.

A patter of stones hit George's helmet, followed by the slithering sound of falling dirt. *Shoot! They've got behind us.* As George whirled his tired brain tried to tell him something, pulling his finger off the trigger. *Behind? How could they—*

Olive drab, not field gray, clothed the legs that nearly knocked into him as Wally slid into their hole. Leroy jumped, and next door, Shorty cursed so loudly that George could hear some of the words over another burst of artillery. Petey was already belly crawling over to hear the news. After a few more choice words, Shorty joined him.

George scootched back to give the new arrival space. "What's the word?"

Wally opened his mouth, but before he could speak a shriek followed by a blast shook their sheltering earth.

The echoes of the blast died away, and George raised his head, nose narrowly avoiding the edge of Wally's helmet.

Wally spat—in their little circle it didn't have anywhere to go, and droplets landed on the toe of George's boot. "It been pretty hot over here?"

George shrugged. "Haven't had any Teds come calling, though they've sent over plenty of gifts."

"Ok. Well, Greer sent me up—he's got some orders." Wally paused, and Shorty started cursing again. "The Jerries are pushing our lines hard to the north—especially up by the Albano Road. It's pretty rough."

Rubbing his tired eyes, George interrupted. "Rough enough that they wanna send the 3rd up there, too?" He waved his arm, encompassing the land in front of them. "Who's s'posed to hold the rest of the line then—"

Wally's mouth compressed like he was sucking on a lemon. "I didn't say nothing about that. Did I say anything about moving up there?" He sighed, his breath another foul smell in their tight space. Leroy pulled out a pack of gum from his breast pocket and handed him a stick. Wally sighed again, then took it. "Thanks. Look, Greer wants to know what's going on over there." He waved his hand towards no-man's land. "They're concentrating the attack up north, but there's been some action all along our lines, and he wants to make sure we aren't caught with our pants down."

George took a last drag of his cigarette and squelched the butt into the mud. "And he figures we're the ones to check it out?"

Wally nodded. "If we don't get attacked beforehand, you four are going on patrol tonight. Soon as it's dark enough. You're gonna take O'Reilly and Hammond—"

"Wait, the replacements? Can't I pick my own guys? Those fellas are fresh out of the repple depple and—"

"And they've gotta learn sometime. Besides, Greer's sending O'Reilly with a bazooka."

"What? On a night patrol?"

Shorty's head snapped up. "Hey, why's a new guy get the stovepipe?"

"Cuz he has training with it, knucklehead. Besides, you aren't to use it unless you get in trouble with tanks. Greer wouldn't mind you fellas scrapping it out a little, but," Wally paused, eyes shifting back over his shoulder, "if you want my advice, get in, take a look at what's over there, maybe grab a prisoner if you get a chance—"

Pete groaned. "It just keeps getting better."

"—and then get back. Make sure you call out your countersign quick—the sentries are probably a little jumpy. They say 'Comin in,' you say 'On a Wing and a Prayer.' Like the song. O'Reilly and Hammond will meet you here as soon as it's dark. Assuming you don't get yourself shot, Novak, I'll see you at company HQ tomorrow."

The other fellas said nothing, but Leroy nodded eagerly, then glanced at George for approval. George forced a grin. "Sure thing, Wally."

After Wally had slithered back up the embankment and Shorty and Pete scrambled back to their own hole, Leroy busied himself with cleaning his rifle. George opened his can of breakfast and stared into it. The beans floating in their tomatoey ooze stared back. He wrinkled his nose at the acidic smell. *I've gotta eat. After all, it's only a routine patrol. I've been on those before.* He swallowed a cold bite, pushing it past the lump in his throat. *Haven't led one...but it'll be fine. In, out, back home again before the Germans even know we've come calling.* He checked his watch. 8 am. *Sunset's early—before 7 tonight.*

And the moon's waning. So. Twelve hours or so to go. A couple hours out, back here before morning.

TWENTY HOURS LATER, George lay in the dirt, machine gun bullets ripping through the air above him. He closed his eyes. *Well God, we're all going to die, ain't we? There's no way we make it back today. But God, if any of us can get out of this, please spare the kid. And please, look after Ma. And Lil... Well, maybe when Lilly hears she'll be sorry.* He felt a flush of shame at the last thought and turned his mind back to trying to find a way out of this mess.

The patrol had started off well enough—just a little later than expected. O'Reilly and Hammond had some trouble finding him in the dark, and once they did there'd been an air raid. After the flares had faded and the planes had gone, they'd finished preparations. They'd left their helmets and extra gear behind—no clanking metal to betray their movements—loaded up their rifles with ammo and their belts with grenades. Painting their faces with sludge, they'd set off—late, but not too late for a quick patrol. George had led with Leroy behind, Pete and Shorty flanked by the two new guys. George had told Shorty to keep an eye on the replacements and had reminded the new kids to stick to the old hands.

They'd made it out quite a ways, the distance measured in slow, muddy footsteps. The countryside was eerily quiet, though distant sounds of battle still raged to the north. George had just been thinking it was time to turn back—he didn't want to get stuck in the open during daylight. But when Hammond blundered into the machine gun, everything went sideways.

I still can't figure how Hammond got ahead of me... but it didn't matter how it had happened. Entering the shadows of a grove of trees, Hammond had stumbled. Something on his kit—something stupid they'd missed—had clanked. In response, bullets ripped through the night.

George pushed his face into the dirt, breathing slowly, marveling at each breath, counting them, as they might be his last. *One. Two. Three.*

He'd reached five when the fire paused. Easing his head up, he searched the dark for the others. Leroy was prone over to his left. Petey crouched to the right—he'd found some cover by a tree. *Good.* Shorty—who knew where he was. *Did he rabbit? No, there he is, in that bush. Whaddya know.* Hammond lay up the slope, the bazooka on the ground beside him. He was silent—dead or just frightened. O'Reilly was nowhere to be seen. *Every time we twitch, we take more fire. If they get a flare up, we're done for. And if we can't get back before dawn—*

His Garand had been partially pinned beneath him. Inch by inch, he slid it out. *Grenades would be better—no decent light to aim by. But if they're where I think they are, I don't know if I can make the throw before—* a shiver ran down his spine. The German MG42 hadn't been nicknamed "Hitler's Buzz Saw" for nothing.

Squinting, George stared at a clump of bushes up the slope ahead. The few clinging leaves quivered in the wind. As the wind died down, they still quivered. *There you are.* He sighted along his rifle, took a breath, and fired.

A cry, a short burst from the machine gun. He fired again, hearing echoing shots from around him—the other guys had joined in. *Seven, six, five, four…* he counted down his shots and stopped with three left. He waited, listening.

Nothing.

He glanced at Leroy—the kid was watching him, eyes questioning. The kid jerked his head towards the bushes, silently asking, "Should I go check it out?"

George shook his head. *Nope. Not you.* He took one more breath, then began to crawl, elbows pulling him forward and to the right. A gnarled olive tree stooped over like a weary soldier and offered some cover. From there, he stood. Took another breath. Bent his head and rushed the bushes.

His feet pounded the same rhythm as his heart as he sprinted. He flung himself into the shrubs, to stumble and fall flat on his face.

Feet and hands scrabbling, he pushed himself up. He paused as his fingers met fabric. He relaxed. He'd just tripped over the ammo belt of one of the dead Germans that lay on the ground next to the machine gun.

Leroy crashed through the underbrush, then, seeing the situation stopped and gave a shaky laugh. "Looks like we got 'em."

"Yep. No time to lollygag though—go get the other guys. Quiet-like, ok? These fellas weren't alone."

With a few whispered calls and shuffling feet, the patrol reassembled. Hammond and O'Reilly were last, O'Reilly carting the bazooka, Hammond with his arm hanging at an odd angle.

We're all alive. We're all still alive. The wonder of it made him pause, then he shook himself. *For now. Someone's gotta be heading over to check out the commotion.* He leaned in, and they huddled with him. "We're heading back. Try to keep moving. Spread out, keep your eyes open, and don't forget…" his voice trailed off.

Something rumbled, an engine, throttled down but still audible. Something heavy that moved with muffled clanks. Something that sounded like it was right between them and their escape route.

"Get down." He was pleased that his voice didn't shake. They crouched low to the damp earth, listening.

"What's that?" Shorty hissed.

"You idiot, that's gotta be a tank…" Pete began, but Shorty interrupted. "Theirs or ours?"

"Quiet." George reached for a smoke—nothing there. "We'll wait here until it passes."

Six heads turned to follow the sound of the tank's progress. It was opposite them, down the slope. The noise grew, rumbling low. Louder, louder, and then at last, quieter. George sighed, then took a breath to order the guys up and on their way. A new sound caught his ear, and he paused.

Pete whispered, "Is that…is there another one…?"

"Sure sounds like it." George settled back on his haunches. "Just sit tight."

The next tank passed. Then the next. Five furtive behemoths crept past. A few soft voices accompanied them. The eastern sky was beginning to turn from black to charcoal when the sixth came level with them. The tank's engine sputtered—stopped. Silence fell. George could hear his heartbeat in his ears and the first sleepy twitters of early-rising birds.

Shorty's whisper sounded like a shout. "Why's he stopped? Think they know we're here?"

"Let's keep quiet and not clue them in, ok?" Despite George's impatience, the same questions raced through his mind. *What're the odds he'd just happen to stop in our escape route?* The seconds ticked by turning to minutes, which would soon turn to treacherous dawn. Nothing happened.

We can't just sit here. So. He waved the others closer. "Ok, fellas, we're going down to take a look. Keep down, no chatter. Let's see what he's up to and if we can't slip around."

Nods all around, even from Hammond whose pinched face gleamed with sweat.

Keeping low, George led the way. The dew-wet grasses soaked through his muddy uniform, the wool clinging to his chilled skin. A shiver wracked his body as he eased forward, half cold, half fear. He avoided a clump of bushes that might betray him with crackling twigs and belly crawled to a spot by a lone cork oak where he could get a look at the clearing beyond.

Petey slid up beside him. "Jesus save us. Look at that thing…" His rosary beads hit each other softly as his fingers trembled.

George reached behind his ear for the smoke that wasn't there. "Ain't much else to see, is there?" They were still about ten yards away, but the looming, boxy shadow dominated the view. Even still and silent, it had a predatory look, like it only waited for the unwary to come near enough for it to pounce.

Someone crept up on his other side—Leroy. "Is that...a Tiger?" The kid's awed whisper was almost reverent. They'd all heard tales of the Tiger Tanks— and curses muttered by the men who'd survived encounters with them.

Finding his voice, George answered. "Could be. Look at that gun. 88mm."

Leroy said, "George, why's it just sitting there?"

"Might be stuck? Might be radioing in for help or something? I dunno...My question is does it have infantry to back it up?" George fingered his rifle, then pushed himself back. The others followed until they reached the shelter of some fallen timber to huddle behind.

"What you thinking?" asked Leroy.

Shorty answered for them all, his voice a low hiss. "We should leave it."

George snorted. "What, just stroll past?"

"We could try to sneak."

Shaking his head, O'Reilly said, "And if he sees us?" He hefted his bazooka. "I didn't haul this thing all this way to not fire it."

George looked speculatively at O'Reilly. "Sure, but Hammond's in no shape to help you load. Besides, I've heard these big cats have enough armor to shrug off even those rounds. And if we fire it, we give away our position."

Leroy poked his arm. "So. What's the plan?"

George hesitated. The light was brightening—he could feel time ticking away from them. Past the tank was open ground, deadly to cross in daylight. But the kid was watching him with eager eyes, trustful eyes, and if he made the wrong call...*You wanted this. You wanted to lead. Now you gotta make a decision, Georgie boy.*

Ok. We're up against a ticking clock, one tank, and whoever's inside. Maybe infantry around too. Quiet but quick's the way we've got to go. But we should make sure we've got some insurance...

He leaned in, "Ok. Here's the plan. We're going to divide up into two groups. Anyone besides O'Reilly here have training with the stovepipe?" The others shook their heads. "Shorty, didn't you fire one back after Salerno?"

"Well, sure, once, in training."

"So same as me. Petey? You and Leroy take Hammond. Circle around to the left, behind the tank—give it a wide berth. Then, head back towards our lines. Remember, sing out quick for the sentries. Comin' in on a Wing and a Prayer." He pointed at Shorty. "We'll give them a minute head start. Then you, me, and O'Reilly will scootch around to the right. If the first group gets off clear, we'll follow. If there's any trouble..." he patted the bazooka. "We'll give the Jerries a little surprise."

Shorty shook his head, cussing up and down. "Why've I gotta go with the diversion group? Can't you and O'Reilly—"

"No. Having both of us there gives us a better chance of getting a shot off if we have to."

"I'll swap with Shorty," Leroy said.

"Nope." *If nothing else, I'm gonna get you back safely, kid.* "I know I can count on you to get Hammond back to our lines. Now, let's get moving."

Silent nods all around. Leroy, Petey, and Hammond slipped away. George counted one hundred beats of his thumping heart, then set out in a half crouch, Shorty and O'Reilly trailing behind. He had played it cool for the fellas, but the worries clamored loudly through his mind. *There must be infantry around. Where are they? No way the Teds'd leave this beast just sitting here. What's the game?*

He circled around to the right until they were well ahead of the stopped tank's position. Then, forward, one footstep at a time, a cautious race against the dawn. Reaching the last cluster of trees, he paused, straining his eyes and ears for any sign of movement.

There was nothing. He stepped out, into the open.

Five more steps along, his ears caught a voice—no, two voices. Whispering. O'Reilly and Shorty? No, the sounds were wrong... *There you are, Jerry*. He dropped to the earth and hoped the others followed suit.

There was only one way to go—forward. George belly crawled, inch by inch. The tank didn't stir. It was all buttoned up—a silent steel monster. It looked blind and deaf, like he could just stroll up to it, but he wasn't going to try it. Big gun aside, he could just make out two mounted machine guns.

A flurry of wings buzzed past his head. With a painful zing, a bug flew up his nose. *Oh, for the love of—* He pressed his face into the mud, quelling the crazy urge to sneeze.

Whatever it was flew out again. Wrinkling his nose, trying to ease the itch, he raised his head slightly. *Only a few more yards...*

A shot echoed through the dark. Voices rose from the far side of the clearing. From the direction the other group had gone. *Oh no...* George dug his toes and knees into the muck, trying to crawl faster.

With a mechanical whirr, the turret of the tank swung about, pointing towards the sounds of disturbance. Another rifle shot rang out from the dark woods, then a third.

George grabbed one of his grenades and got his feet under him. He pulled the pin, holding down the spoon. *If I throw back in the direction we came from, maybe it'll distract them—but where've Shorty and O'Reilly got to—*

He froze in a half crouch as the tank's lid opened with a groan. Silhouetted by a dim light from within, a blonde head rose into view, followed by a field gray shoulder. The form leaned over to call to someone in the trees.

George jumped to his feet. He'd been quarterback his senior

year—was that only five years ago? It seemed like an eternity. He threw the grenade in a nice, even arc. Miraculously, it slipped beneath the tanker's arm. A muffled thump echoed from within the metal monster. The tanker screamed. Grass and leaves around George began a sudden dance in a hail of bullets.

He threw himself down and hit the ground with a thud. Twigs and briars tore his clothing and skin as he crawled. Under his mud and blood-streaked hands, the earth rumbled. A cluster of trees loomed out of the shadows ahead.

George found his feet and, bent almost double, ran. Mud stiffened his pant legs, weighted his boots. His back muscles clenched waiting for the burning strike of the bullet that would end him. His frantic eyes scanned the dark ahead of him, hoping to see the others, then hoping he wouldn't—that they were already clear.

A couple of dark shapes moved in the shadows. *O'Reilly? Did they get ahead of me? Well, if he and Shorty wanted to take a shot, now's the time.* Another burst of rifle fire split the night behind him. Shouts echoed from the forest, but he was too disoriented to tell from which direction they came. He put on a new burst of speed.

There! Shorty stood ahead between two trees, firing back into the clearing. A sharp crack echoed from behind George. Shorty fell. Racing up, George found him—alive still and shaking. George grabbed him under the arms and hauled him behind one of the trees. He scanned the dark beyond. "Where's O'Reilly?"

Shorty shook his head.

A flare lit up the sky, revealing not O'Reilly, but Leroy. The dumb kid knelt twenty yards to the left, shooting back into the clearing. Petey and Hammond were nowhere to be seen—the kid was alone, except for the swarms of approaching field gray—

Head down, George charged, firing his last shots wildly towards the Germans. His momentum carried him into Leroy's arm. Pushing Leroy down, he rose. *Not the kid, God...*

The world burst into brilliant light, then went black.

A DULL THUNDER in his head dragged George out of the comfortable darkness. Smell came back first—the world smelled wrong. Enclosed, dank and musty, like Grandma's storm cellar. Felt like it could be Grandma's cellar too—the surface under him was hard, cold, and smooth, like packed earth or cement. His nose wrinkled. That wasn't right. He'd been outside.

The little movement—the nose wrinkle—brought the thundering closer, focused it on two points behind his eyes, throbbing and aching. He gasped, and a sharper pain pulled at his chest, searing, deep.

He remembered feeling the tearing pain of impact, or was it a bullet? Right now, it felt like a whole shell.

Forcing his sticky eyelids open, he heaved his body, trying to sit up. He flinched in the dim light, headache sharpening, and the pain in his chest and neck screaming.

Strong hands grabbed his shoulders and pushed him back down. Frantic voices irritated the pounding in his head.

"Keep him still, do you hear me? He'll rip it back open again."

George opened his mouth and tried to cry out, but his tongue was thick and useless, like a wad of cotton. He croaked and started to gag.

"All right, it's all right. You, elevate his head a little." A cool hand smoothed his brow. An arm slipped under his shoulders and raised his head. The voice continued—a woman's voice. "Easy now. I'm going to give you some water. Just a sip, no more."

The cold tang of metal touched his lips, and he slurped eagerly from the canteen. The water was warm, metallic and stale, but at that moment it was heaven. George's tongue loosened. He tried to speak but gagged again.

"Quiet." The word was more order than request. "Here. Have another sip."

He tried to reach up for the canteen, desperate for the moisture, but it was pulled away. "No. You'll make yourself sick."

Another voice came from behind, from the person holding his head. "Just listen to Nurse Hoff, buddy. She's gonna get you all patched up."

Leroy? He swallowed again and managed to groan, "Leroy? That you?"

A hand squeezed his shoulder. "Sure is."

"Where…?"

"Weeeellll..." The hesitation in his voice told the story.

George let his head slump back into his friend's arm as the woman—Nurse Hoff? —prodded first his ribs, then a painful area where his neck met his shoulder.

At the moment, the pain didn't bother him—it was smothered by a blanket of despair.

They've got us.

The light dimmed and narrowed to a single spark, and he slipped away.

Part Two

Six

Leroy tried to hold back the words, but they slipped out in a whisper. "Um, Nurse?"

She didn't respond, head bent, fingers busy undoing George's buttons.

"Um, pardon me?"

"Hmmm."

He wasn't sure if the neutral syllable was directed at him or at the exposed dressings over George's ribs and neck. A few dark blotches had seeped through the fabric. Leroy swallowed hard, closing his eyes.

It didn't help—he could still see George splayed on the muddy earth and crushed weeds, blood soaking into his uniform. Could still feel warm blood pulsing out no matter how hard he pressed. Could feel his throat tearing as he'd screamed "Medic! Medic!" all the while knowing it was no good. There was no medic. And then fear had clutched his belly and rattled down his spine as he realized who had come, even before his eyes rose to look down the barrel of a German gun. The fear took over then, leaving him with nothing but physical impressions—the stink of German boot grease, the claustrophobia as he was surrounded by the enemy barking orders, the cold remembrance that George didn't want to be a POW, but raising his hands anyway in surrender, because the Geneva Convention meant that maybe the Jerry medic might help his buddy.

George groaned, and the nurse muttered something under her breath as she lifted his dressing. Leroy edged closer, trying to see. That got her attention—she shot him a warning look over her shoulder. He stepped back, working his sweating hands, and almost tripped—he'd forgotten that the Texan was dozing behind him. The Texan just grunted something unintelligible and went back to snoring. Leroy stepped over to the wall and leaned one shoulder against it, trying to look more relaxed than he felt.

What could I do, huh, George? What could I do? You saved me...How could I not pay you back? This time when he closed his eyes, he went further back, to the day they'd arrived on Anzio. He felt again the blackness of the water closing over his head, the panic, the pull of the cold and the abyss. He shivered. *I couldn't just let you die. Surely you'd rather be a POW than dead...?*

The jitters spread to Leroy's legs, and he wanted to pace, like an expectant father waiting for the doc's news, but the shack was too small, maybe ten feet across and half again as long, and there were the other guys in it—five of them. Like the Texan, most sprawled around on the dirt floor or leaned up against the cold stone walls. One—the man with the dark brown skin and pilot's clothes—squatted near the door, hands folded, watching it like if he stared hard enough it might fall. George was laid out parallel to the back wall.

The others who were awake were watching the nurse or pretending not to watch her. This was her second visit since they'd been brought here, but she'd rebuffed any attempts at conversation, saying only she'd found herself behind enemy lines and wound up captured. She'd checked a few scratches and sore ankles on the other guys, but George was the only seriously injured prisoner, so she focused on him. *Wish she'd unfocus just for a minute and tell me what's going on. What if George...Dear Lord, he's been like a brother to me. Please spare him. Since my first day in Italy— What would I do over here without him?*

The nurse sighed and sat back on her heels. Leroy counted to ten silently before stepping forward again, sidling up to stand next to her. George looked better—pale, but not white like he'd been while his life pulsed out under Leroy's fingers. He was sleeping or unconscious, and his breathing seemed shallow, but even. Leroy's eyes darted back to the nurse—"His nurse" he'd secretly called her when he allowed himself to think of her, though he knew he had no right. His angel of mercy in the hospital…here.

How could that have happened? She was supposed to be safe in the hospital—well, safer than us.

Her movements were slow and deliberate. Leroy tried to wait patiently, but as she straightened she frowned—just a little line between her eyes—and he couldn't bear it.

"Nurse—lieutenant I mean—I gotta know. Is he…how's he doing?"

She closed her eyes, and he could swear she was counting to ten.

He rushed to apologize. "I'm sorry. I know I shouldn't keep—"

"No." She took a deep breath. "It's alright. I'm done." She rocked back on her heels, but the frown didn't go away.

"And…?" he prompted, despite his resolve to keep quiet.

The eyes she turned on him were cool, but not angry. "I think…" She hesitated. "I think he's going to heal up just fine. Given time and rest."

Leroy sighed, a whoosh of relief. "Are you sure?"

"I said, I think," she snapped.

He stepped back, but as he opened his mouth to apologize again, she shook her head quickly and spoke over anything he might have said.

"I'm sorry. It's…I can't make promises. But the surgery went well, and I don't feel anything suspicious. The ribs looked like they're only fractured, so as long as he gets a chance to rest—" She shrugged and, meeting his eyes, gave him a small, real smile. "If you'll help look after him when I'm not in here, I think…well. We can't know, but I think he should pull through. Thank God he didn't get hit any lower." She emptied a little water from her canteen onto a handkerchief.

"Thank God." Leroy echoed her quietly. She glanced at him, her eyebrows quirked in a quizzical arch, then she bent and used the handkerchief to wipe a bit of residual blood off George's face.

George turned his head and gave a little groan of protest but otherwise didn't move.

The nurse frowned again. Then, looking back at Leroy, she forced a reassuring smile.

He returned it. "Thanks, nurse…I mean lieutenant…'

"Nurse is fine."

"Thanks so much, Nurse Hoff."

She nodded, then rolled to the balls of her feet and stood as the door creaked open. The German soldier who'd escorted her into their little prison was back, ready to escort her out to…somewhere.

Her face didn't change at his entrance, but something about the way her hands clenched at the sides of her pant legs prompted Leroy to ask, "Hey, nurse, are you…are you ok out there? Are they being decent to you?"

Her eyes met his, and she hesitated, then nodded. "Yes. Thank you. I'll be back in a few hours. Assuming they let me..." And then, she was gone.

THE NEXT TIME George woke, his face didn't feel so sticky. *Well, that's something.* The thunder still beat in his head, and he kept his eyes closed. He stretched his muscles tentatively, looking for damage.

He found it, burning lines where his neck met his shoulder and across his scalp. Another around his chest—tearing, stabbing pain that made him want to curl up on himself like a pill bug. He tried to slow his inhales and exhales, to keep them shallow so they wouldn't hurt so much.

Whew. Well, something sure hit me. It's kinda familiar—but from where? He tried to think, but that made the thunder in his head stronger. He let it go and focused on breathing—*not too deep*. The answer drifted up on its own: that time he fell out of a tree when he was seven. He'd been trying to get Norrie's kite down. Fractured his collar bone. This was worse, and lower. *Ribs, I suppose.* Gingerly, he felt the sore spots at his neck and head. Bandages—maybe the pull of stitches underneath?

Where'd those come from? For that matter, what even happened? More memories floated up. There'd been the tank, sitting there. He'd had them split up, and then…then what happened?

Well. This ain't Anzio. And I'm not dead unless heaven—or for that matter, the other place—is lots different than Sunday School said. So. Where am I?

Cold seeped through the thin pad under him. The musty smells of wet earth and stone surrounded him, mixed with the familiar aromas of unwashed human and latrine. He shifted. Whatever the ground was, it sure didn't give much—his hips and rear ached but rolling over seemed to be too much effort. Even opening his eyes felt like too much effort. A man coughed. Some kind of steady drone sounded from over to his left. No, not a drone; a steady, wheezing snore. If it didn't hurt so much, he'd have smiled. *Leroy. So. What is this? A prison? Maybe. S'pose I could just ask.*

He opened his mouth and tasted blood as his lips cracked. He tried to lick them, but his thick tongue held no moisture.

New noises—the creak of hinges, a heavy door opening, a deep voice speaking German. George closed his mouth and worked on opening his eyes instead, then wished he hadn't. The light from the doorway stung and started those bongos in his skull again. Leroy's snores stuttered and stopped. Narrowing his eyes to slits, George tried to make out what was going on.

Footsteps approached. He smelled kerosene and heard a clack as a lamp was set down next to him. An arm slipped under his shoulders, lifting, and the cold metal of a canteen touched his lips. He gulped eagerly.

The voice was soft, clipped, commanding. And feminine. "Not too fast now. How are you feeling?"

George's eyes snapped wide open. When they could focus, they met the cool green eyes of a woman. She could almost pass for German. Light hair—just a little too dark to be blonde—fair skinned face smooth, calm, and inscrutable. But she spoke English, and her olive drab collar held pins for the U.S. Nurse Corps.

Where've I seen that face? The nurse—the one from Hell's Half Acre who Leroy had a thing for. How in the world....? No. First things first. "Where...?" The word came out as a croaking gasp. He coughed, and his ribs protested violently.

Leroy's face floated into his periphery. A large bandage covered his right cheek. "Hey, George! You awake?"

"Shush." It was unclear which of them the nurse was shushing, but Leroy's mouth snapped shut. She pressed the canteen back to George's lips, and he forced himself to sip slowly. "You've been captured. This is...well, a shack or shed. It was here already, along with a couple of other buildings, right by where the Germans set up a...they called it a *Hauptverbandplatz*, which I guess is something like one of our clearing stations. You and some other American prisoners are being kept here temporarily."

Licking his lips, George said, "Then?"

"I...I believe they plan to send us to a more permanent camp."

Panic gripped him, dulling the pain. *No. Nope. I'm not getting shipped off to Germany. I was gonna make it big or go down fighting—God, why this? No way I'm going to just stay put—*

He pushed himself up onto his elbows. Crippling pain shot through his ribs, neck, head, and he couldn't stifle a low cry. Spots swam before his eyes.

Leroy's hands found his shoulders first. "Hey, cut that out. Here, let's get you back down—"

The nurse was talking too, her voice short and irritated. "Don't rush. You lost a good bit of blood from that neck wound. Thankfully, they're letting me in to check on you regularly. Lie still now." She reached down to his unbuttoned shirt, probing the bandages that wrapped his chest.

Even in that cold room his skin shivered back from her frigid hands. He refocused on what she'd said. "They?"

"The Germans. There's one doctor here, a surgeon, who—he's a decent man. He helped me patch you up. Some of the others…don't care to waste resources on prisoners." Her voice lowered to a mutter. "Ribs still seem ok, but I wish…"

A wave of pain washed over him, and the world wavered.

Leroy's voice buzzed like a radio losing signal. "Hang in there, buddy. Just hang in there and let Nurse Hoff check you over. You're gonna be fine, just—"

George closed his eyes. "Sure kid." *I'll be fine alright. Soon as I get out of here, I'll be just fine.*

Blinking in the early morning light, Jean tried to push down her fears as she watched the Wehrmacht soldier shut the door on the American prisoners. It might not be a real prison, not yet. Still, the solid stone walls and wooden door effectively shut her away from the only people here that weren't "the enemy."

A firm hand grasped her elbow. Jumping, she shook her arm free and gave her guard an icy glare. Stony-faced, he gestured towards the hospital tents.

Tall as she was, she had to stretch her legs to keep up with his quick step. Ambulances bearing the wounded had churned the dirt lane into a muddy morass. She passed a few parked vehicles, then tents pitched for the medical staff and a larger stone structure—maybe a ruined barn—that had been converted to a laundry.

Jumping another rut, she wished she could turn back. Wrench that shed open, gather up the other prisoners and run for it. *Be sensible, Jean. What good would running do?* Of the seven men kept inside, several were wounded—one badly. *A stupid move like that would just get me shot. Them too.*

Still, her heart screamed that running was better—maybe even being shot was better—than what might wait for her here. Reflexively, she looked over her shoulder as another German hurried past them. Not Him. That should be good news, but she felt like she was in Uncle Burt's pastures, out on the farm at Sun Prairie. You always looked for the bull, not because you wanted to mess with him, but because it was better to know from which direction the danger might come.

"*Fräulein,*" her guard said, then continued, more hesitantly, "The doctor, he say he have many jobs for you today."

Squaring her shoulders and facing forward, she nodded and increased her pace. Time to get back to her "duties."

Alongside the regular hospital tents—familiar, and yet unfamiliar to her American eyes—a sprawling house still stood. The largest room on the ground floor had been cleared and cleaned and repurposed for a surgery, with other rooms providing some office space for medical staff and storage for instruments and medical equipment.

Her current guard was really an enlisted man who worked in the hospital area. Knowing her routine, he took her to the farmhouse kitchen to wash up. He'd seemed surprised the first time she'd insisted on washing after checking on the prisoners—apparently, the German aseptic procedures were less stringent than the ones she was familiar with. As she poured water into a basin—there was no running water in the house—and scrubbed, he stepped into the hall, talking with one of the other men.

She took a deep breath and kept one hand splashing in the water as the other reached toward the tidy rows of packaged medicines and dressings lined up on the kitchen's counter. *We'll see if this works.* With trembling fingers, she pulled out one of the boxes and extracted an aluminum tablet tube of what she believed was the German equivalent of asprin. She slipped it into the roll of hair at the nape of her neck, then replaced the box.

Her hair had always been too baby-fine to manage popular styles, so, like many other women, she'd saved the strands that were left tangled in her brush to make a "rat"—a little bundle of hair to wind her actual hair around so that she could roll it up decently. When she'd gotten orders to overseas, destination still unknown, she'd debated cropping it short. Then, Major Barnett heard she'd be heading over.

Overcome with a desire to share advice, she'd sat Jean down and recounted her adventures as a nurse abroad. Grudgingly, Jean listened and found herself impressed. Barnett had left the Philippines just before the Japanese attacked, before the nurses on Bataan were taken prisoner. She made an offhand comment about how, as tensions in the world escalated, she and her friend had planned on using their "rat" for smuggling medicines out. "Honey," she'd said, waving her cigarette near Jean's nose, "no fella would think to search a girl's *hair*."

Jean hadn't cared for the "honey" or the unwanted advice, but, despite her skepticism, she'd kept her hair. Life in the service had been hard on it, and she'd nearly taken a scissors to it many times. Today, it might prove that it had been worth the hassle.

Hastily, she patted the loose strands into place, feeling for any telltale bulges. *I wonder if I could fit one of those vials of iodine, too?* A shiver passed down her back as she imagined what might happen if she were caught. *Maybe next time.* She'd found a sharp stone on a visit to the latrine and scraped a shallow hole under her bedroll. Any bits of medical supplies she managed to scrounge would go there, with the hopes that when she was transferred, she might still be of use to other prisoners. *Who knows what medicines actually get to the POWs?*

Though the theft only took a few seconds, she was keenly aware of every heartbeat, every moment she was out of her guard's gaze. *How long do I have before he becomes suspicious?* She began unloading the little satchel she used to carry supplies into the prison shed.

"*Warten Sie, Fräulein!*"

She kept working, pretending not to understand.

"*Ich sage, Sie sollen warten!*" A scarred hand seized her wrist and pulled her around. Her guard's brow was furrowed, his translucent blonde eyelashes giving his red, angry face an alien look.

Staring at him, eyes as wide as they would go, she opened her mouth in an astonished "o." She didn't have to try to make her voice tremble at his furious look. "I'm sorry, were you talking to me?"

He sputtered, but then a hand gripped his shoulder, and Doctor Schmidt pulled him away. He leaned in and spoke quietly in her guard's ear. The only words Jean could make out were "...auf Englisch!"

Her guard nodded and grunted something Jean's way that might have been an apology, and the doctor released him. "Surely you remember, Nurse, that Pieter will need to see all of the supplies you bring back, just as he checked the bag when you left." The doctor's English was very good. He'd explained that he studied at Oxford.

"Oh, is *that* what he was saying? I'm sorry, Doctor. I—I forgot, and I couldn't imagine why he was so upset."

Doctor Schmidt gave her a bland smile. He was about Stan's age, and some of his mannerisms reminded her...but too many tears lay down that road. Instead, she focused on his fading brown hair, sprinkled with threads of gray, especially around his ears and in his bushy eyebrows. "We cannot all change our language to accommodate yours, my dear. Now, I have just finished surgery. Would you please see to sterilizing some instruments?"

"Yes, of course."

He turned, and as he walked away, one foot dragged a little behind the other. This had been the first feature Jean noticed as she sat huddled in the back of the ambulance that had carried her here, eyes fixed on the ground, trying to pray. Carefully shined brown shoes contrasted with the surrounding military boots, one foot dragging behind the other as he hobbled over to her, and then the voice, low and kind... but how could it be kind? He was the enemy.

But he's not, not really. He's as good as said he wants the war to end. He's trying to save lives—just like the doctors on our side. His dedication to his work had been evident from the start, as he struggled to save the American prisoners with the same diligence he did the German wounded. That, and his dislike of military procedure. It was by his own request that she referred to him as "Doctor," eschewing military rank.

Pieter finished his check of her satchel, and returned it to her, then went to bring in the instruments from Doctor Schmidt. She accepted them with a twinge of conscience. When she'd worked in the nursing unit on Anzio, she'd patched up numerous German soldiers. Stubborn, the lot of them, many of them too stubborn to be carried in on stretchers, and once they were in, they'd refuse to lie down. Their determination to show their toughness didn't so much impress her as remind her of her very German Grandmother Hoff refusing to allow her children to coax her out of her massive old house when she became too frail to care for it.

Still, while it was one thing to treat a prisoner—just like Doctor Schmidt and his enlisted men had quickly and efficiently treated that corporal over in the shed—helping the enemy's medical team in their own camp felt wrong.

More wrong than letting someone die when I can help? Of course, if they're alive, they can go and cause more casualties on our side. She swallowed, then carried the tray of instruments to the sterilizer. *Doing odd jobs can't hurt, and while I help, I can stay near Doctor Schmidt and away from Him.* She couldn't help another glance over her shoulder, out through the front window looking for that flash of gold hair and those broad shoulders—attributes that in a different place and time might have been handsome. They were spoiled by the scar pulling his cheek into a perpetual sneer, by those cruel hands clenched at his sides, and by the things he said to her when he caught her alone.

Jean's throat tightened. After three days as a prisoner, she had already learned who to fear. He...he was an obvious one. Others she was less certain about. *The doctor's been kind, but...* But she couldn't forget that he *was* the enemy, or at least working for the enemy. However kind he seemed, she'd better not push it. She prepared a tray of clean instruments and carried them towards the surgery.

When she saw the boy on the table, all moral compunctions and all fears of her surroundings evaporated. Here was a life—a life that needed saving.

The poor boy looked like a German propaganda poster—blue eyed and blond haired and healthy and strong, except for where his belly had been torn open.

Doctor Schmidt bent over him, sponging up blood and repositioning the boy's intestines and muttering to himself—the same litany Jean had heard multiple times. "What a waste—all of our young men trying to kill all of your young men until who are left? Just the old men like me..." Then he turned to Pieter who'd come in to assist and switched to German, urging him to hurry.

Though she had no real right to be in there, she stood in the corner and watched until the end of the procedure. *Even Stan couldn't have stitched him up so well*—her throat tightened at the thought, and she slipped out.

Pausing in the hallway, she stared out the window, past the trucks, to the hills rising just behind them. *I wonder where I am, exactly. I wonder how I could find out...*

No convenient maps waited for her in the kitchen, but after a few more hours of odd jobs and organizing supplies, the time came to check the prisoners again and change the dressings on Corporal...*I didn't ask his name, did I?* She ought to have—Stan would rag her about it if she didn't even know their names. *Oh Stan*—something rose in her throat, and she couldn't tell if it was a laugh or a sob. Swallowing it down, she grabbed her satchel.

"Child," Doctor Schmidt called, "Put the kettle on, won't you? After a morning like this, a lull calls for some tea."

"Of course." Pausing in her preparations, she went to the little portable gas stove. The kettle was already full, and it was only a matter of turning the heat on. She lined up her supplies on the counter for Pieter to check, then watched the kettle until it began to steam. The doctor would not boil water in a kettle that whistled. "Too upsetting for some of the men," he'd explained. When she saw the telltale plume, she called to him, and he left his desk in the adjoining room—once the dining room—where he'd been filling out paperwork.

"Doctor? It's boiling. Would you like me to—"

"No, no, thank you. I believe you were going over to check on the other prisoners?"

Other prisoners. She swallowed at this reminder that, despite her liberties, she was a prisoner, too. "Yes," she managed, "once Pieter comes to check the supplies. Unless you need anything else?"

"Only to make one thing clear." He dropped a tea bag into one of the chipped white pottery mugs he had lined up neatly on a shelf beneath the burner and slowly poured the scalding water over it. She scanned his face—something in his voice worried her—but he looked down into his cup of tea, swirling it around as if he could read the leaves. "You know how I feel about this war, how it is a waste of young lives?"

"Yes, sir, I have heard you speak about it—"

He met her gaze. "I do think that, but my family...my family is in Germany. My wife. My sons. *My* daughter. Do you know what would have happened to them if I had refused to serve?"

Jean swallowed. "I don't imagine it would have been good—"

"I am here to do a job, and I will do it. For them. And I won't let anything endanger that job." His eyes pierced her., "Anything. Do you understand?"

"Yes, I understand."

He turned away from her, setting his cup near the stove. "So. You must return whatever you have concealed."

Shoot! Her hand floated up towards her hair, then she pulled it down as he turned to her. His eyes, usually kind, were hard.

Don't give him anything. Maybe he's just checking. "Concealed?" She was vaguely impressed that her voice didn't waver or tremble despite the pounding of her heart.

He sighed heavily and pointed to her pants pocket.

"What…" Reaching into it, she discovered an extra dressing left from her last visit to the prisoners. "Oh! I forgot!" She handed it over and grinned sheepishly. *Whew. No, I wasn't trying to smuggle those yet.*

He took it with a grunt. "Be glad that I was the one who noticed. Something as small in the wrong eyes…might give them excuse."

"Excuse?"

The doctor shook his head and turned away.

Seven

The squeak of door hinges penetrated George's cocoon of sleep. Pain came first, then awareness of where he was. Voices welcomed the newcomer. "Hi, nurse," "Hey, any news?" Someone shifted on the ground next to him—probably Leroy. He didn't say anything. *Probably just gazing at that girl—the kid's hopeless. I don't hear Shorty grousing, don't sound like Petey either. Wonder who we're stuck here with?*

One guy had a slow Texas drawl. George could hear the ingratiating smile in his voice. "Howdy again, nurse. Sure is a pleasure to see your sweet face again."

The nurse answered, "Let's take a look at your arm."

"Of course, ma'am, whatever yououch!" Someone sniggered, and the Texan shut up.

"Looks ok. Just try to keep it clean."

"Yes ma'am. Anything you s…"

Footsteps—she was already walking away from him. "What about you, pilot? How's the ankle?"

There was a long pause, then a deep bass voice answered, "It's fine." Another pause. "Any word on what they're gonna do with us?"

"Nothing they've told me."

Clink. The light was set down near his head. George kept his eyes closed, telling himself he was picking his time to enter the conversation, but deep down knowing he was saving up his energy to speak.

Cold fingers undid his buttons. He ought to be making some kind of crack about that, but the drums were still pounding in his head, and he couldn't think of one. The nurse probed the bandage on his neck, his head, his ribs—*uf. Dang it, that hurts.*

Leroy's eager voice started in. "George's been sleeping since you came last, nurse—whatever you gave him sure helped."

"Good." She felt his forehead—there, at least, her cold hands felt good. "He still feels a little feverish."

Leroy's frown carried through his voice. "Is that bad?"

"It's not unusual after surgery. Still..."

"Can't we get him somewhere...I dunno, warmer, or...?"

"I've spoken to one of the German doctors." She probed his ribs again, gently. "He's looking into it—maybe he can work something out."

"That's it?" The Texan's voice was clear—he and the others had shuffled over. "Maybe?"

The pressure of the nurse's hands on his chest lessened—she was probably shrugging. Another poke at his ribs, and George couldn't stifle a groan.

"George?" Leroy's hand pressed his shoulder. "You awake?"

Peeling his eyes open, George curled his fist into a thumbs up. *Lifting an arm shouldn't be this hard.*

The nurse turned to Leroy. "Here, help him sit up a little—careful." Leroy slid his arm under George's shoulders. Getting his hands on the floor, George pushed himself up, trying not to flinch as his ribs complained. He ended up almost sitting, propped against the shed wall.

Placing her canteen to his lips, the nurse said, "Here. Remember, not too fast."

He sipped—*dang, I'd hoped the water wasn't as bad as I remembered. Better than nothing, though*. Swishing the oily liquid around, his tongue unglued from the roof of his mouth. A couple of molars felt loose. *Great. Wonder what the German POW dental care is like.* Taking another sip, he smacked his lips together and gingerly tried a grin at the kid. "Hello again."

Leroy returned a relieved smile. "Hey there. This is Nurse Hoff. Remember?

Turning his eyes to the nurse, George decided his face felt mobile enough to try a real smile—the good one that hadn't failed to get him a dance since before he'd needed a razor. At the attempt, his dry lip cracked, and he could taste salty blood on the jagged edge. His wince must have spoiled the effect because she just looked down at him, cool expression unchanging, and offered the canteen again.

Huh. Well, it appears Nurse Hoff is immune. Too bad. He accepted the drink, but as he was less thirsty, the taste was more offensive. He coughed and spluttered. "Whew. Thanks. Wonder where they found motor oil to spare for us to drink."

The nurse's lips tightened.

Ok. Maybe it's too soon to joke. "Anything to eat?"

Leroy produced a rather grimy hunk of dark bread from a pocket. "Here, I've been saving this for you."

Saliva flooding his mouth, George fumbled to accept it with a muttered, "Thanks." His front teeth bounced off the crust. He switched to his canines, careful to keep it to the left, away from the loose teeth, and tried to force the dry hunk far enough into his mouth so he could chew.

The other guys seemed to lose interest, at least as far as wanting to stand around and watch a hurt guy eat. They drifted back to slump against the walls of their prison.

The nurse busied herself organizing the canvas satchel she'd brought. She shifted her weight, as if she might stand, might leave.

No you don't, not yet! She was his only link to the outside world. He hustled to swallow and coughed. She paused, offering him another drink. When he could talk, he said, "Thanks."

She screwed the lid back onto her canteen. "This medical area isn't properly set up for prisoners—everyone's in a hurry. Hopefully, the food will be better regulated once you get to …wherever they send you all."

"Ok, but—" His bleary brain focused on one thing she'd said, "Wait, what about you? Aren't you being sent somewhere?"

Those cool eyes broke contact. "Well…"

George's spine stiffened. "What—you haven't gone and signed on with the Krauts?"

Her gaze snapped back to meet his. "No. Of course not. I was captured, just like you."

For a moment panic more painful than his sore ribs clutched his chest. "What—we didn't, we didn't *lose*…The Germans didn't make it all the way back to the hospital—"

Shaking her head, she said, "No. I was…I was in a jeep with a surgeon friend of mine. Our driver…We must've wound up too far forward."

Too relieved and irritated to be tactful, George summed up his feelings with one word. "Stupid."

She dropped her gaze to the floor. "Stan never held too much with rules and regs…but we weren't really going that far forward, and he didn't expect the attack. And when…and when Stan was killed…" She bit her lip.

Leroy twitched towards her, then stopped himself.

"Anyway. I was brought here. Lots of wounded coming in—ours and theirs. The doctor—surgeon, really—he realized I was a nurse and set me to work. Of course I pitched in. It's my job. I helped patch *you* up. Since then, I've just been doing some odd jobs. Sterilizing equipment, trying to help in here—"

George said, "So, they'll use you while they can, then ship you off to a POW camp?" Her face remained cool. George was surprised that she didn't rise to his needling. *I'm losing my touch—must be sicker than I thought.*

She shrugged. "I suppose so. This isn't an ideal situation for any of us. I don't think they quite know what to do with me." As she resumed packing her things, she added, "Anyway, it should be soon. They're moving a lot of personnel around."

"Seemed like they were shipping an awful lot of them toward the front a couple of days ago."

"Yes. Everything's tied up. They shipped some prisoners back already, but the vehicles and drivers are so busy some of you've just been, well, sort of stored here for a few days. Maybe, when you go, I'll go out with you. That would be good." Her voice dropped at the last.

She's scared of something. Beside him, Leroy stiffened, frowning. *He caught it too.*

Gathering herself, she pressed a couple of pills into George's hand. "Here. It looks like you're healing up all right. Still, I think you might be running a bit of fever. I should have brought a thermometer. Take this. Sulfa for infection, and this for the pain."

He took his pills obediently, just as a heavy knock shook the door. A spasm of fear passed over the nurse's face again, and she glanced over her shoulder. Two voices came from beyond the door, then a harsh laugh. "*Fräulein*, are you finished yet?"

She called back, "Just about." Turning to George, her face remained calm, but her voice sounded brittle. "You should sleep if you can. You're recovering still, and who knows when they'll want you to move out."

His aching ribs affirmed her assessment. "Ok." Leroy helped ease him back to his blanket on the hard floor, and she muttered something about how she was going to ask the doctor again about cots.

Leroy scrambled to pick up her satchel for her. The way the kid smiled at her made George chuckle to himself, then he wished he hadn't as his ribs grumbled again.

He reached behind his ear—nothing. "Don't suppose you've got a smoke?"

She shook her head. Several of the other guys in the shadows groaned.

"Once you're at a real camp, the Red Cross ought to be able to find you—send some aid packages."

A fist pounded on the door. *"Fräulein?"*

Leaning in, she whispered, "They're edgy. I don't think their offensive is going so well. They don't really want us here."

The door thumped again.

Pushing himself up onto his elbow, a flash of curiosity blunting the stab of pain, George hissed, "Why—what makes you think—"

She shook her head, scooping up her bag just as the door was flung open. The man who was standing nearest it jumped back to avoid being struck.

The guard's broad shoulders almost filled the narrow doorframe. Just another German—a big, beefy blonde. But something about this fellow had the nurse clenching her fists at her sides.

"Who's—" Leroy began in a whisper, but the guard spoke over him. *"Fräulein*, what could you be doing in here that takes so long?"

"I'm ready now." Her voice didn't shake, but her feet dragged, reluctant to move across the short distance to the door. When she reached it, the big man didn't move. The nurse moistened her lips. "Please, I'm ready to go."

"Yah, after you."

She raised her chin and turned sideways, sidling through the narrow gap. Her back had to scrape the doorframe so that she could get through without touching him. His eyes followed her the entire time. Close to George's ear, Leroy's knuckles cracked.

The German lingered in the doorway, turning his attention back to the prisoners with a leer. "Nice girls you have there on that beach." The scar on his cheek pulled his lip off to the side. "When we push the rest of you back into the sea, maybe we keep some of those around to entertain us." He jerked his head back toward where Nurse Hoff had gone. "Maybe I keep this one no matter what."

Leroy stood, fists clenched, but George grabbed his trouser leg and muttered, "Easy, kid." Raising his voice, he called, "Whatsamatter, Fritzie? No girls back home'll have you?"

The guard stared him down—the smile now looked more like an animal's bared teeth. Without another word, he left, the door closing with a final thunk.

George sighed and lay back down. *He didn't need to say anything—he knows anything I say don't matter to him.* Helpless. He hated it—he'd vowed never to be helpless again.

Leroy spun on him. "Didja see him? Did you see the way he... he ..."

"Settle down, kid."

"Settle down?" Leroy spat. George blinked—he'd never seen the kid this hot under the collar. "He's got no right to look at her like... and did you see the look on her face?"

"Leroy. Quiet down. He was trying to rile us up. He hears you, he wins."

The kid's voice dropped, but it dripped with anger. "She's scared."

George pushed with his arms, his legs, and managed to sit up, his ribs screaming at him. He tried to keep his breaths shallow, tried not to show how much it hurt.

His movement distracted Leroy. "What're you doing? She said you'd better rest."

"S'ok."

"George, you look awful. Don't do anything stupid, not now after everything—"

"Yeah. Everything. What happened?" George scanned the little group of prisoners. Two huddled together, talking. One sat on his own, tossing something up into the air. A fourth, a tall, broad man with deep brown skin wearing a pilot's jacket examined the door, and the last fella across from him leaned against the wall and examined him right back. None of them looked familiar.

Leroy settled down next to him. "Well, the rest of the squad got away, I think. Shorty got hit, then rabbited right off."

"Can't blame him."

"Well, *you* wouldn't've. Petey stuck it out longer, swung by and grabbed Hammond for me." Leroy shrugged. "Anyway, when O'Reilly went down and the Teds started swarming—"

"You ran up to cover them so they could get away, all on your own. Kid, you're crazy."

"You'd have done the same. Anyhow, you were hurt bad. All your right side was blood, and it was just coming out your head and your neck—" he swallowed. "Anyway, the Germans came up, and I was outta ammo, and I threw my gun down and hands up and asked for a doctor." He squirmed. "I…did I do right? You…you looked real bad. It opened you right up—"

"Sure you did right. You kept us alive." *Your life's worth saving anyway, kid.* He shifted, trying to find a position where he could breathe easier. "Now we just gotta decide what we do next."

"Next?" laughed the lone fella who had been playing catch with himself. His drawl gave him away—he was the Texan who'd tried his charm on the nurse. The object fell softly into his hand—a lucky rabbit's foot on a short bit of chain. He tucked it into his pocket and strolled over. "I figure what we do next is get shipped off to a POW camp. Unless you figure they're gonna give us options?"

George sized him up. Even from sitting he could tell the Texan was a good head taller than he'd be on his tiptoes, even taller than Leroy. One of those fellas dirt didn't really stick to. Didn't look soft, though. He held himself like he knew what he was doing. His left forearm was bandaged.

George decided to risk frankness. "Nope. Don't imagine they'll *give* us anything, except maybe a chance to work in one of their camps." He reached behind his ear, searching for that cigarette that wasn't there. He mustered a smile and held out his hand. "Before we start bickering, we might's well know who we're fighting with. Hey, weren't you part of Humphrey's squad?"

The tall man nodded. "Yeah. Hank Parker. And you used to hang around Growly Wally, didn't ya?"

George laughed, then flinched. "Sure did. George Novak. This is Leroy Anderson. Those other guys with you?"

"Yep—well, those two are. Same squad, what's left of it. Hey, Chuck, Barry!" The whisperers looked up and, at Hank's gesture, drifted over. The other guy who'd been watching everything joined them. The pilot turned from his examination of the hinges and leaned against the wall.

Hank did the introductions. "This fella's Chuck Wilson."

George reached up and shook hands. Wilson didn't have much of a grip for his build. He was a short, broad blonde kid—looked like he'd played football. When George asked, though, he shook his head. "Naw. I'm better with tools. Was just about to be moved back to HQ to help with communications operations, when..."

George grimaced. "Dang, you were almost home free. Bad luck, huh?"

"Dunno that we've had any other kind." Chuck kicked at the earth floor.

Hank clapped him on the back. "Eh, at least you didn't end up like Frankie—" He met George's eyes with a sardonic smile. "Squad leader. Pretty much swallowed one of the 88s. *Psheeeew!*" He made an explosive gesture with his hands around his head. Chuck looked ill.

One of the other guys smacked Hank on the arm. "Hey, knock it off." He stuck his hand out to George. "Barry West. I played football."

"Really?" asked Leroy. George could understand his skepticism. Barry was a weedy brunette with a different drawl than Hank's and taped-together glasses. He didn't look like he could take much of a hit.

He caught their skepticism and answered it. "Small school. Coach told me I'd better learn to be faster than the bigger guys so they didn't just sit on me." He shrugged. "So, I did."

The third guy, Ed, was a driver.

Hmm, interesting. "What've they got you driving?" George asked. "The deuce and a half trucks?"

"I've driven 'em, but I try—tried—for the jeep jobs. Loads more fun."

"Hey, buddy, what about you?" George called over to the last prisoner. The other guys shuffled aside, looking a little uncomfortable. George had grown up over on Lansing's west side—darker faces than his weren't a new sight. If accents said anything, it sounded like at least a couple of these guys were from the deep South—probably used to segregated everything. *But if we're stuck in a 150 square foot shed together, they'd better get past that quick—especially if we're gonna have a shot to get out of this.*

The man stood up straight. That deep, bass voice George had heard before rolled out of him. "Michael Roberts. 332nd Fighter Group."

A fighter pilot, hmmm? Well that could be handy.

Barry muttered, "They're letting them fly now?"

Roberts shifted his feet, mouth going grim. George spoke up quickly. "Say, were you in that action over Anzio end of January?"

"Yeah."

George whistled. "It looked pretty hot up there. Thanks for keeping the Teds off our backs. How'd you get grounded?"

"Shot down just north of here."

"Take any of 'em with you?"

That got a grin from Roberts, teeth bright white against his dark face. "At least two."

George grinned back. Refocusing on the whole group, he tried to ignore the nagging pain from his wounds. "So, fellas, here's the serious question." He paused for drama. "Anyone, please, got a smoke?"

There were chuckles all around, then miraculously, Chuck Wilson pulled a cigarette out of his breast pocket.

"For him, but not for me?" said Hank, scowling.

Wilson shrugged. "I was saving it, and, well, you didn't come in all torn up."

Hank muttered some colorful names for Chuck and his family, but George ignored him, fingering the cigarette lovingly. It was almost too good to be true.

Before he could ask, Leroy pulled out his ever-present book of matches. "Hey, George, you sure you want it now? Maybe you should lie down first."

Don't nursemaid me, kid. George held out his hand for a match. Lighting up, he closed his eyes and savored the taste. Foul things, Ma had called them, made him promise that he'd never pick one up. By now he'd broken so many promises he figured one more wouldn't matter.

If I ever get home, I'll quit. I swear, Lord, I'll chuck 'em all. But for today... He inhaled again—not too deep—and leaned back, closed his eyes, and thought about what he'd learned.

Three more dogfaces—one good with building and radios. Plus, a pilot and a driver. If we can all just get along, maybe we can make something of this.

He shifted and grimaced. Even with whatever the nurse had given him and the soothing nicotine, he was going to have to lie down again soon. Taking another drag, he considered the nurse's words. *Hmph. So they'll ship us out soon. Off to a real POW camp, barbed wire, guards and gates, the works. Won't get officer privileges either—could be forced labor. For Hitler. Don't sound appealing.*

Neither did the image of Frank's cold gaze that danced behind his eyelids. Frank would tell Lil all about it, no doubt. How good-for-nothing George had gotten over here at last but hadn't managed to do anything at all except get his squad captured. Never even made it past corporal—after everything, he wouldn't even have another stripe to show for all those months away. The months when she'd drifted off and he'd lost her.

No. No. He wasn't going to let it happen. He wasn't going to rot in some POW camp. No way. Pain lanced through the wounds at his neck, his head, his ribs, and he couldn't suppress a groan.

Leroy was right there. "Ok, that does it. Time to rest." He helped ease George back down.

"Thanks." *How's the kid going to do in a POW camp?* His jaw clenched. Lying back, exhausted, his weary mind kept whirring.

Ok. What advantages have we got? One: This is only a temporary camp, not equipped to hold prisoners. Two: The Germans are tied up in an offensive, so everyone's busy and preoccupied. Of course, the offensive will have to end sometime, one way or another. Either the lines will break at Anzio, or we'll hold. My money's on our boys. Sure, it's a tight spot, but a cornered animal always fights hardest.

If the Germans were repelled, there'd be transports available. He and the others would be hauled out lickity split. Maybe all the way back to Germany. Far away, with the only escape routes long, winding through enemy territory, and the only places to run—where? Britain? Sweden maybe?

His cigarette was spent, just like his strength. *If I just had some time to heal up*—that was the real problem. There just wasn't time.

Once we're shipped outta here, I might just have to admit that I'm out for the duration.

But if I have my way, I won't be around here that long.

EIGHT

BACK STRAIGHT AND FEET SWIFT, Jean fixed her eyes ahead. For the first time in ages, she allowed herself to think about Joe—his memory was about the only thing strong enough to combat the fear that stalked behind her. If she just remembered hard enough, she could feel him there. His ghost stood at her shoulder, watching her with those beautiful, intense eyes, ready to comment or correct or guide.

Pain seared her heel, and she flinched as *He*—Private Grüber—trod on the back of her shoe. He walked so close she could feel his breath on the back of her neck, hear it when he leaned a little closer and smelled her hair.

Deep breaths, Jean. He can't do anything to you. Suppressing a shudder, Jean reached for Joe's memory—her talisman.

It eluded her. Reality was too sharp, and she couldn't forget that if she turned around, looking for comfort, looking for those arms that made her feel special, made her safe, she would find nothing. *It's not that different from when he was alive, is it?*

Grüber's boot bumped her calf, and she quickened her step. *Better his feet than his hands.* She didn't turn around to ask him to back off. When she'd tried before, he just laughed. Came closer. *I just need to get to the doctor. He wouldn't dare do this with an officer around. As long as I stay near the doctor, I'll be fine.* Her toe caught on a clod of earth, and she stumbled. *If only I wasn't so tired*—but last night he must have been patrolling. Through the thin wall her cot rested against, his voice had intruded on her sleep, creeping, insidious, until she'd startled awake. He'd whispered things that still made her skin crawl—detailing what he'd do when he got her out from under Doctor Schmidt's nose.

She clenched her fists and hurried on. Past the smell of wet wool and steam from the laundry. Past the latrines—she considered stopping there for a moment of privacy. They'd allowed her to use the officer's, which at least had walls. Though her feet hesitated, she didn't stop—a plank wall wasn't nearly enough between her and those eyes and that scar-stretched grin.

By the time she'd covered the distance from the prisoners to the farmhouse, her heart was pounding so hard that she might have run a mile. It certainly felt like she was crossing the finish line. The doctor waited at the door. Was it her imagination, or did he frown when he saw that Grüber was her escort? If he did notice her distress, he said nothing except to greet her and put her to work. Organizing piles of dressings, Jean's hands slowly steadied. A motor approached and stopped outside. The sound barely registered in her mind—just another ambulance.

"Hallo? Schmidt?"

Jean tensed, then the voice registered in her memory, and she relaxed. *It's just the Oberst.*

Leaning back, she peered around the edge of the doorway. The doctor was hobbling out to meet him. The contrast between them struck her—the unassuming medical man with the twisted leg facing the tall German officer, still powerful despite the bit of gray above his ears and the first hint of a paunch under his immaculate uniform. The Oberst beamed at Doctor Schmidt and held out his arms as if he were greeting a dear friend. The doctor smiled back, but Jean thought she saw some hesitation. *Maybe I'm just imagining it, but I'd guess they aren't as buddy-buddy as the big guy pretends.*

Willing herself invisible, Jean bent her head over her work. The Oberst had visited before, on the first day of her captivity, and hadn't shown much interest in her except to wonder aloud why she'd been brought here. Still, he was a high-ranking official—something like a colonel—and he might bring news.

The two men stepped into the doctor's workspace. Through the doorway, Jean could just see the doctor's shoulder as he pulled over a rough wooden chair. It scraped across the floor, and the Oberst sat, his back to her.

She slowed her work, straining her ears. Their voices were low, sharing nothing but polite inquiries. A match hissed, and the smell of their cigarettes drifted over. She began wiping down the counter for the second time.

Finally, with a sigh, the Oberst started talking. His German was measured, voice a deep, rich baritone which projected naturally through the thin walls. Mercifully, he wasn't a fast talker. Jean closed her eyes, going back to when she was Jeannie, visiting Grandma Hoff for the summer. Every week, they'd attended her very traditional Lutheran church, and Jeannie, legs dangling over the edge of the pew, listened as Pastor proclaimed the gospel in German. Every summer she'd struggled to attend to the unfamiliar words. She'd tried asking to go to the English services once—only once. It wasn't worth incurring Grandma's horror and wrath at her wish to avoid the "proper" service again.

Now she was grateful for the old woman's insistence. Her German wasn't expert, but it was passable—a fact she had concealed from her captors. *Wish I'd spent more time listening than worrying about if Grandma was going to make me eat blutwurst again. If only I could hear them better!* She tried to breathe more quietly.

The Oberst was saying—no, he was asking—how the doctor liked being here, back out of all the excitement.

The doctor said something like he'd rather be here than in hell— *I guess he means being farther up? Unless he means literally.*

The Oberst laughed and agreed that it was better. Then his voice lowered, and his chair creaked. "I told you I'd look after you. Now, what will you do with your…" *Ach! What's that word…oh! Pet. Pet?* The doctor sighed and replied that he'd just as soon send her back.

Her? Oh, he's talking about me! Jean bristled. *Pet—really? Just because I've pitched in a little doesn't make me—* She pushed her anger down—the Oberst had asked something.

The doctor responded, "I would like to, but the opinion of an old cripple doesn't hold much weight. The Oberst snorted and answered that maybe it should…It sounded like he was going to try…something.

C'mon, c'mon! I could really use some more Biblical terminology. She strained her ears—the Oberst's voice had dropped even further. Still, he wasn't whispering—why should he, when the only other person around couldn't understand him?

They were talking about the Kriegsgefangener—*what? Oh, the prisoners*—how they needed to be transported elsewhere. The Oberst sounded apologetic—his men were all busy, trying to drive out those—*wow, I haven't heard* that *word since Grandpa Hoff was working on the car. Grandma sure chewed him out for saying it, too*—Americans and the British. The vehicles and men were tied up. The Oberst lowered his voice a little more, but the words were coming more easily to Jeannie's mind now.

"Things are winding down. I don't think we'll take them this time—stubborn Americans. Must be some German blood out there." He chuckled drily. "Once that happens—a few days and we can get you some transports, get them to a camp. Maybe she can go along with them? Continue caring for them—that's usual."

"Maybe." The doctor sighed. "I have some concerns." He muttered something—too low for her to hear, and the Oberst responded with a grunt.

Things are winding down—we're winning? That's good news. But that means the prisoners might be heading out soon...so what happens to me? Do I spend the rest of the war in a POW camp? Goosebumps rose on her arms. *I'd like to help the boys there but...* She swallowed, picturing the reports that had come out after the surrender at Corregidor—filthy conditions, no medication, no food... *But those nurses were in the East. Japan isn't even following the Geneva Convention. It might not be like that here. And even if it is, I ought to have the courage to suffer what the boys are suffering. Please, Jesus, give me more courage—*

"Nurse Hoff?" It took her a moment to realize the doctor was really talking to her, that he had switched to English.

Keeping her movements deliberate, she straightened one last scalpel, took a breath, and walked over. "Yes, Doctor Schmidt?"

"How are the prisoners?"

"Well enough, I think. The conditions are really not very good in there—it's damp and dirty. They have nothing but a blanket each to sleep on."

The doctor turned to the Oberst who raised his eyebrows. He muttered something like "Our own, first." The doctor sighed and turned back to her. "Yah. Do what you can. We will talk more of this later. Were you able to finish organizing the supplies?"

"Yes."

"Well done." Another engine rumbled as an ambulance drove up outside. "I think that we will have need of them."

GEORGE SAT, eyes closed, counting his breaths. If he sat just so, and didn't breathe too deep, the pain was bearable. Listening to the quiet sounds of his fellow prisoners, he considered his first move.

Soft voices drifted from his left—Barry West and Chuck Wilson, squatted by the wall, talking about their hometowns. Barry did most of the talking. Across the way, the clockwork-steady *swoosh* and *thwap* of

Texas Hank's rabbit foot being tossed and caught measured the minutes. As a counterpoint, Leroy's snore wheezed at his shoulder—the kid could sleep anywhere. Over near the door, Ed was asking Roberts something about the engine on his fighter. Roberts answered with a deep rumble.

Where to start? Leroy's in the bag. Tex seems like he wants to be chief—could cause trouble. Dunno about the others, but if I had to guess…

Barry and Wilson had fallen silent for the moment.

Better start with Wilson. George opened his eyes and began. "So, Wilson." Chuck looked up eyes wide. George shot him an easy grin. "I was just sitting here, thinking. You were saying you like tools—right? How'd ya wind up a dogface?"

Leroy woke with a little snort. Sitting up, he yawned cavernously.

Wilson dropped his eyes and fiddled with his boot laces. "I dunno. My buddy Phil and I signed up after Pearl Harbor, and we just got sent where they sent us. Guess they needed infantry. Phil'd wanted to sign up at the Navy recruiter, but the line was longer. Better for me, I guess. I can't swim too good, so…" he trailed off and shrugged.

Barry laughed. "I dunno if any of the Navy boys can swim either—my brother sure can't, and he's been in since before the war started. His signing up seemed like a fool thing to me, but…When I signed up, I figured if I were going to fight, I'd rather be on solid ground." He patted the cold, packed earth. "No regrets, either. Especially when they started firing on us on the boat ride over here. When the shells started flying, I sure wished there were some way to dig in!"

George barked out a laugh, then flinched as a dagger of pain flashed through his chest. *Dang it—I keep forgetting.* Leroy chuckled a little, but George could feel his eyes watching, assessing. *Sorry, kid. You're not gonna like any of this.*

The other guys had turned toward the conversation. Ed was still grinning from Barry's little joke. Texas Hank threw his rabbit's foot extra high. Roberts, guarding his turf by the door, didn't react. Wilson managed a weak smile.

Wilson's awful nervous. Not much spirit. Barry then. As long as he doesn't make trouble with Roberts, he might be my in. "You sign up after Pearl, too?"

Barry nodded. "Yup. Hank too, right Hank? Ol'Tex there was with me since basic training—almost got into officer school too, didn'tcha Hank?"

Texas Hank just shrugged, a frown etching his forehead, and turned his attention back to his game of catch. George couldn't suppress a little grin. *Yeah, I had you pegged right, didn't I, Tex? Guess I wasn't the only one with different ambitions.* He turned his attention back to Barry. "Yeah, Pearl got me—and Leroy here—in line too." *Not entirely true, but close enough.* "Funny, innit, how many of us signed on to fight the Japs and wound up here in spaghetti-land instead?"

That got a couple of laughs. *Good. Keep 'em laughing; keep it easy.*

"I didn't sign on after Pearl," Ed volunteered, stretching his arms above his head, joints popping. "Weren't no jobs around home for years. Tried the CCC for a while and liked it—didn't mind the discipline, liked building stuff. Especially out west—you guys ever see Yellowstone?" The others shook their heads. "You gotta see Yellowstone when you get back home. It's crazy—those geysers and all that stuff. Don't look real."

"Why'd you leave?" Barry asked.

Ed shrugged. "Well, I'd been working at Yellowstone—helped with some building, cleared some trails—but I wanted to drive. So, I looked into the army. Seemed like an ok deal. I got to drive, and the pay's not too bad, especially since I don't have to buy the gas. Able to send something home for Ma and the other kids." He shrugged. "That was in '39. Kinda figured we'd end up in the war at some point, but sure didn't figure on anything like Anzio."

There was a somber pause.

Leroy muttered, "Nowhere's quite like Anzio."

"Well," George shrugged, trying to lighten things back up, "not since the last war anyway—feels like what the old fellas said about the trenches all over again. Awful place…" he paused, timing it just right. "I sure hate to think of all our buddies there, still waiting to break out, while we sit here."

The others nodded, except Chuck Wilson who didn't so much nod as shrink further into himself. Hank hadn't volunteered anything, but he fidgeted— maybe he suspected where George was going. *Smart, that one. Yeah, he might be a problem.*

Scanning their faces, George decided to give them a harder nudge. "I sure wish I weren't out of it. Always promised myself I wouldn't finish the war in a prison camp."

Leroy squirmed next to him. "Gee, George, I…"

George forestalled him with a wave of his hand. "Naw, Leroy, you did what had to be done, and I'm grateful to you." He refocused on the others, the ones he needed to convince. "I'm just trying to figure out what to do now."

A heavy quiet enveloped their little prison. Ed nodded, his face open and easy. Roberts and Barry were tough reads. Texas Hank just scowled and threw that blasted rabbit foot in the air again. Wilson was back to fiddling with his bootlaces.

No one's biting. Well, if a nudge won't work, let's try a shove. George squared his shoulders, and then, with every bit of strength he'd been conserving, he stood. Leroy scrambled up beside him, watching as if he thought he might collapse. George shot him a warning look. *Sorry kid. I know I oughta rest, but I can't do this sitting down.* All eyes were on him. Putting all the little energy he had left into his low, urgent voice, he made his pitch.

"So. What I'm wondering is, are you fellas alright with being out of the war? Shipped off somewhere away from the fighting, away from all our buddies?"

Barry and Wilson glanced at each other, then away.

Texas Hank snorted, snatching the rabbit's foot out of the air and pocketing it. He stood too, leaning against the wall. "Not really, but what were we supposed to do? Our patrol got surrounded—a whole platoon of Krauts. Squad leader went down, like I told ya before—probably all the other guys, too. What were we supposed to do, go down in a hopeless shootout?"

George let the silence linger, then conceded, "No, it doesn't do anyone any good to be stupid. The question is—" he paused for effect. "What do we do, now we're here."

Hank's eyes narrowed, but George kept going. *Don't need naysayers. Not yet.* "What about you, Ed? How'd you get caught?

"Me? I was running some supplies and a brass hat to the HQ up toward Cisterna and popped a flat. Hopped out to fix it, and that's when the shots started—must've been a Jerry patrol. The fella I was driving got shot. I tried to hold 'em off, but one snuck up behind me. A gun to my head convinced me that I'd just as soon live to fight another day."

Here goes. "How ya gonna do that, locked up somewhere?"

"I dunno. I'll figure something out though. Don't intend to be Fritzie's lap dog if I can help it." Ed grinned, showing all his tobacco-stained teeth.

The others grunted in assent.

Good. "Any of you thinking of escaping?"

"Whoa, whoa, whoa," said Texas Hank, pushing himself off from the wall and coming to stand in front of George. "Just what're you proposing here, *corporal*? Cuz from where I'm standing, I'm hearing a seriously wounded guy hinting around at something pretty stupid that's likely to get himself and anyone who goes along killed. Am I hearing right?"

Trying to look nonchalant and ignore the fire blazing through his ribs, George grinned. "Well, Tex, all's I'm saying is POW's never been an appealing option for me. I was just thinking, they sure don't seem prepared to keep us here for the long term. What if we just took advantage of that and the fact that we can't be more'n a few miles from our lines and—" he mimed running with his fingers through the air "—skeedaddled before they get themselves more organized?"

With a guffaw, Hank shook his head. "You can't be serious. Where would we even go? And you with a hurt like that…escaping would be—"

George shushed him, low. "Easy now, let's not advertise." All eyes flicked towards the thick door.

After a moment, Texas Hank opened his mouth to start again, but Ed leaned in first. "Look, sure, I've thought about this some, but what did you have in mind? Door and walls are pretty thick. Hinges pretty rusty. Place is too small to burrow or tunnel, and it don't sound like we'll be here all that long."

Now this *guy I like.* "Right. But since they aren't planning on us staying, I figure there aren't that many guards."

Barry nodded, slowly. "Yeah, it's mostly just the same two guys checking up on us, and the nurse."

Leroy muttered, "Wouldn't mind taking a swing at that big blonde one."

Texas Hank leaned his head against the wall. "Great plan. Fight the guards. This sounds like a great way to get us all shot."

"So, you'd rather stay here?" George asked.

Hank bristled, then relaxed. "Nooooo." He hesitated, fingering that rabbit's foot. "I'd just as soon not. I've heard about some of those camps—"

"But those aren't for POWs." Wilson interrupted, sounding like he was trying to convince himself.

Roberts snorted—hardly a breath. He had kept to the background, still near the door—not diffidently, but independent, aloof.

"Whaddya think, Roberts?" George asked.

The other men turned to look at the pilot. Ignoring the stares, Roberts walked over. He looked George straight in the eye, sizing him up. Then he stepped in close, his deep voice low and smooth. "Whatever the rest of you do, I'm not planning to stick around to see what they do to someone like me in their camps. I hear tell they don't much like folks who don't fit their blond, blue-eyed picture. Like some others." His cold gaze raked over Barry, who raised his chin a little, frowning. "Besides, I got over here to fly. Plan on getting back to that as soon as I can."

George nodded, slowly. "Fair enough. You figuring on getting out of here all on your own?"

Roberts grinned, mirthlessly. "Isn't that what the army wants us to do? Fight but make sure we stay separate?"

Barry muttered an affirmative under his breath, but George spoke over him. "Maybe that's what the army wants, but I don't see how that signifies here and now." He scanned the room, meeting the others' eyes. "We're all Americans. We're all caught. If we wanna get out of here, it's gonna take us all working together." He looked back at Roberts. "I'm game if you are." He stuck out his hand.

Roberts just looked at it. "Maybe. Depends what you've got in mind."

"Yeah, I think we'd all like..." Hank began, but George wasn't about to let him take over.

"Look." George's knees trembled. Hastily, he lowered himself to the ground, then used his finger to trace imaginary lines on the dirt, as if he were mapping out plans rather than showing weakness. The others seemed to buy it, crouching around him in a semicircle huddle. "We don't wanna wait out the war as POWs. You guys agree?"

Four heads nodded. Wilson hesitated. Barry elbowed him, and he nodded too. Texas Hank didn't move. George continued. "We get sent to a camp, even a work camp, and you know what that'll be like. Fences, barbed wire, guards, alarms, maybe dogs." He looked over at Roberts. "Maybe worse. We could cause some trouble, work slow, maybe escape, but our odds—" he shrugged. "Here, they're not ready for prisoners—isn't that right? I was out, but you guys saw it. Are there any fences, anything except this shed and a couple of guards?"

Shaking his head, Hank said, "It was dark when we came in…"

Ed chimed in. "Not me. I got a look around—there's none of that. Lots of ambulances in and out; the hospital area's busy, and it looks like there were more troops camped here, but they've gotta be in the offensive. Doesn't seem like anyone's got much time for us—I figure it's like the nurse said, we're just here temporarily. If they weren't so busy pounding away at our lines, we'd probably have been moved out already."

George nodded and smacked his fist into his other hand. "So? This is our big chance!"

Leroy, at least, was nodding. Ed didn't look too skeptical. Barry was listening, while Wilson wouldn't make eye contact. Roberts was impassive. Hank…George couldn't look at Hank just yet. *Get the other guys first.* "We can't be that far from our lines—"

"Wait, wait, wait!" Unwilling to be ignored, Texas Hank held his hands up. "You…can you even walk? You can't even stand that long; don't think I didn't notice."

George forced a grin. *Ok, Hank won't wait. Better let him think he's in charge.* "Don't worry about me. What do you think about getting out of here?" *C'mon, big guy, you wanna be an officer, it ain't gonna happen here or in a camp.*

Hank didn't bite. "I can't *not* worry about you—think about it. We try to make a break with a fella who can't even run—"

George laughed. "Who needs to run? We got a driver!"

NINE

"*Fräulein*?"

Jean knocked a roll of bandages onto the floor. She spun around, but the man standing just behind her wasn't Grüber; it was the short one with the pockmarked face.

The German raised his eyebrows, then jerked his head in the general direction of the prison shed.

Nodding, she willed her knotted muscles to unwind. "Ok, yes. Just a minute, please." She fumbled to pick up the bandages, scanning them to see if they'd gotten dirty. *It's alright. He's never given me any trouble. It's fine; just breathe. I've got to settle down. If only I weren't so tired...* When she'd turned in last night, she'd found a lewd drawing left on her blanket. Though her body clamored that she needed sleep, terrible images waited in the darkness behind her eyelids.

There was no time for weariness. She still had a job to do. Swinging the satchel of medical supplies over her shoulder and grabbing the lantern, she passed the guard and headed down the familiar path. With an effort, she kept her eyes straight ahead and didn't scan the camp for Grüber's shadow.

A low drone buzzed deep in her bones, and she cast her gaze skyward.

Silhouettes of five planes crossed a narrow strip of blue overhead. *I wonder if they're heading towards the beachhead or away from it? Anzio—I never thought I'd wish myself back there.*

But did she? In spite of the dangers of her imprisonment, was Anzio a better option? Images from the hospital, evidence of just what it meant to die by man's cruel technology flashed through her mind. She shuddered.

But at least on the beachhead I was working for *something. Helping, making a difference. Even Joe didn't get to do that.*

The guard at the shed stepped aside, and the door creaked open. A thick wall of stench hit her as she stepped over the threshold. Body odor, dirt, the latrine buckets in the corner, and the sour smell of illness.

She breathed through her mouth. *Keep it together, Jean. It's not their fault—seven men crowded into this little place. Besides, I'm not exactly fresh.*

"Howdy, nurse!" called a voice from the dark.

Mastering herself, she answered. "Good afternoon, soldier." The door swung shut behind her and left her blinking, waiting for her eyes to adjust to the dim light of the flickering lantern. As she waited, she listened. Boots scuffled on the packed earth floor, and wool rustled against dirty skin. One man grunted as he stood.

The Texan's drawl came again, near her elbow. "Any word from the outside?"

"Not much. How're you all holding up?"

Various muttered assurances or complaints came her way, but she wasn't really listening. *Not like I can do much for you anyway, boys.*

Shuffling through the dimness, she reached the far end of the shed where the wounded man lay, his watchdog at his side. *Leroy? I think his name was Leroy.* Whatever-his-name-was jumped to his feet as she came over, smoothing his hair back. Even in the poor light, she could see his grin as he ducked his head and stammered, "Hello-hey Nurse, Lieutenant Hoff."

Casting her eyes heavenward—*C'mon, fella, settle down*—she nodded, then knelt next to the injured corporal. Leroy made way for her and crouched next to her, but not too close.

The corporal was sleeping, and she paused before waking him, listening to his breathing. It sounded alright, though she wished for a stethoscope. *Maybe the doctor will let me borrow his next time.* "How's he been?"

"Better, I think. Whatever you gave him sure helped." The admiration in his voice was so thick that it made him clear his throat.

She had a sudden flash of memory: Her mom had caught her staring out the window at Joe and her brothers throwing the football around the yard with a forgotten dishtowel hanging limp in her hand. Mom had smiled knowingly and nodded. "Puppy love, hmmm?"

Jean came back to the present and sighed, starting on the patient's buttons.

The prone man's eyes opened. "Well, hello again, Nursey."

"Hello, soldier. How're you feeling?"

"Pretty good." He grinned and made as if to sit up, but then he shivered.

Frowning, Jean felt his forehead, then the incision site where his neck met his shoulder. Heat radiated off his skin. "Hmmm. You still feel warm."

The patient shook his head. "Look, I'm fine. It's just chilly in here is all."

The big blonde guy in the corner spoke up. "He's got a fever? Hey, it's nothing catching…is it?"

"You think shrapnel's catching?" the brunette with glasses said with a laugh.

The Texan drawled, "Sure. There was a bad case of it going around last week."

Ignoring them all, Watchdog Leroy asked, "Any word on us moving somewhere else—or at least getting him a bed?"

"I've spoken again to the doctor. He says maybe they can sort something out in the next day or two." *There's no use telling them what the*

Oberst said—it's still all indefinite.

Tex moseyed over to watch the proceedings and leaned against the wall. He made as if to spit on the floor, then thought better of it. "That's what you said last time. Still maybe, huh? Any word on what's going to happen with the rest of us?"

"No." She busied herself with changing the dressing on the patient's neck. Checking again, she couldn't deny it—the flesh felt warm around the stitches. *We don't need an infection here, especially with no penicillin to treat it.*

Next, she finished unbuttoning his shirt and probed the bindings over his ribs. He flinched, then pulled on a painful grin. "Hey there, honey—whatcha digging for?"

"Can you sit up?"

Pushing up with his elbows, he did so. The shadow of sharp pain crossed his face, but Watchdog Leroy didn't move over to help him—odd, almost as if he just figured his buddy could do it, as if he'd seen him do this before. She asked, "You haven't been getting up on your own, have you?"

He flashed her a smile that was meant to be innocent. "Well, ya know, nurse, a fella can't really lie down for some things." He nodded towards the bucket in the corner.

And if that's the whole story I'm Judy Garland. She eyed him and nodded slowly. "Ok. Just don't overdo it."

"Sure. I'll be good. Scout's honor. 'Course, I might not have too much say in it." He reached behind his ear. "No chance you found some smokes?"

"Sorry, no. Well, everything looks alright. We'll keep an eye on the fever. Here's something for the pain. Make sure you rest."

"Look, Nursey—"

Weary as she was, she straightened her shoulders. "Lieutenant Hoff or Nurse Hoff will do, soldier." The Texan snorted.

The corporal grinned, unintimidated. "Sure sure, *lieutenant.*" His tone reminded her of Stan. "Look, I know you're in a tough spot. But stuck in here…we just kinda wondered if there was any new word. When we might be moved out, that kind of thing."

"I really don't know. Hopefully, you'll be in proper medical surroundings soon." She glanced over her shoulder toward the door. They'd be coming for her soon—but who would it be?

"That's not exactly what I meant." His low tone caught her attention. He gestured for her to move closer. Curious despite herself, she complied. "It's just that, any details of just where we are and when we might be moving out could be pretty handy in the right circumstances. I wondered if you happened to hear anything apart from what they're telling you directly—get me?"

Leaning back on her heels, Jean sat silent for a long moment. Her eyes flicked towards the door. *Well. What've you got up your sleeve, I wonder? Still, if I can trust anyone here, it's these guys. But can the guards hear through the door? Heaven help me…* Slowly, clearly, she said, "It's not like they tell me anything, you know. Too bad they all speak German."

At the last, she locked her eyes onto his and widened them, raising her eyebrows.

Comprehension flashed across his face, and he grinned. Aloud he said, "Too bad, nurse. I sure would like to know what's going on."

"Sorry." She busied herself repacking her satchel, and he leaned toward her. Tex and Leroy crouched down on either side.

"You know German?" The injured man whispered.

She nodded.

Tex grinned. "What've you heard?"

She glanced over her shoulder, then leaned down and breathed, "I don't know what they can hear through that door, but don't you think they'll notice if there's no noise in here? And if the door opens and you're all right around me—"

"Right." The wounded man pointed at the big blonde and the

brunette with glasses and waved them over towards the door. "What were you saying, Barry, about that last concert you went to? Was it USO, or..." Taking the hint, the two planted themselves between the nurse and the door and started discoursing loudly. The lanky guy with the lighter hair started talking with the Negro pilot about plane engines. Tex stayed stubbornly by, and Watchdog hovered, naturally.

Jean said. "Ok. I overheard the doctor and an Oberst—like a colonel, I think—talking. They're planning on moving you all out soon."

The injured man shook his head. "We need more."

Tex asked, "How soon?"

"It sounds like they're still pressing their offensive against the beachhead, but it doesn't sound like it's going well."

A huge grin spread across Leroy's face. "I knew we could hold 'em," he whispered, giving his buddy's shoulder a light punch. The wounded man nodded and held up his hand for silence.

Jean continued. "A couple of days maybe? And then, once they've got vehicles freed up and are sure they aren't taking anyone else, they'll ship you out. I imagine you'll be out of here by the end of the week. Maybe. I just catch snatches."

Tex said, "Ok. So after that—"

Leroy interrupted, leaning farther into the huddle. "Have they said what'll happen to you?"

Cold clutched her belly. She tried to shake it off. "I...don't know. The doctor said something to the Oberst, but they haven't said anything to me, and I didn't catch all of it."

The wounded soldier huffed in frustration. "Don't catch much, do ya?"

She snorted, nerves gone as she raised her chin. "I learned German from going to church with my Grandma. Not many military terms in *Stille Nacht.* Wanna switch uniforms and see if you can do better?"

He waggled his eyebrows. "Maybe."

Oh for—She poked at his ribs. "I should check—any pain here?"

"Ouch!"

Watchdog Leroy was still concerned. "So…you might be left here? Or do they have women camps or something—or would you be sent out with us?"

"Maybe? I hope that's how it goes—that I just get shipped out with you all. At least then I can still spend the war taking care of our troops, and I'd be out of here…" Her voice broke, and she hated herself for it. They noticed—well, maybe not Tex. He was frowning, thoughtful. Watchdog Leroy did, though. His eyes were worried, and he opened his mouth like he was going to ask more questions.

The wounded soldier was eyeing her, too, but his face was impassive. He interrupted his buddy. "Sure. I'll bet that's how it goes. For the time being, though, could you try to keep your ears open? Maybe you could get an answer if you tried acting like I'm hurt more bad than I am, and you'd like me to get to a better facility and you wonder how long it's gonna be."

Rolling her eyes, her voice turned brusque. "If you're already trying walking around on the sly you are hurt 'more bad' than you think you are." His eyebrows twitched. "But…that is a good idea. I can try. Now come along. It's high time you were resting."

"Alright. Any word you can give us as far as location, guards… anything would help." He grunted as he lay back. "Also, any chance of smuggling in a little extra medication? Enough for a couple extra days?"

"But don't put yourself at risk," said Watchdog.

Very aware of the roll of hair at the back of her head, Jean hesitated. Then the request registered clearly in her brain, and she frowned. "Maybe I could…but why do you need medication for just a couple of days? I may have some odds and ends squirreled away—figured if we're going to a camp, extra might be helpful, but—"

He tried that grin again, the one he obviously thought would charm her. *He's gonna lie. But what's he got to lie about? Unless…* She narrowed her eyes. "What are you…you aren't trying to get out of here, are you? Trying to plan some harebrained escape?"

She didn't even need to look at the wounded man's expression—Watchdog's face gave them away at once. Heat rushed up her neck. "That's a terrible idea. In your condition? You're stable, but do too much and you run the risk of that rib shifting. Puncturing something. Ever see someone bleed out internally? I can't believe—"

"Shhhhh," hissed Tex, louder than any noise she'd been making. They all froze, listening—had that been the door creaking?

Nothing happened for several long moments, then the wounded soldier flashed her that grin again, covering for the annoyance in his eyes. "Don't worry about me, Nursey."

"It's my job. We dragged you out of death once. I'd hate to find out you're too stupid to appreciate it."

Watchdog didn't say anything—just looked uncertain. Tex snorted a laugh.

To her surprise, the wounded man laughed too, though a spasm of pain crossing his face cut it short. "Getting attached to me, are ya?"

"I just hate to see hard work wasted."

"Don't worry. I'm not planning on wasting it. But look, we can't just—"

CREEEAK! The door swung open. One man swore as it smacked his arm. He leapt aside, and Jean swung about to look, and there Grüber stood, silhouetted. Shards of sunlight highlighted the furrow of the scar across his cheek.

Closing her eyes, Jean turned back to her patient. *Calm. Keep Calm. He can't do anything.* It must have been her imagination, but she felt the skin across her back crawl, and fancied it was at just that moment his eyes found her.

"*Fräulein*, you have been in here a very long time. Are these men bothering you?"

Still. Be still. She pictured the little cottontail rabbits they'd get in their yard, huddled under the bushes to avoid the hawks sitting on the telephone lines. She'd held one that Joe saved after its mother was caught. Its little heart pounded against its ribcage and beat into her fingers as if it would burst. She thought she finally understood the creature's terror as her blood pounded in her ears. *Please, God, help me be still!* And she was. Her hands were the only things that moved as she collected her supplies, and she watched them to be sure they did not tremble. Without looking back, she answered clearly, "No. I'm almost finished."

The smirk came through in his voice as he answered. "Good. We must hurry back. Schmidt can't do without your assistance, it seems."

She nodded and rose. The wounded soldier wasn't looking at her—he stared at the ceiling. Watchdog caught her eyes as she stood, though—his eyes wouldn't let her go. Nice eyes, even with those ears to distract from them. His mouth was one thin line. *He knows—he knows how scared I am. He really is a Watchdog. He'd like to protect me…* A sudden fear gripped her. *Dear God, don't let him do anything rash. I'll bet Grüber would make him pay for it.*

She threw her satchel over her shoulder and grabbed the lantern. She turned, hands stiff at her sides, and took the first two steps towards him, though every beat of her frightened rabbit heart urged her to run the other way, to hide in the dark corners, to freeze until the danger had passed. *Just keep walking, Jean*—but she couldn't.

He blocked the door—his bulk nearly filled the doorway, dimming the light. He stood, legs apart, hands behind his back with elbows out, and leered at her.

The foul air in the little hut felt thick. The prisoners watched silently, but Jean could almost feel the low hum of discontent emanating from them—a deep bass rumble. Her chin went up just a little higher, and she continued forward—one more step, then two, three—until she stood just in front of him. "Excuse me."

With a nod and a half bow, he moved aside. It wasn't enough room, really, but she stepped to the side, ready to pass.

His hand snapped out, grasping her upper arm, pulling her close.

Her cheek bumped the rough wool covering his shoulder, and his hot breath seemed to burn her neck and ear as he started to whisper. The same words, the same threats, the same images—she squeezed her eyes shut.

"Hey!" someone cried—Watchdog, of course it would be him—and there were sounds of a scuffle. Other voices joined in. In a moment there would be trouble.

But the moment didn't come. As quickly as he had seized her, Grüber's grip on her arm propelled her out the door. Heat flushed her cheeks, and her hands ached from being balled into fists, and fury beat against the fear in her heart. The guard outside the door gave her a curious glance. Grüber didn't follow at once. She didn't wait for him. Stiff backed, she walked briskly across the yard, back to the surgery. *Let them shoot me if they're going to shoot me!*

"Is THIS A DEMONSTRATION of the brave American soldier?" the guard laughed, then spat on the floor.

With the nurse out the door, George allowed his eyes to leave Leroy. He glanced at the guard, who stood, scanning the room, waiting for a reaction. He hoped the other guys wouldn't bite—he had his hands full. Leroy wasn't trying to pull away anymore, but he was like a dog straining at a leash. Only George's hand kept him in check.

It's not worth getting shot, kid. Not worth drawing attention. He hasn't done anything... not yet.

The guard opened his fat mouth again. "What, nothing to say?" He laughed. "I didn't think so. Goodbye, sons of Jews and cowards!" He stepped through the door with a mocking wave and slammed it shut.

Leroy pulled out of George's grip and let loose with an uncharacteristic curse.

"Simmer down, kid." George leaned back with a sigh.

Leroy spun on him. "Simmer down? Whaddya think that big baboon was saying to her, huh?" He kicked the wall, then the fight left him, and he flopped to sitting, hanging his head.

Texas Hank joined him. "Yeah, I'm sure he had some things to say, but did you notice, he was looking right at us. He was just daring you to do something so he'd have an excuse."

"More like telling us we couldn't do anything." Leroy ground out.

"And," George interjected, "just now, he's right. We attack a guard, at best we'll be under scrutiny. Maybe separated. Maybe worse."

"So, what?" Leroy's glare cut into the door. "We just don't do anything?"

"We stick to planning," George kept his voice low, soothing. "You heard her—we'll be shipped out soon. Her too. She's got a doctor—an officer—looking out for her, and didn't you notice Fritzie's uniform? He's just a private. If his superior's keeping an eye on a useful prisoner, you can bet he won't try more than whisper."

Leroy nodded slowly. "Maybe."

The other guys made their way over to listen as George continued. "For sure. He was just showing off for us. Trying to get a rise out of the enemy, trying to get a shot at one of us. Looks like the kind of guy spoiling for a fight. If we give it to him it doesn't help her or us. Once we're out of the picture, he'll probably lose interest in her too, as he can't get anything out of it."

"You think so?" Ed asked, looking skeptical.

"Sure," Texas Hank said with a nod. "Anyway, she seems like she can handle herself. As long as Germany keeps following the Geneva Convention, she should be just fine."

Leroy shook his head once. He turned and looked straight at George. "Look. You know I'll go with you if we can figure this crazy plan out. But I don't like the thought of leaving her behind."

George sighed. "Kid, she's better off."

"But..."

"Trust me. What we're gonna do..." he shook his head. "She'll be safer here."

Ten

Jean watched Doctor Schmidt through the corners of her eyes and debated. He'd been hard to get away from today—busy in the surgery, checking supplies, barking orders to the other German staff. Even when he took a moment for a cup of tea, he invited her to join him.

Now, he worked at his desk, his pen scratching across rough paper as he muttered to himself. Provided he stayed there, she was out of his line of sight. This could be a chance to sneak the extra supplies the corporal had requested. Or, perhaps, should she try a more direct approach?

He's been so kind. He might let me assemble some things if I explain that I need them—if I tell him that I'm worried about being able to help the guys once we're shipped off. But I suppose he's got his superiors to answer to. His warning from the other day flashed through her mind. *And he's as good as told me that he's going to stick to his side of things, however he feels about it all.* She clenched, then unclenched her fists, uncertain. *And if I do say something and he refuses, he'll be more likely to suspect that I'll try to smuggle some out on my own, and then the fellas'll be outta luck.*

Her eyes drifted to the square window above her workspace, beyond which lay her path to the prison shed. *What are they planning, exactly?*

If they're really going to make a break for it...talk about crazy.

But...not THAT *crazy. After all, didn't I think about running, too? There aren't that many guards, and they're distracted. There are always trucks and people coming and going, but it's all a temporary station—and most of the staff is busy working the hospital wards—I know all about that. If they're going to try an escape, now's probably the time.*

Of course, it'll probably kill their ringleader. He's not ready to travel. Probably. Maybe he's tougher than he looks. Just that he was on his feet again already is impressive. His buddy, Leroy the Watchdog, must be helping him—

I wish I had a friend like that right about now.

A hand landed on her shoulder. She jumped, but it was just Doctor Schmidt. "Child, are you well?" Her resolve to say nothing wavered. His smile certainly looked like a friend's.

Taking a deep breath, she slid a cool smile over her face. "Yes! Yes, I'm all right."

A sharp, barking laugh and a snatch of conversation filtered through the drafty window frame. She recognized the voice without turning, but she saw the Doctor's keen glance over her shoulder to where Grüber passed. "No troubles with the men?"

She hesitated. *Seems like he knows already. Maybe, if I tell him what Grüber's been up to, he can do something.*

But what? What could a limping medical man past middle age do against the hulking, leering soldier? The doc was an officer, but she'd already noticed his aversion to rank—it seemed like he hardly ever left his surgery or talked to anyone but the Oberst, herself, and a couple of the other staff. Besides, speaking up would draw attention to her activities, and maybe to the other Americans. It might jeopardize their chance to escape.

And...maybe, my chance too. The thought had been hovering at the edges of her mind, but she wasn't ready to consider its implications. She tucked it away for later.

The doctor's sharp, blue eyes narrowed. She gathered herself and formed her response carefully. "No. Nothing, really. Except..." she hesitated, then decided to go for it. *Just ask.* "The man who was wounded the worst..."

"Yah. The corporal—remind me, what's his name?"

"Uhhh..." Jean wracked her brain. The soldier's name wasn't there. She'd heard it once—probably—but hadn't bothered to recall it.

"You've never asked? Child..." He closed his eyes, shook his head, and muttered something in German, looking for all the world like Stan, lecturing her on her bedside manner.

She clenched her fist until her nails pinched into her skin. *He's NOT Stan. He works for the people who killed Stan.* Steeling herself, she took a deep breath. "No. I'm afraid I'm not always the best at getting to know patients. Anyway, he's been trying to overdo it."

"What, has he been trying to walk?"

Thinking fast, she said, "No. But he has stood with help—I think he was trying to impress me." There. Honest need for medication, but not giving away that he could probably be mobile if he really wanted to be.

"Hmmmm. Has he pulled the stitches?"

"No, but the site felt a bit warm, and his ribs were hurting him terribly. He could use some extra pain medication."

The doctor shook his head. "No. If he is overdoing it, we should lessen the pain relief. Then he won't be tempted."

"Oh." She snapped her mouth shut. It was a sensible solution, but she hadn't seen it coming. "But—"

He winked at her. "Old trick. You learn after a while how to make a patient rest, whether they will or no."

Nodding, she could have kicked herself. *Shoot. Well, I guess I'll be stealing pills after all. Of course, now he'll be watching for it.* The crazy possibility came to mind again, and this time she allowed it to linger. *But...but if I go with them, I could just grab things at the last minute. And then I'd be along to help him if there were complications—*

Grüber's strident voice stabbed through the walls again, followed by peals of laughter from another man.

I also wouldn't be left alone with him.

The doctor was saying something. "I'm sorry, what was that?"

"I said I'll send Hans and Pieter along with you next time with a stretcher. They can bring him back here, and we'll take a look."

"Oh. Oh, yes. All right."

Well, he'll get his look around at least. I wonder how that *will go.*

"No thanks, fella." George enjoyed the incredulous look on the German medic's face as he stood. Sure, Leroy was right there to help if he couldn't make it, but he stood on his own. *If the Teds can refuse stretcher bearers, I sure can too.* He just hoped they didn't notice the flinch as his stitches pulled and as the ribs sent stabbing pain through him again. It would ruin the effect.

The nurse was glaring daggers at him—*dang, she's good at it too. Haven't seen a glare like that since Ma found out about the split with Lil. Not that it lasted long once she heard about the circumstances.* He shook the thought off. Silly stuff to think about at a time like this. Irrelevant.

"What are you doing?" she asked, all sharp, angry edges.

"Walking on my own feet." He took his first step, taking shallow breaths. Grinning to show that standing didn't hurt that much. Hoping they wouldn't notice how hard he was clenching his teeth.

She lowered her voice to a hiss. "I thought you were hurt badly enough to need the doctor to look at you?"

"Sure. But that doesn't mean I can't walk on my own two feet." *And besides, Nursey, it'll help with stage two of this new, brilliant scheme of mine. Just wait.*

Arms crossed, she backed off. The German with the white-blonde hair shrugged at the other one. He took the stretcher back outside, while his companion came over and offered an arm. George refused it. He limped out, pretending he couldn't hear the nurse muttering to Leroy, "Could you please tell your friend not to be so stubborn?"

Leroy laughed—a tight, nervous chuckle, and answered, "I'm not sure the president himself could convince George to do something if he didn't wanna be convinced."

George got to the door of their prison and paused just outside, grasping the door frame, and breathing. His eyes scanned everything in his periphery.

The distant, rolling thunder of battle thrummed against his ears—they must be back a ways for it to be so quiet. He couldn't imagine a place without the sound of fighting in the air—well, maybe back in the U.S. Maybe there it was quiet. *Sheesh, do I even remember what quiet sounds like?*

Straining his ears, he quieted his breathing, stretching for the sound of the sea. Nothing. No scent of it, either. He glanced upward at the sun, trying to gauge their location, but could make little of it.

Across the way to the left stood a scattering of tents—some "upgraded" into shacks, though they obviously hadn't been there long. They had boxes and crates for furniture, with a few odds and ends piled up here and there. *This was probably just thrown together as a response when we landed—support for one of the groups that rushed down to block us.*

No fences, not as far as he could see. Rutted mud road ahead—at the end of it, what looked like a stone barn maybe, once? Steam and the smell of boiling wool drifted from it. Beyond that a farmhouse. Teds walking in and out, an ambulance parked in front. Regular hospital tents around, farther on, what looked like tents for the staff.

There! Just beyond the laundry, between it and the hospital tents, under some camouflage-draped trees sat a welcome sight. Vehicles. The motors he'd listened to each night with hope. Looked like some ambulances, a couple of jeep-sized vehicles, a couple of bigger trucks. No fence around them, either.

With the staff spread out so thin and all those vehicles just waiting...if we can get on board one of 'em, we could be back within spitting distance of home in—

Home?

When had Anzio become home? He shook his head. It hadn't. Couldn't be. But it was where he was supposed to be. There was nowhere else he had a purpose. His friends were back there, his orders, his chance to make something of his life. *My chance to show them that I can build a new life.*

One of the German's hands touched his arm, steering him forward. The nurse stood by, tapping her foot. "Sorry. Just had to catch my breath." He shook off the helping arm and shuffled forward, counting his footsteps to the rutted road.

It seemed to take far too long to reach the farmhouse, and he didn't need to pretend to be out of breath. The nurse kept making irritated sounds behind him, like a frustrated cat.

The papers piled up on a desk over in an alcove off the examination area looked promising. The doctor, waiting to examine him, was a surprise, though. *Whew! Hey there, old fella!* Easing himself onto the examination table, George studied the doctor's sparse and greying hair, his lined cheeks behind half spectacles, and the white coat over his uniform—almost like a civvy doctor back home.

However, his eyes were sharp. His gaze stripped George to the bone, then he turned to Nurse Hoff. "Well, nurse. He walked on his own, hmmmm? I suppose we ought to see if he's undone any of our work." His tone caught George's attention. Friendly, colleague-like. Almost fatherly.

That could help us out. Or it could be a problem. He tried to shift to a more comfortable position and winced.

Doc noticed. "Overdoing it, soldier?"

George sighed and shook his head. "Naw, doc. I appreciate your stitching me up and all that. I wouldn't waste your effort. Besides, I gotta get strong so I'm ready for the work camps, right?" He grinned, showing his teeth, watching to see the good doctor's reaction.

The doctor didn't give him much. Just a muttered "Humph. Let's see."

George obediently started unbuttoning his shirt, then gave the nurse a sly wink. She raised her eyebrows, then busied herself at the table that held all those shiny metal instruments. Briefly, he fantasized about what he might do if he got ahold of one of those scalpels. *Might get home sooner, rather than later. Or get dead. Hold it together; stick with the plan.*

"Hey…ah, doc, I don't' suppose you've got any smokes?" George asked. He ruined his façade of casual calm with an "OOF!" as the doctor's icy fingers probed the stitches beneath the bandages.

"No."

"Hmmmm. Anything to wet a fella's whistle?"

"Nein."

"What about some extra blankets?"

The doctor muttered something to himself in German. George wished he'd learned a few more words of the enemy's language, but he only had a handful: stop, surrender, hurry, and girls.

The doctor switched back to English. "Breathe in."

"Huh?" The cold stethoscope made him jump. "Yikes, Doc! Couldn't blow on it a little or something?"

The doctor ignored him. "Breathe in."

George complied.

"Hmmm. You have been overdoing it."

"Are his lungs…?" The nurse bit her lip.

"No, his lungs, they are clear. But this…" he poked George's neck wound.

George yelped.

"This being so tender—this worries me. I do not think that it is infected, not yet, but it needs time. Time resting, not trying to be the big man in camp." He waved a cruel icy finger in George's face. "I used valuable supplies on you. Do not waste them by refusing to rest and dying anyway." He turned and walked away.

George slid his feet back to the ground and began to stand. "Ok, Doc. I get the messa… Oh crud…" His legs buckled, and he sank to the floor.

"Nurse!" The doctor rushed over, the nurse on his heels.

They tried to heave a groaning George up, but he moaned. "It hurts—please, doc, don't pull me."

The doctor pointed at the nurse. *"Geh schnell!* Go get Hans. He was going to the laundry."

Nurse Hoff wrung her hands. "I…I can't! I don't have a guard, and if I get caught running through camp without one—"

Good little liar, isn't she? George thought as he groaned.

The doctor pursed his lips, then hustled out the door, calling for the absent Hans.

He didn't go far—George could hear his voice through the open door, talking to another soldier. They wouldn't have much time.

He had no intention of wasting it. "Keep watch." Pushing himself to his feet, George made for the desk. Nurse Hoff positioned herself near the door. "I can't see anything!" she hissed.

"Well, keep your ears open, then! Let me know when they're coming."

He rifled through the papers, fingers weak and trembling from pain, from hunger, from weariness. He blinked hard, trying to comprehend what he was seeing. Forms, handwritten notes, some sketches. Those caught his eye—anatomy, a few plants, and one was labeled. "Hey! Nursey, can you read German too?"

With a backwards glance toward the door, she hurried over. "They're just flowers. He likes botany, science."

"Yeah, but he labeled this one. What's it say?"

She whispered the words aloud. "*Wild gewachsener Rosmarin, in der Nähe von Velliti in Italien gefunden.*" That's "Wild Rosemary" I think, and "found near Vellitri, Italy." She looked up at him, eyes wide. "This sketch—it's dated just a few days ago. Vellitri, do you know it?"

"Shhhhh." George closed his eyes, reconstructing the maps he'd pored over whenever he had the chance. There'd been a good one at the CO's office, and he'd had a few minutes, memorized the surrounding cities...just in case. "Vellitri. That's...that's north of Anzio. North and a little east. Right up by the Alban Hills—seems to fit our geography."

"Close to Rome?"

"I'm not going to Rome."

"That's not what I—"

"Shhh—you hear?"

He grabbed her arm, and the two of them flung themselves across the room and back to the floor, he with his head on her lap, clutching his ribs and groaning.

Not a moment too soon. The doctor and Hans barreled into the room.

While they fussed and prodded, he pretended to be much worse than he was—or maybe more accurately, acknowledged just how crummy he'd been feeling. Through the pain, he considered what he'd learned.

Vellitri's right on the road to Rome. We're a ways out of the town, of course, but if we're close enough for the doc to visit... He closed his eyes again and pictured it. The hills behind the hospital area must be the Alban Hills, so to get to the road they'd want to head south, maybe southwest a little. That road would lead north to Rome...but to get back to the beachhead, he'd probably have to cross it and go straight south. Unless they tried to circle around north, towards the coast. Cross the Moletta River, come in by the British-held side. *Might be fewer Teds there, by the coast they'd be too vulnerable to our Navy guns. But...would that be the best place to make contact? That side's where things have been hottest. Would we be able to let them know who we are before someone took a shot at us?*

"THAT'S THE QUESTION though, innit?" asked Texas Hank, spitting. Apparently, he only had qualms about doing that on their prison's floor when there was a lady present. "Just what are you saying we oughta do? You've given plenty of vague hints—seem pretty sure you oughta be the leader of this venture, too—but it seems like if we're going to do something, we'd better get down to brass tacks. Do you actually have a plan?"

George snorted. "Of course I have a plan." *Most of one anyway.* "It's like I said. We're gonna drive right out of here."

"But how're you gonna—" started Barry.

Texas Hank interrupted. "Of course we are! Cuz you've got a jeep stashed under those bandages."

"Wouldn't be much good. We couldn't all fit in a jeep, could we?" George replied coolly. "With a real driver at our disposal, I think we could do better than that, don't you, Ed?"

"Sure, I'm a driver," said Ed, "but I dunno where you're figuring to get something for me to drive."

"Well," George leaned forward, hands folded. He had them curious, listening. Leroy would back him, he just needed the others. "There's a whole line-up of trucks and ambulances out there. Not fenced in or anything. Think you can drive a German vehicle?"

Ed hesitated. "I haven't, but it shouldn't be a problem. As long as there's the crank starter and it's not chained up or something. Or worst came to worst we could hotwire it—"

"Do you know how?"

Wilson said, "I do."

They all stared at him, then Barry laughed. "What, Chuck, where'd you learn that?"

Wilson shrugged. "Sometimes on the farm there wasn't a whole lot to do but mess around with the truck and the tractors—"

"Ok, ok." Tex held up his hands, a judge asking for order in his court. "Let's say we get this truck—just steal it out from under the Jerries' noses, I suppose. What then?"

"Then? We get back to our units. Back into it."

Dead silence fell. Finally, Tex managed to find his voice. "*Anzio*? You wanna go back to...If we go back to Anzio, we gotta go through the German lines, their offensive, *and* our lines and maybe mines and barbed wire and..." Hank ran out of words for a moment. His mouth worked, then he said, "I'm all for getting outta here if we can, but if we head that way, we're just as likely to get kilt by our own men as theirs."

"That's one opinion, Tex," George answered.

"No, that's the truth," Wilson said. He scrubbed his hands through his blond hair, then folded them, staring into his palms. "I got family back home—I...I got a girl. I'd like to get outta here, but not if we're just gonna get shot."

"So whaddya wanna do? Head south?" asked Ed. "We hold all the south—"

Barry said, "Yeah, past the Gustav Line. So, same problems, except this time we'd be escaping through heavy German fortifications—"

"Which won't be pointed towards us—" Ed retorted.

Hank interrupted, "Until we're past them. Then they'd be pointed at our backs. Much better." He ticked off the problems on his fingers. "And then we'll have to get past all of their forward patrols and mines, all of our forward patrols and mines and through our lines." He folded his arms. "No. way. I'm not going along with a suicide run."

"Ok, smart guy," said Leroy, "What've you got in mind then?"

Texas Hank nodded for emphasis. "Rome."

"Rome?" They all echoed, incredulous.

"We head north. To Rome. No one'll be looking for us. We can make it."

There was a long moment of silence as everyone considered.

George nodded first. "Ok, maybe we could make it to Rome. But, what'll we do there? Rome's Axis."

Hank shook his head. "Naw. It's an open city, and anyway, Italy's outta the fight."

George laughed. "Sure don't look like Italy's out, or what's this hunk of land we've been bleeding on?"

"You know what I mean. The Italians are out—they don't want the Nazis here. Met a Limey who'd escaped from a plane going down. He said word is there're places for people to hide in Rome. The Catholics aren't any friend of Hitler, even if he's talked nice to the Pope so far." Hank grinned. "We could hide out. Be ready to meet our guys when they finally break through."

Barry was nodding, Wilson too, though he stared down at his hands. Leroy looked to George to see what he'd say. Ed kept his own council.

"So...we go to Rome and hide out. What good's that do?"

Hank sputtered. "What good? Seven prisoners that the Germans lost, that they'll have to waste time looking for, and that they can't make work in some mine or something—"

"It's not a bad plan," admitted Leroy. Barry nodded. Now Ed was watching George.

George nodded slowly. "It's not a bad plan. But my buddies are on Anzio." He hesitated. "A cousin too. My fight's back there, and I can't think of anything I'd like better than to show up back there to thumb my nose at Fritzie. Get to Rome the right way—over all these lines that've tried to keep us back."

Leroy frowned. "I never knew you had family over here."

George grinned, holding eye contact. "Yeah. We aren't close, but still... you know how it is." It wasn't the first time he'd lied to the kid—trying to keep him optimistic, focused on the fight, wanting to live. It was the first time he'd lied for selfish reasons, though, and he didn't like the taste in his mouth.

He tried to reason it away. *I might call him a kid, but he's not. It's his choice, in the end.*

But that nagging voice of conscience he couldn't quite silence—though he'd tried, tried to live his life with no regrets, just like *she* had—whispered in his ear. *Sure, it's his choice, but you know he trusts you. He'll choose to follow you. If he dies doing it...*

He closed his eyes. *I just have to make sure that he doesn't.* He looked around. One man had remained silent. "What about you, Roberts?"

The pilot looked up. He had been standing at the edges, listening to the talk but not contributing. He shrugged. "You all can do whatever you want."

"Whaddya mean? You're planning on coming, right?"

"Oh, I'm planning to get out of here. There's just no real debate for me. Whatever the rest of you do, I *have* to go to Anzio."

Ed frowned. "How you figure?"

"I got into this war to fly. Worked my butt off to get to where I am. Word was we were getting moved up to Ramitelli, over on the Adriatic. From here, across the mountains…that's gotta be a hundred miles or more. On foot, I don't figure my odds are too good. So, if I'm gonna get back to the 332nd, I need to get back to Allied held soil. Catch a boat or plane. Anzio's my best bet."

George nodded. He looked back to the others. "That answers for him. What about the rest of you? What do you think about getting back to your buddies? Back to the fight?"

Ed and Leroy nodded. Barry didn't say anything, Wilson was back to looking at his hands. Texas Hank cursed. "Look, you think you're the big leader here, gonna get us all out. Well, I was here first. These guys"—he nodded to Wilson and Barry—"they were part of my squad, and I was in the group longest."

"By about one day," muttered Barry, but Hank's momentum couldn't be derailed.

"No way am I leading my squad back to that death trap. No. Way."

George looked him up and down, measuring. "You scared, Hank?"

The other man wouldn't be baited. "What if I am? Anzio's a hell hole. No one in his right mind would go back there. No one in his right mind would ask his friend to go back there with him. If we run, I'll run. But I'm not going back there."

In the following silence, George dropped his gaze. *Hank's right.*

He knew it deep inside, but it didn't matter. Didn't make a lick of difference because he knew what he was going to do.

He locked eyes with Hank. "Ok. Well, if that's settled, I guess we can go on with our plans, and I know where you stand. Maybe I'm crazy, but there's no way I'm tucking tail and heading for Rome. The other guys can follow you once we're clear or can come with me, cuz whatever the rest of you do, I'm thinking the same as Roberts, here. I've spent two months trying to break out of Anzio. I'm ready to see if I can break back in."

Eleven

Doctor Schmidt knew. Whether they'd left his papers too untidy or whether he'd known all along that the corporal faked his fall—it didn't matter how, Jean was certain that he knew.

Polite as ever this morning, he gave her tasks to do, requested tea during lulls, smiled his same patient smile. Jean smiled back, pretended she was as relaxed as he, but couldn't force the knot between her shoulder blades to loosen. *Why doesn't he say anything? He must figure we're planning something. Has he told anyone else? Is he just waiting to catch us in the act?* She jumped as his voice snapped her out of her reverie.

"Nurse? Have you those instruments I asked you to sterilize?" From his tone, it wasn't the first time he'd asked.

"Here, Doctor. Sorry."

He nodded silently, but the look he gave her before returning to his work... Not cold, certainly not unkind, but there was danger in it—danger in his cool cleverness.

If he figures out just what the men are up to, will he betray them? She bit her lip, considering. *He's been sympathetic. Doesn't seem to like me being here too much. He might let me go. Maybe. But the fellas...* She boiled water for more tea, picturing the doctor's face. *I feel like he's got "duty" stamped right between his eyes.*

She scrubbed her hands, the unfamiliar-smelling soap one more reminder that she was far from home. Loneliness rose in her throat, almost choking her. Again, she pushed it down. *Just keep doing your job, Jean. And when the boys go—*

Will they be able to make it? I don't like the look of that corporal's incision site, and his ribs are rough. He shouldn't have tried to walk on his own. I don't know if he'll be able to pull this off.

Of course, if I were to go along with them—

She paused, hands dangling over the basin, water running off her fingertips. Drip, drip, drip—the splashes measured time to her thoughts.

I can't avoid the question anymore. If they're going, if I *go... well, I could make sure he doesn't overdo it. Be of use if anyone got hurt in the escape. It would get me away from Grüber.*

As she examined the question, the engine of a jeep rumbled, pulling up outside. She craned her neck to look out the door of the aid station. *The Oberst again? I wonder what he wants.*

JEAN WAITED until the door was shut on the guards and she was sealed into the prison shed. She took a deep breath, then said, "We've got two days to get out of here."

There was a long silence. Tex whistled, soft and low.

Watchdog Leroy took a step towards her. "You sure?"

"Yes. The Oberst came to visit with the doctor today. The German offensive is all but over. He said he could promise transport for the prisoners in two days. If we're going to get away from here, it'll have to be soon."

"We?" The wounded soldier said the word slowly. He was sitting up, leaning against the wall.

Squaring her shoulders, she drew herself up to her full height. "Yes. We."

"You mean you're coming with us?" asked Leroy, his voice somewhere between worried and hopeful.

"Yes. I want to get out of here too." Jean was pleased to hear that her voice didn't quiver despite the way her stomach flopped over.

"Well, Nursey. What you want doesn't really signify." The corporal used the wall to push himself to his feet.

"What do you mean?"

"I mean you're not coming."

Her stomach roiled, but a rush of anger strengthened her. "Try to stop me."

Even in the dim light she could see the red suffuse his face. Tex stepped up, hands raised. "Whoa, now, let's—"

"Look." She pointed at the injured soldier, giving him her coolest glare. "You need me. You need medical help. You shouldn't even be walking yet, much less planning some ridiculous prison break—"

"Ridiculous—but she wants to come along." He rolled his eyes heavenward.

Barry said, "I've always said it was pretty ridiculous—"

"Shut up, Barry."

Barry. She remembered what the doctor had said. She ought to try to learn their names—maybe if they knew her, they couldn't leave her behind. "Look. Maybe I'm doing this the wrong way." She thought of Stan, thought of getting out of here, and dredged up a smile. "I don't even know all of your names yet. So…you're Barry…"

The others introduced themselves, except for the wounded soldier. Leroy did his introduction for him. She shook hands all around and repeated the names to herself over and over, trying to fix them in her mind. "I'm Jean. Jean Hoff."

"Hey!" Leroy grinned. "You're Jeannie with the light brown hair!"

She closed her eyes. *Oh no.*

Hank laughed, seized her hand, and started singing. Chuck and Barry linked arms with him and joined in. The corporal shook his head and sat.

"I dream of Jeannie with the light brown hair—"

"Please..." she managed, but it came out a whisper—only Leroy heard her, head cocked, eyes questioning. The others didn't notice and sang on with gusto.

The tears surprised her. At least they were hot, angry tears. Not weak. She wasn't weak anymore, but to get out of this place, she could be civil.

"Please." Her voice came out a hard, harsh croak.

They paused, mid-note, staring at her.

"What's the matter? We outta tune?" asked Tex, trying a grin.

"No...well, yes, but...please don't sing that song." She let her voice break.

Leroy was right there. He reached out to touch her arm. "Jeannie, Nurse—what did we...I'm sorry..."

She pulled back. Shaking her head, she took a deep breath. *Keep it together.* "My fiancé. He used to sing that to me. He died in North Africa and—"

Understanding dawned on their dirty faces. A muttered chorus of "sorry!" swept the little room. The only one who didn't look repentant or sympathetic was the wounded one—George Novak. He just shook his head.

"Tough luck. Still, if you don't wanna join him sooner than later, you're better off sitting tight."

"George!" Leroy sounded shocked. "Can't you just—'

"Tell her the truth, kid? Yep, that's what I'm doing. We don't have time to play games here." He raised a steady hand and pointed it at her. "We might get outta here unnoticed. They don't check on us much, and it's not like they've got much use for us. We can blend in, rough it out, and make it back. She," he pointed again for emphasis, "is a liability. Being all chummy with the doc, living over there where guards are checking up on her." He shrugged. "They'll notice she's gone right off."

Tex frowned. "That's likely true. 'Course, the way we've been planning, we wouldn't get much more of a head start going it alone—"

"Sure, sure. But even ignoring that, once we're out, what are we gonna do with a girl?"

Jean raised her chin. "What? Think I can't rough it? I camped with my brothers for a week every summer. I know how to shoot, how to hike, how to fish, how to live rough—"

Novak laughed. "Ok, but what are you gonna do about that?" He waved his hand, gesturing from her head to her toes. "Maybe, *maybe* you're capable, but you're still a girl. You'll stand out anywhere we go."

Tex muttered, "He's got a point—"

Wilson cleared his throat. "Well, Nurse…Jean…I mean, there wouldn't be any… um… privacy, really, if you know what I mean—"

"But we could make it work," argued Leroy. "I mean…she says she's gone camping, and it's not as if the nurses have had it so easy over here, and…and how many miles is it? We're figuring we don't have too far to go—that's one reason this whole scheme oughta work. She's not expecting her own suite or anything, are you?" He gave her a hesitant grin.

"Of course not. I haven't had anything like privacy in months. And I know I'd have to trust you all to…well, to be respectable." Novak snorted and muttered something that sounded like "Good luck," but she ignored it. "I'd trust you all a lot further than some others."

Novak shook his head. "No. Look, it's not safe for you—here you've got the doc, and there are procedures…conventions…all that. Out there, you're a target. I'll risk my own neck—"

"And ours," Tex said.

"But I'm not going to be the guy who okays a nurse into no-man's land and gets her shot. Not going to happen."

She eyed him, trying not to let her irritation boil to the surface. She failed. "I suppose I could just order you, soldier."

He threw back his head and laughed, then winced and clutched his ribs. "Really? You think the rank the U.S. government gifted you makes any difference at all in here, *lieutenant?* What, they even pay you as much as me?"

She stepped forward, lowering her voice. She held up one finger. "I speak German. Better than any of you." She held up a second. "I can get a better look at the lay of the land than any of you." A third. "You're counting on me for supplies. Suppose I don't cooperate?" A fourth, but he interrupted.

"What? You think threatening us—"

"FOURTH. That blond lummox that keeps eyeing me up? Private Grüber? Frankly, if I get shipped out of the doctor's line of sight, I'm not sure what he's going to do. He's certainly painted some interesting scenarios, whispering through my tent walls at night and through the cracks in the latrine walls this morning."

That got his attention. Leroy clenched his fists till his knuckles cracked. The other men stirred—angry, worried.

Not Corporal Novak. He nodded, then asked, "Anything on that list worse than dying?"

She paused. Was it? She nodded. "I'd rather die than live scared."

He raised his eyebrows. "Very courageous of you, I'm sure. But you know, it might not be dying. We hit a mine field, I've seen guys lose legs, arms…you might not even keep that pretty face."

Swallowing hard, Jean hesitated again. She'd thought about all these possibilities but hearing them aloud made it all suddenly, terribly real. Closing her eyes, she bit her lip. *Lord, am I doing something foolish?*

She didn't know what His answer might've been—instead, she thought back to that night when Joe told her he was leaving.

They'd rocked, slowly, porch swing chain creaking in the soft summer twilight. There were a few mosquitos about that had crept through cracks in the screen. A slap occasionally punctuated the silence.

His arm was around her, warm, but heavy. She wanted to curl up under it, to feel like it protected her again, like when she'd fallen in the creek as a teenager and he'd helped her out, wrapped a blanket around her, and his arm had stayed a little longer than necessary when he told her how worried he'd been.

He didn't tell her things like that anymore.

But surely he'd let her tell him. "Joe…Joe, are you sure you need to go *now?* There's so much work for you here, just getting the new office open. Dad and Stan…they could really use you."

He shifted, and his arm felt heavier than ever on her shoulders. "How can you say that? How could I just sit at home?"

"You wouldn't be sitting; you'd be helping people. People here need good doctors too."

He'd laughed, a hard sound. "What, deliver a few babies, bind up a few broken bones, while all of the other men—thousands of them—are over fighting? What a waste. You really can't want me to waste myself like that, Jeannie."

"But…" she twisted the ring on her finger. *But you promised* me, *promised me that we'd be together. I took those nursing classes for you. I stayed here instead of moving to that job in Rochester for you.* She couldn't say any of it out loud—she knew how he'd react. "Maybe…then, if you really feel like you must—"

"It's not a feeling. It's something I know. I thought you understood that."

"Yes, ok. But if you've got to go now, maybe we should move the wedding up? We could get married before you go over."

He was shaking his head. "No. I go over, married to you, I'd be distracted. Thinking about being home with you and…all that."

You won't be thinking of me if we're not *married?*

He was still talking. "No. We need to wait. I'll come home when this mess is done, and we'll pick up where we left off. Our own practice, you and me working together—at least until the babies come, then you'll need to stop and take care of them." He squeezed her shoulders. "It'll be just like we've talked about. Just like we've dreamed."

Sure. Just like you've dreamed.

He'd noticed her silence, eventually. "You wouldn't want me to be any less than I can be—than God wants me to be, would you Jeannie?" He removed his arm, gesturing expansively into the starry night. "Just think, think how many lives I can save! And with my training, I'm almost guaranteed to be working in one of the surgical hospitals—Stan thinks so too—so you see, I'll be out of the line of fire and really be *out* there, really be free to do what I was meant to do."

He had finally looked at her and noticed the tears streaking her cheeks.

Reaching over to wipe them away, he sighed, then kissed her forehead. "Aw, Jeannie, I wish…I wish you could try to be a little braver about this. For me."

Novak's voice called her back to the present. "Nursey? You in there?"

She blinked and returned to the dark, dank storage shed, to the stink of unwashed men and the decision before her. *A little braver, Joe? I'll show you braver.*

Raising her chin, she said, "I'm going with you. One way or another, I'm not staying here." *I'm not being left behind again.* She looked around the room, challenging. "Anyone object?"

Leroy stepped to stand beside her. Tex shrugged. "Naw, I figure it's your choice." The other men murmured assent.

George said, "Well, looks like I'm outvoted." The look he gave her, though, made her suspect that he'd only given up for the time being. Then, he brightened. "Hey!" He studied her and Leroy, and his eyes gleamed. "Hey, how tall are you?"

She and Leroy looked at each other—eye to eye, though he was a little over six foot, and she was only just—then back at George and chorused, "What? Who?"

LEROY SCRAPED the dirt floor smooth with a rock, then gathered up the other mapping materials—a sharpened stick and some pebbles.

They'd spent the hours since Jean left scribbling, trying to visualize their prison area and how best to put their plan into motion.

The light was failing—what little light there was from cracks and chinks in the walls. Soon it would be time for Jean to check in again and for the guards to deliver their dark bread and watery cabbage soup. Leroy's stomach grumbled. The food was never enough, but George had encouraged—ordered, really, with a smile—all of them to save their bread. It would be "something to walk on tomorrow night." Leroy's stomach rumbled again. *He's right, but it's sure going to be hard not to eat it all!*

He hefted the rock in his hand a couple of times. Rome or Anzio—neither of them sounded like a great option. But then, neither did staying here. *Naw, even if we weren't friends, I'd stick with George. He usually* is *right, after all. Hope he does make officer someday.* As he bent to pile the stick and pebbles in a corner, an unpleasant thought crossed his mind. *Maybe that's why he's so set on going back to Anzio? Figures if he gets us all back he'll get a promotion? Dangerous way to get some stripes...*

Leroy frowned, realizing that this train of thought put his friend in an uncomplimentary light. Then he shrugged and tossed the larger rock into the corner to join the rest. It bounced back, bumping Barry's shin.

"Hey!" Barry let loose a couple of curses that Shorty would've approved.

Leroy held up his hands. "Sorry." He squatted against the wall beside George and continued thinking it all through. *'Course, if he masterminds an escape and someone does take notice, I suppose that's fair enough. And I don't figure he means to lose any of us along the way. Probably why he'd like us all to head to Anzio together. He's always been a good friend, and a good squad leader. Besides, I owe him.*

He leaned his head against the wall, slipping back to that first day, feeling again the tossing and rolling of the sea. Climbing down the side of the ship to the smaller landing craft had been harder than it seemed like it ought to be. The ship bucked and kicked, and his sweaty hands shook. His heavy pack swayed, pulling on his balance.

He'd set his teeth, set his grip. Then, midstep, the ship tilted.

He hung out over space.

His hands slipped free of the ladder.

The world froze, trapping him between sea and sky.

Then the waves slapped him, trying to knock the air from his lungs. They pulled him down. A rush of cold water covered his head.

He floundered, trying to swim, trying to pull himself towards the direction he thought was up—waiting for the life belt to do its job.

Nothing happened. No movement. No air. No nothing.

His lungs burned. The gear and wool clothes were so heavy, and the life belt—did it have him upside down? His arms swung sluggishly through the slowing water.

Dear God—I'm going to drown...

A hand grasped his collar. His first instinct was to fight whatever sea monster was dragging him, dragging him down.

Then, with a heave, he broke out into light and air—glorious air! He gulped and got some spray in his throat. Coughing and spluttering, he pulled in another breath. Voices cheered, and someone called his name. George answered from just behind him, "Stop hollering and pull us up, Petey!"

When they were both safe aboard, he'd tried to thank George through chattering teeth. The other man just laughed and clapped him on the back. "Well, you loaned me those smokes yesterday. I figure we're even now." Then he'd patted his pocket and frowned. "Dang, I'll bet they're soaked."

Yep, George had been a great buddy, but more than that, he'd always had more courage than Leroy. *This whole idea, it's kind of crazy. But if anyone can pull it off, it's George.*

He glanced to where his friend sat breathing heavily from the exertion of bickering with Texas Hank again.

Hank'd like to be the big man, but I wouldn't follow him. He'd look out for himself. That's not George. The only problem—

The only problem was Jeannie. He was almost sure that it was their duty to get the nurse out of here...almost sure, but heading back to Anzio with her? That didn't seem right. Certainly not safe.

And even though George didn't want her to come along, if she *did* come, there was the way George was with girls.

He shook himself. *What're you doing, Leroy? Worrying about girls when we might be dead tomorrow? Stupid. That's why you're not the leader. Jeannie—see, you can't even get her name right—Jean being safe, here or back there, that matters. Whether she and you ever...* he swallowed. *Well, that doesn't really matter.*

The door creaked, and in she came, along with the guard dropping off their food. Leroy's mouth watered as he went over to collect his portion as well as George's.

By the time he returned, Jean had joined Texas Hank and George over in the corner, ostensibly checking his wounds but also throwing her two cents into the debate.

Hank had leaned in close to George, whispering furiously. Leroy could imagine what he was saying. *We've got to go for Rome, Novak! Heading back to Anzio's just plain dangerous.* Something like that; the same tune he'd been singing all along.

George responded, his whisper a little louder. "Sure, we could circle north...throw 'em off...but if we cut through the woods..." The woods. George was still considering sneaking through the woods and coming in on the north end of the beachhead. After all, The Allies had had a hard enough time securing that particular area—if German spies could sneak around in there, why couldn't a small group of Americans do the same?

Hank whispered something—more like a hiss, and George responded with a harsh laugh, though he kept his voice low.

Jeannie interrupted with a sharp voice that all could hear. "Please, put your hands down while I'm changing your dressing."

George obeyed, but he didn't stop talking. "Look, Hank, you know there've been prisoners escaping on both sides. Where we came through wasn't too hot, and if the Teds are withdrawing, we ought to be able to get pretty close—"

"Pretty close isn't good enough. You really wanna get shot by our own guys?"

"Naw, we just need to get close enough, find an American patrol, and we're in."

"If they don't shoot us first."

"Look…"

Jean interrupted. "None of it matters if we can't get out of here. We've only got two days to work with—remember? And today's almost gone."

That sobered everyone. Two days. Two days until a proper camp, lots of guards, farther distance to their army.

Without warning, George pushed himself to his feet. The nurse jumped up beside him. "You still need to rest…"

He shook his head. "I need to see if I'm strong enough to even do this, Nursey."

She sat back on her heels and glared at him but said no more.

Leroy scanned George's face. He smiled so easily, but there was strain around his eyes and mouth. *Can he make it? I've been worrying about Jeannie—should I be worrying about my buddy instead?*

George said, "Ok. For the moment, let's ignore our destination. What about the rest of the plan?"

Jeannie set her face in a mule-stubborn look. Leroy grinned. She had a will—he liked that about her. *Still, is that a good thing just now? Running's gonna put her in danger, but if she stays, she'll have Grüber to contend with.* He could almost smell the fear on her when the big beast of a German came around.

If he hurts her, I'll kill him. Before, he'd wondered if he *could* kill someone else, pull the trigger when he needed to, or if he'd choke. *I guess I still don't know—I fired some shots and then surrendered to save my friend. Not much of a battle record. But, for Grüber —*

That leering face, those thick, greedy hands. No matter what, he'd find some way to protect her.

And the only way to protect her from the German was to get her out of here—even if George's plan sounded more than a little like it sprang from his meds rather than his usually clever brain. *But it's the best plan we've got. God willing, it'll be enough.*

He snapped back to reality on hearing George swear—swear at Jeannie.

"Hey!" he cried, bristling. *My buddy or not, he shouldn't talk to a girl like that.*

George ignored him. Low anger rippled under his words, and his face was flushed. "What, so now you're all buddy-buddy, you're going to bow out? I thought you said you had enough grit for this job." He jabbed his finger toward her nose, then winced.

Jeannie stood straight and tall as a statue. "I do. I have enough *grit* to do whatever it takes to get out of here. I'm just saying that I want to be careful. Doctor Schmidt is a good man—"

"He's a Nazi."

"No, he's not. He hates the war—hates Hitler."

"What, he's told you so, has he? Nursey, if that don't make you suspicious—"

"No, he hasn't told me directly, but I can see it." She leaned in. "What he *has* told me is that he joined the Wehrmacht—regular army, not the SS by the way—because he was pressed into it. If he'd said no... He has a family. Children, a new granddaughter—"

George pinched the bridge of his nose. "Look, Nursey. I've seen he's a good doctor, and he's been decent to you. Maybe you're right about his beliefs—I'm not saying you aren't. But I *am* saying that he made his bed when he joined up. If he's not out of the way, we can't get out of here. None of the rest of the plan'll work."

Jean wavered, twisting her hands into the sides of her pant legs.

"Yes, but if we just adjust it a little—"

"We don't have time to adjust the plan. Not now."

"But, if I mess up the dose… He's a good man. He might be our enemy but he's a good man."

"Sure." George snapped. "And how many good men died because *other* "good men" didn't have the stomach to stand up to Hitler and his goons? How many families have died in how many countries since the "good men" joined up instead of saying no?"

Jean bowed her head. George nodded in satisfaction.

Leroy wasn't so sure he'd won, though—that set of Jeannie's jaw—

Through gritted teeth, she asked, "Does that mean someone ought to die, just because they aren't as brave as you? If you call this brave—being willing to risk other people's lives so that you can get back to a losing beachhead—"

George's face went dark, angry. *Uh oh.* Leroy had only seen that expression once, back in Naples just before he slugged Shorty—knocked him clean out. George had gotten in some trouble over that, but Shorty'd had no right to nose around George's past. He'd sure never mentioned it since.

Leroy didn't think George would hit a woman, but he stepped between them anyway, holding up his hands like the referee in a boxing ring.

"Whoa, Jeannie—I mean, Nurse Hoff." He put his hands on her shoulders. She shrugged them away, and he let them drop to his side, glad the dim light concealed the flush he could feel heating his neck. "Look. George's my buddy, and while I might not agree with all of his ideas—"

George snorted.

"—you shouldn't talk like that. If anyone's brave—why, he saved my life. Dragged me right outta the ocean. And he's been a good squad leader. Looked out for all of us." He shrugged. "I've followed his lead so far. I still would."

She was still stiff, unhappy, but she nodded. He turned to George. "And, George, you gotta think about what you're asking her to do."

"What? Dontcha think she's got the guts…?"

"Courage has nothing to do with this. Heck, she's stayed alive this long, brought us lots of info, and the way she handles that Grüber…but this doctor, he's been protecting her. Kind to her. Saved your life too."

He turned back to Jeannie. "J… Nurse. Do you think that, when the time comes, you can…just sort of sneak your part by the doctor without getting caught?"

She nodded. "Yes. I think I can."

"Ok. If you can manage it, fine. BUT." Leroy held up one finger. "You gotta have stuff on hand in case you get caught. You gotta have a plan. We won't be out yet to help you if this goes sideways."

To his relief, Jeannie nodded. "I already have some sedatives stashed. I'll get some more ready…in case."

George huffed and sat down. He was tired, but he couldn't give anyone the satisfaction of knowing it. *Cuz of course we'd be satisfied to see weakness. Stubborn—*

The door swung open, and there loomed Grüber.

Leroy braced himself for the inevitable. This time, as Jean walked past, the German moved at the last moment so she bumped against him. His polite excuse was said with a smirk that made it sound profane. As they exited the room, he grinned at the prisoners and gave a suggestive wink.

It was just as well he closed the door quickly. Leroy didn't know he was running for it until his shoulder slammed into the wood. He heard a harsh chuckle outside.

Chuck grabbed his arm. "Calm down…he can't do nothing…"

The rage bubbled up in Leroy's throat, choking him. "Who says? Who says he can't do anything? He's got all the power—just cuz he hasn't yet—"

"Leroy," George's voice was steady. "Kid, it's gonna be alright. We're moving on in a day. Unless you do something that'll draw attention—get his dander up too much, and we miss our shot. And don't forget," he nodded toward the door, "now it's her shot too."

Twelve

Despite the reassurances he kept giving Leroy, George was worried.

He forced himself to stay awake while the others slept and probed his neck wound and his ribs, trying to assess his state.

Nothing felt like it was healing—not fast enough. Sitting, standing, walking—he could manage them, but he had to face facts. He couldn't move well, not nearly as swiftly as he needed to. Because of this, too much of his plan depended on a cold, angry nurse.

And he wasn't sure of her.

She said she could handle it. In his experience, people said plenty of things when they were desperate. He'd played along—another lie to Leroy. He had to keep the kid focused—couldn't waste time feeling bad about it, but he did. The kid was so trusting.

This escape was my idea. I've gotta hold 'em together. He coughed, and his chest pain flared. *Course, I can't even keep myself together.*

The door opened, admitting the nurse for his evening check-up. The other prisoners didn't stir. All the planning must've worn on them.

He tried for a jaunty whisper, "Running late, aren'tcha, Nursey?"

She walked over and handed him his meds. "Sorry. The guard was late, and then there was a local woman in labor—the doctor asked me to assist."

"Don't care." He didn't want to hear what a nice guy Herr Doktor was. It'd just make it harder if things went wrong.

"Sorry. I forgot what a tough guy you are, how you don't care about anything."

George eyed her. "You think I'm some kind of nice guy under it all? I'm sure not."

"Seems like you look out for your buddies. Just too bad for me I'm not on that list."

"Heh. You aren't my type. I like my girls alive."

"You got me there. I haven't been alive for a long time." Her hand moved in the dark—she was playing with that ring around her neck. "But maybe I don't deserve to be treated like the enemy. I've been taking care of your sorry hide, after all."

"Maybe not. But it's still a stupid idea."

"What?"

"You coming along. You should be fine—the Teds usually play by the rules."

"Sure they do, except when they accidentally bomb hospital boats or Hell's Half Acre."

He closed his eyes. Deep down, he agreed with her—he didn't want to leave her here, alone, trusting in some German doctor that she wouldn't quietly vanish. But he couldn't risk the others for her sake, either. *She's not my responsibility.* "So, you're really not scared of getting shot? Stepping on a mine? Blowing up that pretty face? I've seen some things…"

"I'm a nurse. I have too. I know the risks. Why are you so set on scaring me?"

"Because—" Leroy's snore paused, and George stopped speaking. He most definitely didn't want the kid awake for this exchange. When his friend's breathing had resumed its steady cadence, he continued. "Because. You think I'm not scared, I don't mind dying? Not true. I want to live. I want to get out of here, get back to it, and live. And I want to go home at the end of it." *Go home alive and a success.* "I'm not gonna risk my life and my buddy's life by taking you along if you can't take it. So. I have to be sure. Can you handle it? Can you handle these risks?"

Lips tight, chin raised, eyes like green ice. "Yes."

He nodded. "Ok." *No turning back.* "Think you can still get to the laundry tomorrow?"

"Yes. I've already mentioned the idea to the doctor. It's obvious that I'm a mess. I should be able to get in there, and then…well, they're understaffed too. I'll be quick, and I'll get that uniform."

"How're you gonna convince the guys to look the other way?"

"I'll flirt with them." She said it so grimly that he laughed.

"Yeah, you're quite the Jezebel!"

"Just because I don't doesn't mean I can't."

"Honey, sorry, but I'm skeptical."

She stood. "Well, you'll see tomorrow when I deliver the goods, won't you?"

"Sure."

She turned to leave, but he gave a low whistle. He motioned her close. "One other thing. Go easy on Leroy. Don't let him down till this is all done, ok?"

She drew back. "What…what do you mean?"

"Let's not play games. You've seen how he is around you. If you give him the cold shoulder, you think it won't affect him? Sad Leroy is Careless Leroy is Dead Leroy. Don't shoot him down till no one else will."

She stood, statue-still for a full minute. Then, she said in a cold voice, "I don't intend to do anything to jeopardize this plan." She turned, tapped on the door, and was released back into her personal captivity.

OF ALL THE THINGS that could have gone wrong, Jean hadn't expected Doctor Schmidt to be suspicious when she asked to do laundry. Under his piercing gaze, she felt like a child again, crumbs and powdered sugar from the Christmas rosettes on her cheeks, her grandmother reproving her while Grandpa laughed.

The doctor wasn't laughing, though. Brows drawn down, he watched her as she stammered, trying to wash his suspicions away with a stream of words. "Since I'm to be sent…well, somewhere soon, I just thought…maybe I could borrow some clothes and get mine washed before…I go. Wherever I'll be going."

"Clothes. We have no women's clothes. You want…what, a uniform?"

Oh dear, he wasn't supposed to put it together that quickly. Stupid, Jean, you ought to have thought this out better…if only I'd gotten some sleep the last night! If only Grüber would leave me alone— Here, in the cold, clear morning light, her clumsy attempts at subterfuge seemed laughable.

She considered backing down, trying again later. George Novak's skeptical face flashed across her mind, and her resolve hardened. *No. No, I've got to do this today.* She scrambled to gather her scattered wits. "No, of course not!" *Not if you're going to ask specifically anyway.* "Just… isn't there something in there that I might be able to borrow, or—"

She hated to do it, but she thought of Joe, of Anzio, of Stan, and the tears came easily.

"I…I'm just…I don't know where I'm going, and nothing I'm wearing is clean…and hygiene—I'll be taking care of other troops, and how can I do it if I'm this filthy and…" She swallowed a sob.

"Oh, well..." The doctor blustered a little and produced a handkerchief and a pat on the back. "Of course, of course, child. If you go at once, you ought to be able to find something, and they should have your things ready for the morning."

She blew her nose, then the words sank in. "The…the morning?"

"Yes. The Oberst said that he will have a truck ready in the morning. You'll be sent off with your American men, collect a few other prisoners along the way, and get to somewhere more permanent."

She swallowed. *It really is now or never.*

He was asking something, but the roar of a truck pulling up drowned out his voice. "I'm sorry, Doctor, what?"

"Do you want me to come along to the laundry?"

It would require her being a bit sneakier, but it would eliminate any questions. "Thanks…if you don't mind?"

Shouts echoed from outside, footsteps thumped in the doorway. The doctor barked at Hans, who hustled over and directed the stretcher bearers.

As the first patient was carried past them, the doctor sighed. The amount of blood soaking through the man's shirt didn't bode well.

Jean sighed too—laundry would have to wait—but he stopped her with an outstretched arm.

"No, you go. You haven't much time. Here. I'll have Hans walk you to the building, and..." He scrawled a quick note. "Give this to the men at the laundry. They'll give you what you need."

"Thank you, Doctor." *Perfect! Finally, something's going right.*

Hurrying off, with Hans trailing behind, she crossed the muddy ruts of the road, back towards the laundry. The sky was cloaked in heavy gray clouds, the smoke from cookstoves and the scents of the encampment surrounded her—the smells of fuel and oil and men. Strong, but not nearly as pungent as on the beachhead. *Of course, these troops can get moved out and get supplies moved in. Clean clothes. Medical care.*

What I wouldn't give to be back in a real rear echelon. And an actual field hospital, with an operating room that didn't get bombed all the time… and I'm heading back to it. I'm actually going along with an escape back *to Anzio.*

I am out of my mind.

As they reached the low stone structure that had been converted to a laundry, Hans gave her a hasty farewell and hustled back to help the doctor with a promise to come for her shortly.

She stood alone in front of the yawning, dark door. It was quiet—there didn't seem to be the usual groups of men milling around. A couple of soldiers stood talking off at a distance, but her weary and preoccupied brain barely registered them. The aromas of the building gusted out to meet her. Laundry soap and the piles of sweaty, dirty clothes bagged to be washed mingled their scent with the smell of wet wool and fresh ironing.

I could turn around. I could just walk back, tell the doctor I don't need anything after all. Or I could just get myself a change of clothes, have mine washed, and then tomorrow I could go when the truck comes to take me away.

She clenched her fists, willing herself towards courage. *If I stay until tomorrow, if I don't go with the men, I'll be waiting. Again. Waiting for other people to decide my path, in the hands of… who knows. Left behind, again. Alone.*

Closing her eyes, she embraced the wave of pain that always came with that word. Pain and anger. She opened her eyes and stepped forward. It was time for her to make her own decisions. *Even if they're bad ones?* She felt like she ought to stop, to pray for guidance, but what did it matter? She'd already chosen.

Back to Anzio she would go. If she didn't die trying. *Or get horribly wounded.* She forced her feet forward before she could think much further down that path.

The laundry was quiet. The gray light illuminated the weathered stone walls and mercilessly scrubbed board tables. The workers had strung lines from the ceiling, and the clothes that had been washed were all hung in tidy rows. She looked down one row, then the next—she couldn't see anyone.

Maybe they've gone to lunch?

Just to be sure, she walked down one aisle completely, to the back of the building where they'd set up large vats for boiling the clothes. The bubbling pots of wool soup struck her as odd, but she supposed that even stubborn lice couldn't survive a good boil. Steam wreathed the shadows and drifted out through open windows near the ceiling.

She considered leaving the doctor's note on the ironing board but decided that it was best, since no one had seen her here, to leave as little evidence as possible. She turned to search the racks of ironed and folded clothes. Whatever else you said about them, the Wehrmacht were tidy. She held up a pair of woolen pants. Too big. So were the next three pairs.

Wish I had my musette bag still. Maybe the doctor will let me use some surgical thread and take a pair in. She gave an almost hysterical laugh as she held up the fourth pair—finally! A man who was tall enough but not so broad. The shirt was easier—baggy would help sell the illusion.

But as there's no one here, maybe I can do one better.

Quickly, she seized an extra shirt and another pair of pants, much too big, but she'd be able to tie them off. There was a white undershirt hanging, still slightly damp. She grabbed it as well.

Now what? She hadn't thought past getting the clothes—the ones for now, the ones for later. Should she leave her uniform here? Take it along?

Well, I'm certainly not going to change here. Besides, less evidence sounded better. *With luck, or God willing, I'll be able to get a clean U.S. issued uniform to wear in a couple days.* She rolled up the well-fitting clothes inside of the larger ones and headed for the door.

Rows of hanging laundry blocked her way, letting only scattered beams of light past. Ahead, one shirt shifted as if in a slight breeze.

She froze. Silence. Nothing more moved, no footfalls sounded.

I have nothing to worry about. I'm allowed here. I've gotten permission and everything. Still, her scalp prickled. She hurried forward. Damp wool brushed her cheek as she ducked under a shirt. *Maybe Hans will escort me to my tent so I can change. I bet the doctor will loan me a bit of rope or a bandage to tie the britches up if I ask him on the way. And then I can hide the extras until—*

Coming up, she slammed straight into a bulky, uniform-clad chest. With a half-shrieked gasp, she jumped back.

Grüber.

She tried to retreat, but he seized her arm. "Fraulein. I'd been hoping for some time alone with you." His hot breath stank of cabbage and cigarettes and alcohol. He stepped towards her. Stumbling back, she twisted her arm, trying to wrench it out of his grip. Tightening his fingers, his leer grew. "Careful—you might hurt yourself."

Sidestepping to avoid the shirt she'd stepped under before, she pulled harder. "You let go of me right now. Do you understand?"

He laughed. She yanked her arm, stepping backward. Off balance, he followed but didn't let go.

Another step back. Her hip smacked the edge of the shelf where she'd found the clothes. The pain fed her fear and anger. "Let GO!" Trying to find an angle for a kick, she pulled back hard again, and again he stumbled.

Her back hit the rear wall. *He was letting me pull him.*

The momentum of his stumble carried him into her. His bulk crushed her into the wall. He laughed, a coarse, harsh sound as his arm snaked around her waist and his thick lips caressed her ear. "I thought I'd have to wait until tomorrow when you were finally out from under Schmidt's thumb." He pulled her tighter, choking off the scream she tried to force out. "Old fool keeping you for a pet and never learning your tricks. I'll bet…" he let go of her arm, thick fingers touching her hair, "…you've got some good ones, haven't you?"

Her hand was free.

A bubbling vat stood just beside her. She stretched her fingers as he pressed against her. They wrapped around the hot metal rim—scalding pain lanced through them. She gritted her teeth and pulled as hard as she could.

Grandma Emmerson had believed in angels. In their protection, their guardianship. Jean had doubted since Joe was killed, but she knew that that vat was too heavy for her to move. One handed, at that angle—there was no way.

It tipped.

The water wasn't quite boiling hot, but the wave of it that splashed his trousers, just missing her, must have been close by the way he howled.

He leaped back panting and cursing. He seized the wooden paddle out of the laundry vat and spun towards her.

She wasn't there—as soon as the water splashed, she ducked under his arm, slipped between the shelf and table, and ran. The paddle whistled past her head—he shouldn't have missed, being so close, but maybe pain or anger distracted him— *"For He shall give His angels charge over you, To keep you in all your ways…"* sang Grandma's voice in her head. *Whoosh!* It passed overhead again as she ducked and ran through a row of shirts. Her heart thumped in her ears, echoing his pounding boots. She dodged to the right, then the left. Past a stack of pants. Past an ironing board. The door was just ahead. His harsh breaths gasped out raging curses just behind.

Bursting through the doorway, she stumbled. The world spun around her as she fell. She stumbled and fell, right into the arms of Hans. Her heart beat so hard in her throat that she thought it must burst.

"Nurse, what…" He looked at her, those German blue eyes wide and confused, then he looked over her shoulder at Grüber, wet, panting, and still holding the paddle in his hand. Grüber stopped, his face beet red. He looked as if he were debating whether he could get away with going through Hans to get to her.

Hans was no physical match for Grüber—the kid was maybe nineteen, and it could've been his clothes that she'd stolen, but as he looked from Jean to Grüber, his jaw set. The look in his eyes changed from confusion to swift comprehension and anger.

"Nurse Hoff. Go. The doctor needs your help with the last patient." He pushed her gently behind him.

"I…" she whispered.

He barked at her, "*Beeil dich*. It is a difficult case."

She ran for it. Stumbling on the ruts, she realized with shock and gratitude that in the crook of her left arm, she still clutched the bundle of clothes.

Oh, thank you, God. Any indecision she'd felt was gone. *There's no way I'm staying here any longer!*

THIRTEEN

IN THE FEW DAYS Jean had known Doctor Schmidt, she'd seen him kind, cool, professional, suspicious, and yes, even angry at the waste and death around him.

She'd never seen him enraged.

Hans had returned unscathed and given his report. The doctor had sent for Grüber. His lieutenant had come instead. Doctor Schmidt had begun talking calmly. His German had rapidly sped up until he screamed.

Busying herself cleaning more surgical tools, Jean tried not to look as if she were listening desperately to every word. The lieutenant listened in silence until the doctor had shouted himself out, then he replied. Even without seeing him, Jean could hear the casual shrug in his tone. Grüber was a hothead, he said, and maybe not always best with the ladies. He'd already talked to him—he said he'd just tried for a kiss, and she'd attacked him like a wildcat, spilled boiling water all over him. The lieutenant laughed a little, made some comment about feisty American women.

The doctor made some uncomplimentary observations in return.

The lieutenant answered, "Sir, we all know you and the Oberst are friends. If you want Grüber dealt with, you may as well talk to your friend. I'm not qualified—do you know who his uncle is?"

The doctor cursed and shouted, "I don't care who his uncle is—having a Party official as an uncle—"

"Gives him a certain amount of protection," the lieutenant finished.

The doctor lowered his voice, but his tone was frigid. "He will not be on the transfer detail tomorrow?"

The lieutenant sighed. "His uncle wants him moved closer to home. Austria. He is supposed to go along, guard the prisoners—"

Jean had heard enough. Glancing over her shoulder to make certain that no one was in sight, she eased open a carton of medication. She flinched as the movement pulled the burns on her palm and fingers. Doctor Schmidt had tutted over them and bound them carefully, talking to Hans over his shoulder in German, trying to get the whole story, then looking back at her with eyes that made her think of Dad or of Stan, sad eyes, as he asked if she wanted to talk, asked what Grüber had done to her, whether she needed...he'd hesitated there...anything.

She tucked another stash of pills into her hairdo, carefully patting it into place. *Keep it together, Jean. Not too many at a time. Nice and slow.* Deciding it was worth the risk, she pulled out a small pile of dressings, slipping them into her pockets.

Then, she took a deep breath and pulled out a syringe.

Pulling back the plunger, she watched the pentothal sodium fill it, hoping she'd calculated the dosage correctly. If she had, the injection shouldn't hurt him. She hoped. After all, it was in common use in the German surgery as an anesthetic. *Still, giving the dose all at once, and not being able to monitor his breathing or heart rate afterward... I don't like to do it, but what else can I do? I'm not getting on that truck.* She closed her eyes and prayed. *Please, God. I know he's made choices that... but he's a good man. Please, look after him.* She slipped the syringe under the counter where there was a gap between the board that made the work surface and the drawers beneath. A little securing adhesive on the overhanging lip of wood made a perfect hiding place.

"Nurse Hoff?"

She jumped, and her hand whipped out from under the counter. *There's no way he didn't see that.* She took a breath before she turned, trying to smooth the worry from her face. "Yes, Doctor?"

For a small eternity, he looked at her with an unreadable expression.

DOCTOR SCHMIDT washed his hands, scrubbing them under the quickly cooling water, soaping to his elbows and between each finger. His skin ached under the meticulous cleaning, but it needed to be done. He needed to be clean.

The American nurse worked behind him, the soft clink of instruments being taken out of the sterilizer the only sound. He'd offered to let her go and rest, but she'd said that she'd rather work than sit.

She's a good girl. Quiet, professional. Like his Birte when he'd first met her. Back when she was Birte Friedman, working as a nurse, and he was just Frank Schmidt, another student working on his medical degree at the University of Göttingen. It was 1913, and they'd been so young, so full of hope.

Before the world went mad. Before the mud and trenches of France.

Back then, he'd viewed the future with anticipation. Science—science was the way of the future. Away with superstitions, away with the squabbles of nations. Men of reason would lead the world to great new heights. Man's baser passions were finally under control.

Then, a shot in Austria killed that insignificant Grand Duke and the world went mad.

Frank Schmidt had kissed Birte goodbye with a new ring on her finger and shipped out, certain that even now, even in the field, he could do good. In the end he came home, unlike so many others. He came home crippled in body and teetering on the edge of a broken mind, but at last he knew the truth.

They were wrong—they'd all been wrong. There was to be no great ascent to the heavens for Man. Like Icarus, their wings of wax had melted. If God were merciful, perhaps they would not destroy themselves as he had.

Frank had hoped, but deep down he knew it wasn't the end when the armistice was signed. When the world punished Germany, Germany took it grim-faced, but he knew what lay underneath. Men spoke of peace as his land went hungry, as the economy suffered, as resentment simmered in every heart.

The people muttered about the unfairness of it all. Why should Germany pay for a war the great nations had all participated in? Why should their country—their fatherland—be punished for trying to do what all the other great empires had done?

And how could they ever repay the debt? How could they ever, ever hope to be a strong nation again?

The façade of peace was thin indeed.

Frank had tried to ignore it, burying his worries as he flung himself into work. He scrimped along, kept his head above water—only just—and read the newspapers from abroad that spoke of a peace he could only hope for.

He heard the whispers, but never joined in. What good did whispers do? Did they put bread on the table, shoes on the children? No, he did that, by accepting how things were. Frank worked. Kissed his wife. Kissed his four babies and watched them grow. Tried to sleep at night. Surely, surely if he just kept working, just kept out of it, he and his family could live in peace.

Even a bitter peace was better than what he'd seen in France.

Then, Henrik, his brother's son, had come to visit. Frank hadn't thought much of it when Herman's letter arrived, indicating that he felt it just as well the boy left Berlin for a while. That was no surprise. Frank and Birte had settled in the Sudetenland to be away from the unrest of larger cities. Nor was he concerned about taking Henrik in for a while. On their rare family visits Henrik had shown himself a smiling, hard-working boy with a keen interest in medicine. As Birte was ill again, he would be able to help with errands and little tasks around the house that might be a challenge for his aunt.

All the arrangements were made, and late in the fall of 1933, little Henrik—not so little anymore—stepped off the train to be greeted by his uncle. Frank smiled and embraced the boy.

Henrik was the picture of his father—tall, blond, smiling, and ever-talking. Almost as soon as he was in the door of the Schmidt home and had greeted his cousins, he babbled about the changes that were happening in Berlin, about the progress of the Party, and about how the German people would soon be able to raise their heads again—to be strong.

When the boy paused for breath, Frank seized the opportunity. "But what use is strength if it brings more bloodshed?"

"Uncle," Henrik had replied, blue eyes shining but voice world-weary as if he'd heard it all before. "That's the talk of Jews and Communists. Not strong, German men. You were in the last war—you must remember what we were before we were betrayed."

"Betrayed?"

"Surely you know about the Jews?"

"Jews?" Birte asked, coming down the stairs, leaning heavily on her cane. "What have Jews to do with anything?" Her eyes shone as she embraced her nephew, murmuring about how he'd grown.

He gave her a quick hug, then continued his chatter. "Jews, Auntie—Jews are the ones who lost us the last war—and the Communists. Here." Henrik dug through his rucksack and produce a tattered book. Frank read the title silently to himself—*Mein Kampf. My Struggle*. "Look! The leader of my *Jungvolk* group loaned it to me... It explains everything about how our country—our great nation—was contaminated and betrayed. Herr Hitler wrote it himself! He's just the man to fix everything—to put bread on our tables and guns in our hands again! I'm only in *Jungvolk* until I get back, then I'll be able to join the *Hitler Jugend* and really learn some things."

The boy finally paused. Frank's gaze darted to Birte. She was frowning, a little crease between her brows, and he knew, he *knew* what was going to come out of her mouth once she opened it. She would ask what made the boy think so ill of the Jews. Their nephew didn't know that his aunt was a Jewess.

She'd chosen to be baptized and to attend his family's church shortly after their marriage. She'd stroked her swelling belly and blushed as she explained, "I don't want the children to be torn between us. Besides, my family is far away, and yours is here. Where you go, I'll go." She'd embraced her new faith, and no one except his own parents had been told her background. At first, it hadn't seemed necessary to bring up. As times had changed, Frank had been deliberately cautious to avoid questions. After the sackings of Jewish employees at their old university this spring, he had gone through their house, checking for signs that might hint at her background. The only evidence that remained were a few articles in a chest at the foot of their bed—her mother's Sabbath candles and a black copy of the Torah in Hebrew. She also kept a photo of her parents sitting by her bedside. Her father looked very much the German – light haired and serious. Only her dark-haired mother might have been viewed with suspicion. Apart from these few things, her past was hidden. Unless, of course, she informed her nephew of it. What would happen then? A prickling shiver ran down Frank's spine.

As she opened her smiling mouth to answer Henrik—all innocence and honesty, his Birte—he interrupted.

"Henrik, why don't you go get your auntie a cup of tea? I think there is some in the kitchen. Hilde will show you." His daughter nodded and led her cousin off. Grateful, Frank took his wife's elbow. "Here now, Birte, you sit there." He guided her over to a soft chair and smoothed an afghan over her knees. "You know you shouldn't strain yourself to come downstairs yet. Ach, what's the good of being a doctor if my own wife won't listen?"

For the rest of the evening, Frank kept the conversation on safe paths. The book was forgotten by the others, and he pushed it out of his mind until night, when the house was dark and full of quiet breathing.

While Henrik slept the deep, peaceful sleep of a child who doesn't know much of the world—so naïve, so easily led—Frank took the book. He sank into his chair by the fire—the chair where he'd read stories to his children, stories of monsters and magic and happily ever afters for those who did good. To the flickering light of a candle, he read.

He read the words, though his brain could hardly believe them.

When he closed it at last, the candle's flame was guttering, nearly drowned in the wax. He watched it fade, dim and blue, then with a final gasp of life it flared up tall and sputtering. He whispered, horror clutching his heart. "This…this will light them all on fire. And we will all burn."

He had debated how best to warn Birte—his little nurse who'd never been afraid of anything, her heart too full of love to make room for fear. She'd never imagine evil of anyone, especially not Herman's boy. When Herman's family had lived closer, she and Henrik's mother had been expecting their children at the same time—Nata her first, Birte her youngest. They'd planned their babies' wardrobes, picked names together, nursed their infants together.

How could he tell her that she mustn't tell this boy who she held the same day he took his first breaths that she was Jewish? That he might hate her for it. That he would almost certainly betray her.

How could he warn her that he feared the madness was back, a flame licking and gnawing at the edges of the world they'd built and labored for—that it would all crumble soon?

"But I *will* save her," he whispered aloud. "Whatever I must do. Birte and the children—I will not let this fire touch them. I swear."

He'd warned Birte at last, finally resorting to bluntness. She'd wept, refused to believe him, but when he mentioned the children—how their lives might be changed if they were branded, how they could be limited in marriage and employment—she agreed.

Her parents' picture, her mother's Sabbath candles, her Torah—all were taken from the house. She refused to let him burn them, so he snuck out at night like a criminal and buried them in the vegetable patch. At dawn, he made certain he was out digging so the neighbors could see that he really *was* gardening—hastening to get in some work before going into the clinic for the day. The neighbor was out in his own garden early having a smoke, and they laughed about wives and their demands.

After six months, Henrik was returned to his family, and Frank tried to resume his life. The evidence was safely buried unless someone were determined enough to come digging through their garden. *Or through genealogical records back in Hamburg—or perhaps wedding licenses.* The thought worried him, but he tried to convince himself that it wouldn't happen. *Who would bother?* He was only a small-time doctor, uninvolved in politics, careful to display Germany's new flag, careful to keep his head down, to follow all the forms. *It won't happen. We are safe now.*

The war came, as he had known it would. The Sudentenland was taken. The fire spread, but this time it came as lightning—the Blitzkrieg launching itself across Europe, scorching the earth, burning all who tried to contain it until the Belgians were swept over, the French capitulated, and the British were driven back over the Channel.

Their sons weren't able to sit quietly by, though perhaps, he reasoned, that was for the best. *Honorable service keeps other eyes off them.* They'd had to pass some screening to enlist, but nothing had come back. Birte's family had been small—if any relatives lived, they were distant and unknown and her parents long gone. And after all, she was Christian now.

Gustav went first. He signed up for the Luftwaffe. He'd always wanted to fly. Kurt followed shortly after, though he chose the Navy. Frank held Birte as she wept.

Then Hilde, who was still unmarried, was called away to a factory in Hamburg. She had itched for something different to do for years and did not complain.

Ralph was still young—only just seventeen—but he was strong, and as the British and Americans held on stubbornly in North Africa, the doctor watched his son and tried not to worry.

They were scattered, but undiscovered. They heard from the boys and from Hilde frequently. They survived, untouched by the fires of war.

Then, one Tuesday, just after dawn, it all fell apart.

Hearing a knock at the door so early, before he'd even left for the clinic, surprised Frank. He didn't have any patients who'd visit him at home anymore. Fearing that traffic at his house might attract unwanted attention, he'd stopped accepting anyone like that years ago.

When he went to the door, there stood Obergefreiter Meyer. Not an Obergefreiter anymore—he stood tall in the uniform of an Oberst, a far cry from the weedy little nineteen-year-old the doctor remembered from 1917.

While Frank stared, hand frozen on the door, Meyer stepped through, his shining boots solid as polished stone on Birte's immaculate floor. He wore a broad smile stretched across his narrow face like a man wears new shoes that haven't been broken in yet. "Frank!" he exclaimed, clapping his old medic on the shoulder. "You're looking good! Won't you shake hands with an old friend?"

Woodenly, the doctor held his hand out, then flinched at Meyer's grip. He'd forgotten how the man could latch on, his fingers strong enough to make bones ache. For a moment, he was transported back to the muddy trenches, young Obergefreiter Otto Meyer clinging to him with pincers for hands as he strove to extract a last piece of shrapnel without hitting the femoral artery.

Meyer owed him his life. Surely, he couldn't have forgotten that. Surely, that might inspire a visit if nothing else did. Frank found his voice. "Meyer. It's been a long time. Or should I say *Oberst* Meyer now?"

Meyer laughed. "Yah, the leadership knows how to value a man with some experience. At least in the Wehrmacht. Some of these others—" he shrugged.

Frank nodded. "Well, come in. Would you like some tea? I was just finishing breakfast." He led his old...friend? Yes, he supposed that Meyer had been a friend. You couldn't save a man's leg and life, take a hit and sit with him all night in a shell hole keeping him alive, trying to keep your own sanity in the crashing cacophony...You couldn't go through all of that without forming some kind of bond.

Birte was still in the kitchen, and if she were discomfited by the early morning visit she didn't show it. She welcomed Meyer, smiling her beautiful smile and hurrying over, eager to greet a friend of her husband.

Did he imagine it? Did Meyer hesitate before taking her hand?

Perhaps, or perhaps not. But he didn't imagine the way the other man's eyes followed Birte as she moved around the room, gathering tea things then carrying them to the table in the adjoining room where the men could sit in comfort. There was no expression on Meyer's face, just quiet watchfulness. That familiar prickle travelled down Frank's spine, the same one he'd felt at Henrik's unthinking words. Again, he felt the shadow of a rising storm that could sweep their lives away. Under the surface, under the Oberst's smile, danger lurked.

Swallowing down the fear, he tried to tell himself it was unfounded. Meyer was nothing but polite, complimenting him on his home, asking about his practice and about the years they'd not seen each other. He lifted a glass when he heard about the children who were serving and shared a few stories of his own children and the exploits of his newest grandson. All seemed well, but that prickle wouldn't go away.

The shapeless fear came into painful focus when Meyer mentioned his eldest grandson. The Oberst leaned back in his chair, fiddling with a couple of coins he'd found in his pocket. "Of course, Gunter gets into trouble. He and some friends were caught breaking shop windows in Berlin the other night—out after curfew too. Looked very bad. But the officer that brought him home mentioned that the shop belonged to a family that had been hiding some *Juden*." He shrugged. "Well, knowing *that*, who can blame the boy's spirit, even if his actions pushed the limits?" He laughed, but his eyes watched Frank.

The doctor managed a smile and nod. He was grateful Birte was working in the kitchen, out of Meyer's line of sight. The set of her shoulders spoke volumes.

The men sat silent for a few moments, the clatter of dishes the only sound besides the sipping of tea and the munching of kuchen.

Frank dreaded to ask the question but knew he must. He cleared his throat. "So, Otto. What brings you to our little home after all these years? Surely with your busy life it was out of your way to just," he took a sip, "pop in?"

Meyer smiled again, but it did not reach his eyes. "Ah, Frank. You always did like to cut to the heart of the matter." Without warning, he stood to intercept Birte who was passing through the room.

She jumped. Frank gripped the edge of the table until his knuckles were white—

—but all Meyer did was bow, small and quick. "Thank you, Frau Schmidt, for the refreshment. It does a man's heart good to visit a house like this, a home that reminds us of just what we fight for.

Birte's cheeks flushed, and she smiled through trembling lips. "Thank you, sir."

Meyer continued, speaking over her. "However, I do have some private business which I wish to discuss with your husband. If you would give us this place alone…?"

"Of course." She started for the stairs, only meeting Frank's eyes once. She smiled, just for him. *She feels it too. Our doom has found us.*

Otto Meyer, the Oberst, sat again and folded his hands on the table.

When he spoke, he spoke the words Frank had dreaded to hear, and he knew—*he knew*—what Meyer would say before he said it. "Your wife. She's a lovely woman." The pause for effect, the look up to meet his eyes. "It is too bad, really, that she is a Jewess."

Frank didn't flinch—he couldn't. He had to play the game through to its inevitable conclusion. "Whatever do you mean?"

Meyer leaned towards him, face grim. "You know exactly what I mean, Frank. Your wife was born Birte Elizabeth Friedman, only daughter of Joseph and Rebecca Friedman, members of the *Verein der Neuen Dammtor-Synagoge* in Hamburg." He lowered his voice. "You know what that means. Your children are half-breeds. Your grandchildren will still have enough Jewish blood to count against them. You won't practice medicine anymore, unless of course you renounce her—though I'm not sure that would save any of you."

Frank drew himself up. "Where is the evidence of this? I certainly haven't seen any evidence of my wife being anything other than a loyal German woman. She goes to the Lutheran church for goodness sake. She was just talking about choosing Christmas gifts that we could send to the children—"

His bluster didn't make any difference—they both knew it, but he had to try.

Meyer grimaced, a much more natural expression for him than the forced smiles. "Keep spinning this *Blödsinn* as long as you need to, Frank. The fact of the matter is, if your family's history comes to the notice of the wrong people..." he shrugged.

God, oh God. Why have you delivered me into this man's hands?

But then, a ray of hope. Meyer continued. "It's fortunate for you that I'm the one who uncovered your wife's records."

Silence. Frank spoke, treading carefully. "What...exactly... are you planning to do with them?"

Meyer sat back and pursed his lips. The doctor in Frank wondered if he suffered from heartburn or indigestion—it would account for the perpetually sour expression. Or maybe that was just part of working for the Third Reich.

"I have no strong political convictions, Frank. I don't think that you do either. But the fact of the matter is, the government has put me where I am, and I am happy to be there. I'm not going to stick out my neck."

"So. If you're not here to protect my family, are you here to threaten me? What's this game you're playing, Oberst?"

"I don't forget a debt. I may not be a patriot or a moralist but—Frank, I haven't forgotten. You saved my life. Stayed with me at risk to yourself. I've followed your career. You haven't set a toe out of line, but you've protected and helped our citizenry." He looked down at his folded hands. "I have no wish to see you suffer. I conveniently buried your wife's records in Hamburg—"

Frank opened his mouth wide, but Meyer held up a forestalling hand.

"It was a simple enough thing to do. No risk to me. However, if anyone digs ..." He shrugged.

"So?"

"So. I'm in need of some good medical staff in my new command. You're in need of a show of patriotism—something to keep eyes off you and your family." He leaned back. "I want you to volunteer for the army."

Frank couldn't help it—he laughed aloud. "What do you think that will solve... If anything, wouldn't it draw more attention? And an old fellow like me, with a limp no less—"

Meyer pulled out an envelope containing a small stack of documents. "I've arranged everything. Well, my aide has. Good boy, not too bright. Very patriotic. Thinks that you already volunteered and that I'm meeting to congratulate you and to get together with an old friend."

He flipped one page over and pointed out some handwritten notes. "And these records will vouch for you—that you've been examined. That your family lines are pure." He leaned back. "Just go along with it. Enlist, and if you're lucky no one will feel the need to look any further into your lineage."

Frank nodded, slowly. "And you get out of this…?"

Meyer shrugged. "Like I said, I owe you. It was only a matter of time before you were found out." He pulled out a cigarette. "Do you mind?"

Filthy things. Not good for Birte's lungs, but do I dare mind? "No. Go ahead."

The Oberst lit up and took a contemplative puff. "Besides, I'd like a competent fellow like you around, Frank. There aren't many of these young fellows, foaming at the mouth for war, that I'd trust as far as you and me—members of the Old Guard. We're short surgeons too. I know, you haven't been practicing surgery exclusively for a while, but we both know you're capable." He held up his cigarette in a half salute. "I'd be honored to have you. Oh!" he slid another piece of paper over. "And I've seen to having your daughter sent back from the factories to look after your wife. It gets her out of the public eye as well—pity she was born with such dark hair."

Frank nodded, not really listening. So. It had come, but it was not as bad as it could have been.

He would have to serve, but he could still be a doctor. That was something. After all—whatever else he thought of this war's foolishness, of all the darkness that was spreading, he could help the young men who had been injured.

The decision wasn't difficult, and for that he was grateful. He was tired of difficult decisions.

A CLATTER behind him brought him back to the present. The nurse made a frustrated sound in the back of her throat. He turned—she was picking up a scalpel off the floor. The light flickered off the shining blade as she set it aside. Her bandaged hand was shaking.

Poor child. She wasn't that much younger than his Hilde, but harder, colder. She had known pain.

And now...now he was certain that she knew fear as well.

"Nurse Hoff?" He did not really want to ask, but he needed to—he had to know for certain just what this girl had been doomed to.

She looked up, her eyes red-rimmed and weary but her shoulders straight. "Yes, Doctor?"

His courage failed him. He could not ask about Grüber's attack—not directly. "You seem tired today, Nurse. Are you well?"

She hesitated. Her eyes flicked downward, and he could see the thoughts moving rapidly behind them. *What is she deciding?*

"Nurse?"

She met his eyes and answered, "I *am* a little tired. And my hand..."

"Are the burns painful?"

"Not terribly. But it makes me clumsy." Her eyes dropped. "I'm not sure how much use I'll be to you today. Not that I suppose it matters so much, but I had hoped to leave things tidy before I go."

He put his hand on her shoulder—the first time he'd touched her except for bandaging her hand. He shouldn't have. Her thin shoulder, rising and falling with her breath, convicted him, reminding him of her frail humanity. She was a child who he was allowing to be shipped off. To an unknown destination. With those who wished her harm. He pulled his hand back, wiping it on his pants leg. *Focus on Birte. She's well, her last letter said. And the boys. And—*

"Why don't you rest for the remainder of today?" he said. "If you're to be going somewhere with fewer medical facilities, it would be best if you keep that burn clean – you don't want an infection." *I'll sneak some sulfa along with her, just in case. It's the least I can do.*

She didn't answer, weighing something in her mind, though she kept her face smooth. At last, she moistened her lips and said, "Thank you. I should be careful—though they are not bad burns. I'm sure they will be scabbed over soon." Her hands trembled, and she clasped them. "I will rest, but I feel like I should check on the American soldiers again. With them moving out tomorrow...I..." she hesitated, choosing her words.

The doctor shook his head. "Hans can do that. I can do it myself if it will make you sleep easier."

"No, thank you." Her answer was a little too quick. "I don't think I could rest without seeing them. After everything we've gone through in the last few days, well, they're my patients really and will likely be for a long time. Assuming we're sent to the same place."

Hmmm. The suspicions that had started when that American, Corporal Novak, had faked his collapse returned. It had been a good performance, but the rifled papers on his desk had revealed the "attack" for the ruse it was. *What have they talked you into?*

He opened his mouth, intending to let her know that he knew, intending to put a stop to the foolishness, but she reached up to brush a strand of hair into place with her bandaged hand. He hesitated. "Alright. Go and see to them, but don't stay too long, and make certain you get some rest. It will be a long day tomorrow."

He watched her gather her supplies and considered how best to act.

FOURTEEN

TEXAS HANK MET HER just inside the shack's door, taking the lantern from her and surveying her new field gray ensemble with a grin. "You got the clothes!"

"Yes."

"Um," Barry looked her over. "You still don't look much like one of the fellas."

In answer, she dug deep into her satchel under bandages and medication and pulled out the tightly rolled larger pair of pants, shirt, and undershirt. "I'll wear these over the top. Hopefully, with them being a little loose, and with a bit of padding…" She met their skeptical eyes, stomach roiling. "And it'll be dark. Don't you think…?"

"Sure, that should help," Tex said, though he couldn't stop fingering his rabbit's foot. Barry shrugged one shoulder. "Here," Tex said, "I'll tuck 'em over in the corner until they're wanted."

She handed him the bundle. "I'm sure it will work," she said again, as if by saying it, it would be so.

Leroy came over. "'Course it will. Maybe we can snag a coat off one of the guards too. Don't worry. We're going to pull this off."

"Yes. Yes, of course." She tried to infuse her voice with the same confidence.

Leroy scanned her face. "What's wrong, Jea…Nurse Hoff?" He reached out and touched her bruised arm.

Flinching, she pulled back. "Nothing." She swallowed down the memory of her terror in the laundry building and added, "I found out for sure that they're moving us tomorrow morning."

Chuck, crouching in the corner, muttered a curse and kneaded his hands together. Ed and Roberts, who'd been quietly talking, fell silent. Roberts whistled, low.

In his usual position at the back of the building, George just nodded. "So. It will have to be tonight." He reached for his shirt buttons. Taking the cue, Jean hurried to give his checkup. He needed to be as fit as he could be. The other men dispersed, each to his job. Tex, Ed, and Roberts worked on the hinges while Wilson and Barry talked loudly next to the door to cover the noise.

Probing George's neck wound, Jean frowned. There was some seepage around the stitches. The flesh looked puffy and red. "How are the ribs?"

"How do ya think?" He pulled on a grin. "Don't worry, Nursey. I'll manage. So. Tonight. Give it two hours, then we'll call."

Nodding, Jean reviewed the plan in her mind. "Ok. I'll let him know you're doing poorly when I go back, so it seems more plausible. Then, when I hear from you, I'll…" she swallowed. "I'll take care of the doctor."

Leroy squatted beside her, meeting her eyes. "Jean—you're sure?"

She nodded. "Everything's ready. Unless the opportunity comes to just slip away…well. We have to get out of here. This is our chance. So. I'll do it. He…he should be fine." She rubbed her right hand against her forehead, forgetting the bandages.

Of course, Watchdog Leroy noticed. "What happened to your hand?"

Whipping it back down into the shadows, she busied herself with rearranging her bag. "Nothing. It was...it was nothing."

George craned his neck, trying to get a better look. She took note of how he didn't move his torso more than he had to. *He's not healed up enough for this. Not that I'd be able to convince him. Not that I'd dare to at this point.* She shivered—she had no intention of being here in the morning.

George raised his eyes and met hers squarely. "You're a crummy liar, Nurse Hoff."

"Did *he* do something? Grüber?" Leroy's voice shook. The look on his face startled her. He wasn't a big guy—a little taller than her but lanky, wiry but no muscleman. With his sappy grin and those ears, she hadn't taken him too seriously. But the look on his face...It said plainly what he'd do if he caught Grüber trying to hurt her. Seeing him so protective touched her, but it worried her, too. She recalled George's words. *Don't let Leroy down too soon. Sad Leroy is Careless Leroy is Dead Leroy. But, if he's thinking of going up against a guard for my sake, maybe he's in even more danger if I* don't *let him down.*

Gently, Leroy took her hand. It surprised her so much that she didn't object. He turned it over. The worst of the burns were covered, but a bit of shiny red flesh showed where the bandage gapped.

"What happened? Jean?" He leaned forward, and his eyes didn't look angry anymore, just worried, and safe. She found herself wanting to lean on his shoulder and tell him everything.

"It was just... when I was getting the laundry..." her throat clogged. *Stupid girl. Keep it together. You don't know this guy, and likely he'll be dead soon. Just like you. Just like all of you.*

She looked down at his hand holding hers and pulled away. "It was an accident. Just an accident while I was getting the laundry. Burned my hand on a hot water vat."

He leaned back on his heels. "Sure." She breathed a soft sigh of relief before he continued. "Ok. And the vat hurt your arm too?"

Shoot. He noticed. "This doesn't matter. We need to make plans. Tomorrow..."

"Tomorrow nothing." Leroy leaned forward. "Nurse Hoff, we can't do this if we can't trust you."

Stung, she sputtered, "What?"

"This isn't the time to start lying, keeping secrets. If there's something we don't know—"

"No—I just don't want to—" She closed her eyes, then opened them, putting all the assurance she could into the next few words. "You can trust me."

George snorted. "Sure we can. Far as you can any woman, I suppose."

Leroy frowned at his buddy, but George shook his head.

"You just haven't known enough of 'em, kid—let her be. She's being as honest as she can, I figure."

The old, cold anger rose in Jean's heart, and she welcomed it. It was stronger than the fear—maybe it could give her the strength she lacked. "What do you know about me?" she spat. "I've faced all the risks so far. I've done the scouting. I got you into the doctor's papers. I got the uniforms. When have I ever done anything to—"

"Will you three shut up?" Hank hissed, just as the door creaked open. The guard was there—not Grüber. He scanned the room, frowning. His eyes rested on Jean, George, and Leroy, huddled in the far corner.

"*Fräulein*? Is all well?"

Jean stood. "His fever has spiked. I'm giving him some medication, but he seems to be delirious."

George swung his fist, gasping, playing it up. "Delirious nothing, you cold-hearted white-hatted iceberg of a…n...nurse."

Leroy grabbed his arm, easing him back down. He looked up, and though the quick glance he gave Jean was probing, the limpid eyes he turned on the guard couldn't have been more perfect. "He's really bad. Nothing he's saying makes any sense, and he keeps going from hot to cold." He looked down. "I can't get a read on him at all."

Filled with the uncomfortable feeling that he wasn't really talking about George, Jean tried not to squirm. *Stick to the script.*

"I'll have to come back in an hour or two. If he isn't better," she had a flash of inspiration, "I'm not sure we'll be able to move him tomorrow."

The guard gave her a shrug as if he thought any reprieve was unlikely. *Aaaand he's probably right. But at least it's some groundwork laid.*

She turned to Leroy. "I'll see to him again soon. Try to keep him quiet, and," she paused to give him a meaningful look, "try not to worry."

He met her eyes. "I'll try not to, Nurse. I know he's in good hands."

She nodded, her throat tight. She hoped he was right.

A welcome fresh breeze greeted her outside, and the dark enveloped her. The rumbling of the distant battlefield was almost imperceptible—or maybe she'd just become too accustomed to it.

The silence was broken by the crunch of tires. An ambulance—she could just make out the red cross painted on the side of it. Casualties. Her heart sank. Here was another piece on an overfull chessboard. *Shoot. If we get busy tonight, it might be harder to slip away. Of course, the doctor* did *give me permission to rest. With these hands, I'm not much good anyway. And, if there end up being a lot of casualties in, he might be busy, not able to pay so much attention to me. Maybe I won't have to deal with him after all.*

She stood for a moment, watching the ambulance park, watching the men hurry over with stretchers and start unloading patients. Harsh words in German echoed through the night, and she counted stretchers—one, two, three, four, five...

Her guard grunted something at her which she mentally translated as "Let's get going" though she didn't know the actual meaning. She started walking, and he didn't object, so she figured she had it close to right.

The dim lights inside the house were bright to her eyes. The doctor came bustling past, looked at her briefly, and shook his head. "Nurse, you know you're supposed to rest."

She hesitated. On a stretcher near the door was a young man, leg mangled and torn beneath a tourniquet, misery on his face, hair the same color of blond as Joe's had been. "If you need me…"

The doctor was bending over the young man, checking his pupils. "We don't." he answered shortly. "Go. Rest."

She hated to interrupt him but had to plant the seeds. "Alright. I will likely need to check on the Americans in a few hours. The surgery patient seems to be taking a turn for the worse. He's feverish."

The doctor nodded impatiently. "Fine. Whatever you need to do." He barked something at her guard, who plucked at her elbow. "Pieter will take you to check on them in two hours. Go now."

She obeyed, shadowed by Pieter until she came to her little tent. Crawling into her cot, she told herself that she ought to rest. *What a plan. Is there* any *way this is going to work?* The steps—and what might go wrong with each—kept spinning through her brain as she tried to force her weary eyes closed, tried to force herself to sleep.

I've got the uniform. I've got what supplies I can, and they're ready. The fellas have the door fixed. They can handle one guard. Quick, easy.

And the doctor? The only one who was really watching her movements—well, except for Grüber. *Hopefully, he's still nursing some painful burns.* The doctor was busy. And if something changed, if he became suspicious and if he wouldn't let her be the one to check on the men, she'd knock him out.

Or maybe it was if he caught her trying to steal supplies. Or…It had all gotten muddled in her mind.

And now there was no more time to try to get it all straight. They were out of time.

STANDING BY THE DOOR in the dark, Leroy flexed his hands, waiting for the signal. *I sure hope everything's ready. Time's up.* At George's nod,

Leroy started pounding on the door. The other guys huddled in the shadows feigning sleep, dark forms in the darker room. George lay, sprawled on the floor, panting and moaning. They'd used a little of their precious water to smear his face to simulate sweat, just in case the guard came to check.

At last, the guard called through the thick, closed door. "Yah?"

Leroy didn't have to pretend to make his voice tense—he was sweating like a pig.

We're crazy. We are out of our gourd crazy. God, have mercy on us!

Aloud, he shouted, "My friend. He's...he's really bad. Please, the nurse said she'd come and check soon, but I don't think he can wait. Please, can't someone go and get her?"

There was another pause, then the door opened a crack. The guard looked through, rifle at the ready, scanning the room's shadows. George groaned and muttered something unintelligible. The guard stared at him for a moment, face impassive.

Come on, buddy. Everything's fine. We'd be stupid to try to make a break for it—you know it, we know it. Not that that's gonna stop us, but still, just take the bait, c'mon.

The guard opened the door a little wider and clicked on his flashlight. He trained it on each of the "sleeping" men. Ed and Roberts kept still in the shadows behind the door. Hank rolled over and cursed. Chuck sat up, then lay back with a grunt. Barry rubbed his eyes. "Leroy, can't you just shaddup? I'm trying to sleep here."

The guard's eyes flicked over to where George lay.

He watched George move restlessly in his sleep, breath rasping. His cool eyes flicked back to Leroy.

Shoot—what if he says no?

The guard nodded.

Leroy repressed the urge to exhale loudly in relief. The heavy door closed silently on its freshly cleaned hinges, and the wooden bar fell into place.

Plastering his ear to the wood, Leroy could just make out one set of footsteps walking away. No conversation first—he just went. *Good. He must be the only one on duty.* He turned back to the room and gave a thumbs up. "Ok!"

Stealthily, the men rolled to their feet, gathering up their meager bundles of possessions, moving to the wall beside the door, where the shadows would fall the darkest when the door was opened.

They waited.

As the minutes ticked by, Leroy tried to silence his brain. He failed.

What if he grabs the doctor instead? What if Jeannie couldn't get the meds? What if she tried and got caught? What if… He closed his eyes, waited, and prayed for her safety.

JEAN WAS WAITING for the call. Sleep stayed far away, and her thoughts wandered back to Joe. Not to their courtship, or their farewell. *What was it like for him, at the end? What about Stan?* He'd dragged her along for that talking to—this was all his fault, really. *The old coot, always trying to do things his own way, always thinking that somehow it would all work out.*

She tried to muster up some anger at him to burn away the ache and because, if she were angry, she'd be too busy to be afraid.

Tonight, the anger, always close to hand, so easy to find for the last couple of years, wouldn't come.

Tonight, the fear was stronger.

She closed her eyes, trying to pray, reciting the old psalms from Confirmation.

The LORD is my shepherd; I shall not want. He makes me to lie down in green pastures; he leads me beside the still waters. He restores my soul: he leads me in the paths of righteousness for His name's sake. Yea, though I walk through the valley of the shadow of death…

Death. Am I ready to die? Really ready? They might shoot me if I'm caught… I don't think they're supposed to, but especially with this dumb disguise idea… This is a bad idea, isn't it, Lord? Maybe I should just—

The call she'd been waiting for nearly made her jump out of her skin. She hated how her voice shook. "Yes?"

The guard answered, his English labored. "Frau…Nurse. Come. The *Amerikanischer Soldat*—he is bad."

"All right. I'm coming." She prayed that he wouldn't comment on the bulky satchel she carried. Mercifully, the guard's eyes were tired, and he hardly looked at her. He moved rapidly ahead, back towards the prison shed.

As they passed the farmhouse, she hesitated. The way Novak had been looking today, she felt like they needed some morphine, just in case, and she'd only been able to manage to sneak out medication that came in pill form. Not to mention spare dressings and gauze—they could use it all. *It's now or never.* "Excuse me—he will need medicine." She pointed toward the door, hoping the guard would understand.

He nodded. Better yet, he stood on the stoop outside of the doorway and let her go in alone. *Ah, he's watching the shed—he must be the only one on guard duty. Terrific.*

There was still a lot of business and bustle from the other rooms of the house where the patients were lodged, and it sounded as if the surgery were in use as well. However, her workspace in the kitchen was quiet. Hopefully she could get through this unnoticed.

She slipped inside, fighting the urge to sneak. *You have every right to be in here. You're caring for one of your own troops. There is no reason anyone should suspect you. Look confident, Jean. Confident!*

For the moment, there was no one in sight. Hastily, she began filling her bag.

"Nurse Hoff?"

She froze, one hand in the satchel, the other reaching for a stack of gauze. *The doctor.*

Letting her fistful drop back to the counter, she daintily picked up just one packet instead, looked it over, and placed it in her bag before turning. *Calm. Don't look rushed. Don't look guilty. You're here for a good reason. Calm, Jean, calm! Please God, don't let him have seen that first grab—*

She looked him right in the eye and smiled. "Doctor. You're up late."

He did not smile back. "So are you."

"Yes. Remember, I'd told you the surgery patient—Corporal Novak—was doing poorly. And you said that I could go and check on him later when the guard came. The guard came for me. It sounds like the corporal's quite ill—feverish. I'm concerned about infection. I was in a bit of a rush to get over there to check him out." *Too much. I'm talking too much.*

The doctor waited, silent. Then he nodded, slowly. "Stubborn man. It's a pity he can't just wait and allow himself to heal. All this impetuousness—it's more likely to get him hurt than just accepting where he is."

He watched her watching him, his expressionless face mirroring hers, giving nothing away. But his words…Her heart fluttered in her chest. *He knows. He knows they're running. Maybe he knows I am too. What will he do?*

With a deep breath, she willed herself calm. *C'mon. Hold it together.* "Yes, I'm sure you're right." She half turned back to the counter, frowned as if thinking carefully, then pulled out a couple more bandages. "Just in case…I can always put them back later," she muttered to herself for his benefit. Then she looked up and smiled. The doctor still stood, watching, between her and the exit. She hoped he didn't see her lips trembling. "I'd better be off—the guard is waiting for me."

"Not Grüber?"

The way he said it…he knew her fear. Shared it, maybe. He'd always been so kind. *I hope he won't get in trouble once I'm gone.*

You can't worry about that, Jean. "No. Not Grüber. The other one who's usually outside the door."

He nodded. "Good. I'm …sorry that…" He closed his eyes and shook his head. "You'd better go, I suppose."

"Yes, they wanted me to hurry." She grabbed one more dressing. *If he's suspicious anyway, I might as well.*

"I'll come along."

Her hand froze over the drawer. "Wha…what?"

"I'll come with you. To check the patient."

She looked over her shoulder, searched his face, but he stared at the floor, his arms crossed. He added, "Not that I don't believe you can handle it, but I would like to make certain of the situation. I hate to see my hard work wasted."

Oh no. Oh no. He can't. They'll…he's not young, and what if—" She pasted on what she hoped was a reassuring smile. "Oh, no, doctor, if you're done in the surgery for now, why don't you go get some sleep? I'm sure we'll be ok without you having to come—you'll have a busy day tomorrow I imagine, especially after all of the rush this evening."

He shook his head. "No. I'd like a look at him before he's sent off anyway." He started for the door, but she didn't follow, frozen in place, trying desperately to *think* even though her brain refused to process this turn of events.

Turning back, he gave her a long look. "Hurry, Nurse. I thought you said it was urgent?"

She nodded. "Yes. Yes, I suppose we'd better.…"

He turned to the door and continued walking. She paused, and her hand groped under the counter behind her. Ever so carefully, she removed the syringe she'd secreted there. She slipped it into her sleeve.

Fifteen

On hearing the heavy door beam slide upward, Leroy gave a sigh of relief. *Thank goodness, she's here.* Much later and they'd risk their attempt being interrupted by the next guard coming on duty. Besides that, her reluctance to tell him the truth earlier had shaken his confidence.

The door pivoted inwards, and Leroy readied himself to deliver his lines, to start yelling for the guard to come in and to hurry. Then the other fellas would do their bit and they'd be off, home free—

His mouth snapped shut as not one, but two shadows came through the door. Jeannie wasn't alone.

Oh sheeeeoot. The doctor.

The guard stayed outside, but the doc didn't hesitate. Holding a flashlight, he walked right over to George, his frown deep enough to be visible even in the dim light. Jeannie trailed in his wake. Her eyes met Leroy's, and she widened them, expression screaming "What now?!"

Leroy grimaced, then mimed slamming his fist into his hand. *Sorry, Jeannie, we're probably gonna have to use some force.* She shook her head and held up her arm. He couldn't see what she pointed to, and the doctor was already kneeling next to George. Leroy slid over to them. The other fellas held their positions, waiting and watching.

Good old George was doing his best to sell it, groaning and moaning and clutching his ribs. If Leroy didn't know better, he'd think it was all real. However, the doc didn't seem to be buying it. His frown deepened as he passed the flashlight over George's face, checking his pupils. He put his hand on George's forehead and looked up at Jeannie.

"You're sure that he's doing worse? He doesn't feel warm."

"I…well, doctor, he certainly looks sick, doesn't he?" she asked. "What do you think of the neck wound?" Her voice was calm, but her hands shook as she stepped back, positioning herself in the shadows behind the doctor. She reached up her sleeve. She drew out a syringe.

Leroy closed his eyes. *Ok. Here we go. Better keep him distracted.* "Hey there, doc. Thanks for comin'. He…he's been feverish—"

"No. He hasn't." The doctor's voice was soft but cold.

"Wha…Whaddya mean, doc?" he stammered. Behind the doc, Jeannie mouthed something. Leroy squinted at her, and she pointed at her arm, then the doctor. Her lips formed the words again—*His arm! I need his arm!* He nodded, but before he could move, a voice called from the doorway. Leroy couldn't understand the German words, but it sounded like a question, like someone asking if the doctor needed help.

Two shadows now stood framed by the doorframe. Leroy's heart sank. *Two guards now. Great.* Little bits of scattered light glinted off the metal in their hands.

Dang it. It's all falling apart… C'mon, God, won't you throw us a bone here?

"Nein," said the doctor. He rattled off something in German, and the guards laughed. They withdrew and stood outside the still-cracked-open door, talking softly and laughing again. However, the doctor's face was grim as he turned cold eyes back on George. He rolled up his sleeves. Leroy's breath caught in his throat. The doctor probed George's ribs, hard. George just moaned.

The doctor leaned in close to George and breathed, "You're going to get her killed."

He knows. Oh shoot…

George didn't take the bait, he just moaned again. "Ugh it hurts… Ma? Mom, are you there?"

The doctor gave him another poke, and he coughed. "Drop this ruse, or I'll alert the guards."

George opened his eyes to slits. He hissed between his teeth, "And whaddya think Grüber'll do to her when you're not around?"

The doctor rocked back on his heels. His face was pale in the reflection of the flashlight. He muttered something that sounded like an oath, then half turned and looked at Jeannie who stood very still, syringe mostly hidden in her hand. Finally, he leaned in again. "You'll all get killed."

"Doc," whispered George, and he pulled one of his most winning smiles. "You play along, and I give you my word, no one'll get killed tonight."

The doctor hesitated again, then he closed his eyes and muttered "In Gott…"

He stood, then turned. Leroy was almost certain that his eyes locked on the syringe before he half stumbled into Jean. Whether it was she or he who pushed the needle into his arm at the last wasn't entirely clear, but the doctor didn't cry out. The world froze for a few silent seconds, then his eyes rolled back in his head, and he went down. Leroy caught him as he fell. He also caught the painful twisting of Jean's face as, with tears leaking out of the corners of her eyes, she cried out, "Doctor? Doctor Schmidt?!" She didn't lose her presence of mind though. She threw the syringe into the dark corner of the room for the guards to find later—proof that the doctor hadn't been complicit.

"Help!" called Leroy, easing the doctor to the floor, then snapping off his flashlight. "Guard! The doctor—poor old guy must've had some kind of fit!"

One guard came rushing in while the other covered them. *Dang it. Smart move, fellas.* The guard who'd come in remained watchful as well. Rather than bending down to check the doctor himself, he stayed standing, pulling out a sidearm and watching as Jean scrambled for the doctor's pulse.

Her panic sounded real as she said, "I can't see anything. Please—he dropped his flashlight—can't we get more light?"

The guard obliged, pulling out a flashlight with his left hand, though still holding the pistol with his right. *Click.* He trained the beam on the nurse and the doctor, not moving the light around the room. The guard standing outside said something, and he replied with a few words, his brow creased.

Jean looked up from the doctor's prone form. "I think he's had a heart attack—please, quick, *schnell*? We have to get him to help; I have to try to help him!" She pointed out the door frantically. "Hospital! Hospital! *Schnell*!"

Whatever else he understood, the guard understood the urgency in her voice. He holstered his sidearm, then called to the second guard who answered and took a step through the doorway. He paused just over the threshold, next to the heavy door.

The first guard bent and tried to rouse the doctor, but the man was limp, dead weight. He barked at Leroy, but Hank stepped up to lift the doctor's feet. Moving fast, Hank edged his way around so that he'd be first out the door. The guard followed, holding the doctor under the arms, and Jean trailed a few paces behind.

As Hank got close to the door, just before he passed into its shadow, he stumbled. He dropped the doctor's feet, cursing. The guard's eyes followed him, so he didn't see the heavy door tilt. His friend did—the first guard tried to call out. It was too late. The thick slab of wood hit the second guard squarely on the head.

His helmet took the brunt of the hit, and he gave a strangled yell. Hank was ready, aiming a sharp kick at his face. His rifle clattered as it fell.

The first guard gave a grunt—Barry and Chuck hadn't waited for him to realize what was happening. He sprawled on the ground, and

Hank relieved him of his pistol.

Without pausing to speak, they got to work. Ed and Roberts emerged from the shadows behind the door and heaved it back into place, replacing the hinge pins. Chuck and Texas Hank dragged the guards farther into the shed. Barry pulled the doctor back as well. Jeannie had already scrambled into the far corner and was pulling on the baggy uniform clothes in an attempt to disguise her figure. Leroy hustled over to the first guard, who was wearing an overcoat, and rolled him over to relieve him of it. George joined him, and they searched the guards' pockets. "C'mon, fellas, one of you's gotta be a smoker," George muttered. The guard moaned, and Hank's arm swung up, holding the sidearm. "No!" hissed George. "No gunshots." Hank settled for another crack to the guard's head. The German lay still.

Leroy handed Jeannie the overcoat. She slipped it on, then pushed her hair up under one of the steel helmets the guards had let fall. Hank handed her the rifle. She snapped it open, checking if it was loaded, then grabbed her medical bag.

"I'll take it," whispered Leroy. "Don't see many guards with luggage." He looked her over. *She still doesn't look much like a man, but in the dark, here's hoping she'll pass.* At least the bulky clothes and overcoat broadened her shoulders a bit.

"Door's all set," whispered Ed. He looked Jean over and grinned. "Good thing you're so tall."

"Mach schneller," she grunted, making her voice as deep as she could.

George eased himself up to standing. Leroy tried not to worry about how heavily he leaned against the wall. At least his voice was strong, if low, when he laughed. "Better try not talking, if that's as deep as you can go, *sir.*"

"Just hurry up," she replied.

Treading softly, they exited the stuffy shack into the cold night air. From the darkness within the prison shed, someone groaned. Quickly, Leroy turned to swing the thick door shut and pull the heavy locking bar down. The guard wasn't usually relieved again until morning. With any luck, their absence wouldn't be noticed until then.

The men fell into line, hands on their heads like good prisoners. Leroy placed himself at the back, closest to Jeannie. Wrapped in her disguise, she marched behind them, rifle pointed at their backs.

They shuffled towards the motor pool, but not too quickly. Like George had said: "Running calls attention. Eager prisoners, too. Don't lollygag, but we gotta get to that ambulance and get moving."

The motor pool wasn't far from their little prison, and they'd pinned their hopes on its ambulances. It would be perfectly ordinary to see one of those driving towards the front. *Of course, prisoners getting on board wouldn't make any sense, so here's hoping we don't get spotted.*

Providence seemed to be smiling on them. Cold gray haze shrouded everything. No one was stirring in their corner of the dark camp. They marched forward—not too fast—and entered the shadow of a truck. An ambulance was the next over. Though the knot of fear didn't leave his belly, Leroy's heart rose. *Maybe we're gonna pull this off after all!*

"*Was ist hier los?*" The voice, much deeper than Jeannie's faux male tones, came from the shadow between the two vehicles.

The fear in Leroy's belly pulled taut. The line of prisoners stopped short.

The red embers of a cigarette cast a dim light on the German's face, throwing the angles of his cheekbones into sharp relief. He took one last drag, then flicked the butt down to hiss in a puddle. George's head turned to watch it fall with a regretful sigh. The guard called something over to Jeannie again, a string of gibberish that ended with "*...morgen abfahren?*"

Jean grunted something unintelligible back and nudged Leroy's back with the rifle, steering him towards the right. He understood and gave a small nod—the ambulance wouldn't work for a prisoner transfer. With the guard right there, watching them, it would make no sense for them to board it. *On to plan B.*

Roberts, at the front of their lineup, glanced back. Jeannie gestured towards the canvas covered truck. He nodded and climbed up. The others followed. *Quick, fellas, quick, before the Jerry thinks this situation through or gets a good look at our guard.* A raindrop slithered down his neck as the haze turned to a drizzle.

Stepping away from the shelter of the vehicles, the German pulled his jacket collar up and strolled over. Even in the dim light, Leroy could make out his frown.

Shooting a glance back at Jeannie, Leroy saw that she was ignoring the guard. Standing straight and tall, she kept her attention fixed on her "prisoners." Roberts and Ed were up, though they'd planned that Ed would need to shift up front to drive. Then Barry vaulted in, followed by Chuck, their back up in case they needed a hotwire job. Hank and George awaited their turns. Leroy shuffled forward slowly, trying to stay unobtrusively close to Jeannie.

The guard came up beside her and let loose another string of German—it sounded like the same words, then a whole bunch of other words.

Jeannie responded in kind, her voice steady and calm, and way too feminine despite her attempt to lower it. Some of her words seemed to confuse the guard—he leaned towards her, frowning, and asked another question. She responded, and Leroy caught the name "Grüber." He could see her hands tremble as they clutched the rifle.

The name seemed to convince the guard. He laughed and pulled out two new smokes. He offered one to Jeannie. She hesitated, then took it.

Leroy glanced up—everyone but George was on the truck. Hands reached down to help him up, but he had turned to watch the guard.

The guard held out a match to Jean, sheltering it with his hand to keep the rain from dousing it. Again, she hesitated. Muttering what were presumably thanks in German, she leaned forward. She tried to keep her head down, her face away from the flame's small illumination. Leroy held his breath. He took half a step toward them, hands balling into fists.

The guard frowned. He leaned forward, scanning her face. He asked a question, and his voice rose—

–then he fell to the ground as George's fist impacted the back of his skull.

Leroy exhaled, torn between relief and a little annoyance that his buddy had acted while he hesitated.

Jeannie threw the cigarette down. "No, wait..." cried George, but his wild reach was a moment too late. "Dang it, woman! I could've used that," he hissed.

"Sorry. And thanks." She leaned down and grabbed the German by the heels, dragging him back into the shadows—Leroy hustled to help her.

Ed vaulted back out of the truck and grabbed her helmet. "Hey, Novak, should we switch back to the ambulance?" He accepted Jeannie's rifle and coat—it would be best for their driver to look as German as possible. Chuck climbed out of the truck and hesitated, waiting for the decision to be made.

A gust of wind carried voices and a laugh from over toward the farmhouse.

"No—no time. This'll work."

"Your call. C'mon, Chuck." Ed led the way to the truck's cab.

Leroy spied the guard's rifle and grabbed it. Jeannie snagged his canteen.

Then he, George, and the nurse climbed into the back where Roberts, Hank, and Barry waited.

The engine roared to life. Shouts echoed from over towards the prison shed. Leroy glimpsed lights. Ed threw the truck into reverse.

GEORGE BRUSHED AWAY the nurse's steadying hand. His teeth rattled as the truck jolted backward. Each jounce burned through his injuries.

The last meds the nurse had given him were only a thin cover for the pain. *Punching that Ted probably wasn't the best move either.* But, what else could he have done? Forcing the pain aside—there'd be time for it when they were out of here—he groped in the darkness hoping for a spare rifle. A pistol. A shovel. Anything.

Leroy peered out over the back of the truck. He held the rifle from the motor pool guard, poised and ready. Hank crouched beside him with the guard's pistol in hand. Barry half stood, silhouetted on the other side of the opening.

Then, Ed spun the wheel. The truck tilted, tossing them like dice in a cup. Leroy tumbled onto his hip with a grunt. George half fell on the nurse. She yowled like an angry cat. Barry nearly rolled out the back. Roberts caught his sleeve, steadying him.

The engine complained as the gears shifted. Forward, gathering speed over the ruts. Not enough speed. *Hurry it up, Ed!*

The first shot poked a hole in the canvas. It shone like a tiny, dim star.

"Get down!" George pushed the nurse flat. He and the others followed in a tangle of limbs. Harsh breathing vied with engine noise. Shots and shouts called from outside.

George raised his head fractionally. Leroy had his head down but still crouched near the back. More dim stars peppered the dark walls. *I wonder how many are hitting up front. I should be up there, not hiding in the rear...* A jolt knocked his chin into the floor. Salty blood flooded his mouth. *C'mon, c'mon Ed. This is going to work. It's got to—*

A shadowy form loomed at the open back, grabbing the edge of the canvas. It pushed past Leroy.

Leroy pushed back, swinging the rifle.

George tried to rise. Another jolt threw him off balance.

The German raised a pistol, took a shot, but he was off balance too.

George kicked out hard with both feet. He hit the German in the shins. The German grunted, swayed. Roberts's shadow loomed up as he shoved him off the truck.

George gasped, trying to keep his breaths shallow. *Uf—ribs didn't like that!* Still, he had to know what was going on. He heaved himself to a crouch.

The shapes of the camp were receding. Flashlight beams crisscrossed in the hazy air. No other vehicles were following, not yet.

This is gonna work. Anzio, here we come.

BAM.

The truck swerved, throwing them about like rag dolls.

"We hit?" cried Leroy.

"The engine—" Roberts said.

"Sounded like—" George gasped as Barry's knee bumped his stitches.

"Oh shoot, we're gonna get shot—" Barry whimpered.

"Get off me," grunted Hank, pushing Barry aside, trying to get his pistol arm free.

George tried to rise, but another jolt threw him back. The nurse was thrown against him. She cried out something that sounded like a garbled prayer. George grabbed her arm, trying to steady the both of them. "Lee—can you see anything?"

"I don..."

The truck gave one last, great jolt. George's head struck the floor. For the first time in a while, something hurt more than his ribs.

It took him a moment to realize that the truck was no longer moving. The floor beneath his head vibrated—*tires spinning. We're stuck. And they're coming.*

"They're coming! We gotta move!" Leroy had found his feet. Hank vaulted down, then Barry clawed his way out. Roberts grabbed George on one side. Leroy hustled back and grabbed him on the other. Jean scrambled along beside them.

George shook his head, trying to clear it, sending a jolt of pain through his stitches. "I'm fine—just..."

"Just shut up," the nurse growled. "Let them help you. Otherwise, you'll slow us down."

The six of them emerged into the night. The truck had slid into a ditch where the camp's dirt track met the larger road. Shouts followed them, echoing through the dark.

George worked to find his footing on the rocky, uneven ground. He scanned the terrain. Ahead of them and to the right, the ground rose towards the inland mountains. To the left, across the road it dropped away, towards the open level land and the sea. Toward Anzio.

Barry was babbling. "Uphill. They won't look for us uphill—there'll be cover—"

George put a steadying hand on his shoulder. "Hold on, buddy, we've gotta check on the others—"

Leroy was already on it. He came jogging back around. "No one in the cab. Some blood on the seat, but—"

"We're here!" Ed hissed from the dark off to the right. He and Chuck crept onto the roadside.

The sound of running feet and voices and the sweep of flashlights came closer.

Ed said, "We gotta run for it."

"North." Hank's voice was firm, decided. "I'm following the road and heading north. Gonna hide out in Rome." He stared George down. "You coming?"

George shook his head. "Nope. I'm for Anzio. Across the road and south."

Roberts, with a nod, headed to the edge of the road, downhill. "I'm not waiting around. See you from the skies, fellas. Nurse."

"Wait!" the nurse called and pressed a few supplies from her satchel into his hands with a few hurried words.

A shot echoed overhead.

"We gotta go—c'mon!" Leroy hefted the rifle and reached for the nurse's arm, then pulled his hand back.

Even now, kid? Aloud, George said, "Ok. Let's go. Ed?"

"I'm with you," said the driver with a grin.

George nodded. "Ok. See ya, Hank."

The lean Texan nodded, then ducked and ran. Wilson and Barry watched him, hesitated, then turned to follow.

"Wait!" cried Jean in a frantic whisper. Chuck paused. She ran over and handed him a little bundle like the one she'd given Roberts. "Sulfa, bandages—"

"Thanks." Wilson managed a weak smile. "Us or them?"

Jean hesitated, looking between the two groups. Another shot rang out. She threw up her hands and turned, following Leroy, Ed, and George.

Sixteen

George led the way, scrambling over the verge of the road and down the slope. A shot echoed—getting closer. He increased his pace. Each inhale burned all around his ribcage. *Better than* not *breathin' though!* The sounds of the others followed—soft grunts or muttered imprecations as they stumbled on the uneven terrain. The rain had stopped, but the footing was slick and treacherous. Rocks slid underfoot. Tangled weeds grasped his feet—perfect trip lines.

The slope ended at a narrow gully. George grabbed a gnarled olive trunk and paused, gasping. "Hold up!" he hissed. The three shapes following him slid to a stop.

"We gotta run, whatcha doin?" Leroy scrubbed his hand through his hair, looking back over his shoulder, towards the road, towards the beams of flashlights crisscrossing it.

"In case..." George pulled in another breath. "In case we get separated, keep heading south, parallel to the road. Don't try to get into Cisterna, but when you can see the outskirts, find a spot to hunker down. We'll try to meet up there. Whoever makes it, wait until...let's say day after tomorrow. Then, whoever's there, try to cross over the open ground that night, back to Anzio.

Ed nodded. "Ok, sounds good. Ow!" He winced—the nurse had taken advantage of the brief lull to check the bloody spot on his arm.

"Just a graze," she whispered, and then they were off, hunching as they ran, trying to crash through the underbrush quietly.

At least there's some cover down here. It almost looked like this had been a farmed plot of land. The gully widened and flattened, and George turned left, down the slope on the far side. Olive trees loomed out of the dark at regular intervals. George wove through the trunks. Despite his ribs, he was feeling better. Maybe it was just adrenaline, but as long as it got him away—

A shot rang out. Angry, guttural voices echoed down from the roadbed.

He skidded to a halt in the deeper shadows under a tree. The nurse reached out and caught the trunk before knocking into him. Ed and Leroy joined them. Huddled in the dark, the four of them paused, panting and gasping and straining their ears.

The voices from above continued, cutting clear through the night air. "Can you tell what they're saying?" he breathed into Jean's ear. Without the German helmet her hair had come half undone, wreathing her face in thin, spectral wisps. Her eyes were wide and frightened.

"They're…they're splitting up. Some uphill, some down…" she paused, straining her ears. "I think…I think someone said dogs."

Ed muttered a soft curse, then apologized.

George gathered his thoughts. "Ok. We gotta keep moving, but keep it as quiet as you can, ok?" Three heads nodded in the dark, and off they went, sliding through the shadows. The three soldiers' training kicked in—it was always hard not to bunch up on patrol, but it was safer not to present a big target. They spread out, a few trees between each of them.

The nurse hadn't done this before, and she followed close behind him—*probably trying to make sure I won't just keel over.* Her quick, frightened breaths hissed between her teeth.

He searched out the others in his peripheral vision. Leroy to the left and a little behind, Ed to his right—a dark shadow behind Ed. Was that another tree or—

Crack!

Ed's shadow jerked, then fell without a sound.

Behind him, Jean gasped but didn't yell. George swung behind the tree just ahead. "Get down!" he tried to yell quietly—it came out as a croak. He crouched in the long grasses, heart thundering in his ears. Leroy and Jean must have listened—he couldn't see them. Couldn't see anyone else either. Seconds ticked by like hours.

Maybe I didn't see someone. Maybe they don't know where we are. Maybe it was a lucky shot.

A twig snapped, over near where Ed had been. A flashlight clicked on.

His eyes dazzled, George could see nothing but a dark, hulking form. *How'd he get here so fast?*

The German soldier's flashlight skimmed over the leaves and branches. All was quiet.

George prayed that the tree's thin concealment would be enough. As the flashlight moved along the ground, he spotted the nurse. She huddled behind a clump of grass. Good girl, she was keeping perfectly still. Hidden, hopefully. Still no sign of Leroy. *That's a good sign, though. The kid would've hit the dirt right off the bat. He's got to be fine—*

The flashlight clicked off.

Why's he not calling for backup? Whatever the reason, their pursuer made no noise. Echoed calls still sounded from the roadbed, but their little valley under the trees was silent. The four of them were alone, each their own little island in the dark.

Small sounds became magnified.

Boots brushed the grass.

A twig snapped.

A rustle came from a different direction.

Another Kraut? Maybe not—it was over about where Leroy should be. *Whatcha doing, kid? C'mon, just wait it out. We'll get out of this yet.*

The boots continued forward, then stopped.

George didn't move, didn't breathe. He wished he could slow his heartbeat. Wished he had a weapon. Wished he could see the danger.

Then, to his left—a scuffle, a shriek. The light flashed on. Grüber held it.

He also held the nurse by the hair.

With a thick chuckle that held no warmth and without releasing his grip, Grüber bent to lean the flashlight against a tussock. The light shone into the nurse's eyes. She flinched, tried to turn her face away, but he held her head in the beam. His free hand drew a Mauser.

"Ahhhh." Bending, he pulled her face close to his. "The others are all searching along the road, but I thought I smelled you. Where are the others?"

"I'm alone." She spat the words, her cool façade cracking, but not broken. He jerked on her hair, and she winced.

"Try again, *Fräulein* . Though I could wish you might be telling the truth…you and I, we've been waiting for some time alone together." He put the gun to her temple.

With a snarl, Leroy rose out of the dark, the flashlight magnifying his shadow to tremendous proportions.

Grüber swung around, tried to aim.

Leroy swung the rifle at Grüber's head like a club.

The German stepped back, taking the blow on his shoulder. He held on to the pistol and the nurse—

—but now his back was to George. Lunging, George got ahold of the arm that held the nurse. The big German, hollering for all he was worth, pivoted and struck him in the side with the gun barrel.

Pain seared George's torso. He lost his grip, dry heaving. Unable to breathe, he fell. Dimly, he saw the nurse struggling free, then grappling for the gun. The Mauser slipped from Grüber's hand.

But now Grüber held Leroy's gun barrel in his other hand. More lights were flashing down the hill. The German shook the nurse loose. She fell with a sharp cry. He reached for his hip and pulled out a wicked-looking knife.

Leroy was too close to dodge.

Oh God, not the kid, not the kid—

Crack.

Grüber stood stock still for a moment, then slowly slumped to the ground.

Jean knelt in the beam of light, the gun in her shaking hands.

"I…I…is he…?" she whispered, barely audible over the cries of their approaching pursuers.

The German lay, limp and still.

Giving a little cry, the nurse dropped the weapon.

Leroy doused the flashlight, grabbing her arm. "C'mon, Jeannie. It's ok. He's gone now. C'mon, we gotta—"

He turned towards George. His eyes widened. "George? Georgie? What...are you gonna…can you run?"

George tried to give him his old grin, but it took so much effort. "Sure, kid. Sure, just…help me up."

He allowed the kid to pull him to his feet. *Breathe. Just breathe.* Each inhale was agony. The nurse watched, dazed. She said, to no one in particular, "I was never gonna kill anyone—"

Her eyes locked on his torso, and she came back with a jolt. She found her voice, shaky though it was. "You can't run."

He looked down, feeling the warm wet of the dark stain that was slowly spreading. *Gotta breathe.* He sucked air in through his nose. "Sure I can, Nursey. I gotta—" His legs gave way, and he sank back to the ground. "I gotta—"

"Shut up, George." Leroy's voice was hard. He looked at Jean. "Is he gonna make it? Can you patch him up?"

She stared back at him. "I…well…"

Leroy grabbed her arm so hard she jumped. "They'll be here in a second—*can* you?"

"Given time, we could get him moving, I think, but there's no time—"

The kid's jaw locked. Nothing about him looked laughable in that moment. "I'll get you time." He grabbed George's shoulder. Everything was hazed with pain, but the kid found his eyes. "Look. You. Let her help you. No fussing, no fighting—you LET her. Then the two of you head south—toward Cisterna, right, but stopping before you get there—for our meet up, ok? I'll meet you there."

George swallowed. *No, this wasn't how it was supposed to be!* "Kid, wait, you gotta…"

Leroy shook his shoulder, gentle but urgent. "Look after her, Georgie. I'll…I'll meet you. Day after tomorrow. Otherwise, you just get safe. I'll—"

The shouts were too close. Leroy shook his head; there was nothing left to say. He grabbed the nurse's hand and gave her a look that said everything. She stared at him eyes wide. "Le…Leroy?" she stammered. He turned away and grabbed the German's flashlight and the rifle.

The approaching lights were maybe ten, fifteen yards away.

"Hey! Hey George, wait up!" Leroy hollered, and off he ran at a right angle, crashing through the underbrush.

The approaching footsteps veered after him.

Two shots rang through the night.

George felt the nurse's hand, resting over his wound, twitch with each shot. He tugged on her arm. She put her head down by his mouth. "He's bought us some time. Come on."

She shook her head. Moisture touched his cheek. She was crying.

With a groan that he couldn't quite muffle, he rolled to his knees. Pain shot through his body so hard it nearly doubled him over.

That seemed to wake her up—she grabbed his arm and hissed in his ear, "You shouldn't move until I can get a look at that."

He matched her tone, grim fear clutching his heart as he answered,

"If they catch Leroy, or realize he's alone, where do you think they'll come?" He nodded towards where Grüber lay. "And what do you think they'll do?"

"You don't..." her whispered voice shook. "You don't think they caught him...do you?"

No, they can't have caught him. Not the kid. His mind flashed back to his kid brother's lifeless body, Norrie's wide, empty eyes. George forced the image down. *Not NOW.* "I hope not, lady. But if they did, it's even more important that we get you safely outta here. He ran because of you."

"Because of me..." she whispered. The words carried a bitter weight that cut through the night.

"Get the gun. Then come on. Help me up."

She obeyed. The gun went into her satchel, then George used her arm to pull himself up. Good thing she was so tall. George could stand straight with his arm around her neck and her arm around his waist.

They hobbled off into the dark.

It was a nightmare journey. Branches caught at George's feet. Pulled at his legs. Whipped him in the face until he wasn't sure if his skin was wet from the rain-soaked leaves or from new cuts. They heard no nearby sounds of pursuit—it appeared that Leroy's ploy had worked. *God, whatever happens to me, he's gotta be ok. We just have to get to the meet-up.* What was the plan again? *Day after tomorrow. We'll have to hustle.* His boot caught in an animal hole, and he stumbled. He grunted—so did Jean. Her labored breathing rasped in his ear. He tried to lean a little less heavily, but his injuries screamed.

It seemed as if the night would never end. Just when it seemed he couldn't take another step, he noticed a lightening in the east. The sky slowly changed from black to charcoal to gray. "We'd better find a place to hunker down during daylight," he gasped.

Jean nodded, "Where are we going to—" and then they broke through a line of trees. Before them, standing in a small, weed-filled clearing and lit up in the early morning sun like a Sign, stood a rundown stone structure. No light shone through the black, empty doorway, and no road led to it.

Jean slid his arm off her shoulders, easing him down to sit in a clump of weeds beneath a tree. "What…" he started to ask.

"I'm going to scout it out," she whispered. She pulled out the pistol, holding it gingerly.

George was too tired to argue—besides, she was right. It needed to be checked. *Stupid to make it away and then to be caught trying to find a place to hide…I'd do it myself.* But he knew the truth, even if he couldn't admit it. He couldn't stir another step. "You can handle that?" He nodded toward the gun.

She took a firmer grip and nodded.

As the nurse crept across the clearing and as her slim form was swallowed by the dark door's mouth, George tried not to think about what Leroy would say if he were here. He counted the seconds and couldn't repress a relieved sigh when she reemerged. On her return, she whispered, "I think it'll do. Looks like it's maybe used for storage. Not recently, though. Doesn't smell like animals, no signs of people. There's a bit of a road behind, but it's overgrown. There's stairs and a little loft."

"Sounds like the Anzio Hilton."

She grinned, but it wobbled on her face. "C'mon. Let's get you in there and see about that bleeding."

Gritting his teeth, he mustered his last strength and hobbled along beside her. It looked like she was right—the building appeared long abandoned. *Seems almost too good to be true. Of course, if they're searching this way, an old abandoned barn would probably be high on their list of places to check. Safe or no, though, this'll have to do.* Inside, George collapsed against the rough stone wall and leaned his head back. He pulled in breath after fiery breath. Through the haze of weariness and pain, all he could think of was Leroy. *God, please don't take the kid. Please, let Leroy have made it through the night.*

Seventeen

Leroy crashed through the underbrush. Twigs slapped his face and tore at his skin. He didn't holler anymore. Too obvious—a smart pursuer might figure out that he was trying to decoy them away. He'd thrown the lit flashlight away, hoping it might serve as a distraction. Had dropped the rifle, too. Speed was his only chance. Crisscrossing through whatever patch of undergrowth looked loudest, he hoped he was making enough noise for three.

A bullet buzzed overhead.

Well, at least someone's following.

Another bullet thunked into a tree nearby. Lungs burning, he gulped air and pushed his legs harder. *Just like running sprints in track.*

Well, not quite. Shouts and wavering flashlight beams followed him. Too close. A stitch burned in his side.

Pretty soon, I'll have to quiet down. Get out of sight. Hopefully, they'll go right past me. Just gotta find a good spot. He scanned the brush ahead, looking for cover.

A dog barked.

Through the sweat coursing down his back, Leroy shivered. *Shoot. Lord, they've got dogs—* So much for going to ground. His pulse pounded in his ears.

"Ugh!" Something grasped him around the ankles. His feet stopped, caught, while his body continued forward. Arms pinwheeling, he struggled to keep his footing. A half-stumbling leap carried him over the ensnaring brambles. His left foot found solid ground. His right found a rabbit hole.

Pop.

Pain seared through his ankle as it rolled. He bit back a cry, hopping back to his left leg. The next step onto the right brought tears to his eyes—*Sprained? Broken?*—but he could not stop.

A beam of light shot over his left shoulder, followed by a crack and the whine of a bullet. Another C*rack!* Searing pain burned across the top of his scalp. *Oh God, they can see me—*

One of the flashlight beams caught an area of deeper shadow over to the left. A depression in the land—maybe a stream? Water. If he could lose his scent in water—

Limping, leaden legs pumping, he veered. His breath came in gasps. Fear and adrenaline could only carry him so far. The searching lights beamed back and forth, gilding the tips of leaves and casting sharp shadows. Another deep bark echoed through the night, followed by a shout.

He stumbled forward, skidding through loose rock and scree. The land dropped sharply away—it was definitely a stream bed. If he could just get down into it…what good would that do? They'd seen him. They'd be right above him in a moment. He could envision what would happen next. First the lights would beam down the gully. He'd get a little farther maybe, while they aimed. Then the shot would come—right between the shoulder blades. His body cringed at the imagined impact. He pushed his legs harder but couldn't outrun the image. Would he bleed out first? Or would they just let the dogs tear him up—

One of the flashlight beams grazed his shoulder. A triumphant cry echoed through the night. He pulled in another deep breath. Maybe his last.

The lights went out. All of them. Pitch dark dropped over the world. All was silent except for his too-loud boots and rasping breath. He stumbled from the wonder of it. *What in the…?*

Then he heard it. A hum, a low drone. It approached rapidly, growing louder by the moment. But not behind him—overhead. *Planes!*

The engines whined low overhead, and a gust of wind stirred his sweat-soaked hair. *Thud thud thud thud thud*—bullets hit the dirt behind him, near where the lights had been. The dog barked fiercely. An oath and a cry rang out. The engine passed away behind them.

One of ours—oh thank you, Jesus and the U.S. Army Airforce! Then, he became aware that the engines were growing louder again. They were coming back for another pass. The guns opened up again, coming towards him this time—

A black pit opened before his feet. He stumbled as he half ran, half rolled into the gully. Salty blood filled his mouth—he'd bitten his tongue. He came to an abrupt stop at the bottom, a rock banging his shin and his hand splashing into a trickle of water. The engine of the plane roared overhead, then away, into the night.

He lay still and breathed. Through the thudding of his heartbeat, he strained his ears for barking dogs. Voices. Engines. Anything.

A breeze hissed through the dry grasses above the gully's rim. Nothing else stirred. No lights flashed. Not a whisper or a whimper carried through the dark.

Could the plane have gotten them all? He listened a little longer, his heartbeat slowing. *Maybe. But I'd better not count on it. They might just be lying low, like me. Don't figure they'd want their lights on for a little bit, just to be sure the plane's gone, even if they are still breathing.*

He eased his hand out of the water. *Cold. Must run down from the mountains.* Not very deep, but it was something. Pushing himself to his feet, Leroy stepped into the stream, boots and all. Even in the dark, he half crouched as he limped off. He followed the streambed uphill. Hopefully, he'd throw any remaining pursuers—or dogs—off his scent.

Slimy rocks rolled under his feet, and he stumbled, praying no one was around to hear the splashing. *Careful! No good turning the other ankle.* The streambed was slick with muck, the water barely reaching over the toes of his boots. *Hope I'm not just leaving a nice trail of footprints for someone to follow come dawn.* In the dark, he couldn't tell. He'd just have to hope that the current would be enough to wash away any sign before daylight. *Don't think about it. Just keep moving.*

The little stream's course rose steeply, and he used his hands as well as his feet to pull himself along. Water seeped into his boots and wet his sleeves. He shivered as the sweat on his back dried. Every stumble, every dislodged stone made him pause, listening. Were his pursuers dead? Had they given up? Or were they just waiting for him, ready to spring out of the dark?

Or worst of all, had they given up on him and gone back to find easier prey? Had George and Jeannie been able to get away?

It sure sounded like they all followed me, but what if someone stayed? Or what if Jeannie couldn't get George moving again? Dear God, help them, he's so hurt. And Jeannie... Jeannie's shocked, pale face flashed across his mind, twisted with terror as she dropped the gun. *She wasn't kidding—she does know how to shoot.* Brave girl, she'd handled the escape but when Grüber'd shown up... *She shouldn't have had to deal with him. Served him right, but I should've been the one to stop him. I should've been able to do something—*

His ankle gave out.

With his last ounce of strength, he gripped the stones beneath him. Pulling himself to the far side of the stream from his pursuers—if he still had pursuers—he collapsed onto a flat patch of sandy soil.

He closed his eyes. *If they're going to catch me, they'd better just do it. I'm done.*

Lying still—blessedly still—allowed his body time to complain.

His ankle throbbed, and his calves burned, and his mouth felt as dry as sandpaper. *At least there's water.* With a grunt, he leaned over the stream. Scrubbing his grimy hands under the icy water, he then used them to scoop some into his mouth. It made his teeth ache and left sandy grit coating his throat. He tried to filter it through his teeth, hoping it was just sand dirtying it up—he had nothing to treat it with. *Wouldn't it just figure if I ended up with dysentery after all this?*

The cold invigorated him. He splashed his face, scrubbed his hands and arms, then braced himself to investigate his injuries. First, he gingerly probed his scalp. The bullet wound burned. His fingers found the sticky spot where blood had matted his hair together. Pausing, he took a few deep breaths. Forcing himself to probe the area further, he relaxed. It didn't seem to be bleeding anymore, didn't seem to go too deep. *Guess it's ok.*

Now to the ankle.

It throbbed, and he tried not to jar it as he worked on his stiff, muddy bootlaces. Gritting his teeth, he pulled off the boot, then the sock. Flakes of skin peeled off with it. Disgusting. *If I ever get out of here, I'll never take clean socks for granted again, Lord.*

He felt the ankle, turning his foot gingerly. *Probably just twisted, maybe sprained. Not broken, I hope.* It had started to swell and was tender to the touch. *Hey, coach, can I get a bag of ice? Well, maybe I've got something that can do the same thing.*

Easing his foot back into the cold water, he felt with his toes until he found a deeper hole—somewhere he could immerse the injured joint. He leaned forward and swished his filthy sock in the water. *Wish I had something to wrap the ankle with. But maybe if the sock's cold enough, it'll help a little. Too bad I didn't get some bandages from Jeannie.* He wished he could ask the nurse's advice, wished he could see her and George, wished he knew for sure that they'd gotten away, that they were still alive.

I've gotta try to find them. He inched his sock back onto his foot, then the boot. The swelling made it hard to lace, but he gritted his teeth and pulled it as tight as he could. Using one of the boulders in the streambed for support, he pulled himself up. The ankle complained—so did most of his other muscles—but it held him. Favoring it as much as he could, he scrambled to the top of the bank and peered into the night.

The problem was, in the dark, he had no idea where he was. Running as fast and far as he could, weaving through the landscape to try to throw his pursuers off, he'd gotten himself completely turned around. He scanned the sky, but haze cloaked it, concealing any stars. He pivoted. If he could just get a look at the mountains…nothing. They were hidden in the deep dark.

Leroy pushed down rising panic. *Ok. It's probably a couple of hours before dawn. No way to tell if I'm headed in the right direction. So. What do I do?*

Follow George. That's what he'd always done, ever since he set foot on this shore. But George wasn't here. *I could head downstream, cross over it, try to find the two of them.* But they'd said they would head south, parallel to the road, toward Cisterna. There was no guarantee that they were where he'd left them. Even if they were, what chance did he have of finding them? *I could head back to the road, find where we left it, and then…* And then, what? Give himself back up to the Germans?

No. Gotta stick to the plan. Find the road, but don't get too close. Follow its line south until I'm around Cisterna. Meet the others, cut across no-man's land, get to our lines.

But I still don't know where I am. And the odds of actually finding them… The panic rose in his throat again.

Settle down. Think it through. What are my options? One, go back the way I came. That's a good way to get caught. Maybe get George and Jeannie caught too. Two, stay here. I feel like I ran forever, but I'm probably not nearly far enough away from the camp, especially with all that zigging and zagging. Besides, wouldn't anyone following figure we'd head for water?

No, this isn't a safe place to be come daylight.

Ok. I'll have to keep going. Not too fast, so I can keep my ears open. Try to find some shelter, and then when it's daylight, get my bearings.

Now, which way? If the stream was heading uphill, likely it was coming from the mountains, so he wouldn't want to go that way. If he headed forward, at a right angle to the stream—that ought to be north. He hoped so, anyway. *And if it is, I shouldn't have to worry about minefields or patrols. At least, that was what Hank figured.* Then, tomorrow he could circle back around to find the others.

He hobbled off through the dark, angling away from the stream without letting it get too far behind—not yet. Using his hands and his good leg as much as he could, he tried to keep to sturdy stone and the scattered shelter of tree trunks. Off to his left, the land sloped downhill a little. His ankle didn't like the uneven ground—between that and the pain in his head, his stomach roiled. *Good thing there's nothing in it, I guess.*

The night seemed like it would never end. One step, then another. The silence was broken by occasional sounds of artillery—distant, but still audible on the edge of hearing. Leroy's skin cringed a little at each blast. His brain might realize that it was far away, but his body remembered the fear.

His wet sock chafed his throbbing ankle. Cold sweat dripped into his eye, despite the chill that made little clouds in front of his mouth each time he exhaled. His ears and shoulders ached from the tension of listening, always listening. Loneliness wrapped around him in a cold, empty embrace. No George to follow. No Jeannie. No squad. No orders. No family or foreman or—

A twig snapped.

Leroy froze.

Something rustled in the woods behind and to his right, in the direction of the streambed.

Maybe I'm not so alone after all.

Might just be an animal, out looking for food.

Might not.

As quietly as he could manage, he turned towards the left, away from the gully. His feet were reluctant despite the fear creeping up his back to his scalp. The streambed had been his trail in the wilderness, something that would lead him back to his friends. Some connection. Leaving it meant truly being alone. *But that's what I chose—to go alone. To give them a chance.*

For his friends, and for his safety, he turned towards the aloneness and crept, slow, careful, and nearly silent, into the dark.

THE NIGHT WANED. The stars had emerged, then paled. The eastern mountains, behind Leroy, stood dark and solid against the charcoal sky.

He stumbled, his feet so numb that he hardly noticed the twinging ankle. Leaves and twigs crackled underfoot, but it didn't seem to signify. He hadn't seen or heard anything for the last hour, or two, or twenty—time wasn't measured in hours anymore. It had narrowed and refined itself to the action of lifting his bad foot, placing it carefully on the firmest piece of ground he could find and supporting it with the stick he'd picked up as he swung his good foot forward. Place. Step. Repeat.

His dragging foot caught. Stumbling forward, his hand shot out to catch himself. It landed on something smooth and hard that bit into his palm. Recognition pierced his foggy brain. *Wire?*

Barbed wire! He yanked his hand back, expecting to feel the pain of metal spikes tearing his skin. To his surprise, he felt nothing. To be sure, he felt his palm with his other hand, then raised it to his eyes. Dirty, but not bleeding.

He reached out a probing finger. The wire was smooth. He followed it, trailing his finger along it lightly. *Booby trap? Maybe. Or...* His fingertip came to a narrow wooden fence post, then a bit of plant hanging over. He couldn't see much, but it felt familiar, long and thin, with a little curlicue hanging off it. Recognition flashed through his weary brain—it was the remains of a *vine! This must be a vineyard!* They didn't grow grapes up on the Iron Range, but he'd seen pictures of them in Dad's old, illustrated Bible.

A vineyard meant shelter, maybe food. His fingers scrabbled over the vine, hunting for a cluster of grapes. Nothing. Too bad it was winter. But nearby there must be a house, a barn. Maybe people.

He hesitated at that. Italy was out of the war—they'd surrendered back in the fall, months ago, when the Allies first invaded. Some Italian partisans had joined up with the Allies. Most of the people he'd met in Naples had been happy to see the Americans coming through.

Still, what if the farmer still had…sympathies?

Or what if the Germans had already taken over the farm?

Or what if…

The thoughts swirled around. He wished George were there. George always had a plan, always had a way to work things out to their advantage. *But George isn't here. He's somewhere with Jeannie and broken ribs, and I gotta find them again and help them.*

So. He needed a place to rest. His ankle and hungry belly and dizzy head told him so. He staggered forward, following the fence line.

A dark shape loomed up to his right. A barn.

He staggered up to the wooden double doors. Pulling up the beam, he tilted his head, trying to get a look inside. The warm smells of fodder and animals wafted out, and it was all he could do not to fling himself through the door at once. *Settle down. Could be booby trapped. Shorty was talking about Jerry booby trapping barns so we'd get blowed up when we try to sleep…but this should be ok. I'm behind their lines still…I think.* His head was too fuzzy, and he was no planner. Not like George. He'd just have to do it. He muttered a little prayer, ending with "Thy will be done," and ventured in.

The barn was dark and blessedly warm. Something rustled over to the side. He squinted—a cow stood, watching him from her stall.

Shush now, Bessie! I'm nothing to fret yourself about. "Bessie" seemed unconcerned. She swished her tail again and blinked at him.

A pile of hay waited in the corner. Without another thought or worry, he collapsed into the prickly softness and was asleep at once.

He didn't wake up for hours—not until the sun had pulled itself over the horizon. It wasn't the sun that woke, him, however, but a voice.

"*Americano*?"

EIGHTEEN

"WELL, IT DOESN'T LOOK TOO BAD," Jean lied, leaning back on her heels and contemplating George's colorful torso. The early morning light shone through their shelter's stone doorframe, tracing pale streaks through the suspended dust. The whole structure smelled of damp and dust and the old brown straw that had sifted down from the loft above. For a moment, she was back in the faded red barn on Joe's family property—she and her brother helping rake it out, Joe talking about his plans, how they were going to fix the place up. The three of them still just gangly kids, with the whole world ahead of them—

"Nursey? You there?"

She blinked. "Yes. Stitches first."

Obediently, George tilted his head, exposing the line of stitches. He couldn't conceal the flinch that stretched his face into a brief grimace. The flesh around the wound was still red, still warm to the touch. Jean bit her lip. *What I wouldn't give for some penicillin.* She dug out some of the precious sulfa and pain medication that she'd managed to smuggle out from under the doctor's nose. Although, judging from those last moments before their escape, perhaps he'd known what she was doing all along. *I hope I got the dose right. I hope he's ok. Please, God, don't let me have killed him, too—*

Realizing that she still held the tablet in her cold, grimy fingers, she said, "Here. Take this."

George eyed it. "What is it?"

"Just something for the pain. Why?"

"I don't want anything that's gonna knock me out."

"Well, let's take a look at your ribs." Her mouth twisted into a wry grin. "You might change your mind."

Yesterday, before the escape, she'd been pleased to see that the massive bruises sheathing George's torso had started to fade from deep, angry reds and purples to browns and yellows. The old bruises still looked better, but the spot on his left side where Grüber had struck him stood out, dark and painful. The area sported a spectacular array of unnatural colors that were painful to look at and crusted in blood. Whether there was any damage underneath, whether he'd suffered any internal injuries...that was the question. She reached toward the wound, but George caught her wrist with his right hand.

"Hey, Nursey! Let's just assume it hurts and leave it alone, ok?"

"Fair enough." He released her, and she stared at the spot, picturing the anatomy charts. *One of the lower three ribs. Hopefully just one. Probably not just fractured anymore—and in a good position to puncture something.* There was plenty of soft tissue in there—liver, stomach, spleen.

At least we found a spot to rest. They'd decided to wait through the daylight hours and head out again at night. Theoretically, if they were where they thought they were, they ought to be able to get the few miles south and meet up with Leroy in plenty of time. Assuming they were where they thought they were...but that was another worry for another time. For now, she needed a better idea of just how able the corporal would be of travel when night fell.

His breathing sounded all right—a little strained, but not like the boys who'd come in with punctured lungs—and he seemed to be handling the pain all right. Not begging for morphine anyway. *Pity. If he'd just take some medication, maybe he'd get sleepy and shut up. He's been nothing but ornery and angry...* As she had the thought, he started in again.

"I'm just saying that, since we had Fritzie down anyway you should've checked his pockets. Who knows what else we could've found? That knife of his, for one thing. It could've been handy." He scratched behind his ear. "Some cigarettes too. That would've been nice."

She pulled out bandages. There was nothing to be done about internal injuries, but she could wrap the ribs, offering some compression and stability. "You couldn't smoke here. The smell would give us away."

"To who? Looks like we've run right into the middle of nowhere." He grunted as she put a bit of gauze against the worst patch of bruising, where the skin had broken.

She pulled his right hand across and handed him the edge of the bandage. "Hold that there, please." His groan as she made him lean forward made her frown again, and he flinched when she touched his left shoulder. She got to the end of the bandage and tucked it in. "There. That's the last of it. I felt like I was filching so much before we ran, and now look. We could've used more. Of course, I don't suppose he—Grüber—would have been carrying any of that..." her voice trailed off. She pursed her lips and looked away, unwilling to think about everything that had happened. She rallied herself, tried to find her old calm. "Anyway. You should sleep while you can."

George snorted. "Not likely."

She worked to keep her voice even. "Well, if you'd LET me give you some morphine, it would ease the pain—"

"And then what'd we do if they come around looking for us?"

"I thought you said we were in the middle of nowhere." Silence. She ventured, "Do you really think they will?"

George sighed, reached behind his ear, then pulled his cigarette-less hand back with a grimace. "Dunno. We're not valuable prisoners—no officers. Well, except you, I suppose." He pulled his shirt around his shoulders, using only his right arm. "But we did leave Fritzie dead… along with any cigarettes in his possession."

Jean couldn't muster exasperation—at the mention of the man's death she could feel her face pale and hated herself for her weakness. *I had to do it. Had to stop him.* She closed her eyes, her empty stomach turning. Her aching scalp felt again his thick fingers seizing her hair.

She could feel the weight of the gun in her hand.

Feel the pull of the trigger when she squeezed.

And then, in the dark behind her eyes, she could see him, too. The night shadows had hidden most of his face, but not his eyes. His eyes—going from vengeful, filthy, to blank and glazed as he fell. The red blood seeping through his uniform, a strange dark flower.

He's dead. He's gone now and he can't do any of those things he said. He can't hurt me. I should be happy. She brushed the tears out of her eyes.

"Hey there, Nursey. I didn't know you cared so much about smokes." George's weak grin faded as he looked her over. It morphed into a frown of frustration. "Just when I was thinking you had some nerve." He turned his head and spat onto the dirt floor. "Should've known better." Easing his body back against the wall, he started to fold his arms across his chest, then flinched and left them at his side. He continued, his voice flat and cold. "So. Is it time for the break down? How're you gonna fall apart on me, hmm? Gonna throw a temper tantrum? Weeping, crying, bringing the rest of the Teds down on us? Then I suppose when they've got a gun to our heads, you'll try to *beg*—"

Her tears turned hot. "Why you… you cold-hearted—" she spluttered.

George affected a laugh. "What a joke. Me, cold hearted. From a girl like you! That sure takes some nerve—"

"What do you know about me?" Jean stood up, her voice rising with her.

"Shhhhh." George motioned her down, glancing out through the empty doorframe. She lowered her voice to an angry hiss.

"You don't know anything about me. How dare you…I came over here to save lives—"

"Ahhh, that's what the tears were for? Fritzie? You're wasting tears on that—" He squeezed his eyes shut, then opened them. "Ok. You came to save lives and you had to take one. That's rough. It is. But you said you could handle this. Whatever came, you were in. If you can't hold it together now—we don't have time for womanly hysterics, here—"

Incensed, she leaned in closer. "I wouldn't expect you to understand. You probably knew all about taking lives before you came over here—I'll bet you were some kind of cheap thug! That's why you think you can just push everyone around. Well, you can't push me, mister... Wha…stop it!"

George was gasping, hands pressed to his belly, trying hard to keep his laughter quiet. Tears streamed down through his squinted eyes. "You…you think…oh lady. You really have cracked."

Like a popped balloon, her anger deflated. She sighed and looked away. *Maybe.* She plopped down on the ground next to him. "Settle down. If you pop your stitches, I haven't got any more bandages, remember?"

He wiped his eyes. "Wheweeee! That hurts, but it's the best laugh I've had since…I dunno. Whew. If the laughs are the only reason they let women into the Army, maybe it was worth it!" He gave her his old 'I'm so charming' grin and a wink.

The anger surged again. Jean asked, voice dripping venom, "So. Those grins and winks usually work on the ladies, don't they? Seems strange since you obviously dislike us so very much. Or is it just me?"

"Oh, I've learned a thing or two about you ladies—I use the term loosely, mind—along the way, and no, it hasn't improved my outlook. But you…well, you are a special circumstance."

"Why? What have I done that's so bad?"

"Nursey, I don't care what you do, long as you don't hurt my friends."

That stopped her short. "Your…but the plan went off. I…thought I did alright too. Saved your skin anyway."

His grin turned cold. "Sure did. After Leroy and I saved yours."

Heat flushed her cheeks. "Well, yes, I suppose that's true. But," she searched his eyes, trying to figure out where he was going, "I didn't get anyone hurt…did I? I know we all got separated—"

"Forget it."

She sat up, leaning her nose up to his. "No. I don't want to forget it. I've bandaged you, followed your lead, and taken all of this garbage from you—"

"Ha! Sure you have—"

"Fine. But I'm not leaving you alone until you explain—"

"Leroy." He spat the name out, sharp as a gun crack.

"What?" She rocked back. "Wha…I didn't do anything to—"

He jabbed his finger towards her. "You think that kid would've gone off running into the night if it was just me there?"

Jean blinked. "I…" Her mind went back, to that moment before he ran, when he pressed her hand. Back to that look that he gave her. "You mean you really think it's my fault that he's…off, wherever he is?"

George leaned his head against the wall and closed his eyes. "Lady, he's…he's just like my kid brother. Norrie, he was a nice kid too—would've done anything for anyone, but around girls, he just got stupid." He sighed. "Leroy's head over heels for you—I warned you, even. If he's dead from trying to play the hero and save his lady fair, that's on you."

Jean opened her mouth to protest, to tell George that he wasn't being fair, but one word stopped her. *Dead? He can't be dead. He's going to meet us.* She pictured that beaming grin, that last look he gave her before he ran off. *He can't be.* Joe's face superseded his—that last smile, that last kiss. He wasn't supposed to die either.

George, head still back, had opened his eyes to watchful slits. "Aw, has the ice queen got a little sympathy in her after all?"

"That's not fair. You don't know me. You don't know anything about me! Neither did—does—he. I never asked him to...that's not fair, Novak."

George sighed. "Life ain't fair, last time I checked."

Standing, she took three steps towards the door, then turned back. "What about you? How'd he end up here in the first place?" Her voice wanted to shout, but she kept it quiet—a shrill, desperate whisper. "He was in your squad, following your orders, wasn't he? And then he had to surrender to save your hide. And whose, *whose* idea was this whole escape in the first place? Whose fault *is* all of this, George?"

George's face flushed red, and his fists clenched. Even half prone on the floor he looked dangerous. Jean took a step back, but there was no need. After a moment, he deflated. His face crumpled. He sighed and leaned his head against the rough wall, closing his eyes again.

"I suppose you're right. God forgive me. I swore I'd never let him get hurt..." He covered the top half of his face with his hand and just...sat there. Silent. Sitting there in the dirty straw with his torn and bruised body and muddy shoes and messy, dark hair, he was a picture of defeat and dejection.

He looked as rough as Jean felt. Her anger fading, she walked to the door, careful to approach it from an angle in case anyone was watching from outside—a trick Novak had taught her as soon as they took cover. She looked back at him, heart stung by sudden sympathy. *His plan got you this far, Jeannie. And he's just lost one of his best friends. He's scared for him. Not to mention he's got to be feeling awful.* Stan's face flashed across her memory, and she knew exactly what he'd say to her about her unfeeling heart right now. And—she hated to admit it, but she knew the truth. He would be right.

The outside was quiet and still except for a few birds singing their morning songs. Turning back, she surveyed George—he hadn't moved. She hesitated, then moved to sit beside him.

"Look. I shouldn't have said that. None of this is your fault." She hesitated. "He...Leroy, when you were first brought in, while you were still out cold, he told me a little about you. About what a good friend you were. How hard you worked to keep everyone safe. How brave you were." She looked down at her clasped hands. "He thinks the world of you, but I don't think he would've followed you if he didn't want to get out of there. He chose to. We all did. And," she dragged her sleeve across her nose which had begun to drip, "as far as we know, everyone except Ed's still alright. The plan worked."

George snorted, but didn't say anything in return.

Jean wracked her brain for what to say next. *Darn it, Stan, I am a good nurse. Or at least, I'm going to be.* "So. He reminds you of your brother?"

Shrugging his right shoulder, George sighed. "Sure."

"Is your brother in the army, too?"

George's hand came down from his face to scratch his stitches. "Nope."

Jean tried, and failed, to hold her tongue. "Don't do that—you're going to make it harder for them to heal."

He held up his hand in surrender. Jean leaned in to adjust the bandage he'd pulled out of place. "So. Where is your brother now?"

"He's deceased, Nursey."

"Oh." She looked up, stricken. "I'm really sorry. What…what happened to him? Unless," she hurried on, seeing George's brow lower, "unless you don't want to talk about it."

Rather than growl, George sighed. "No. Maybe it's just as well you hear it. He fell into bad company, of the feminine kind."

Heat flushing her cheeks, she busied herself with a thread on her sleeve. "Oh?"

He folded his hands, staring at his cracked, filthy knuckles. "Met this pair of sisters. He dated the younger one. She liked speed. We saved up, fixed up this jalopy together. He liked to drive her around. They took a curve too fast." He shrugged.

A show-off, just like his big brother. She caught herself and pushed the uncharitable thought down. *Jean, you're just as bad as he thinks you are.* Aloud, she said, "Corporal—George, I'm sorry for your loss."

He just nodded at this stiff acknowledgement. They sat a while in silence. The next words came reluctantly from his lips. "Usually we rode together, you know? I could usually laugh him down from showing off too much, but…I wasn't there."

So you weren't *always the show-off?* Suddenly anxious to reassure him, she blurted, "It's not your fault. Sometimes these things…these things just…" *These things just happen. The same, stupid platitudes everyone told me about Joe.* She fell silent.

"I wasn't there cuz I was out proposing to her sister."

Jean's head snapped around, and she stared at him. "*You* were engaged?"

He laughed, hard, hollow, bitter. "Sure. I used to be just about as clean cut and idealistic as good old Leroy. Believed in looooove and… all of that." He leaned away from her and spat. "She said yes. Then we got the news."

"That must have been awful. Did she…what happened? If you don't mind."

He shrugged. "No reason not to tell you. She was pretty broken up. We all were. But we were gonna stick it out. She got a little wild for a while there, trying to cope, but I was helping her. Things were going ok. She needed me around, but we were going to make it. Then, well, Uncle Sam decided he needed me more."

"Oh." Jean hunted for tactful way to ask and came up empty. "I'm guessing it didn't work out?"

"Nope. It's the same old story as lotsa guys. I went off to training, got a letter two months in that she figured we'd made a mistake and she oughta be free. Wouldn't return my letters or calls, wasn't around when I was on leave. Saw the notice in the paper a couple of weeks later that she was engaged to another fella. The birth announcement came out just before I shipped out."

Jean's eyes went wide in spite of herself. "Oh—you mean…I don't suppose, well, the baby wasn't—"

"Mine? Nope. Even though her little boy was born just six months after she broke it off with me, so…" he shrugged.

"Oh George. Oh, I'm so sorry." She meant it.

"I don't need your pity."

Her burst of sympathy was frozen in his glare. Flushing with anger—*I* tried *to be nice, Stan*—she glared back. "Well then, why tell me?"

"Good question. I guess I just needed to get it off my chest after all this time…" He laughed humorlessly. "Anyway. It's all water under the bridge."

They sat silent for a little while. As irritated with him as she was, Jean couldn't resist asking, "Did you ever find out anything more?"

His voice was hollow, the anger past. "Naw. Well, except that the fella she presumably had that baby with since she couldn't stand having me so far away—the fella she married?" He nodded towards the west. "He's out there on that beachhead."

"What, on Anzio?"

"Yep. Buck private, though he's trying to brown-nose his way up. He shipped over a couple of months after me." He laughed. "Ironic, ain't it?"

The thought hit her like a thunderbolt—the question of why he would be so set on getting back to that awful, deadly beachhead suddenly had a different answer. It was an answer she didn't much like. "Is…is that why you're so set on getting back there?"

He was silent.

Pushing herself away from the wall, she stood. "George, is it? What are you planning to do? You're not going to…"

"What?" His voice was challenging.

What indeed? "Well, do anything…*to* him?"

"Go off on some jealous revenge rampage…naw." He hesitated. "But

I can't stomach the thought of her hearing that her man's out there, fighting the fight while I'm just rotting away, sitting on my tuchus—"

"Oh my... You're showing off."

"What?" It was George's turn to stare.

"You planned this whole escape and everything—why? Was it just to show her that you're as good as this other guy? And what about the rest of us? If it weren't for her, would you have even tried the escape? Honestly—"

"Does it occur to you that I've got buddies on that beachhead, too? Fellas who are fighting the fight and need more men back? Fellas I'm responsible for—"

"Sure you do. But that's not who you told me about first." She glared at him. "Are you really gonna let some girl who dropped you rule your life like this?"

His face flushed beet red, then went white. "I don't think you're really qualified to lecture me on letting someone from the past rule my life." He jabbed his finger towards the ring she wore about her neck. "What about that guy?"

Her hand moved towards the ring, then she jerked it back to her side. "I loved Joe, and I keep the ring to remember him. But he's dead, and I've had to move on with my life—"

"Ha! Move on? What part of this..." he waved his hand in front of her, encapsulating her whole person, "...is you moving on?"

She crossed her arms. "What—nursing? I decided to do something to help the war effort. To help save lives—"

"Cuz you couldn't have done that stateside?"

"I didn't want to do it stateside. I wanted to do it here."

"Why?"

"Because. Because...it's a good thing to do."

"You hate it here. It's all over your face. So why really, Jeannie?"

She bristled. "Don't call me—"

"Why are you here? It shouldn't have to be such a hard question—"

"Because he didn't think I could do it." She spat the words out, then covered her mouth.

"What, didn't think you could be a nurse?"

"No. No, I was a nurse because we were going to get married, and he was going to start his own practice, but then—" She tried to hold the flood of words in, but maybe it was the weariness, maybe it was shock from having killed a man, maybe it was just George's mocking grin that said he understood her when he didn't—he *didn't*—that kept the words coming. "He…he left me there, all alone, like he didn't care at all, preaching about duty…and I didn't want him to. I wanted him to stay home, and he…he wouldn't. He said I wasn't brave enough, and he didn't care enough to stay with me. You *had* to leave—he didn't. And he did anyway. He left me…and then he died, the very first day on the beach in North Africa, and didn't help anyone at all, ever."

The tears coursed down her cheeks as the words poured out, words she had never yet said aloud. Spent, she trailed off into silence.

George sat back with a grunt and a satisfied nod. "So. He left you behind, and you never forgave him."

Rallying herself, she straightened her shoulders. "No! I mean, yes… it wasn't like that—"

"Sure it was. You never forgave him for running off to war and leaving you behind, so when he died you came over here too, with a chip on your shoulder."

"No, I didn't. I came—"

He stabbed the air between them with his finger. "With something to prove, and who cares about some poor sap like Leroy who only sees the good you do—"

"Will you STOP?" she screamed.

They stared at each other in the dusty dimness of the old barn. The silence around them echoed. Nothing moved.

They waited for a few moments more. Then George ventured, with a crooked grin. "Well. If you wanted to let them know where we are…"

"Ach!" She threw her hands in the air.

After a long time, the last words he'd said made it through the tumult of anger and frustration and pain rushing through her mind. "Look. Everything else aside, I think you should know. I'm not trying to hurt Leroy. I never had any intention of leading him on or…" she trailed off.

George sighed. "Yeah. I guess."

"He seems like a great guy. I just…after Joe…well. You know. It's not so easy to just walk back into it."

George shrugged. He looked away.

"You know, you should forgive her too."

He looked up, eyes sharp. "What?"

"You said I should forgive Joe…"

"I didn't say anything about it. I know better than to put my oar in. I just said that you hadn't moved on. And that maybe your motives aren't as pure as you'd like to think. That's all."

She bit her lip. "Fine. Well." The words hurt to say, but she forced them out. "You might…be right. But." She jabbed a finger toward him. "If I should forgive him, you should forgive her too."

"It wasn't the same thing."

"Maybe not. But it doesn't seem to me like carrying this around is doing either of us any good."

He closed his eyes.

"What? Don't you think—"

"Shhhh."

"But—"

"SHHHH. My nurse says I should try to sleep."

She humphed. "Fine. I'll keep watch."

"You do that. Now that I know you've got wicked aim, I'll even let you take the gun for keeps. Next guy you shoot, though, check the pockets, ok?"

She sighed. "You just can't let it go, can you."

"Nope. Tenacity is one of my most endearing traits."

"Keep telling yourself that."

He scooched himself into a more comfortable position, and soon his breathing was deep and regular.

Jean was thankful for the quiet, even though it left time for the memories to pounce. They were always waiting for her, just at the edges of the shadows.

Instead of shutting them down as she usually did, she approached the memories carefully. Maybe it was time to reexamine them. Surely nothing he'd said had any real merit… Or did it?"

She poked that hard knot of feelings that she'd buried deep in her heart regarding Joe.

She'd thought they were just sadness, loss, pain…

But there was something else there too. Something that hurt more than the others when she disturbed it.

Resentment.

Was George right—with all his bluster and poking and prodding? There, in the silence of that run-down Italian barn, she closed her eyes and admitted the truth to herself at last. She'd never forgiven Joe.

He shouldn't have left. He didn't have to leave, and he did it anyway. Leaving didn't do a bit of good. Didn't help anyone. He just left and died.

But there was more—a hurt even uglier, even harder to admit.

He didn't just leave; he left me. *He wasn't even sorry to leave me. He should've been sad—should've been sorry. Should've insisted that we get married right away. Should've made me feel like…like I mattered. Why didn't I matter to him?*

And even deeper—*God, why did you let him leave me? Why did you let him die? Why didn't you bring him back to me? I prayed and prayed that he'd come home.*

The tears flowed freely, for the first time in a long time. Choking down her sobs, she glanced at George to make sure he still slept. *Just think how he'd make fun of you.*

Scrubbing her filthy sleeve across her eyes and nose, she took a long, shuddering breath. The loneliness closed in, and she gave herself up to misery, burying her face in her hands and sobbing, hissing angry epithets at the man who hadn't cared enough to stay, and asking God why He'd let it all happen.

It was later, hours later, after the tears had run dry, that a shout from outside brought her back to herself—a shout, followed by a string of words in German.

Her head shot up, hands down as fists at her sides. Her fingers scrabbled for the pistol that waited, cold and hard and deadly. Her tears were forgotten, anger drowned in fear.

They've found us.

NINETEEN

"*Americano?*"

Awareness returned to Leroy in bits and pieces. First his mouth—his mouth was hanging open, desert-dry and gritty. He closed it, tried to lick his cracked lips. His tongue didn't have any moisture to share. Second, the air. It smelled like sun-dried grass, dust, and animals, but the smells were cut by a fresh-air smell, like a draft from an opened door. Next his ankle—a dull, throbbing ache met him there. It made a dissonant counterpoint to the rest of his body which lay on something soft—if a little scratchy—and warm. When was the last time he'd felt warm? As his consciousness clawed its way out of the black pit of exhaustion it had fallen into, the scratchiness increased—little poky pieces of the surface were poking through his clothes. His hand brushed over the surface—hay or straw. He was on a haystack in that barn—

The barn. The escape. Jeannie. George. It all came flooding back to him, and so did that funny word, "Americano." *Who said that?*

Eyes snapping open, he sat up so fast that spots raced in front of them. "Uf." His arms gave out, and he fell back against the hay, his body screaming a reminder that his belly was empty and his muscles exhausted. Deciding it was better to take things slowly, he half raised himself on his elbow. He blinked, waiting for the spots to clear. When they did, when his eyes focused in the dim, dusty light, he found that he was facing a kid. The small boy was perched on a low wooden bench set against the barn wall, watching him with still, black eyes.

Ooooh. Shoot…

Sitting up the rest of the way, slow and easy, he held up his hands. He tried to stretch his sore face into a non-threatening smile. "Hey there, buddy."

The boy blinked once. Otherwise, he didn't move. He had olive skin and thick, dark hair that rebelled from the neat cut someone had tried to give it. His clothes were worn, but clean. He didn't look frightened or angry, just watchful. *That's something, anyway.*

"Um…" Leroy patted his pockets, hoping he'd find some gum or candy—the local kids always liked that—but all he could find were his matches. *I can't really give a kid matches…could I? Maybe they need them…* The boy's mouth opened, and Leroy's hands froze.

"*Americano? Voi siete americano?*" The kid's voice was quiet, calm. As to what he was saying— Leroy patted his pockets again, wishing that his little government-issued Italian phrase book would appear inside them. He was fairly certain it had been left behind on his nice little box table in his nice little dugout. Still, this shouldn't be so hard to figure out—after all, he'd read the thing cover to cover three times in the dull waiting periods between almost dying or drowning. *Siete… that seems like a verb maybe? Americano—well, that's easy.* He decided to risk a nod. "Yep, you betcha. I'm an American."

The boy looked him over again. "*Avete gomma?*"

Leroy remembered that one from Naples. "Sorry…um, *mi dispiace*. I don't have any *gomma*." He'd given Wally his last stick.

The kid shrugged, then gave a very American thumbs up. "Ok."

Something moved to the side in the shadows. It gave a metallic thud. Leroy jumped, then sighed with relief. *Just the cow.* The poor, scrawny thing did nothing but chew her cud at him, her tail swishing and thudding against a metal pail hanging on the side of her stall. *Milk.* Just the thought of it stirred a little saliva to moisten his dry mouth. Mom had kept a milch cow. He'd been in charge of milking Bessie. *Well, It's worth a try.*

He pointed to himself. "Can I…" he pointed to the bucket, then to the cow and made milking gestures in the air "Uh…" the word floated back into his memory. "L-latte?"

The boy cocked his head.

"Um…" Leroy pushed himself up, wincing as his foot hit the floor. The ankle felt achy still, but not nearly as bad as last night. *That's something— not broken, at least.* He hobbled over to the milking pail as the boy watched him, unmoving. Picking up the pail, he gestured to the cow again. "Latte?"

The boy flashed him the thumbs up again. "Ok, Americano."

"Thanks, kid." Leroy plopped down on the milking stool, trying not to look at his filthy hands. He should wash them first, but the spots still danced at the edges of his vision. He didn't think he could make it much longer without something in his belly.

Slowly, he pulled the milk from the cow's udder into the pail. It hissed and foamed against the metal, and his mouth watered more. The cow was thin and must be getting near dry, but he took his time, making sure to strip her well. He made it halfway, then he couldn't stand it any longer—he lifted the whole pail to his mouth and gulped that thick, warm, creamy liquid down. It hit his stomach like a ton of bricks, and he almost retched. He sat, gasping for a few minutes, elbows on his knees, focusing on keeping it inside of him. Holding the pail between his knees, he closed his eyes and savored the taste on his tongue.

"Aren't you going to finish?"

He opened his eyes. The boy—Leroy judged him to be around eight or nine years old—was standing just in front of him, frowning. "Wh-What?" Leroy asked.

"Aren't you going to finish milking her? If you don't, Mama's sure to send me right back out here to finish, and what good does that do?" The boy's English was very clear, just a little accented.

Of course, to him, I probably have the accent. Well, the kid knows more than he was letting on. Leroy grinned. "So, you want me to milk her and finish your chores for you, huh?"

The boy nodded. "Yes."

Leroy laughed again and finished the milking. Giving the cow a pat, he handed the pail to the boy. "Sorry, my hands aren't too clean. Maybe you'd better just drink it down."

The boy handed the pail back. "You have it. I had milk yesterday."

With a grateful nod and a stammered, "*Grazie*," Leroy did as he was told.

The child took the milk pail, patted the cow's neck, and headed to the barn door. On the threshold, he stopped and looked back at Leroy. "Are you coming, Americano?"

Leroy hesitated, then nodded. "Sure I am…but, well, do you have any water?"

The boy tilted his head, then shook it. "For washing? No, it is better if you come as you are."

"But, why—" Leroy began, but the boy had already begun walking out the barn door, silent, and he had no choice but to follow or be left behind.

A gracious farmhouse with a tile roof stood just ahead, looming out of the early morning mist. The damp chill seeped into Leroy's weary bones, stealing the warmth that the hay and the animals had lent him. He shivered.

When they were about halfway across the yard, the boy broke into a run.

Shoot—what's he up to? Leroy's stomach clenched. *Has his mama got a German in there, and now he's gonna turn me in since I don't suspect him? Or maybe—*

But there was no more time for thought. The house door was open, letting out streams of golden glowing firelight and the boy's shrill chatter. "Mama, *ho trovato un americano nel fienile! Credo che sia ferito o che stia per morire!*"

Morire—wait, isn't that something about dying? Shoot, what's this kid saying?

A form showed up in the doorway, lit from behind. Not a German soldier—it was a woman in long skirts and an apron, hair pulled back tight, and hand on her hip. She took one look at him, standing teetering in her yard in a filthy, blood-stained uniform, threw up her hands, and motioned for him to come.

"Voi siete vivo or morto? Avanti!" Though he didn't catch the first phrase, Leroy recognized the invitation to come in, and he walked onward, taking ginger steps on his injured ankle.

Coming abreast of the woman, he noted that she wasn't old—older than him, but younger than his own mother, her dark hair barely touched by gray at the temples. Her sharp, black eyes looked him up and down, then rolled heavenward. Crossing herself, she gestured him over the threshold and then pulled the boy over by his ear. A rapid exchange in Italian ensued, during which Leroy stood, working his hands together, wishing he had a hat to take off or anything to offer, wishing, too, that he could edge a little closer to the fire and the bread he could smell baking. The scent of it set his mouth watering again, and his stomach grumbled.

Maybe she heard it, because the Italian mama abruptly stopped giving her son an earful and turned to Leroy with a wide smile, gesturing towards a plain, wooden chair near the fire. He nodded to her and stammered out, "*Grazie, mille grazie.*"

Sinking into an actual chair by a warm fire was pure bliss. The only downside was that the heat started to make Leroy's head and ankle throb almost at once.

Clucking her tongue, the woman shoed her boy out to get

something—*acqua*. Leroy was almost positive that that was water, and he licked his parched lips in expectation. The boy returned quickly with a pail, then ran for another while his mother hung a pot over the fire on a hook. When several pails had been emptied into it, she pointed to Leroy and made some incomprehensible gestures.

"Huh?" He looked over at the boy. "What…what's she want me to do?"

The boy didn't blink. "She wants you to take your clothes off."

Leroy forgot his ankle injury until he'd leaped to his feet and taken two steps towards the door. He put too much weight on it for the second step and almost went down. "Wait—what d'you—" His ears burning, he looked at the woman, "What—" then back at the boy. "Why?"

The boy did blink then, just once. "She wants to boil them. To kill the lice. And because she says you stink."

He looked back at her—she must have had enough English to understand the basics, because her eyes were laughing. She nodded and plugged her nose and said, *"Sì, puzzate."*

Leroy released his breath with a whoosh and resumed his seat. He shuffled his feet. "Ma'am—" He turned to the boy. "Can you please tell her thank you, and I'd love a wash, but I have friends I have to get back to. I can't wait for laundry. I'm sorry, but that's just the way it is."

The boy relayed the message, and his mother gave him a thin, appraising glance. She asked something in a sharp tone. The boy translated. "Are you running from the Germans?"

Leroy hesitated, then nodded. "Yes. And I've got to find my friends. One of them is hurt."

The woman's lips got even thinner at this pronouncement, but she nodded again, pulled the kettle off the fire, and walked through an adjoining door, calling directions to her son over her shoulder.

"Mama says you should at least wash up. She'll put the water in a basin, and you can clean your wound. She says since you're bashful, you can do it in there. She'll take a look at your head after."

Leroy nodded and muttered his thanks. Following the woman, he found a small bedroom with a crucifix on the wall and a basin filled with blessedly warm water and a full pitcher beside it. Stripping off his shirt, he bathed his face and his hands and whatever else he could get to. The water turned black. He started to carry the basin out to dump, but at a bark from his mother, the boy took it for him. When it was returned, he refilled it from the pitcher and started to bathe his head wound. The water quickly turned pink, then darker red. With a click of her tongue, the mama was there. She made him bend over—she was shorter than he by at least a foot—and probed the wound. Dabbing it with warm water, she called over to her son who translated, "Just a scratch that bled a lot. She says you should use the rest of the water on your feet here, by the fire."

Obediently, Leroy took the proffered chair. When he peeled off his socks, the mama gave a quiet shriek and spouted off a string of words in Italian, including many repetitions of "*Ma – che puzzo*!" Finally, she spoke to her son, who translated, "You must give those to her at once." The kettle was back over the fire. She grabbed the socks without giving Leroy a chance to protest and threw them straight in.

He obediently put his feet into the basin of warm water she provided. Before he even saw it happening, he had a plate on his lap with a thick slice of the bread he'd smelled baking, a bit of cheese, and some kind of dry meat and a glass of red wine in hand— "To make you stronger for the road," the boy translated. The other two sat near him at the well-scrubbed table, though they did not eat. He bowed his head to say grace when the mother did. Though he couldn't understand the words, it made him think of Dad and Mom saying grace back home, and he felt a lump rise in his throat.

He ate, chewing slowly, savoring each bite and sip. The other two didn't try to converse, just watched him silently, smiling when he met their eyes. Squirming a little, uncomfortable with the attention, he turned his gaze to the few family photos on the mantle. One was of a smiling man with the boy's unruly, dark hair.

The boy followed his gaze. "That's my Papa. He's fighting with the Partisans. Have you seen him?"

Leroy shook his head. "No, but I haven't seen much of Italy, yet. Who's the one next to him?"

Seeing where his gaze was turned, the mother muttered something and crossed herself. The boy answered, "My brother. He's dead. He died in North Africa."

"I-I'm sorry. Sorry for your loss." *He died, fighting my allies most likely. And they're still feeding me like... like I was never their enemy.*

The meal done, the mother walked over to the boiling kettle, reached into it with a long fork, and pulled out his socks. Their color looked a bit better, at least. She rattled off something in Italian, and her son translated, "She'll hang them over the fire. You can sleep in the barn for a little longer, and then they'll be dry for your walk."

Leroy opened his mouth, not sure if he was going to protest the extra time it would take, or just thank her, but he froze, listening.

From outside the door, a sound pierced the morning air—men's voices. It didn't sound like they were speaking Italian.

The smile slipped off the woman's face. *"Dio buono..."* she whispered, then gestured violently to her son. He slipped out of his chair silently and took Leroy's hand, finger to his lips.

Heart pounding, Leroy stood on his bare feet. *My boots!* He sped across the floor, ignoring the ankle, and grabbed the boots from where they sat just inside the bedroom.

A fist crashed on the door and a deep voice barked a command.

Faster, gotta go faster— He followed as the boy tugged him through a narrow hall, to a part of the house that looked older than the rest. A stone archway held a wooden door. A key hung next to it. The boy opened the door—it was a mouth into black dark. The smell of damp earth and old wood wafted up on a cool breeze. *Underground. Please*

God, not underground. Leroy shook his head and pointed to the bed in the room they'd just passed. *Couldn't I just hide underneath?* But the boy shook his head—the front door slammed open, and they could hear men's voices and his mother speaking rapidly in Italian.

The boy pulled Leroy's head down and hissed, "It's the old cellar—we use it for the *vino.* Go straight down the stairs, then left past the first set of shelves. There's a stair that comes out in the garden. Hurry!"

Leroy swallowed, hard, then obeyed. He was on the second step, hand brushing the damp, cold stone wall when the door shut silently behind him, plunging him into darkness.

His old fears, his nightmares of the mines, flooded him. Cold sweat sprang up on his brow and under his arms. His heart pounded in his ears. His trembling fingers started to reach for the matches in his pocket—*But what if the Germans search?* A loose match, the smell of sulphur—even little things might betray them. *I can't let that kid and his mom get caught helping me. God knows what they'd do.* Steeling his nerves, he took a step down, then another, the gritty stone cold under his bare toes.

Feeling forward with his feet and the hand that wasn't holding his boots, he descended. Counting every step, he waited for the Germans to open the door and find him standing on the stairs, helpless as a trapped rabbit. *Eight steps...nine...ten.* His foot slid forward, looking for the drop off to the next step. Nothing. Had he reached the bottom?

He shuffled forward, tentative, then hasty. His fingers trailed across the damp stone and earth until...nothing. The wall dropped away, and he stood at the bottom of the stairs, alone. He was alone, in the dark, underground. The deep, dark, rotten smell of the earth closed around him, and his feet rooted to the floor. He clutched the air in front of him like a blind man, trying not to think of Uncle Ernie's funeral after the mine disaster. The closed casket, sitting in front of church like a warning. Closed because there was no body—it was already buried. Buried and drowned and crushed beneath the earth.

Oh God, oh God, help me. There was a sound from above—a creak, a boot on the floor? He found his courage and stepped forward, hands raking the empty dark.

His knuckles scraped against a wooden shelf—*Shelves! The kid said the way out was beyond some shelves!* His hands traced the shelf lightly, hoping there weren't wine bottles waiting to be knocked over and betray his presence. Pushing himself farther into the dark, he found the end of the shelves. *Then, to the left…* He rounded the corner and barked his shins on a box or crate. Biting his lip, he shuffled around it, then forward until his fingers touched a cold earth wall ahead.

A noise—voices carried through the cracks of the door. It sounded like the boy, as well as someone else. Time was running out.

He groped along the wall, and there it was—the way out.

Had the boy called it a stair? That was a generous word for the narrow wooden ladder, crammed between narrow earthen walls. The space was barely big enough for his shoulders. No matter—it was an escape. He scaled the rungs in the time it took for his pounding heart to beat five more times, then put his shoulder to the wooden door in the earth above him, easing it up.

His eyes blinking in the sliver of light, he peered about. Grasses obscured his view—what if all the Germans weren't inside the house?

There was no time for caution. He pushed himself out of the narrow gap between the wooden door and its frame, catching slivers in his wrist and jaw, and eased the door back into place.

Can't stay too close. The house stood a few yards away, and the trap door was situated on a little embankment. He slithered down the slope, head low, not daring to look around to see if he was observed. *If they see me, I'll know it soon enough!*

The cover of a grove of trees was about twenty yards from him, but there were more grape vines at the bottom of the embankment, and the grass was grown up around the fence posts. As he reached the bottom of the slope, a thick clump rose right in front of his nose.

He flopped behind the cover, burrowed into it, and hunkered down to wait. Maybe a break for the trees would be the smarter move, but he couldn't bear to just leave and not know what had happened to this nice little family who'd already lost so much. *Besides,* he reasoned, *I'd need to move around a bunch to get my shoes on, even without socks—*

The socks.

His socks—men's socks, all stretched to fit his feet, still hung by the fireplace in a house with no men to be seen. Labeled with their brand name, in English, stitched right into them.

Twenty

After depositing the American soldier in the cellar, Eduardo considered the key. He could slide it under the door easily enough. Perhaps, with it out of sight, the Germans would believe that the cellar was unused. *Or they might break down the door. Or shoot us, saying we're hiding something.* If it were on the hook by the door, however, it would give the American very little time to get away. He decided on a compromise, slipping next door into his bedroom and tucking the key into his dresser drawer. If they asked for it, he'd give it to them. Then, he strolled back to the kitchen. He would make certain he was there to help Mama, but he wouldn't run—not for the German pigs.

Papa had been right when he said that Il Duce—he always sneered as he said Mussolini's title—should never have gotten in with Hitler. He'd tried to convince Eduardo's brother, Pietro, regaling him with stories from the last war—about how the British and Italians had made good allies, how they'd mopped up the Kaiser, how the old allegiances shouldn't have changed. "Mussolini and his Blackshirts will all be trampled under Hitler's heel, mark my words!"

Then, headstrong Pietro would start spouting off about their *Mare Nostrum*—how Italy ought to own the Mediterranean, how Italy needed colonies too, if they ever wanted to be a great power. "What kind of coward would I be, staying at home and tending vines rather than fighting for my country?"

He'd gone—and in his letters home he talked about how he missed them. How he wished he could come back.

And then, the letters stopped.

Papa had gone silent, raging against the Germans in his heart as he went on with his daily work until Italy's surrender. Then he'd come home and told Mama that he was going to fight with the Allies. He'd spat, described how the Germans had betrayed them, killing Italian troops when the surrender took place so they'd never have a chance to go and fight. "No. The Americans and the British and the Poles and French and Indians…all the world is here, trying to drive the Germans out of our country." He stood up tall and struck his chest. "If we sit and let all the world do this for us, how can we have pride again?"

Mama had grumbled a little about his pride—said it sounded an awful lot like Pietro's foolishness—but she hadn't really protested, knowing, perhaps, that it wouldn't make a difference. He had gone. They'd had word from their uncle that he had joined with some partisans farther south, trying to soften up German lines for the oncoming Americans and British. Since then, there'd been no new word. Only more Germans.

The pigs. They'd visited before, taken the other cow, half of the poultry, and all but two of the bottles of last year's *vino*. He had let them, holding in his anger until they had left, but Mama had still chided him. She'd said, "Be happy that all they did was take a few things. Things can be replaced." But now they were back, and they weren't just hunting for things.

Back hunting that American—curse them. It was all he could do not to spit on the floor when he entered the room and saw Mama at the door, stepping nimbly aside as the two men pushed into the kitchen.

They growled and cursed—likely saying she hadn't been fast enough. Eduardo hadn't bothered to learn their filthy language.

Mama, somehow reading his thoughts, shot him a swift, hard look. He exhaled, letting his anger go. Smoothing his face, he schooled it into stillness. *Wide eyes, quiet eyes, don't look like you know anything at all.*

As the Germans stomped with their dirty boots across his Mama's scrubbed floor, demanding information in their broken approximation of Italian, his eyes scanned the room. Had the American left any sign of his presence? *He took his boots. Didn't have a bag. Mama put the dishes in to wash already—good. And I dumped that basin with the blood. There shouldn't be any sign—*

"*...omicidio...*" The word made him look up. *Murder? They're saying that Americano murdered someone? Is it even murder if it's war?* He mentally shrugged. He didn't much care—he hoped the Americans and British and whoever would sweep the Germans clean out of Italy and let Papa come home. If it took killing every German along the way, it made no difference to him. *Still, if they're saying murder they'll be looking harder.* He scanned the room again. His eyes froze on the fireplace.

The pot of water still hung from a hook. The American's socks hung from another hook. Even from here, he could see the words sewn into the bottoms of the socks—words in English, a name of some sort. *English. If they see those...*

He sidled across the room, not making directly for the fireplace, moving to put his body between the Germans and it.

They'd finished asking Mama questions and were pushing farther into the house. One headed into Mama's bedroom. The other stalked around the side of the kitchen, eyeing the cooking implements. His waist strained at his uniform's cloth. *That one likes his stomach full. I'll bet he's looking for something to eat*—a cold shiver travelled down his spine—*and if he looks in the fireplace—*

For a moment, neither soldier was looking at him. A couple of quick, smooth steps got him over to the fireplace. In the seconds he had, he wracked his brain. *What now?* If they searched him, the bulky socks would betray him. Throw them in the fire? Would they smoke, being damp? Likely. If they didn't, the smell would give them away—a little wafted up to his nostrils as he grabbed them off the hook. Out of the corner of his eye, he saw the German at the sideboard turning and saw Mama watching him. He heard the heavy step of the German coming out of the bedroom.

There was only one place. He put the socks back into the pot.

"Boy!" barked the soldier who'd been in the bedroom. Thinner than his companion, he also looked to be the more alert—and dangerous—of the two. "What are you doing over there?"

Don't move too fast, or they'll know. He turned his head, then his body, blinking. Willing himself to look simple. "Me, signore? Mama just told me to boil water for tea as she's been feeling ill. I was checking on it."

Right on cue, his mother coughed and pulled her shawl a little tighter around her as she stood up straighter. She was the picture of a woman who was sickly but too proud to show it.

The German from the bedroom stepped back a little—*Ah, you don't like sickness, do you?* The other one, the fat pig, perked up. "Tea? I've been feeling poorly myself. Please, signora—don't let us stop you making what you need. And perhaps, once we've finished our search if all is well, I might have a cup?"

Eduardo glanced into the pot. The water was boiling, the socks floating in it. It didn't look like tea, but it didn't look like clean water either.

"*Sì.*" His mother coughed again and pulled on a strained, tired smile.

The big German smiled back, then said something over his shoulder to the other. He strolled off down the hallway, presumably to check the other rooms. *Good. Now, just take your friend with you.*

But as reluctant as the second German had been to stay near illness, he didn't seem inclined to let them out of his sight. He leaned against the wall, fingering the bayonet on his rifle and keeping his eyes on

Eduardo. The boy had to use all his resolve to stand still, willing himself to look innocent.

The German didn't look convinced. "Is the water boiling, boy? We don't want your mother to have to wait too long for her remedy."

Eduardo glanced at the pot. "Mama, what herbs do you want me to put in?"

"I will do it," she answered. She walked, slow and stiff to the sideboard. They didn't have any real tea—supplies had been running low, and Mama was reluctant to let Eduardo venture far. However, Mama kept a variety of dried herbs in a tin on the counter to steep in times of illness. Eyeing the pot, she measured out a generous amount. It looked like more than she usually used, but Eduardo supposed that the big pot would hold much more tea than she generally made, and perhaps enough herbs would cover over other, less savory flavors.

She walked the mixture over to the fire, her face smooth. Eduardo moved out of the way, careful not to look into the pot, not to look as if anything were out of the ordinary. They waited—his mother preparing the tea, him watching his mother, the German watching both of them. Thuds and thumps came from the other rooms of their house, followed by a call from the second soldier.

The guard who watched them responded, then asked Mama, "Signora, there is a locked door at the rear of the house. Where does it lead?"

"Just to the old wine cellar," she answered.

He stepped forward, glowering. "If that is so, why is it locked?"

Meeting his eyes, she answered, "In case one of those filthy American gangsters comes sneaking through." She spat on the hearth. "My husband and eldest son are gone. I must protect what little I can for the one that is left, even if he is a simpleton." Her gaze swung to Eduardo. "Boy! Don't stand there gawking—get the cellar key."

Eduardo jumped, his mouth hanging open, playing the part she had set for him. "Yes, Mama!" He scampered to his room, listening for footsteps behind. *Surely now the pig will join his friend in searching.*

He did not. Eduardo unlocked the cellar door for the fat soldier, saying a quick prayer that the American was long gone and had left no trace, then hurried back to the kitchen. The scene hadn't changed. His mother watched the pot, the soldier watched his mother. The minutes ticked by.

The big German returned, complaining that there had been nothing worth seeing back there and their bird must be flown. Either he hadn't noticed the narrow stairs leading out of the cellar or didn't find them significant.

Then he inhaled. "Ah, that smells very healthful. Come, is it ready, or does it need more time?"

"A little more," Mama answered. Only Eduardo could see her face—could see the pinched line between her eyes and at the corners of her mouth. If the dirty water didn't taste like tea, if they investigated the pot… Eduardo had heard stories of the kinds of retaliation the Germans meted out—arrests, deportations, shootings, burning houses with the occupants still inside—

Finally, Mama couldn't wait any more. The smaller German had started to finger his bayonet, the big one to tap his fingers on the table. Turning to the big one, Mama asked, "Would you still like a cup of tea? It is very strong."

The big German replied in his mangled Italian with a wide grin "Ah! Yes, please, signora. The stronger, the better." As she reached for just one cup, he sat at the table. He gestured towards the seat across from him. "And, I know you mean to have some too. Don't wait on my account. You must come and drink with me."

Mama nodded. Handing the cup to Eduardo, and gesturing for him to take down a second, she walked, careful and stiff to sit across from her enemy.

How her stomach must be turning. Eduardo's was, and the tea wasn't even for him. He ladled a mugful of tea for the German, avoiding the mysterious bits and pieces that floated in the water. He preferred to think they were just bits of boiled herbs. Color-wise, it *looked* teaish enough, at least he hoped so. He ladled Mama's slowly, afraid to put too little in and draw attention, unwilling to make his mother drink more of the brew than necessary.

He carried the mugs slowly to the table under the watchful eyes of the Germans. The fat one had risen to pull out Mama's chair. The thin one walked towards the fire.

Eduardo's hands clenched the mug handles until they shook. *Don't look in the pot!*

The German leaned over to sniff, then wrinkled his nose.

"Sir!" Eduardo cried. The German straightened and scowled at him. Eduardo forced an ingratiating smile across his face. "Would you like some?"

Grimacing, the German answered with mock politeness, "*Nein.* It smells like my grandmother's feet."

Eduardo could barely suppress the mad desire to laugh, but hid it in a shrug, setting down the mugs before Mama and the fat German. "Cold water then? I could get some from the well."

"What, and warn the Americans hiding outside that we're here?"

Eduardo cocked his head, affecting a puzzled frown. *He doesn't know anything. Stupid pig.* "I don't know what you m—"

"Nein," the German bit off the word. "We will get our own water when we leave here."

Eduardo nodded and turned his attention to the table. The German had picked up his mug and inhaled the steam coming off it. Mama held hers. Without changing expression, she bent her head and took her first sip. Eduardo suppressed a grimace. *Maybe she's just pretending?* If she was, she did it well. "Mmmm," she said, nodding.

The German watched her as he raised his mug. Blowing the steam across the top of it, he took a sip. Eduardo held his breath, waiting.

The German swallowed, then smacked his lips, frowning. He took another drink, then stared at the cup speculatively.

His companion spoke up. "Why are you not drinking, signora?"

Mama didn't even spare him a glance. She lifted her mug and swallowed her tea down in three gulps. The fat German laughed, then did the same.

"Whew," he said, when he came up for air. "That's good medicine, I can tell. You know, I think my grandmother had that very same recipe."

Eduardo bent his head as he collected the two mugs and took them to the sink. Only then, with his back to the room, did he allow himself the smile that tugged at the corners of his mouth. *I doubt it.*

Twenty-One

George woke to the nurse tugging on his arm. *Ouch!* Her touch was too near the ache in his side where Grüber had hit him. *Dang. It wasn't a dream. I'd love to get somewhere with some aspirin…and a beer…and a cigarette…Could I have them all at the same time, please, doctor? Probably not.* He tried to pull out of her grasp. The pain flared, jolting his sluggish brain to wakefulness.

As he blinked the crust out of his eyes, she shook his arm again. "Ok, ok, Nursey, what…?"

She clapped a hand over his mouth. Vision clearing at last, he met her eyes. They stared into his, wide and frightened. She jerked her head towards the door.

Voices. Voices speaking in German.

Oh heck, can't we catch a break—

She grabbed him under the arms, pulling him to his feet. Pain seared his torso in a hot ring, the worst focused on his lower left side. Biting the inside of his cheek until salty blood flooded his mouth, he tried to help, to bear his own weight. His clumsy boots scrabbled on the loose stones and dirt of the floor.

A shadow passed before the door. *No getting out that way.* Finding his feet at last, he pulled the nurse towards a narrow set of stairs that curled around the wall to the door's right, leading to the loft.

The barn, if barn it was, was cylindrical in shape—like a mix between the bottom half of the silos that dotted the Midwest prairies and a leftover castle tower from ages past, repurposed for modern days. If the second were true, it had held up well. The masonry was old but seemed sound. *I sure hope that the stairs still are, anyway—*

The steps were made of stones inset into the wall, following the curve of the building. Wooden beams had been propped under them to add extra support—they looked like a newer addition. George supposed it was better than the stairs being of rotted wood that might creak and give them away. Unfortunately, the stones jutted out from the wall at odd angles and were barely wide enough for him alone, much less his supporting nurse.

George gritted his teeth and pushed the nurse ahead of him, heaving himself after. *Gotta make it up. Get hidden. Maybe they'll just go away.* His breath came in painful gasps—he tried to keep his inhalations shallow. *Just one step at a time.*

Four steps from the top, his boot slipped on the slick stone. He grunted as he caught himself, banging his shin and scraping his hand bloody against the rock wall.

The noises from outside stopped. A voice called out.

The nurse's wide eyes and pale face looked over her shoulder from above. He pointed her upward, and she nodded. With a silent scramble and a heave, her legs disappeared into the upper story. With one last effort he hauled himself up too.

Just in time. As his head cleared the edge and he rolled into the shadows, a silhouette of a helmeted form filled the doorway, dimming the light.

Glancing around their hiding place, George felt his optimism dim too. *There's not much chance of hiding.*

Unlike the stairs, the floor of the loft was wooden. The wood was sound, the boards well fitted. The low mounds of hay looked fresh enough that someone must have used it not too long ago. *Maybe this place isn't as abandoned as we assumed.* Still, movement would almost certainly cause the boards to creak. It might dislodge dust and hay as well, to fall on the head of the searcher below. Lying on his back, George closed his eyes and tried to think. *How're we gonna get out of this one?*

Booted feet trod the floor below, crunching over scattered pebbles.

Something rustled in the rafters. George looked up into the eyes of an exceptionally large rat. He bit back a cry. The rat's beady eyes fixed on his face, long tail dangling down far enough that he could probably touch it if he stretched his hands up far enough. He suppressed a shudder. Nothing else bothered him quite like rats. It'd gotten worse since he'd heard stories of the filthy makeshift hospital wards in North Africa, where the rats chewed on the guys who didn't have the strength to wave them off.

The rat sat up, listening to what now sounded like two sets of boots walking around below. German voices softly conversed.

A step sounded at the foot of the stairs. *They're coming up.* The nurse's fingers plucked on his sleeve. He met her eyes and jerked his head towards the shadows, farther into the loft. *Back—keep going back.*

Straw clinging to her hair, she nodded. Clutching her satchel tight to her chest, she scooted across the wooden boards. Slowly, trying not to dislodge any hay dust or to make any sound, he followed. The rat didn't move, just watched him creep along like a demented snail in uniform. He pulled a face in its direction.

Boots scraped on the stone steps. Fritzie was on his way. There was a thump and what sounded like a curse. *Slipped on the same stone I did I'll bet.* That meant he was nearly up.

He reached the nurse. She lay huddled against the back wall. Above her was a little window, set deep into the stone wall. It let in a hazy beam of light in which dust motes drifted lazily. George rolled toward her, following into the deep shadow below the window. He hoped that the light might be enough—just enough—to dazzle the eyes of the searchers and offer them concealment. At his approach, the nurse pressed even farther back, tucking half of her body down in a little divot where the wall met the beam that supported the loft. Sliding in front of her, George positioned himself facing outwards. *If I'm gonna get shot, I want to see the fella that's doing it.* The nurse's quick breaths brushed his neck. He imagined he could feel her heartbeat pounding into his back. Reaching in front of him, he pulled over what hay he could, trying to conceal their huddled forms.

There was no more time. The curved top of a helmet rose above floor level.

One eye peering above the hay, George watched the dark shadow of the German's helmet, turning back and forth, slow, wary. *Wish I could've gotten a little more hay piled up. If I can see him, that means that if Fritzie's looking close enough, he could see me. C'mon, God, just throw an old dog a bone here. Let this guy be the one out there without a flashlight—please!* Behind him, the nurse's—Jean's—breath hitched in her throat.

Poor kid. For the first time he thought of her like a person—a frightened person, who knew what might happen if she were caught again. New resolve gripped him. *No matter what happens to me, I can't let them take Jeannie.* Even in this situation, a grin tugged at the corners of his mouth. *Leroy'd never forgive me.*

The soldier's shoulders rose above the level of the loft's floor. Again, the German's head turned from side to side, scanning the space. George could almost feel the eyes, like searchlights, boring into him. There was no way—none—that he and Jean could escape detection. Especially if Fritzie were to take those next steps, if he were to come up all the way—

A shadow darted through the dark, just in front of the soldier. A flash of long tail and a hint of beady eye were all George could see.

The soldier jerked backward, hitting his elbow on the stones of the wall. He let off a long string of expletives.

Guess he doesn't like rats either.

Voices called from below, laughing at him. He answered them.

And then, miraculously, the head and shoulders disappeared. He'd gone back down, calling to someone below.

Jean clutched his arm from behind.

The sound of footsteps receded. It sounded as if they'd gone back outside. He didn't move, unwilling to risk it. Besides, now that the fear was fading his wounds were throbbing again, especially that fresh scrape on his hand.

Jean's breath was hot in his ear as she whispered. "It's ok. They didn't say anything about us—they're just on…a patrol, I think. Looking for a place to spend the night if they need to, checking out the area. He said he didn't like the look of the loft. Thought it might be dangerous. And have more rats."

George nodded, but didn't dare turn his head—voices still sounded from outside. The voices dimmed. He counted to one hundred, then to one hundred again, slowly. Nothing.

Jean's hand pressed his shoulder, pushing. Slowly, he slithered forward. Then, still cautious of sound, he used his right arm to push himself to sitting—even through the adrenaline, his left ached too much to use. Jean grabbed his elbow. Looking back at her, he had to stifle a laugh. She was good and wedged into that crack by the wall. She grimaced at him, mouthing, "Help me out!" Balancing himself, he reached out to her with his right hand and grabbed her forearm. The relief of their narrow escape was euphoric—her mouth quivered from suppressed laughter. "Wish you'd brought a shoehorn."

He grinned and murmured, "Sorry, forgot to grab one. Hang on. I can't pull you, but—" He pivoted to plant his feet on the wall above her, and she used his arm like a rope to pull herself out.

They sat for a moment beside each other, just breathing. Jean opened her satchel, checking the contents. Pulling out her canteen, she handed it to him. He took a drink, then leaned in and whispered, "Look, now that they've checked up here maybe we should just hunker down for the rest of the day. Head out at dark, then meet up with Leroy tomorrow, like we planned. I don't much like the odds of trying to sneak past a patrol in daylight."

She gave him half a grin. "Will dark be much better?"

"Nah, not really, but they might not see us right away, and maybe we can fool 'em. Especially with you wearing gray and knowing a few words of German...It'd be even handier if you knew some Italian. We could pretend to be locals."

"Sorry. Grandma's German Lutheran church didn't have a service in Italian."

"Too bad."

She shrugged, then said slowly, in the way of someone offering an olive branch, "But maybe I could teach you a few words, so that you could sound more like one of them. My voice is really too high."

He settled against the rough stone wall next to her in a more comfortable position. "Hey, that's a swell idea! I'll bet—"

Their whispered conference was interrupted by a shout from outside. They both froze, eyes wide, foxes catching the first bay of the hounds.

The shouts weren't angry; they sounded like greetings. The sounds of voices moved until they were just outside, below the little window above Jean's left shoulder.

One thing was clear, even to George—all the voices were speaking German. He could tell that questions were being asked, but he couldn't tell much else. He watched Jean's face, though under all the dirt and shadows it was hard to discern her expressions. Was it good news or bad news?

Maybe they're all getting called away. Heck, maybe we've broken through, and they're all falling back.

A burst of laughter from outside made him frown.

Yeah, probably not a retreat then.

Suddenly, Jean clutched his arm, fingers digging in. She hissed into his ear, "It's them—they're from the camp. Warning about escaped prisoners. They're...they're laughing that a nurse got away from the guards."

The voices lowered. The laughter was replaced by a deep, angry rumble.

Jean's hand tightened on his sleeve. "And...and they're being told that we killed a guard. Someone's nephew, someone who's a higher-up...must be Grüber. Oh...they're talking about what they're going to do to us...lovely." She tried for a breathy laugh, but he could feel her hand shake. He covered it with his own and leaned in to whisper.

"Look, don't worry, Nursey. We're gonna get out of here. It'll be dark soon enough—the days are still short, right? We'll meet up with Leroy, and we'll get back to our people. No problem."

"Sure. Easy..." she broke off and cocked her head to the side. "They say that they're watching the road to Rome—lots of prisoners are supposed to be escaping there...They're arguing whether the Pope ought to be left alone—sounds like one of them's Catholic."

"Must not be strict, if he's going along with all of this."

"Mmm. They aren't saying if they caught the others... Oh, I hope that Hank and the fellas made it through all right. And..."

"What?"

"They...they're asking if the patrol checked out the barn. The one who's talking...must not be the same guy...he says he doesn't think so."

George swallowed hard and tried to think through the pain and weariness. "Ok. Ok. Well...if we just—"

"Oh!" It was a quiet gasp, and she put her hand over her heart. "Oh—one of them is saying that yes, they checked the barn."

George closed his eyes. "Ok. Then—"

"And someone else...another one asked if they checked the hay... sounds like he's saying he likes to use a bayonet—"

George started moving before his brain caught up. He jerked his head towards the stairs, and started off, slithering across the boards of the loft. Soft sounds behind told him that Jean was following.

There was no time for stealth, but he tried, wincing as he heard the boards creak under him, heard the small bits of rubbish and dust patter on the floor below, heard his breathing, loud in his ears, and felt the tearing pain in his ribs. *That's what I get for hoping for a rest, I suppose. Please, God, just let me be fast enough.*

He reached the stairs and eased his nose to the edge of the boards, holding his breath. No one there yet. He flipped onto his backside and slid down the stairs as quickly as he could stand, landing on the floor below in a half crouch.

He heard Jean follow him, her breathing quick and frightened. He looked back at her—her breath might be quick, but her eyes were calm, her face set. *If I had to be stuck here with a girl, at least I've got one who's not a coward. She might not be the worst choice after all, Leroy.*

A shadow and a cough announced someone at the door. He pushed Jean back into the shadows behind the little stairway. He knew as he did it that it wouldn't be enough. He moved so that he stood in front of her. *Maybe...maybe he'll just see me. Maybe he won't get her. Maybe... maybe I can make up for my stupidity somehow. God, did I do wrong in bringing her here? In bringing them all here? Should I have just left well enough alone, let them go through the process...at least they wouldn't be dead. But my own stupid pride...I just couldn't see staying, and I figured I was smart enough to make it work, and I couldn't get out on my own... Don't let me get this girl killed, please. If it's gotta be me...just don't let me have gotten them all killed.*

He closed his eyes, as if it might make him invisible. Then he opened them. Hadn't ever worked in hide-n-seek as a kid. Probably wouldn't work now. It would be just as well to see what was coming as to go into it blind. He grinned, baring his teeth. Maybe, if he kept his eyes open, maybe he'd still have a chance to fight back.

The German entered the room. George had a good view of him

between the stones of the steps. He wasn't a huge fella but big enough to put up a fight. Young face, smooth cheeks. Dark blonde hair. Wary face. Just a kid but looked like he'd seen some action.

Normal circumstances, I could take him, but with everything...the wound, the guys outside...the nurse... Hey there, God, it'd sure be convenient if he were to just pass us by...please...?

The German paced away from the door, following the curve of the structure opposite the stairs, peering through the gloom. When he reached the point across from their hiding place, he stopped, staring right at the stairs.

His eyes were level with George's as he looked directly at their hiding spot in the shadows.

George froze. He held his breath. He would have stopped his heart beating if he could, but it continued, thundering in his ears. How could the man before him not hear it?

Were the shadows enough? Could the soldier see the eyes staring at him from between the slabs of stone?

The German's eyes focused. His face twisted in what looked like a triumphant sneer. He opened his mouth.

The German sneezed five times, the sound ringing through the quiet stone building like an explosion. Then he wiped his nose on his sleeve and strode forward to the stairs. He ascended, a step at a time, his equipment clanking.

George closed his eyes, relief flooding his body. A thud came from above—the soldier had slipped on that same step. A grin ghosted over George's face, then froze there. The guard had stopped moving. He muttered one word. "*Blut*!" At first, George took it for a curse, but his tired, foggy brain wouldn't accept it as such.

Blut. Funny word, almost sounds like—

Realization dawned, and he clenched his left hand into a fist—the hand that he had scraped bloody on the wall when he slipped going up. Blood he'd stupidly left behind as evidence.

Blasted stupid fool, what was I thinking, not wiping that up... not that there was time... Will he call for backup or play the hero?

The guard must have been having the same internal debate as he stood still on the stairs. Looking up, George could just see his boots through a gap in the stones. *If he goes up, we can maybe slip out the door. If he calls out, maybe we can just wait. If he goes down for backup... we'll be trapped.*

The seconds ticked by as George stared at those boots. They weren't the tall jackboots from the filmstrips of marching Nazis; they were brown and mud-stained. This fellow was likely just a grunt. *The question is, is he the kind of grunt who'd rather do a job alone, or would he rather get some help?*

One boot lifted.

It stepped up.

George remembered just in time to keep his relieved exhale silent. A few more steps, and the boots disappeared. The wooden floor creaked overhead.

George reached behind him and found Jean's arm. He gave it a little squeeze and a pull, hoping she'd get the hint. Then, stepping as lightly as he was able—imagining that he was stepping on plate glass that could crack at any moment—he crept out from their shelter and darted for the door. Jean's soft footfalls followed. *Just a couple more steps.*

He reached the doorway and gave one parting glance over his shoulder, up to the top of the stairway.

His eyes met those of the soldier, staring at him in surprise.

The surprise turned to resolution. George saw, as if in slow motion, the soldier's mouth opening.

He grabbed Jean's hand, and they ran for it.

Twenty-Two

Jean thanked God for the blessing of each burning breath.

George's rough hand gripped hers like iron. His bent back looked solid as a wall, but his left arm clung tight to his side. Even now, her training kicked in. *He really shouldn't be running*—but they couldn't stop. The soldier's muffled shouts pushed them on.

Other field gray shapes swept into her periphery. Her legs pumped harder, her bag banging against her hip. She and George plunged into the line of spindly trees.

Buzz-thwack! the first bullet shattered a branch near her shoulder. Undergrowth snatched at her feet, and she stumbled. Twigs sliced at her arms, grabbed at her clothing. An image flashed through her mind of Dad and her brother Fred crunching through Minnesota snow, hunting pheasant. Poor birds, roosting quietly until the retriever's bark startled them to fly. They fluttered from imagined danger into real death. Another bullet buzzed overhead. Wings wouldn't help her either—only speed.

A stitch pulled at her side. She let go of George's hand and half stumbled down a hill spotted with evergreens and olive trees. Too thin for real cover. Slick mud and last year's leaves coated the ground.

Another shot shattered a branch above George's head. Bark rained down on them. A piece of detritus stung her eye, and tears streamed down her cheeks.

George darted a glance over his shoulder. His unshaven face looked grey and stretched. He caught her eye. "Just…keep coming. Prove… prove me wrong, Nursey. Keep moving." His clawed fingers clutched his side. Step faltering, he groaned. *He's running on sheer stubbornness. We've gotta get somewhere safe and soon.*

She increased her pace and came abreast of him. "Try to keep up!"

Another shot rang out—a little farther back. There were still shouts, but they weren't gaining.

Why've they slowed down?

She answered her own question as the trees thinned ahead. In another moment, they broke out of them entirely. Before her, a flat, wide expanse of bleak marshland stretched for miles. No cover. Nowhere to hide.

There was no reason for the Germans to run. They knew that there was only so far she and George could go.

George leaned against the last tree, holding his side and gasping. Lunging back to him, she grabbed his arm. "Quick." Stumbling, they made it about a hundred yards south along the tree line before he collapsed against her. Jean steered him into the cover of some brush, pushed him to a sitting position, and went to work on his shirt buttons.

"Can't…keep…your hands offa me, can you?" He grinned, a little of his old spark back.

"Be still, my heart."

After everything, she half expected to see a rib or two piercing his flesh. The bruise on his left looked no better. Other dark bruises radiated out from it. The stitches at his neck were still in place, but the incision still burned an angry red. *We've got to get back to our hospitals quickly.*

Straining her ears for their pursuers, she rifled through her few remaining medicines. "Here."

"What is it?"

"Just trust me. It'll take the edge off."

He shook his head. "The pain lets me know how far I oughta go."

She leaned in close, holding his gaze. "We both know you've gone farther than you oughta go." She held out the pill again and her canteen. With a sigh he took it, then leaned his head back against the tree trunk and closed his eyes.

A sharp crack came from the north, up the slope. *Gunshot or a branch? Doesn't matter.* "C'mon, George, we've gotta get going. Where now?"

He hesitated. His bloodshot eyes scanned the land ahead of them. "I don't…I'm not sure."

The admission knocked her back. "What? But I thought you had this all planned out—"

"Thought I did too. Look at us." He laughed, but it turned into a cough which he tried to muffle in his elbow. "Separated, split up, and lost, with Teds on our tail. And the kid's probably—" He broke off, his eyes closing. "Maybe you were right. Maybe I should've just let it be."

She shook her head. "It's too late for that. We made our own choices." *Was that a voice? It's wait here and get caught or go on. Which? Surrender or run?*

Jean set her jaw. Dad had said that her stubbornness was both God's greatest blessing and greatest challenge for her. Hopefully today it would be a blessing. She gripped George's arm. "Corporal Novak—George—we're not going to give up. We're going to get out of this. I know it. Now. Which way do we go?"

His breath had slowed, but it still sounded labored. He did not open his eyes. "Southeast. Parallel but out of sight of the highway. You know that."

"Ok. And then?" A flicker in the trees caught her eye—did the wind or pursuers move those leaves?

He moistened his lips. "Get too far, we'll run into the action at Cisterna. Too hot there."

"Well, we just take it easy, then. Get in sight of Cisterna and wait for Leroy, right? Just like the plan."

"Yep. Except its daylight. We'll probably get shot."

There was no doubt, indistinct voices carried on the wind from the trees.

Jean nodded. "Ok. Then we'll have to find someplace to lie up till dark. Come on." Ducking under his right arm, she heaved him to his feet. He slumped into her. The knot of fear tightened in her belly. *Please, Lord, if he goes down I don't think I can carry him.* "C'mon, George. A little farther and we can rest a while."

She stepped forward, and after a brief lag he stepped too, quiet and uncomplaining. *He really must be feeling terrible.* Sweat ran down her back and coated her neck under George's heavy arm. One step, then another. She watched the ground, placing her feet carefully to avoid a stumble or the crack of a traitorous twig. George's breath in her ear came in shallow gasps, and her own rasped in her throat.

The world around them had fallen quiet, but it did not feel like the quiet of safety. Other silent feet trod these woods, searching. Every small sound of the forest—tree branches rubbing against each other, the breeze rattling the dried leaves, the squelch of mud under her boots—set her teeth on edge.

George stumbled, and her knees almost gave out. The muscles in her calves and shoulders burned. Behind them another twig snapped. *Dear Jesus, please,* she closed her eyes, then opened them again. *Please. I can't do this. I can't carry him alone. Please. We have to find shelter somewhere.* "C'mon George," she whispered. "Just a little farther—" He gathered himself, and she pushed forward, one agonizing step at a time.

Ahead, the ground dropped and grew marshy as it blended in to the flat, open land beyond. A fallen evergreen tree leaned against a hummock at the edge of the bank. Under the trunk was a shadow. Her frantic eyes rested on the patch of darkness. *That looks promising. Please, oh please…!*

"Here," she whispered, easing George to the ground. She stooped to gaze under the tree trunk. The gap between it and the ground was narrow, but underneath there was a space where the remaining branches had caught on the higher ground, keeping them suspended above the earth. Those same branches camouflaged the hole from above, and the slope of the land hid it from behind. *If we squeeze in tight, it might work.* She closed her eyes. *Thank you.* Swinging around, she grabbed George's knee and shook him. He focused on her, and she motioned to the gap. "Can you crawl in there?"

"I… Sure. I think so."

Once his boots had disappeared, she checked the area for any footprints—any evidence of their presence. It looked alright, at least to her untrained eyes. The long grass was untidy with fallen leaves and pine needles—no mud to show obvious footprints. It was a bit flatter where George had slid through. *I can't do much about that. Unless…* Shoving her bag into the hole, she gathered an armful of sticks and leaves, then slid under the tree trunk, feet first. She scattered her armload after, leaving a small pile of debris blocking the entrance to their shelter. *It's not much for camouflage, but here's hoping it's enough.*

Groping branches scratched at her exposed skin, but by wriggling around she was able to half sit, shoulder to shoulder with George against the earthen wall. Light poked through the latticework of boughs above them, tinted dusky green by the pine needles. Jean allowed herself a sliver of hope. *This could work. If we can just keep still and quiet, and they don't have dogs, and they aren't looking too hard, maybe this will do.* She studied the corporal's face. *If he doesn't get a rest, we're not going to make it anyway.*

He caught her looking. Trying to pull on a smile, he leaned close to whisper, "Nice place you've got here. What's the plan?"

"Here." She fumbled in her satchel and pulled out a piece of brown bread. There wasn't much smell to it, but it was enough to flood her mouth with saliva and to remind her stomach just how much it disliked hugging her backbone. Splitting it, she handed half to him. "We rest here till dark. Then, we head to meet Leroy. Ok?" He nodded. The water in her canteen was running low, so she pulled out the one she'd taken from the unconscious soldier by the truck. Opening it, she took a drink, then spluttered in surprise. It wasn't water but some kind of alcohol.

George grabbed it out of her hand and took a sniff. "Well, I didn't know we had *this* along. Should be a more comfortable rest than I expected." He took a swig.

"You really shouldn't—with medication and needing to heal and—"

"Nursey, you're a better egg than I gave you credit for, but why don't you just leave me be, ok?"

She sighed. "Ok." Accepting it back from him, she took a slow drink. The warmth flowing to her belly felt good. It reminded her of the red mulled wine her grandma pulled out every Christmas, though this was harsher. *And likely much stronger.* She put it aside, determined to both keep her faculties and to stay awake.

At least, she intended to. After a terrifying night and day of running, and with the liquor dulling her body's aches, the rocky earth felt surprisingly comfortable. Her eyes sank closed. *I ought to stay awake so George can rest…or we could take turns…or…* She drifted off.

JEAN WOKE with a shiver. Moisture from the muddy soil had seeped into her layered clothes. Her limbs were stiff and chilled. Blinking, she squinted through their sheltering branches. The dim light had an orangish cast to it, and she realized that she'd slept the day away. Twittering birds somewhere above and behind her sang their evening songs. George slumped beside her, his breathing soft and steady. *Well, that's good at least. Rest can only help him.* She stretched, trying to ease the terrible crick in her neck, rotating her head, her shoulders, her arms in the confined space. Her elbow hit one of the leaning tree branches, making it rustle and showering both of them with dried needles. The birds' singing changed to scolding. A rush of wings reached her ears as they took flight. Jean peered up through the branches. *Huh. I must've spooked them. I wouldn't have expected—*

Then she heard the voices.

They were soft, too soft to distinguish anything other than the fact that they were human, male, and muffled, as if the speakers didn't wish to be heard. Jean closed her eyes as the fear tightened every muscle in her body. *Oh no oh no...please, God, no...*

George gave a soft snore. It sounded like thunder.

The voices fell silent. Had they heard him? Had they just stopped talking? Jean wrung her hands in an agony of suspense. *I've got to wake him up, but quietly.* She reached across her body slowly, slowly, and gently placed her hand over his mouth, increasing the pressure by increments.

George's eyes snapped open, and he grabbed her wrist, eyes rolling wildly in his head. They focused on her, and he relaxed, even managing half of one of those ridiculous grins under her fingers. She drew her hand away and put a finger to her lips, tilting her head up towards the hill behind them. He nodded.

They sat in silence as the minutes ticked by. Nothing moved except the sun, and that they could only tell by the fading light. Straining her ears, Jean bit her lip. *Where are they? Have they passed on by, or are they just waiting?* Still, nothing happened. In the distance, plane engines droned—someone was going to suffer an air raid. Larger artillery pieces sounded off to their left—probably hammering Cisterna, the way their luck was running. *And if Leroy's waiting for us down there—*

George's hand grasped her shoulder, and she jumped inside her skin. He gave it a little squeeze, then inch by inch he eased himself over her until he lay on his belly on the earth. A spasm of pain stretched his face, and she reached for the last pain pill she had stashed in her satchel. Before she could get it, he had crawled out of their meager shelter and was headed in the direction she had indicated, pulling himself along with his good right arm, using his knees to keep his torso from bumping on the ground.

Not without me you won't! Fear clenching her belly, she pushed the satchel onto her back. It pressed on her spine, heavy with the weight of the canteens and pistol. She crawled after him.

The fading light gilded the top of their sheltering tree and the little hillock on which it rested. Jean held her breath as the two of them wormed their way up the earthen slope. George made good speed. *Rest must have helped, but still, I wonder how he's managing—he must be running on sheer adrenaline. And stubbornness.* This time the thought bought a grin, then a frown. Somehow, in all of this, had the two of them become friends? *Well, Stan would approve.*

She pulled herself up alongside him, and they both eased their heads over the bank, scanning for movement, for human shapes, for anything.

It took Jean a minute to see the Germans.

Not ten yards away, two German soldiers lay, sprawled against tree trunks, guns at rest beside them. They didn't move—if not for the subtle rise and fall of their chests, barely visible from this distance, she would have thought they were dead. *They're asleep. On duty? Do they do that?* The troops she had seen were always so disciplined—except Grüber anyway—that the idea of a couple of them on patrol stopping for a nap seemed more than a bit suspicious. And she *had* heard voices, just minutes ago. And the birds had been startled by something.

But the Germans didn't move. There lay their guns, unguarded. And their canteens. And full packs.

By unspoken agreement, both she and George pulled their heads down, back behind the sheltering bank. He knelt, chewing on his lip, considering. Raising his head, he scanned the rest of the area, then looked at her. She shook her head. *There must be someone keeping watch. Why would they just be lying here with our lines so close to theirs?*

George pointed to her, then to the ground, words as plain as if he had spoken them aloud. *You stay here.*

She shook her head again and pointed to herself, then to him. *I'm going where you go.*

He frowned, then pointed towards the men and made a circle in the air. *I'm going to circle around them.*

She nodded, slowly. If both of them went crawling about the hill, it was much more likely that they'd be noticed. He reached for her satchel, and she handed it to him. Rifling through it, he pressed something cold into her hands. The gun.

Fear gripped her heart. *I don't want it. I don't want to touch that thing again.* But he pointed to the gun, pointed to her, then covered his eyes and pointed to himself.

You cover me.

She hesitated, but George was her friend. He was. And she had to help. She nodded. George gave her a thumbs up. Then he pushed his body back down the hill, disappearing into the grasses and tangled undergrowth.

Jean pulled her eyes away from his departing form and aimed them—and the gun—up the slope, towards the clearing and the two sleeping Germans. *Dear Jesus, please let him get back. Please, let him get back safely. Please, don't leave me here alone. And please, please don't make me have to kill anyone else.*

The minutes ticked by. *It's too long—too long!* She pulled in a deep breath. *I'll count. Then I'll know how long it's been. I have to give him...ten minutes. Ten, and then I can start worrying.* She began to count off the seconds—six hundred seconds until she could worry. *One. Two. Three.*

She had reached seventy-five when she heard footsteps coming up from behind her.

Her heart had been pounding before, but now it took on a rhythm that alarmed the detached nurse in her. *Is this what it's like to have a heart attack?*

Frantically, her eyes scanned the surrounding underbrush. Could she creep away, find some more cover? Maybe—but the steps were coming fast, and so close. Jean tried to shrink, tried to press herself into the cold, unyielding earth.

Maybe it's just George. Maybe he saw it was safe and circled around behind, and now he's walking. But that didn't make sense. The steps were coming from the wrong direction. Besides, there were still the sleeping Germans. Every muscle and fiber in her body screamed that this was it. She was about to be caught.

Her hands clenched spasmodically, the cold metal of the gun reassuring and terrifying. Grüber's cold, dead eyes stared at her from the dark recesses of memory. *I can't. I can't—not again. Lord, I don't want to kill anyone…but if I don't, what if he shoots George? But if I do, won't the others wake up? And how many shots are left?* She'd loaded a hunting rifle, a shotgun, and, at Dad's insistence, his pistol from the last war. Theoretically she knew how to check, but she'd never tried on this type of gun. As the bushes rustled and breathing—a man's breathing—approached, she realized that she didn't have any time to figure it out.

Clenching her teeth, she rolled onto her back, bracing herself against the hillside. She raised the gun, aiming at where she figured head height would be. Her weary arms and hands shook. The heavy gun dragged them down. *Hang on, Jean. Gotta wait for a clear shot.*

The shadow of a man appeared between the trees. His light hair was tousled. He wore no helmet. *Good.* She aimed at the thatch of hair, then changed her mind and aimed for the chest. Bigger target.

He stepped out of the shadows. She told her finger to squeeze the trigger. It would not move. His eyes found her. They were wide and brown in his filthy face.

Recognition flashed through them. "Jeannie?"

TWENTY-THREE

WITH A LITTLE SOB, Jean dropped the gun and flung herself at Leroy. He gasped, then caught her and held her tight. Tears on her cheek surprised her as she pressed her face into his collar. She barely remembered to keep her voice to a whisper. "Leroy? Oh Leroy, we thought… Oh!" She let him go, and he stood for a moment, arms still out, dazed expression on his face. Pointing back up the hillock, she breathed, "Two Germans. Sleeping. George is circling around, checking things out, but he's hurting and—"

With a little shake of his head, Leroy found himself again. He nodded and put a finger to his lips, then took her hand and pulled her down. They crouched in the underbrush, listening. The sleeping Germans made no sound.

After a moment, Leroy ignored his own advice. He leaned forward and whispered close to her ear, "You're ok? I didn't think I'd ever find you, but I figured you might stick to the woods as long as you could, so I kept heading towards Cisterna and thought I heard something up here so I figured I'd check…but you're ok?"

Jean managed a quavering smile. "Uh huh—and you are too? We were so worried."

"Sure. I'm a fast runner."

Reaching out a trembling hand, she touched the angry red line that crossed his scalp. "But ..."

"Just a scratch." He smiled at her, the same shy smile that she hadn't wanted to pay attention to before. Now, it felt like coming home. "We're gonna be ok now. We're—" He stopped, staring over her shoulder. There was a slither in the underbrush, then Leroy leaned around her and pulled George into a brotherly embrace.

Studying George's face, all of Jean's worries about his health came flooding back. He was pale, dark circles shadowed his eyes, and his skin looked dry and dehydrated. His grin on seeing his friend was the only thing about him that looked healthy and alive. He motioned the three of them into a football-style huddle, though he did not move his left arm away from his side.

"Hey, kid. Glad you could make the party. There's another couple ahead a few yards, more alert than these, and I think I heard some others digging in. We'd better scoot."

"Sounds good," said Leroy. "Whaddya think? Farther down the Cisterna road or south from here towards the beachhead?"

Jean answered, "We should get back as quickly as we can." Leroy caught her eye, then looked at George with a worried frown.

George nodded, every movement slow. "Ok, south. And then..." he trailed off.

Leroy finished for him. "We'll have to take it carefully. If we're lucky and find a patrol, we let them know we're Americans, and they can get us through with passwords and all."

"Here's to good luck!' said Jean. She scooped up the gun, handed it to Leroy, and the three crept away from the hillock, away from the sleeping enemy, and towards the open ground to the south.

Leroy crouched in the shelter of the last large tree and chewed on his lower lip. The long, flat stretch of land before him looked featureless and empty in the failing light. Far away, the western horizon was nothing but a lighter gray line above a charcoal haze. Almost at the edge of sight, a few tiny white lights sprang into the air like sparks. *Ack Ack fire. Must be an air raid on the ships.*

Closer, just below his concealment, dry grasses soughed in the icy evening breeze. He strained his senses—was it only the wind sighing? Closing his eyes for a moment, he prayed, *Please, Lord, we're so close.* He scanned the ground one more time, then nodded to himself. There, just downhill and to the left, was the answer.

Keeping low, he turned and crept back to where Jean and George waited. The nurse was checking George's dressings, that worried frown back between her eyes. It deepened at his approach. He leaned in and whispered. "Ok, there's still too much light left, but I don't think we're safe waiting here anymore. It looks like there's a depression a couple hundred yards away. Maybe a creek. Whaddya think, George?"

His buddy blinked. After a moment, he seemed to register what Leroy had said. "Sure. Sure, kid. Lots of creeks and things running down to the sea. If there's one to follow, we could find some cover."

Forcing a smile, Leroy nodded. *He's awfully slow. Not like George.* "That's what I thought. So. We'll stick close to the tree line, but not too close. Stay low and get down that embankment as quick as we can. Sound ok?"

George nodded again. "Sure."

The three of them exited their cover. Crouched low, they scuttled through the long grasses. Knowing that they ought to spread out, Leroy stuck to George's side. He didn't care for the way his friend's strong frame wavered with each step. Jeannie clearly didn't either—she kept to George's other side, watching him closely. The nighttime shadows trembled and moved in Leroy's periphery, creating imagined foes all about. He grimaced and wished he hadn't dropped that rifle during his flight. Gripping the pistol tighter, he quickened his pace, ears straining for the first sound of danger.

They arrived at the shadowed depression in the land without incident. Sure enough, it was a low creek bed. There was a little stream of water winding along its bottom, nestled in the center of a bed of thick mud. Leroy slid down first, boots squelching in the morass, his sockless feet chilled by the damp seeping through them. He turned back to help George and Jeannie down. *Not great cover—if we walk upright our heads'll still be in plain view.* Still, it was better than nothing. He led the way, back bent, hand tracing the side of the gully. One step, then another. Each step was twice the work as the mud sucked onto the lifting foot, trying to hold it down. Step. Suck. Lift. Step. On and on, he pulled his body through the sludge. The damp and cold soaked into his bones until they ached.

A hiss from behind made him pause. Glancing back, he saw Jeannie trying to support George. His friend was leaning heavily on the nurse's arm, hunching as if he carried a great weight.

Shoot. Leroy hustled back, handed the nurse the gun, and took over her post at George's side. "Hang in there, buddy, we're almost through this, then we'll get a rest." He took a step forward. George did the same. "Just keep going, get through this mess, and next thing you know, there'll be a patrol, and we'll be scot-free. All you gotta do is hang on." Step. Suck. Lift. Step. Leroy kept the prattle going, soft, mindless, as he pushed forward. George followed him, keeping upright. The encouragements were a thin thread, but they were still something to hold on to. *C'mon, buddy. Just hang on. Just a few more steps. Almost there. Just hang on.*

The last gleam of light faded from the world around them, and with it went the last of George's strength. Without a sound, he slumped against the side of the gully, head drooping to his chest.

Leroy hustled to catch him before he fell. Jeannie hurried back to them. "He needs a rest. Can we get him out of the mud?"

Together, they pulled and prodded George up the stream bank to the long grasses that grew at its verge. A convenient boulder, lodged in the earth at the point they came up, stood like a leftover from God sculpting the mountains to the east and provided a sense of shelter as they huddled together in the cold dark.

Jeannie rummaged through her pack and pulled out a dark hunk of bread. Breaking it into three pieces, she handed one to George and offered another to Leroy. His stomach complained at the sight and smell of food, but he swallowed the saliva down and shook his head. "You two split it. I found a farmhouse while I was running—got some milk and bread there. Lost my socks, though."

"Socks?" Jean asked, but he shrugged. That story would have to wait. For a moment, he saw again the house where he'd left that woman and her son, pictured them standing in the doorway, watching as the Germans drove away. *At least they were alright*—but he hadn't dared return to their home to check on them further or to collect his socks.

Jeannie pulled out two canteens and handed Leroy the one with an unfamiliar make. Leroy took a sip, then spluttered. The nurse's grin showed through the dark. She leaned forward. "Any idea where we are?"

He glanced at the sky, then at the horizon. "Still bearing southwest, which we want, but the stream bends here. I think…I think our best bet is to stick to the high ground now that it's dark and head straight on toward the coast." He glanced at George, who sat, bread still in his hand. "That gets us to our lines fastest. Whaddya think, George?"

Seeming to wake up, George raised the hard bread to his mouth, then lowered it as if chewing were too much work for his weary jaws. Leroy swallowed. *We better get him back, quick.*

Jean reached over and took the bread.

"Hey…" George said, weakly.

"Just wait. Let me make this a little easier." With care, she dribbled a little water from her canteen over it. It crumbled, and she scooped bits into his mouth.

Leroy frowned, eyes darting between the two of them, but when she looked up at him he managed a shadow of a smile. "Well, one thing we could do, Jeannie…I'm sorry…" he rubbed his hands over his face. "Jean. Nurse Hoff…"

She looked down at the canteen. "Jeannie's alright."

He scanned her face. "Are you…you sure?"

She nodded, then grinned. "For you. And you, I suppose," she poked George's leg, and his eyes, which had been drifting, focused on her. "It's better than 'Nursey' anyway. But if either of you sing that darned song I might…I might just slug you." She tried for a fierce face, and Leroy grinned.

"…light brown hair…" murmured George.

She looked at him sharply, as did Leroy, wondering if he were daring her to carry out her threat. No playful grin spread across George's face. Instead, sweat coated his brow, gleaming in the dim light, and his head lolled to the side as if he hadn't the energy to hold it up. Leroy's hands clenched as fear gripped his middle. *No, God, please, don't take him. Not this close—we've come so far!* "Hey, George?"

Jeannie tapped Leroy's shoulder, and he turned his attention to her. Glancing at George, she leaned in close and lowered her voice below the whispers they'd been using. "Leroy, could you…could we talk a minute?"

"Ok—"

George interrupted. "Nope." His voice was clearer. "You don't get to do some sort of doctoral consult without me." He scrubbed his right hand across his face. "What's up, N—Jeannie?"

Jeannie sighed. "Ok. You…it doesn't seem like you're doing too great, George. You've overdone it and then some. I suspect that we're going to need to get you into surgery as soon as possible. That rib might have pierced something, and I don't think—I wish we could rest longer, but I don't think we can risk spending another night in the field."

"Ok then." Leroy tightened his laces and stood. "Let's get moving.

Hopefully, someone will be out and about, but once we get close we'll just make sure we're kind of loud and hope they see us."

Jean stood too. She paused, rummaging through her bag.

"Here we go," said Leroy, holding out his hand to George. George did not take it. His mouth was set in a stubborn line.

"What...what are you doing?"

With a sigh, George shook his head. "I'm staying here. I'm too slow, and my legs...I'm not feeling them so well just now. You two'll have a better chance without me."

"What?" Leroy stared at him. Stepping forward, he grabbed his friend's shoulder. "Don't be stupid. We're not gonna just leave you here."

George flinched at his touch, then looked at him, gaze level and firm. "Sure you are, kid. You get Jeannie and yourself outta here. You'll have a better chance—"

"No. We've come this far together..."

George mustered his strength and spoke over him. "You came this far because I convinced you to. Felt like I had something to prove. I don't have nothing to prove anymore, except that I'm half the friend to you that you've always been to me." He looked away. "Now. Get outta here."

Anger replaced disbelief. Leroy planted his feet, opened his mouth, but Jeannie stepped between them. She reached out to touch his arm. "Leroy...he might be right."

He spun on her, aghast at her betrayal. "What?" *George always said she was cold, but this—* "After he...after everything? You'd just leave him?"

"No, that's not what I..." She paused, grasping for words. "Look. If he keeps going, the walking might...it's not going to help his condition. But if we can move faster and find someone—a patrol, maybe—and send them back for him, we might be able to get him to help sooner."

"What if they won't risk coming out this far? What if we're farther out than we think we are and…" he wiped his eyes and tightened his lips. "I'm not gonna just leave my friend."

"I'm not going any farther." George laughed—it ended in a wheeze. "What're you gonna do? Throw me over your shoulder?"

Setting his jaw, Leroy said, "If I have to."

George sighed. "Look, it's gonna be light again before you know it." He pointed at Jeannie, his finger shaking, but he held Leroy with his gaze. "You wanna get her safe? You need to go and go now."

"You stubborn idiot. I oughta…" Leroy stomped away a few paces, then came back.

"It's gonna be light soon," George repeated, his speech slurred.

"Good!" Leroy exclaimed. "Then the fellas in Anzio will see the three of us."

"Shhh! Not so loud!" Jean interrupted. The men fell silent. "Look. What if…what if we helped you for a ways, George, just got you a little further in, and if we don't find anyone…"

"Fine. That's what we'll do." Leroy strode over, squatted, and pulled George's arms around his neck. His friend's quick intake of breath when he moved the left one made him release it. "Left arm bad?"

"It's…I can't really…" George gasped for a few moments, finding his breath. When he found it, he grumbled. "This is stupid. Not only am I slowing you down, I don't wanna get carried into camp like a kid who skinned his knees."

"Shut up, or I'll slug you and carry you that way." Leroy got his hands under George's legs and lifted.

Jean hurried over. "Let me help." Together, they hoisted George onto Leroy's back, piggyback style.

George still muttered under his breath but held on with his right arm. "We won't get far like this."

"We'll get far enough," Leroy answered shortly.

Jeannie gathered up their meager supplies, and the three of them set off.

THE NIGHT WORE ON. The chill in the air spoke of midnight having come and gone. Though none of them had said anything for the last hour, Leroy was fairly certain that they were all thinking the same thing. *Where have our lines got to? Sure, we're not moving fast, but we should've seen someone by now. Unless we had it wrong. Maybe we didn't start where we thought we did and we're too far north, or too far south. Maybe we got turned around in the dark. Maybe—*

Jeannie appeared at his elbow. He spared her a glance. Sweat dripped down his forehead from exertion—even after short rations and illness, George was not a light load. She whispered, "I've been thinking. Maybe we should cut back towards the left. Try to hit the road? We might find someone sooner—"

The drone of an engine passed overhead—several engines. He jerked his chin up towards the sky. "Ever been strafed at? It's not much fun."

She bit her lip and nodded, her long hair falling out of its pins and trailing down her back.

They continued in silence, trapped in a never-ending, weary march. Leroy paused, repositioning his aching arms. *Dear God, I don't know how much farther I can go, with nothing to eat, no rest... But we can't stop now. We've gotta find someone soon... Please, let us find someone soon.*

Ahead, somewhere in the dark, a man cleared his throat.

He froze. George raised his head. Jeannie almost stumbled into his elbow. They waited, silent.

It's someone...but are we sure we're by our lines? Even if we are, what if it's a Ted patrol? Indecision gripped him.

A moment later, what sounded like the same voice sneezed.

Someone whispered, "Bless you."

In English! They're...they're speaking English!

A third voice shushed them.

The second voice hissed, "Shush yourself."

"Will you shaddup? I thought I heard something."

"You're always hearing something."

The voices were coming closer. Still, Leroy hesitated. They sounded edgy. Probably a recon patrol, just what they'd been hoping for. *Pretty green if they're making this much noise, though. We'll have to watch ourselves.*

He squatted, letting George slide down from his back. Then he stood.

Squinting into the dark, he waited for movement to give them away. *There they are*—three fellas spread out, walking towards him. The silhouettes of their American-style helmets convinced him.

Leroy raised his hands slowly, unsure of what to say. Reaching over for Jeannie, he pushed her behind him. She stumbled and gasped. The nearest member of the patrol froze and raised his rifle. *Better move quick here.* He cleared his throat. "Hello there? Who you fellas with…?"

Everything went wrong.

All three shadows whipped their rifles up even higher. The man nearest jumped hard. Must've been walking with his finger on the trigger. His weapon fired. The bullet grazed Leroy's arm as it passed him. Jeannie cried out.

Leroy flung his arms into the air. "We're Americans! We're Americans! And we have a wounded man and a woman!" The words tumbled out of his mouth, and the forward man's rifle lowered. Leroy spun to find Jeannie lying on the ground behind him. A wound blossomed red out of her side.

One of the men in the patrol cursed, and footsteps thudded on the ground, running forward.

Leroy dropped, tried to lift Jeannie's limp form. "Jean? Jeannie, you gotta wake up. Jeannie—"

Her eyes opened to slits, and her lips parted. "Leroy?" she asked.

Her eyes rolled back into her head.

PART THREE

Twenty-Four

The first thing Jeannie noticed was a piercing ache in her side. The rest of her body felt heavy and sore, as if she'd been lying in one position for a long time. She shifted, and the ache pulled. It felt like... *Stitches. I've got stitches. Why…?*

The memories came flooding back. Stan. The capture. Grüber. The escape. The shot. Leroy calling her name as she fell.

Her eyes snapped open. *Leroy and George! Did they make it?* She wracked her brain but couldn't find the answer. George had been pretty badly off, she remembered that. Leroy…she remembered his face, terrified and angry all at once as he'd reached for her.

But, where are we? We found that American patrol…are we back? Opening her eyes, she looked around her, searching for a clue. She was in a tent, her bed blocked off by curtains. A line led into her arm. The sudden roar of a plane's engine shook the air and ruffled the canvas above her head. In the distance, artillery shells screamed and shrieked and boomed.

Sure sounds like Anzio.

"Jean? Jean? Are you awake?" Her old tentmate, Gladys Grady, appeared, leaning over her. Gladys looked like she'd lost weight in the last week, and her eyes were tired. Her blonde hair rolled into a turban left her looking as matronly as ever. Unlike the last time she'd seen Jean, though, she met her eyes at once and smiled.

Jeannie licked her lips. "Yes. Hello, Gladys."

Gladys pressed her hand. "Oh Jean, we were so worried…" Her lower lip quivered.

"I'm fine." Memories of her behavior before struck her, and a hot wave of shame flushed her cheeks. "Look, thank you. I'm sorry, so sorry, about how I was before. I shouldn't have—"

"Oh don't..." Gladys leaned down and gave her a gentle hug. Though it startled her, for the first time in a long time, Jeannie didn't want to pull away. She managed to get her right arm up to awkwardly return the embrace. Gladys stood and cleared her throat. "Don't worry about it. I shouldn't have been so pushy. Sometimes I really am a mother hen—"

"No, you—"

"Now, Jean, I—" Gladys interrupted, stopped, and laughed. "See? I'm doing it again. But I knew you were struggling, and I should have been more understanding. And then they found Major Larson's dog tags, and the driver said you'd been along—he was wounded, just barely escaped himself. He didn't know what had happened and… we thought…" she bit her lips. "And the last thing I'd said to you… the last thing was me being cross with you." Her voice broke.

Jeannie grabbed her hand. "Please. Please don't. Everything's ok now. I'm fine, and I'll be back at it soon. I promise, I'll do better now."

Gladys wiped her eyes. "Back…? Oh Jean, you're only just stable. You lost a lot of blood, you know. By the time that patrol brought you and that corporal in, you were white as a ghost. Thank God we'd just gotten some plasma, and the boy who shot you volunteered to donate—poor thing, he felt terrible…ow!"

Jeannie's hand had clenched Gladys's hard, fear lending her strength. "That corporal…how is he? Oh Gladys, how are the men who were with me? Are they…?"

Gladys hesitated. "Well..."

Jeannie closed her eyes. "No...Oh no."

"The tall one, with the ears? He's ok. He's been hanging around the hospital tent every chance he gets, asking about you. I ...um, I think he likes you."

Jeannie smiled and closed her eyes. "I know." She took a deep breath. "But the other?"

"Corporal Novak." Gladys nodded. "He's had to have a couple of surgeries. His ribs were broken, and one had punctured his spleen. The site where—was it a German doctor who operated on him? That's what I heard, anyway. It was infected. We had to clean it out, get him on penicillin—"

"But...he's pulling through?"

Gladys nodded, slowly, looking less certain than Jeannie would have liked. "Yes—it seems like he's going to pull through. Stubborn guy."

"You have no idea. But was the damage—really, is he going to be ok, Gladys?"

The blonde nurse raised her eyebrows but didn't ask. Jeannie answered anyway. "He's my friend. Just that and...and he's been through a lot. He's the one who got us away from the Germans. Saved my life at least once. I'd hate to think..." she trailed off.

Gladys put a hand on her arm. "Well, it's going to take some therapy and lots of time. But I think, God willing, he should be alright. He's getting sent to Naples to convalesce. Maybe you two will be on the same ship."

"On the same...what do you mean?" Jeannie tried to sit up, but the screaming pain in her side reminded her that this wasn't a good idea. "I'm gonna heal up, and I'm gonna stay on here...I have to help."

"Oh Jean, I'm so sorry."

"But I've barely done anything...." *Everything—all my plans, my chance to make a difference—gone.*

Gladys took a deep breath. "This is no place for the wounded—you know that. And with all you've been through, getting back on your feet is probably gonna take a while, honey. Now that you're stable, you'll likely be heading out on the next boat. Hopefully tonight."

Jeannie lay her head back down. *So. It's…over?*

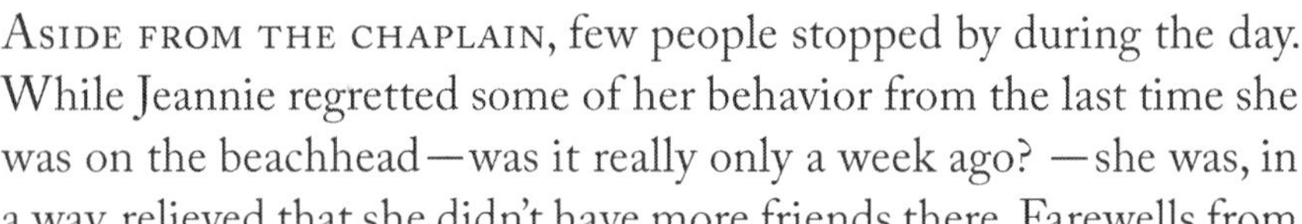

Aside from the chaplain, few people stopped by during the day. While Jeannie regretted some of her behavior from the last time she was on the beachhead—was it really only a week ago? —she was, in a way, relieved that she didn't have more friends there. Farewells from colleagues were regretful—she had been a good nurse, after all—but not emotion-filled.

That was good. She didn't think she could handle more emotion.

The sounds of the hospital, of Anzio, brought back memories of Stan. In the fear and danger of the last week, she'd been too occupied to fully feel her loss. Now…now his absence was everywhere. He should be here, but he was gone. Her mentor. Her advocate. Her friend.

Though her weary body cried for rest, Jeannie resisted. When she closed her eyes, she'd see the hole where he died. Or she'd see Doctor Schmidt, her enemy who'd protected her, collapsed on the dirt floor, unconscious. What happened to him? Did she get the dosage right? Would he return to the family he'd left behind? Or, somehow the worst of the three, she'd see Grüber's leer in the laundry, then his cold, dead stare as he lay on the ground, her bullet in his chest. It was better to stay awake, although the howls and shrieks of artillery and air raids and Anzio Annie made a terrifying counterpoint to the groans of the other patients being treated on Hell's Half Acre.

Around her privacy curtains, she caught glimpses of the men carried in for recovery. Once or twice she almost called out, thinking the passersby wore the face of one of the other prisoners—one looked like Hank, another like Ed. *No, of course, Ed's dead.* Swallowing the lump that rose in her throat, she lay back, wondering how the others had fared. Had they been rounded up by searching soldiers, or had they made it to Rome at last? Did Roberts make it back to fly again, or was he lying on some Italian hillside?

The surgeon who came by to double-check his handiwork on her stitches had confirmed Gladys's opinion—Jeannie would take her own journey down Purple Heart Highway when darkness fell tonight. The thought of the road and of the claustrophobic hospital ship waiting for her made her nervous, but it was all dimmed and dulled under a heavy, overshadowing gloom. *I'm leaving. I'm going away from here.*

She knew that she should be relieved—at least a little. Anzio was a terrible place. She'd never wanted to be here. Only fear of the unknown in a POW camp or under the power of Grüber had induced her to run back. But now that she'd made it, to leave, to be denied the chance to help, left her feeling empty. She realized as she lay there that she didn't wish to stay because of Joe, not anymore. Nor did she wish to stay to prove anything to herself. Now she wished that she could stay for *them.* For the men and the nurses that would have to stay here, whether she left or not. The people who would be suffering in her place.

Off to Naples to recuperate. Then I'll probably be sent back home. Back to sit it out. To wait.

There was guilt and sorrow in that thought, but not fear, not anymore. She was too weary for her fears, too tired for anger, and too fretful to think about any kind of future.

Just after supper was brought around—she had to eat sparingly after her fast, so her food was mostly of the liquid variety—someone cleared his throat. She raised her head, and there was Leroy, standing at the foot of her cot and gazing at her with his brows knit in worry as he tried to smile.

Her smile wasn't forced. "Leroy!" She reached out her hand to him.

He stepped forward and took it, his smile growing. "Jeannie. I… How're you doing?"

She shrugged, then wished she hadn't as the wound in her side pulled. "I'm all right."

He knelt next to her bed, still holding her hand as if he couldn't bear to let it go and hung his head. "I'm sorry. I'm so sorry. I should've moved you farther back or..." He trailed off, and his tortured eyes rose to meet hers.

She shook her head and squeezed his fingertips. "It wasn't your fault. You tried. It was just an accident, and I'm ok. The nurses and doctors say I should be fine. Besides, after everything you did for us—if you hadn't led the guards away at the beginning—"

He shrugged. "That was just—"

"Just about the bravest thing I've ever seen."

His ears flushed, and he dropped his eyes, but not her hand. "Well, I couldn't let them...you couldn't go back...I couldn't let them take you, Jeannie." He cleared his throat. "Besides, with George so badly off I had to do something—did you hear? It sounds like they're hopeful he'll make it. He's still out, and they won't let me in to see him, but he'll be evacuated. Get somewhere decent."

"Yes. I'm so glad—he wouldn't have made it either if it hadn't been for you." She turned her face toward the wall. "It sounds like I'm being sent away, too."

The cot sagged as he sat down on the edge of it. "Yeah, I know. Shipped out tonight. That's good. They'll get you somewhere safe. Maybe back home."

"Home." She said it softly, tasting the word on her tongue like an unfamiliar spice. "You know, before I came here, I couldn't wait to get away from there. Now..."

"Now maybe it won't be so bad?"

She sighed. "Parts of it." She turned her eyes to his, and this time she was the hesitant one. "Only...I hate leaving everyone behind. Not knowing how...people are. If they're safe."

He absently smoothed the knee of his trousers. Freshly shaved and washed, he smelled nice, and his smooth cheek looked better clean than with stubble. "Maybe…maybe some of the nurses will keep you posted."

"Maybe."

He took a deep breath and looked up, meeting her eyes. He moistened his lips and then said, as if it cost great effort, "Maybe…if you didn't mind…"

"Yes?"

His voice was quiet but decided. "Maybe I could write you, too? Let you know how things are going?"

She considered. After everything that had happened since she'd landed on the Anzio beachhead, things had changed. She had changed. And she meant it when she said, "I'd like that."

His slow grin spread across his face. "You would?"

"Mmmhmmm." She looked down at her hand, still clasped in his. "You know, if they do send me home, and you write, you'd have my address."

"So. Maybe when I get back, I could stop by? Check up on you?"

She looked up at him, and for the second time she felt a real smile spread across her face, and she allowed herself a luxury she'd thought long gone: hope.

"I think you'd better."

"Is that an order?"

"Does it need to be?"

"No, ma'am, it'd be my pleasure."

GEORGE'S TRIP to Naples blurred and ran together, like a sidewalk chalk drawing after a rain. The jolting of the truck down Purple Heart Highway to the shore with planes buzzing overhead like bees blended with the pitching of the hospital ship. Even in his dream-state the dark quarters stank of human bodies and medicine and disinfectant. His head filled and echoed with the chatter of the staff and the complaints of the passengers asking for water, for a smoke, for more morphine.

Even in his dreams, George waited for the torpedo to hit. The crunch of metal, the shuddering of the ship, and the cries of the trapped as they sank. He dreamed that it had happened every time he closed his eyes and woke half babbling prayers, convinced that it was his time to go. After all, he deserved it.

The litany of his sins wound round and round his brain. *Almost got Leroy killed. Jeannie…probably dead. Ed, shot. Roberts and Hank and Barry and Chuck, all gone. Squad leaderless, one dead, one wounded, the others scattered…*

But it was all over—his war was over. He'd heard a lady's voice tell him so. He thought at first it was Jeannie, but her voice was a little higher, and anyway, this voice was smiling, so it probably couldn't be. Other words scattered around him. "Fever" was one, and he'd feel something cool on his head. "Infection" was another, and he'd have to swallow bitter drugs or have another needle pierce his arm. They kept trying to force drink down his throat, and he kept trying to tell them that all he wanted was a beer and a cigarette thanks, and then he'd be just fine going down with this blasted truck, or ship, or whatever he was in. The words kept getting lost in his throat, and the sleep kept swallowing him, back to dreams of Norrie laughing and Lilly smiling and ships sinking behind them in blood and flames. The darkness prepared to swallow him—

Cold fingers touched his wrist, and they felt more real, more solid, than anything had in a long while.

With an effort, he opened one eye, then closed it again. The bright light burned.

Not the boat then. Did we make shore? Or maybe it's heaven.

He shifted his body. He was lying in a bed—a real one. It sure felt comfortable, maybe heavenly. The jab in his arm that followed did not. With a grunt, he opened both eyes to slits. Standing over him was a nurse—*Well, that's familiar*—but this nurse was small and brown haired and judging from her posture seemed to lack the chip on Jeannie's shoulder.

"Well!" she said, lips curving upward. They were red, almost too red. The color hurt George's eyes almost as much as the light from the windows. *Windows? Huh, it's been a while since I've seen those.* He refocused on those clown-red lips which were talking in a slow, clear voice. "We've been sleeping a long time, haven't we? It's nice to see you're back with us, soldier."

We? George blinked, squinching his eyes shut, hoping to clear his vision a bit, then stretched them back open.

The room looked like a real hospital, with walls as well as windows, and it smelled clean. He smelled clean, too, except for that "sick" smell to his skin that told him he hadn't been taking care of his own needs for a while. He opened his lips to try to talk, but no sound made it past his dry tongue.

The nurse noticed. "Oh, here soldier, let me help." She slid an arm under his shoulders and lifted him to drink—the sense of déjà vu almost made him laugh. But this time the water was contained in a little cup rather than a metallic canteen, and it was fresh. He sipped gratefully but didn't need her reminder to "take it easy." It didn't feel like his stomach had anything in it to come up, but he wasn't planning on risking it, not over these nice clean sheets. *Clean sheets? When's the last time I saw those?*

Other wonders started to register. His face must've been shaved—the cup didn't hit any bristle anyway, and he thought he could smell shaving soap. The sun poured in from outside the window, and the world was...quiet. Oddly quiet. What was missing? *The bombs. No planes, no bombs falling...it's just* quiet *here.* A few voices here and there, sure. And there—were those planes going over? He strained his ears. Sounded like bombers, but American made ones.

The nurse took the cup from his lips and turned away. He tried to sit up, but it hurt and pulled. *Wonder if they had to do more surgery after everything?* She turned back and saw what he was up to. "Oh no, we're not ready for *that* just yet. Poor thing, you've been through an awful lot."

He licked his lips a few times, cleared his throat, then tried his old charmer grin.

This nurse smiled back. *Not like Jeannie at all, then. Wait, Jeannie—did she get hit, or was that just a dream too?* He tried to sit up again, suddenly alert.

"Hey, Nurse, what about..." but he broke off with a grunt as his injuries screamed, and the nurse fluttered around him, sternly alarmed. Hands on his shoulders, she pushed him back down onto a new pillow she'd tucked behind his head.

"Now you need to settle down, soldier! You're going to pull out those stitches! I'll have to go and get Major Hanley to look at—"

He grabbed her wrist. "Wait, please, Nurse. A couple of questions? Just a couple? Please?" He gave her the grin again, this time with a little apology in it. She pursed her red, red lips, then nodded. Her hair was pinned back so tightly that it hardly moved.

"Alright, soldier. If you promise me that afterwards you'll take a rest. I have to get this blood draw in, too—"

He nodded. "Of course, Nurse, of course. It's just...well, I'm not sure just where I am. And I had some friends I was with. One was a nurse too. I think she might've been wounded."

She gave him a sidelong look. He wasn't sure just what it meant, but his heart sank under a sudden, crushing certainty. *Oh God, please, don't let me have gotten Jeannie killed... She wasn't a bad kid, Lord, and she sure saved my skin. She didn't deserve that.*

Seeing his agitation, she frowned. "I don't want you to become excited. Doctor's orders are—"

He held up his hands. "I'm not getting excited. Promise. I just...I'd just like to know what I've missed, ya know? Then I promise, I'll settle in. No problems at all. I'll be a good boy." He tried the grin again, and she relaxed a little.

"Alright. You're in Naples, nice and far away from the fighting."

He nodded. "What about my friends? Any word on—"

She shook her head. "A lot of people came on your boat. I'm not sure I'd even know—"

"One was just a kid—Private Leroy Anderson. Nice kid, tall, blonde, kind of big ears."

"I'm sorry, I don't know—"

He pressed on. "The other was a nurse, like you. She…if I'm remembering right, I was pretty out of it when it happened…I think she might've gotten shot."

The image came back, though it wavered, like he was watching it through water. Leroy, pushing Jeannie behind him, hands up, talking to someone up ahead. A shot that he felt sure was going to get him, but it didn't. Jeannie's pale form in the dark, sinking to the ground. Leroy turning around, howling her name, and cursing—the kid never cursed. The fool who'd shot her and the whole patrol running forward, everything going black—

The new nurse was nodding, slowly. "Yes, a nurse was sent down from Anzio. She'd been shot."

He almost forgot his promise and sat up again, but he forced himself to remain still. "Is she…?" He couldn't bear to ask.

The nurse put a hand on his arm. "She's going to be fine. If it had been a little lower…but thank God, it wasn't. I understand that yesterday she even came up to the ward to check on you." Giving him a searching look, she continued, slowly, clearly compelled to offer some motherly advice. "Now, while it looks like you'll both be sent back stateside soon, you know you're really not supposed to be fraternizing—"

A cool voice, a little tired but wonderfully familiar, cut into the conversation. "Please, Nurse Carson. If there's any fraternizing to be done, Corporal Novak isn't the man I'd risk it on." Jeannie walked around the corner. She moved slowly, as if she weren't entirely comfortable on her own feet just yet, but her eyebrow was cocked at a crooked angle that said she still meant business.

George threw back his head and laughed aloud. "HAaahOW!" It turned to another grunt of pain, and he put his hand over his stitches. "I dunno, Nurse Hoff, if you bring that kind of charm and charisma over here, you might just tempt a lowly dogface like me to forget my place."

She rolled her eyes, but he noted how she gripped the end of his bed hard to keep standing and how pale her face was.

The red-lipsticked nurse had the good grace to flush a little as she pulled up a chair for Jeannie, but she still cautioned them not to visit too long, and she also told the green-eyed nurse, "And you should get one of the men to push you back to your ward in a wheelchair. You shouldn't overdo it, you know."

Jeannie's lips compressed to a thin line, but she nodded and, to George's amazement, said, "You're right. Thanks. I just hate being cooped up."

The nurse squeezed her shoulder and left them to visit.

Jeannie met his eyes squarely and sized him up. "So. They tell me that you're just too stubborn to die." She smiled then, a little half smile that softened her eyes. "I was glad to hear it, George."

"Aw, shucks Nursey," he said and flashed her a sly wink. "You aren't going soft on me, are you?"

She shifted in her chair, a little flash of pain crossing her face. "Nope. Just after all the time I put in on you, it'd hardly be fair if you went and died, would it?"

"I wouldn't dare waste your time, Nurse Hoff." He lowered his voice, grin melting. "You ok?"

She shrugged, looked away. "Good enough. They're…they're sending me back home this week, sounds like."

"That's fast."

"Figures. One time I'd rather the Army moved a little slower." She smiled a sad smile. "Give me time to heal up more...maybe I could get back out there."

"Still got something to prove?"

She gave her head a slow shake. "No, not really." She looked away. "Just...now that I've seen it, I hate to leave. I was hardly able to do anything at all, and they're still out there, still fighting. I wish...I wish I could help. For them. And for me." She bent her head to look at her clasped hands.

"Leroy." He hesitated, wanting to know but not wanting to ask. "You know how he is? Any idea?"

A little flush crept across her pale cheek. "Yes, he's fine, or was a few days ago. I just got a letter from him yesterday."

He raised his eyebrows. "Reeaaaally?" The flush on her face darkened, and he was tempted to push a little harder, but thought the better of it. "He made it back to the beachhead ok?"

She nodded. "He got us all back, in the end." Looking up, she added with a little proud smile. "They mentioned a promotion for him, and it sounds like he might be your squad's new leader. Oh, and he said..." She fumbled in her pocket.

She's even carrying the letter with her. Hmmm.

"He said to let you know if I saw you that Pete made it back fine and Shorty's gotten another letter from his missus." She looked up, eyebrows raised.

Even though he knew how it would hurt, George couldn't help a little chuckle, raising his eyes heavenward. "Oh my." He quickly sobered. Leroy was alive, for now. But a squad leader on Anzio...that God-forsaken beachhead. George had insisted on going back, and now Leroy was the one stuck there.

He started when he felt Jeannie's hand on his arm. He looked over at her—her gaze was cool, measuring. She knew his fear, knew what he'd been thinking, he was sure.

"He's in God's hands." She said it simply, calmly.

"Maybe I should've just let it be. Or maybe he'd have been better off in Rome… I wonder how those guys ended up."

"Who knows? Maybe when we break out of Anzio they'll be there, waiting. But as for the other stuff, George…You're crazy, you know, and yes, you're a leader, and we followed you. But we didn't have to—we chose to. Maybe we were all a little crazy."

She stretched out her long legs, then drew them back in with another grimace, hand going to her side. At his concerned look, she just grinned and shook her head. "And now…now we are where we are." She looked around at the hospital walls. "God only knows where we'll be next. But he's given us another chance at life and you and me…I figure we've done enough fighting against where he's put us, and we've both had enough bitterness."

"Maybe you're right, Nursey. Maybe…" He hesitated, searching for the right words. "Maybe it's time to try forgiveness. Try moving on for real."

"Wouldn't that be something?" She stuck out her hand to shake with a smile—a real, normal person smile, not cold or controlled at all, and for the first time he understood what Leroy must see in her. "Whether I see you again or not, George, I hope we're friends now."

He took her hand and shook it. "Friends. And who knows what'll happen, Nursey. The world's a funny place."

Twenty-Five

The calendar on the wall read July 10, 1946. Jeannie had circled the date in red, with a big question mark under it. She tried not to look too hard at that question mark as she pinned her hair for the third time. It wouldn't behave itself today, no matter what she did—too tight the first time, too flyaway the second. She growled in frustration around the hairpins she held in her mouth and tried again to get the victory roll she wanted in front just right.

After more than two years, she wanted to look presentable.

Leroy's letters sat piled on the oak chest of drawers that served as her dressing table. The piece of furniture was too big for the space—calling the apartment she and her roommate shared "modest" was generous. Still, it had been enough for a couple of single nurses working busy shifts at all hours. Gina was a few years younger and still stared with wide eyes at Jeannie's scar when she caught sight of it. She asked lots of questions about going abroad—the Army Nurse Corps hadn't taken her because of her asthma. *A couple of rejects, the both of us,* thought Jeannie, but there was no real bitterness in the thought. Maybe the bitterness had been left behind at Anzio, or maybe the surgeon's knife had cut it out with the bullet. Anyway,

Jeannie was grateful for the good work she'd been able to do since returning, and today—

Well. Today should be interesting.

She glanced down at the letters. The first one to catch her eye was one of the earliest.

June 5, 1944

Dear Jeannie,

Well, we're here. Camped right outside of Rome. Now that it's been 'liberated' I hope I get a chance to check out some of the old ruins and things. (I guess we'll see what the enlisted guys like me are allowed to do, huh?)

It was really something, getting off that beachhead, looking down from the hills to where we sat for all those months. I wrote George, too. I think I could even see the little gully where our old dugout was situated. It was quite a sight.

Once we headed north, I was able to find that farmhouse where the family helped me when we were running—did I tell you about that? If not, let me know, and I'll write more—anyway, looks like the family got through ok, and the mom just wouldn't rest till I'd taken along a new pair of socks she had knitted. She told me some stuff about what happened after I'd gone. What a joke, you'd hardly believe it—

The rest of the text was covered by the letter that had come the following week.

Dear Jeannie,

What do you think? I ran into Roberts, the pilot, yesterday. He made it back and has been flying raids again. You wouldn't believe the stories he had to tell—

Another overlapped it from later in the month and carried some news that had surprised her.

Dear Jeannie,

I hope you're well. Thanks for the pictures—Shorty finally had to admit that you're real.

How's being a civilian nurse? I'll bet even a big place like Mayo Clinic is happy to have someone with so much experience. I'd bet you could get dozens of letters of recommendation from fellas over here if you needed them. I'll bet you didn't need them, though.

It sounds like George shipped out last week—permanent discharge, but he said he's up and running again pretty well. It also sounds like he's taking a war bride home with him—can you figure? She is a girl he met in Naples before we hit Anzio. I guess he looked her up while he was recovering, and that was that. I never figured George would settle down!

Shortly after, George had sent a wedding picture—himself and a pretty woman with dark hair. The inscription read: *Mr. George and Mrs. Gia Novak in wedded bliss. Sorry, Nursey. We'll always have Anzio.*

She hadn't heard more from George personally, though Leroy had mentioned him just a couple of weeks ago. George and his wife had settled near Detroit, and George had made manager at the auto plant. He'd promised to have a job waiting for Leroy if he wanted it. Leroy had closed with, *It sounds like a pretty good deal. How do you feel about Michigan?*

The stack of letters had grown large over the years, but the top letter covered the rest.

Dear Jeannie,

We docked today! I'm planning to catch the train, and I should be able to see you Wednesday if I've got all the connections right.

Love, Leroy.

Love. It had taken a year for that word to replace the innocuous "your friend" or "sincerely" at the end of his letters, a little longer for it to show up on hers. But it had been there for more than a year now.

Still, today—today she would see him again. She told herself she wasn't nervous, but she just couldn't get her hair right, no matter how she'd tried, and she'd smeared her lipstick too. At least she'd managed not to run her new stockings.

The little alarm clock on her side table rang, and she spat out the hairpins. "What? Already?" It was time to get to the station. She looked in the mirror in despair and jabbed the last pins into place. It would have to do.

Her feet flying, she raced down the stairs, heels clicking on the wooden floor. Her landlady, Mrs. Hanson, was just walking through the hallway, carrying a vase of flowers. With a gasp Mrs. Hanson stopped, pulling up against the wall. She laughed as Jeannie jumped back as well, dodging a splash of water.

Jeannie laughed too. "Oh, I'm so sorry Mrs. H. Here—can I help you?"

Mrs. H. just raised her eyebrows, looking over Jeannie's new green floral-print dress and carefully pinned hair. "Well, don't you have somewhere you need to be? Isn't this the day?"

Flushing, then paling, Jeannie nodded, the butterflies rising in her stomach.

"Here." Setting the vase down on the sideboard, Mrs. H. pulled out one big white shasta daisy, pinching off the stem with her fingernail. "Bend down, won't you, dear?" She reached up into Jeannie's pins and pulled one just a little loose, tucking the flower into the right side of the rolled tresses. She puttered for a minute, standing on tiptoe. "And stand up."

Jeannie obeyed. Her landlady nodded in satisfaction. "Perfect. Your brother didn't come after all?"

"Oh no, he was just joking about coming by to scare Leroy—at least I think he was..." She trailed off as she looked out the beveled window in the front door. A dark car had just pulled up—was it a taxi? It was a rare event to have any vehicle stop at their quiet lodgings, even if the gas ration was off now. *Fred couldn't have really come to check on me, could he? No, surely not…besides, he'd be working today.*

But someone was getting out of the car as she turned the doorknob and headed outside. She blinked, the bright afternoon sun shining full in her face. He stood just as tall as her brother, but as her eyes adjusted, she realized that his hair was lighter. And…he was in uniform.

Jeannie froze, one hand on the banister, one foot halfway down a step as Leroy turned around. He looked older than she remembered—a man, not the boy with the bashful grin. The ears were still there, but his face had leaned out, and he looked…different. But good.

Her confused brain tried to grapple with the fact that he was standing there. "I…I was just going to the station…" she stammered stupidly.

He stood there just looking at her. Clearing his throat, he found his voice. "My train got in a little early, and I had a ride, so I thought I'd surprise you." He smiled. She tentatively returned it, though neither of them moved.

Then the window of the car—not a taxi, and it had Michigan plates—rolled down. George leaned over an attractive dark-haired woman in the passenger seat. He called out, laughing. "Well? What're you two waiting for? You know I'm taken, Nursey, so you'd better not still be pining for me."

Jeannie's jaw dropped, and Leroy flushed. They looked at each other and laughed.

"Hi, George." Jeannie called, waving.

The woman beside him pinched George's cheek and laughed. "You bet you're taken, though if you don't watch out, I might trade you in yet."

"Oh really?" He pinched her nose in return, but Jeannie wasn't really paying attention to them anymore because Leroy's feet had unfrozen and so had hers. She descended the stairs and met him on the sidewalk, standing close enough that she could smell his cologne—not too strong, nice stuff—and see the new little weary crease lines around his eyes. They deepened as he grinned at her, looked down at the cap in his hands, and looked up at her again. His eyes said everything, and she didn't hesitate anymore.

Jeannie closed the gap between them. Her arms went around his neck, and his rested perfectly around her waist as she leaned to whisper in his ear, "Welcome home."

THE END

AUTHOR'S NOTE

While my main characters and their personal experiences are entirely fictional, most of the events surrounding them are not. Following are a few points that I thought might be of interest.

-Anzio's hospital area was nicknamed "Hell's Half Acre." The bombing of the 95th Evacuation hospital and the death of two nurses in their tent on the day the replacement medical staff arrived on the beachhead were true tragedies. During the months that the Allies were hemmed in on the Anzio beachhead six nurses lost their lives, along with many patients and other medical staff.

-While no nurses from the Anzio area were taken prisoner, some WWII nurses did end up as POWs. The largest group was held captive by the Japanese after the fall of the Philippines in 1942—11 navy nurses and 66 army nurses. They were not released until 1945.

-Stephen Foster's "Jeanie With the Light Brown Hair" was penned in 1854. Due to disagreements between radio stations and one of the music industry's major copyright holders in 1940/41 "Jeanie" was dusted off and played on the radio incessantly. The song has been rerecorded by numerous artists over the years. (For this story, I've chosen to use the longer version of the song's title, and to spell "Jeannie" in the longer variant some artists have used.)

ACKNOWLEDGEMENTS

I ALWAYS FIND that the true stories in history are far more compelling than anything I could imagine. There is so much more to tell about the Anzio beachhead and the real sacrifices that took place there than a novel like this can touch on.

I owe a great debt to histories such as Evelyn Monohan and Rosemary Neidel-Greenlee's And if I Perish: Frontline U.S. Army Nurses in WWII and Rick Atkinson's The Day of Battle: The War in Sicily and Italy 1933-1944 as well as the many online resources provided by the U.S. Army, the Office of Medical History, and WW2 US Medical Research Centre.

Even more, I am grateful for the first-person accounts of people who lived the Second World War, such as Avis D. Schorer's A Half Acre of Hell: A Combat Nurse in WWII, Ruth G. Haskell's Helmets and Lipstick, June Wandrey's Bedpan Commando: The Story of a Combat Nurse During WWII, Audie Murphy's To Hell and Back and Bill Mauldin's Up Front.

This book could not have come into being without the support of many wonderful people I'm blessed to have in my life.

Thanks to Abbi for reading through the early, ugly drafts and cheering me on. Thanks to Mara and Dad for beta reading and sharing thoughts as the story began to turn into a book.

Thanks to fellow authors Joy Neal Kidney and Gail Kittleson who were kind enough to beta read and C.F. Yetmen, Angela Petch, and Chrystyna Lucyk-Berger who were amazing translators for German and Italian phrases. If there are any errors left in those languages, it is my fault! Thanks also to the other members of the Second World War Authors group who offered help with resources or historical odds and ends that I couldn't seem to pin down.

Thanks to Jen Italiano for her amazing editing skills which aided my poor math and found the occasional missing character. Thanks to Amanda Ruehle who took my rough documents and turned them into this beautifully formatted and covered novel.

Thanks to Todd, my right arm. For reading, kid-wrangling, encouraging—without you, none of this would be possible.

And, finally, thank YOU, Readers, for coming along on this journey with me. If you'd like to travel farther, please visit me at my blog where I write about World War II history, fiction, and other odds and ends:

thenaptimeauthor.wordpress.com

Soli Deo Gloria!
Anne Clare

Also By Anne Clare

Whom Shall I Fear?
Christmas Stars (available in *Wartime Christmas Tales: A WWII Flash Fiction Anthology*)

Made in United States
Orlando, FL
07 November 2021

10248711R00201